THE GRUMPY PLAYER
NEXT DOOR

PIPPA GRANT

Editing by Jessica Snyder
Cover Design by Lori Jackson Designs
Cover Image copyright © Miguel Anxo

Tillie Jean Rock, aka a woman who should probably get her eyes checked

There's a fine art to revenge, and today, I am arting the hell out of it. I'm talking cackles of glee, evil cartoon overlord-style, rubbing my hands together while bouncing on my toes. Reminding myself to *shut up* because my brother will be home from his morning workout any minute now, and I don't want to tip my hand when he doesn't know I'm waiting for him here in his house up on the mountainside.

You would think he would've learned to engage his security system more often by now.

But he hasn't, which means I'm here, armed and dangerous and ready, and I'm cackling with glee all over again.

I know, I know. *Is this really how you want to pay him back for having a box labeled "dildos" delivered to you at your parents' house in the midst of all the pre-wedding activities for your other brother last week?*

Yes, actually.

Yes, it is.

It's payback time.

Also?

I have zero doubt Cooper will have mad respect that I'm doing this.

Sort of like while I was pissed when he replaced my coffee beans with roasted goat poop before he left for spring training nine months ago, I very much respected that he pulled it off, even if I wasn't pleased at having to admit that that was the prank that took him over the top to win in our annual off-season prank war.

But this winter?

This winter, my brother Cooper "Stinky Booty" Rock is going down.

The universe told me so. Why else would it have hand-delivered that video into my social media stream to inspire me right after I finished figuring out where to donate an unopened box of dildos?

I cackle again.

And then I slap my hand over my mouth.

He's home.

There's his dark head, bent toward the knob, beyond the tempered glass panel beside his front door. He's dressed in Fireballs red, which is more orange than it is red, and he's probably worn out from lifting at the gym.

Yesterday was cardio day.

I know, because he ran past Crusty Nut, our dad's restaurant where I'm the manager five days a week, at least two dozen times without stopping in once to say hi.

I haven't seen him since the wedding several days ago, which either means he's avoiding me and the revenge he knows I owe him, or he has a stick up his butt and has forgotten the little people.

Or, possibly, he's distracted, in which case, he needs this.

I squat into position at the top of the stairs, as hidden as I can be while still seeing my target, Nerf blaster locked and loaded, waiting while he fumbles with his keys.

For the record?

It's not easy to hide at the top of a curved staircase. I'm on my belly now, half-angled behind the wall of the hallway to his guest bedrooms, peering between the slats of the banister, hoping all my target practice pays off.

Steady, TJ. This is what you trained for.

The lock clicks.

I flatten myself lower and take aim.

The door swings open.

Dark hair in the foyer. *Go go go.*

I squeeze the trigger, sending a rapid blast of modified foam darts at the six balloons floating in the space above the door.

The needle sticking out barely an eighth of an inch in the tip of the first dart connects. One helium balloon pops. Then two more, followed by the fourth and fifth. The sixth shifts after getting hit, like it's a tough guy balloon. It's the ninja of balloons, and it doesn't want to participate in my dastardly plans today, but that's okay. The other balloons are bursting in a sparkly, shiny, beautiful pink glitter spray that's splattering on the walls, exploding from its nylon shell and raining down like a spring shower, coating the walls, making the air sparkle, and dusting all that dark hair as Cooper's lifting his head. "What the—"

And in the span of a heartbeat, before he can finish that sentence, I realize my mistake.

My terrible, horrible, very bad miscalculation.

If I were a superhero, I'd be sucking all that glitter into my lungs and redirecting it into my brother's bedroom, which is likely what I should've done in the first place— hindsight, right?—but I didn't. This was so much more dramatic and didn't risk me having to find out which local he's screwing around with in his spare time, as she'd be coated in glitter too after rolling around in his sheets, except my prank has failed.

It has failed *spectacularly.*

"*Oh my god,*" I gasp.

That's not Cooper.

That is *so* not Cooper.

Yeah, Cooper has dark hair. But he also has an easy smile, blue eyes, a quick sense of humor, appreciation for a well-executed revenge plot, and a tall, lanky body.

The man staring at me is tall. And dark-haired.

But he's also thickly muscled. Growling without making a noise. Aiming dark eyes at me. And I have no idea if he has any respect for pranks.

Harmless pranks.

The ones where no one gets hurt.

Even if it means he's gonna look like a pink vampire in the daylight for the next three weeks.

Or, you know, *forever.* Because it's *glitter.*

I swallow hard while those brown eyes silently bore into me from a face that's as chiseled and manly as they come, and which also looks like it was decorated at a birthday slumber party for a fourteen-year-old.

What's he even doing here? He's not supposed to be here.

This isn't where he's staying this winter.

But he *is* here, and this isn't good.

This isn't good at all.

"Hi, Max." I lift a hand and wave, realize I'm still holding the Nerf blaster, and toss it down the hallway.

It hits the corner of the wall instead and clatters to the wood floor.

Stupid thing doesn't even have the decency to land quietly on the hall runner.

Max Cole, right-handed starting pitcher for the Copper Valley Fireballs, is six feet, four inches, and two hundred twenty-five pounds of steely baseball perfection. He's been with the team four full seasons, two of which were record-setting years.

And not in the good way.

Any guy who wasn't begging his agent to be traded away from the Fireballs during their sucky years is okay in my book —professionally speaking, of course—and Max stuck around to help pull them from the worst team to ever exist in professional sports to the underdogs who took the playoffs by storm this past season, even if they didn't make it *all* the way.

Not that Max is ever willing to do anything beyond glare, twitch, and ignore me when I'm around him.

Possibly spending four years incessantly flirting with him to annoy Cooper—and Max, if I'm being honest—wasn't the best build-up to this moment.

But possibly him ratting me out to Cooper after—you know what? I don't want to talk about it.

Let's just say Max and I started our acquaintance on the wrong foot and haven't ever recovered.

He lifts a hand too, but instead of waving back, he swipes at the glitter coating his face.

"That was supposed to be for Cooper. Obviously. I didn't expect you. How could I have expected you here?" I'm not gulping.

I'm not shrinking into myself.

I'm not quivering in my belly.

And also possibly my lady bits.

Okay, *fine*.

I'm borderline terrified of what this prank-gone-wrong might've just incited, and I am *not* immune to that many feet of muscled baseball perfection, despite the number of times he's rolled his eyes or grimaced at me when I've flirted with him the past four years, and despite exactly how furious I was with him over what he did the day we met.

And who's furious now?

Max.

Max is currently furious.

He's a massive, glittering, growly bear of *if this crap isn't the kind that comes off easily, you better not be planning on sleeping again for the next three months, Matilda Jean Rock.*

Prank industry secret: There's no glitter that comes off easily.

I might've misread the universe's instructions when it came to how to get Cooper back.

"He shoved his dirty gym socks under the seat of my car when he was home on the all-star break and it took me three weeks to figure out what the smell was, and before he left for Florida last year, he hid rum cakes all over my house and Grady's goat kept breaking in to find them and ended up staggering all over downtown wearing one of my bras on his head while bleating this weird monologue that sounded like a Garth Brooks song after pooping on my kitchen table. *He taught Grady's goat to poop on kitchen tables.* I thought you were Cooper. This is Cooper's house. You were supposed to be him. That glitter was meant for my butthead brother. I swear."

He still doesn't say a word.

I gulp and try a new tactic.

At this point, it's habit, so why not go with it?

I smile and wink. "So how was morning workout? Did you flex all your studly muscles and show the rest of them how to do a squat?"

He bends forward, runs a hand through his dark hair, shaking his head and making bright pink glitter rain down onto Cooper's wide plank wood floor, and making me wonder if that's how he rinses his hair in the shower.

When he's naked.

And wet.

It would be lovely if my body would cooperate and *not* get hot flashes when my brain goes rogue and pictures Max Cole in the buff.

It would also be lovely if my brain wouldn't go rogue every time I saw him.

It would also have been lovely if *Max* wasn't the guy on the team who'd end up renting the house next door to me for the entire off-season. And you'd think that seeing him in long baggy workout pants and T-shirts and light jackets wouldn't inspire all the fantasies—it's not like he's walking around shirtless in November—but I cannot help the way I'm wired, and I'm wired to think that Max Cole is hotter than a bacon grease fire.

Even despite the way we met.

His personality sucks, brain. Stop fantasizing about him.

Yeah, but have you ever seen him joke with his teammates, Tillie Jean? He's a sexy, fun man-beast until you walk in the door, my brain replies.

Stupid brain.

The vacuum. I should get the vacuum and help clean the floor so he can—

"*Erp,*" I croak as my cerebral functions scramble again.

He's still bent over, but now he's pulling his warm-up jacket and everything underneath it over his head in one smooth motion, revealing bulging muscles and taut skin and that phoenix tattoo on his left shoulder, and my mouth is dry.

Desert dry. Like, so dry I think my tongue just saw a mirage.

He straightens, tosses his clothes on top of the glitter, and uses it as a stepping stone to reach the first stair.

Max Cole is shirtless and stalking up the stairs to kill me.

Move! Run! my feet yell.

If we have to die, the scenery will be good while he's choking us, my vagina replies.

I'm still flat on the floor, which means by the time he's halfway up the stairs, I'm having to lift my eyeballs to track his movements. When he hits the landing, my brain cramps because my eyes aren't supposed to go this high.

"Are you gonna kill me?" I whisper.

He pauses and looks down at me, and when he speaks, his chocolate silk voice reminds me—again—of exactly how attractive Max Cole is no matter what he's doing. "Oh, Tillie Jean. You have no idea."

MAX COLE, aka a guy who's not really the glittering type. Or the painting type. Or the Tillie Jean Rock type. For the record.

THERE ARE SEVEN THOUSAND THINGS I HATE ABOUT TILLIE JEAN Rock, and I'm not talking about the seven thousand bits of neon pink glitter that are still in my hair hours after my glitter shower and will likely still be in my hair on the day I die, even if I live to be a hundred and twenty.

That's just *one* reason I hate Tillie Jean Rock.

Right behind *flirts with me to annoy me*.

And *joined the Lady Fireballs even though she's not dating anyone on the team.*

And then there's *is always perfect, no matter what.*

Always. Fucking. Perfect.

"Oh my gosh, Dita, look at her baby belly! She's so adorable. Mom, seriously, you *nailed* the ears. LaShonda! *For shame*. You did *not* put lipstick on that baby dragon." All the women in the bar's back room break into titters and giggles while Tillie Jean, the object of my abhoration—no, not *adoration*, I really do mean *abhoration*, and if that word's not in the dictionary, it should be—circles the party room that I'm trapped in, complimenting everyone's paintings here at this god-awful *paint the new mascot* party while she sips from a glittery gold travel coffee mug that Luca Rossi's girlfriend gave her for saving her life at a party a couple months back.

Which I only know because Luca couldn't shut the hell up about it.

Not because I pay that close of attention to what happens in Tillie Jean's life.

If I had my say in it tonight, I'd know nothing at all about what Tillie Jean was up to right now either.

Also, *reason number four thousand, six hundred twelve: Tillie Jean effortlessly saves other people's lives.*

Shouldn't be a reason I hate her, but it is.

So. Fucking. Perfect. All. The. Fucking. Time.

And I'm the moron who chose—who *chose*—to move to her hometown for the off-season, which is how I've ended up here tonight, sitting between her brother Cooper and Trevor Stafford, relief pitcher for the team, drinking iced tea in the party room of The Grog, a local bar which feels like the inside of a ship after a night of pirate debauchery, while Tillie Jean instructs us on how to paint our own Ashes.

Yes, I said *Ashes*. Not *asses*.

Ash is the newly-hatched next-generation dragon mascot of the Copper Valley Fireballs, who's adorable as hell with her pudgy baby arms and little ear sprouts.

Usually.

She's not nearly as cute when I'm being coerced into painting her with Tillie Jean Rock's instructions. My version looks like an angry green blob with a face and a diaper, and not because I hope management ages her up to breathe fire and be a scary mascot so our reputation doesn't get soft after all the work we put in over the last year to go from zeroes to heroes.

"Dude, check out your Ash eyes." Cooper leans into my

painting and grins. He's two beers deep, which means he's fully relaxed and in his happy place. Not that Cooper's ever *not* in his happy place. Does that mean he's in his happier place? "She looks like she wants to murder someone."

Trevor leans over from the other side and whistles. "Pretty sure that's not what management was picturing when they asked us to do this. We want people to bid on these for charity, not run screaming from the demonic baby dragon."

I point to his painting, where his Ash's eyes are making her look terrified. "And what happened to your Ash?"

Cooper peers past me and cracks up. We've been teammates for four years. He's seen me at my absolute worst—not long after I joined the Fireballs, matter of fact—and I'd hate him if it wasn't so easy to like him.

He's basically just like his sister, except he doesn't flirt with me, which makes him tolerable.

Okay, *more* than tolerable. He's a good dude. Probably the best friend I've ever had on any team.

"She get kidnapped by the loser mascots?" he asks Trevor. "They holding her for ransom in the dungeon at Duggan Field or something?"

Three of the women in front of us turn around. *Their* Ashes look like actual cute baby dragons.

Apparently Tillie Jean runs Ladies Painting Nights monthly here. Yes, *of course* she also knows how to paint, and *of course* she uses her skills to help the people in her pirate-themed hometown in the mountains. She can also drive in the city or the country, tell pirate jokes or recite Shakespeare and switch seamlessly between the two, and sprinkle glitter all over the town without getting any on her.

And she still looks *right* in a paint-splattered smock with her cinnamon-brown hair swept back under a Pirate Festival bandana, her cheeks glowing, her summer sky eyes bright and cheerful, and her lush pink lips spread in a perpetual smile.

11

She's such a pain in the ass.

I have zero doubt that all the stories about this town being founded by a pirate who raced his treasure inland to hide from the authorities however many hundreds of years ago are true, nor do I doubt that pirate blood still runs in her veins.

Annoying wench.

Come paint the new Fireballs mascot with us, Robinson Simmons, the Fireballs' utility man, said this morning at the end of our workout. *Management signed off. It's all this guided painting thing so we don't make her look bad, then we sign the paintings, and then we can auction them off for my niece's foundation.*

Who says no to two hours spent painting a baby dragon mascot to be auctioned off in support of kids with Down syndrome?

Assholes, that's who.

Tonight, I wish I'd been an asshole. Instead, I'm a glittery pitcher posing as a guy who likes to paint baby dragon mascots for charity.

Any other night, with any other instructor...

"You can use my painting and say it's your own, Trevor," one of the older ladies says with a wink in his direction.

"Thanks, Dita, but I don't think anyone's gonna be buying my Ash no matter how she looks."

I scowl at him.

Cooper punches him in his non-pitching arm. "Shut up. Yes, they will. You're a *legend*."

Trevor snorts.

I refrain from punching him in his non-pitching arm too. If I punch anything, I'll send it through a wall.

"Trevor, I love her." Tillie Jean, painting goddess of Shipwreck, Virginia, the godawful pirate town that would be charming and welcoming and everything a small town should be if *she* didn't live here, steps into our row and leans over my buddy's shoulder, close enough for him to sniff her, and yep, I should not be here.

She even *smells* good. Like a flower that's not too potent mixed with a sea breeze or something.

Reason number six hundred ninety-four...

"She's not as good as yours," Trevor says to TJ.

She puts a hand on his shoulder and squeezes, and my blood pressure threatens to choke me.

"It took me eight times to get her perfect," she tells him. "You practically nailed her the first time around."

"Yeah, but your Ash *glows*."

"Like Max's hair?" Cooper asks.

I do punch him in the arm.

That glitter bomb was for him, and if I hadn't left my wallet at his place last night and gone to retrieve it before lunch instead of taking him up on his offer to cover me, *he* would be the one sparkling right now.

"Max, you should lean into your painting and rub your hair all over it," Cooper's grandmother says from the row behind me. "You can have a glittery ass. *Ass. Ash!*"

"Too much punch, Nana?" Tillie Jean asks.

"Jus' right," the grand dame of the Rock family replies, hefting a stein with *Nana* sprawled over an image of a pirate wench on the side of it. "*Arrr!*"

Cooper lifts his own custom stein, which has a picture of himself as a pirate holding a baseball bat that serves as a flag-pole for a pirate flag. "*Arrr!*"

Everyone else in the room lifts their custom steins too. "*Arrr!*"

Trevor's spent a few off-seasons here in Cooper's home-town, so he has his own custom stein with a painting of himself—yes, *done by Tillie Jean*—as well.

Only Robinson and I are drinking out of plain pint glasses.

And Tillie Jean and her coffee mug.

She leans over my shoulder and peers at my painting. "Nicely done, Max. I can *feel* the emotion."

Her voice has that coy, flirty quality again, like she wasn't squeaking in terror when she realized I wasn't Cooper a few hours back, and as usual, my junk doesn't know how to react.

A woman getting throaty and purry with me? We gear up for fun.

Cooper's sister brushing her boob against my shoulder? Full-on retreat.

You don't touch Cooper Rock's little sister.

As if I'd want to.

And do you know how it feels when your junk wants to get hard and also asks your nuts to retreat back into your body at the same time?

Hell.

It feels like hell.

"Leave him alone, TJ, and come tell me I'm perfect." Cooper reaches around me, and Tillie Jean disappears from my side like he yanked her away.

I grab my tea.

Trevor eyes me and shakes his head, but doesn't say anything.

"We about done?" I mutter. Tillie Jean's telling Cooper his brush strokes are imprecise or some bullshit, and he's laughing because that's what they do. They give each other shit, but they also have each other's backs.

Trevor studies me for half a second, then looks past me to the happy siblings. "Yeah. Darts?"

"I'm in for darts," Cooper says. "Sign your paintings, mateys. That's worth more than your art. *Arr!*"

"Is he like this all winter?" I ask Trevor.

"Only the first few times he drinks. He'll get it out of his system when he realizes spring training starts in three months. We usually get four."

14

Cooper drops his stein and stares at us in horror. "Oh, fuck. We only get three months."

Tillie Jean pats his head. "I think you'll be fine, Stinky Booty. Robinson. Let's see this beauty. *Oh*, look at you. You cover all the bases *and* you paint circles around your teammates. I'm having words with management if they ever trade you away."

He gapes at her with horrified brown eyes. Kid just finished his rookie season in the show and liked it. "Don't jinx it, TJ."

She winks. "No such thing, Robinson. I wouldn't do that to you."

I sign my painting and head out into the main bar. I need to get away from this room. Trevor stretches his pitching arm while we cross past the pool tables.

I shoot him a look.

He ignores me.

Guy's older than I am, and he fucked up his shoulder good about two years ago. Wasn't sure he'd have a comeback, and he hasn't been the same since. Plus, his contract's up. He's here for off-season workouts because he's optimistic.

No idea if his agent's blowing smoke about being able to get him another deal, but we'll see before spring training starts.

I nod to his glass. "Refill?"

"Hell, yeah."

"Grab a dart board. Be right back."

Max

THE DART BOARD ISN'T COOPERATING.

And I don't mean my score. My score is fine.

But the dart board isn't making it easy to ignore the laughter coming from the bar running the length of the far wall, where Tillie Jean and all her aunts and cousins and grandmother and mom and friends are sitting around, shooting the shit, having a better time than I am.

I should go home.

I should've already gone home.

Spending three months in the same town as Tillie Jean Rock? *Not* a good plan.

Spending those three months renting the house next door to her?

Even worse.

"Cole. Dude. You still surfing that pissed-off wave with TJ?" Cooper looks up from the closest table, where he's catching up on all the Shipwreck gossip with a handful of locals now that the last of the paint night activities are over, and he eyeballs my dart.

It's just a normal dart.

But it might've hit the board the way my fastball lands in a catcher's glove.

"Just playing darts, man."

"You just looked at the bar and then looked at the dart board like you want to eat it."

Tillie Jean and her mom explode in laughter again. My whole body tenses, and I actively force my muscles to relax on a subtle exhale.

I shake my head at Cooper. "Off night."

His brows furrow as he tips his chair back to study me with a clear view like he hasn't had a single drink tonight, even though he's taken a few shots after his painting beers. "You wanna get out of here? I got glow-in-the-dark balls. We can—"

"Your balls glow in the dark, man?" Robinson looks up from the table where he's spilling to Cooper's local friends about the time this past season that we got roped into an engagement gone wrong on a road trip in Cincinnati.

Trevor snorts next to me. "Gotta see a doctor about that. Or maybe a nurse. You have pretty nurses here." He's on beer number five and feeling fine.

Whereas I know better than to touch a beer or a shot or anything stronger than unsweet tea tonight.

Definitely time to leave.

I thought I could hang out here and ignore the only irritating part of this town, but I can't. Every time I start to relax into the game, she laughs that magical fairy laugh that makes the glitter in my hair feel like pixie dust.

Or someone says her name, which should be annoyingly country—*Tillie Jean*, it's so old-fashioned—but instead sounds like fucking music.

Or I accidentally look over at her and catch her tucking her perfect hair behind her ear.

It's not too short or too long. Not too curly, nor too straight. And it's this magical color of cinnamon with some caramel sprinkled in between, and I have a serious problem.

I fling another dart at the board.

This one hits so hard it breaks in two, and the pieces go flying in opposite directions.

One lands in Robinson's drink. "Touchdown," he crows as the guys around him explode in laughter.

Cooper keeps staring at me.

"Let it go," I mutter to him.

"I'm serious. You want to take off, I haven't hit Scuttle Putt yet for midnight minigolf, and the fresh air's good for plotting revenge."

Right.

Revenge.

If she were one of the guys, revenge would be a no-brainer. We pull shit on each other all season long, and yeah, a glitter bomb would be epic and it would require an epic plan for retribution that would make the sports pages.

But she's not one of the guys. She's Cooper's sister. And while Cooper might be the best friend I've ever had in baseball, possibly one of the best guys I've ever met in my entire life, I'm damn certain he wouldn't say the same about me, which means no matter how fucking perfectly annoying his sister is, I keep it to myself.

I keep *everything* to myself when it comes to Tillie Jean.

Because I like having Cooper Rock as one of my friends.

"I don't want revenge."

He grins. "Hate to tell you, but you don't get a vote. Ever since the great tea towel incident all those years ago, it's tradition for us to entertain ourselves one-upping each other all winter. She got you. You have to get her back. But don't even think about doing it with nudity or spit-swapping or I'll kill you."

I'd be offended, except I wouldn't trust me with his sister if I were him either. I have a longer relationship with my jock-strap than I've ever had with a woman, and I like it that way.

"What's the great tea towel incident?" Stafford asks.

Half the locals gathered with Cooper laugh, and the other half sigh. Tillie Jean and her crew pause and glance our way.

She winks at me.

I twitch.

Stafford snorts.

And Cooper, who doesn't notice his sister flirting with me —not that it's unusual, since she likes to do it to irritate both of us—shakes his head. "Sorry. Rock family secret. I've already said more than I should."

"Hey, Coop, speaking of family—you related to the bartender?" Robinson wiggles his thick brows at the woman running the taps in front of a cracked mirror etched with a pirate ship.

"Yeah, she's my aunt, and she's married with three kids."

"Aw, hell, no. No way."

"Aunt Glory, Robinson's got a crush on you," Cooper calls.

A collective groan goes up around the bar.

"Join the club, kid," an older guy at the pool table calls back.

"His beer's on me," another older guy at a booth hollers.

"She's such a heartbreaker." Cooper's in his element, smiling and laughing and pulling everyone in the entire bar into his orbit. He loves being here, and they love having him. Not that there's a place on earth where it's not true. It's just *extra* true here.

"Marriage or birth?" Stafford asks.

"Both."

That would be hilarious any other night of the week, but

tonight, my shoulders bunch again, and I turn and try to concentrate on the dart board while Cooper keeps going.

"Just pulling your pegleg. She was born Glory Rock, married a Johnson, and now—"

"Quit talking," I say as I miss the dart board completely.

"What? She didn't hyphenate. She hated being Glory Rock. Pop and Nana didn't think that one through. Teenage boys, man. They all wanted to climb Glory Rock. But I was gonna say, we've got some Johnsons up our family tree if you go back a few generations, so even though we're pretty sure it's not incest, we're not *sure* sure."

Tillie Jean pushes a chair in between Cooper and Robinson and hands the rookie a beer, sloshing the liquid over the side as she puts it down. "Tough break, kid, but you're not the first to fall under her spell. Aunt Glory's half the reason for the huge rivalry we have with that dumb town up the way that I'm not allowed to call dumb anymore now that Grady's married to someone from there. Max, I didn't get to tell you earlier—I love your shirt. It really brings out the muscles in your—*a-wah-wah-wah*."

Cooper jerks his chin at me while he holds a hand over her mouth. "Got your back, Max. Starting to understand what's wrong with the dart board, and it's not the dart board, right?"

Stafford lines up a shot and comes within a hair of a bull's-eye. "Yeah, the problem's totally not the dart board."

Robinson scoots his chair further from her. "TJ, why don't you ever compliment my muscles?"

"*Boo-da-fwa-wa.*"

Her eyes are dancing again, clear as day despite the late hour, and it briefly makes me wonder what she's sipping out of her glittery coffee mug before I remember I shouldn't wonder about her at all.

I'd still bet my favorite glove she's talking nonsense behind Cooper's hand, though, and also that she's probably going to lick it any minute now.

He yelps and jerks his hand away.

Stafford snickers. "Can't handle a little lick, Coop?"

"I hit his tickle spot," Tillie Jean whispers loudly, lifting a hand smeared with dried green paint and wiggling her fingers. She follows it with a giggle. "And don't worry, Max. I'll get him back for you taking his glitter bomb. TJ's on the case."

Cooper laughs. "What, you're gonna tie your own shoelaces together?"

"Not telling. But you are going *down*, my dear brother. So, *so* down."

"*You're* going down."

They need to stop talking about *going down*. And yeah, that's one more reason I hate Tillie Jean Rock.

"If you'd been the one to walk through your front door like you were *supposed* to be, *you'd* be glittering, and Max would still be secretly in love with me."

They both look at me, Cooper like *dude, I'm sorry I have a sister*, Tillie Jean like *c'mon, Max, what's it take to get a reaction out of you?*

I jerk my head toward the bathroom. "Back in a minute," I tell Stafford.

I'm not coming back. I'm slipping out the back door. The bar's too crowded, the people too happy, and I'm on edge.

Happens sometimes.

Shouldn't be here. I'm in a mood. Need to get back to the house I rented for the winter, read a little, write some shit down, breathe, and start fresh in the morning.

But I need to take a leak first, and when I walk out of the john, I bump into Cooper's dad.

He smiles, just like he always does, and once again, I'm reminded of all the reasons I hate Tillie Jean.

She has no idea how good she has it with a father like hers.

"Hey, Max. Good to have you here." He claps me on the

21

shoulder. "I know you kids are planning on working hard, but don't let the pressure get to you. Already proved yourselves this year, and you know baseball. Never know what'll happen."

Relax relax relax. "That's half of why we love the game."

He chuckles. "No matter what next season brings, you boys made us all proud."

Hello, sucker punch number two.

It's not that I didn't play my heart out on the field.

I did.

It's more that it's always someone else's dad telling me they're proud. Not sure why that one hurts tonight—I let it go a long time ago—but there it is.

It's one more cosmic smack in the junk on a night that I should've stayed home.

I nod to him, step around him, and head toward the party room and the back door to freedom, but I barely get inside before I bump into someone again.

And this time the bump comes with a hint of rum and a subconscious twitch between my shoulders, followed immediately by a cold splash of something all down my shirt and jeans.

"Oh, crap!" Tillie Jean leaps back, looks up at me, and makes a face that would be hilarious on any other woman in the world. Lips pursed out in an O, eyes bulging under wonky eyebrows, *you're gonna kill me now, aren't you?* replacing her usual *hey, big guy, what's up?* swagger. "Oh, crap crap crap, I did *not* just do this *again.*"

"TJ, give the guy a break." Cooper rises from his spot halfway across the room as Tillie Jean grabs a napkin and attacks me with it.

"I know, I know, you're gonna start thinking I'm doing this on purpose," she mutters while she swipes my shirt.

My favorite Boring Distillery T-shirt that's been washed the exact right number of times to make it soft as butter, and that they discontinued a year ago, is now coated in brown paint water.

Ruined.

Fucking. Ruined.

"You—" I cut myself off with a grunt as she goes south of the border with the napkins, and I leap back. "I got this. It's fine. I'm fine."

I'm not *fine*.

My pulse is kicking up and my muscles are clenching and there's that itchy spot between my shoulder blades that I can never reach, getting itchier by the minute.

Bar's too crowded.

I know they're all good people. I know they mean well. I know tomorrow is a new day and everything will be fucking *fine*, but I'm not into it tonight.

"Hey, Aunt Glory, send me a bill, yeah?" Cooper calls to the bartender as he nudges Tillie Jean out of the way. He makes eye contact—*panic attack, man? I got you*—and jerks his head at the back door. "C'mon. Let's go goat-tipping."

"Stay," I mutter to him. I'm not having a damn panic attack. I refuse. I'm just pissed. "Just need clean pants and a new favorite shirt."

"Sure. Then—"

"Then I'll see you tomorrow."

He holds my gaze, and I want to punch him. Again.

Not because he's an asshole.

More because I am.

After an eternity that's probably only half a second, he nods. "Nine at my house. Mountain sprints, baby."

"Can't wait."

I wave to Trevor and Robinson, nod to the bartender, and escape as fast as I can without looking like I'm trying to escape.

The cold post-season air hits me as soon as I step outside, and I suck in a full breath that doesn't quite quell the agitation. Ripping my shirt off and basking in the chill doesn't help either. I'm still too hot.

I'm always too hot, but tonight, it's worse. I'd rip my pants off too if I thought that would help, but it wouldn't.

No sense asking what's wrong with me.

It's always the same.

Fucking anxiety.

Usually I have it under control. But since we made the post-season, it's been sneaking up and hitting me worse.

Not hard to figure out why.

Play for a team that finishes with the worst record in baseball nine years out of ten, people don't expect much of you. You still work hard, but you get to play hard too without much thought. Even before I was with the Fireballs, I played for a team that underperformed.

But you play for a team that goes from zero to hero in under a year, with more press than the team that won the whole damn thing, all of us getting near-daily calls from our agents with sponsorship and endorsement offers, interview inquiries, and discussions of next year's salary negotiations, and there's pressure.

Get stronger. Faster. Throw harder. Every day counts. Your body is a machine. Rest. Lift. Run. Stronger. Faster. Harder.

Win more.

It hasn't been a full week since we got here for winter training, and the pressure's solid. People think the season makes you.

They're wrong.

The off-season training makes you. And I'm starting it wrong.

Fuck.

I'm a block away when I realize I'm going the wrong direction, and when I turn, there she is.

Again.

"Go away, Tillie Jean."

Her brows are furrowed as she stands there right outside the bar. "You heading back the long way?"

"Yes."

"Hey, I'm sorry. I didn't mean to glitter you. Or throw the paint water all over you. Or—no, wait, okay, I did mean to flirt incessantly with you to annoy you and Cooper." She smiles.

It's a friendly smile. An olive branch smile. The kind that promises she'll quit trying to annoy me if I quit making it so easy for her to succeed.

She glances at my bare chest, then starts to shrug out of her Fireballs hoodie. "Do you want my—"

I cut her off with a grunt and cross the street. No idea if she drove or not, but I discovered two seconds after I unpacked my suitcase that she lives next door to the house I'm renting here for the winter, which means if she's done for the night, she's probably going the same way.

And yeah, if she's going the same way, I'm taking the long way.

The *very* long way.

My pants will dry eventually, and then they're going in the trash too, right next to my favorite shirt.

Dammit.

"We could call a truce, you know."

"Go away, Tillie Jean." Not sure why I think that'll work the second time I say it, but it's all I have in me.

Her footsteps sound on the empty street as she jogs along behind me. "I'm not saying I don't deserve having my house toilet papered. Or something way more creative than that. It's a rule. I get it. I glittered you. You get to pay me back. I wouldn't even argue if you got me back for the dirty paint water, even though that really was an accident. But maybe it's time we call a truce on the *other* thing."

And she just went there.

Of every memory I have in my adult life, the memory of

the first time I met Tillie Jean is one that I have apparently not actively scrubbed hard enough out of my brain. And there it is again, popping up in technicolor glory, with all of the complicated shit that went with it. "Don't know what you're talking about."

"Of the two of us, I'd be giving more here."

It's forty degrees, I'm shirtless, in soaked jeans, and I'm breaking out in a sweat. "Go back to the bar."

"*Max.*"

I swing around and glare at her. She's three inches from me, all blue eyes and dark hair and tight shirt over breasts that I regularly pretend I've never seen while she holds her hoodie between us.

"What?" I snap.

"Can we *please* call a truce?"

"Why?"

"Because you're here all winter and it's frankly exhausting pretending to like you all the time. Also, if we call a truce, you might not growl and glower every time you see me, and then Cooper might start wondering if there's something going on between us, and what's better than torturing Cooper?"

She smiles again, eyes lighting up with mischief and an offer of friendship, which is something she gives so damn freely without having a clue how much of a privilege it is for her to be safe and happy and loved in this adorable little town where she *can* offer that friendship without hesitation.

Reason number three hundred seventy-six why I hate Tillie Jean Rock.

"Fine. Truce. Whatever."

Her lips purse. They're painted a deep rose, and I should not be looking at Tillie Jean Rock's lips when I'm on edge. I don't do smart things when I'm on edge.

I don't date. I screw around.

And if Tillie Jean wasn't Cooper's sister, I would've screwed around with her a long, long time ago.

She's living, breathing temptation when she's not talking, which, thank god, she does all the time.

Reason seven hundred forty-four and reason sixty-two.

She crosses her arms over her shirt—her *clean* pink Anchovies Pizza T-shirt that's so tight I can see the outline of her bra under the streetlamp, and *fuck me*, it looks lacy.

I rip my gaze to the sky, turn, and stroll away again.

And again, she chases after me. "I grew up as the baby after Grady and Cooper. I know when I'm being told something just to shut me up."

"It'd go a long way toward a truce, then, if you shut up, wouldn't it?"

"Chicken versus egg. Are you cranky because I flirt with you, or do I flirt with you because you're cranky? And why's it only *me*? You flirt back with everyone, but not me."

My fingers twitch. My palms are getting clammy. And I can't slow my heart rate. "I'm cranky because you flirt with me."

She jogs along beside me. "So if I quit flirting, you'll quit being cranky?"

"No."

"That's not how truces work."

"We don't need a truce. We need you to shut up." And I need to get home. Shower. Breathe.

Quit being such an asshole.

But she laughs.

She *laughs*, and it's pure joy and uninhibited happiness dancing through the night and leaving dents when it bounces off my personal bubble.

Reason five hundred.

"If you only knew the number of times my brothers told me to shut up," she muses. "Pro tip: that doesn't work on me."

Of course it doesn't.

"Now, if you'd—*mmph!*"

I'm possessed.

Possessed by the anxiety devil that wants peace and needs quiet and sees only one possible way to make a woman stop talking for three damn seconds.

You kiss her.

You kiss her, because she can't talk when her mouth is busy, and she's been flirting with me for four damn years, and yeah, there's no small part of me hoping she'll realize this is a bad idea and rack me in the nuts.

Nothing distracts a guy from worrying about stupid shit months down the road like immediate pain.

But this is Tillie Jean Rock.

And I have underestimated her.

She's not kneeing me in the nads. Nor is she shutting up.

She's making gaspy little moans as she leans into the kiss, her tongue darting out to swipe at my lips, tasting like coffee and rum and temptation under the stars, her hot, silky hands settling gently on my bare chest like she's afraid if she touches me, I'll melt away like cotton candy in the rain, and kissing isn't enough.

I want to pull her behind the nearest building and rip her shirt and pants off and screw her hard and fast. The only thing better than a solid racking to knock an anxiety attack out of the ballpark is a good hard screw.

My hands are on her hips, ready to lift her and carry her around the corner when a noise breaks through the haze.

Voices.

Fuck.

I'm in Shipwreck.

I'm in Cooper's hometown.

I'm kissing his sister.

His *very off-limits* sister.

Reason number eight hundred ninety-nine…

Wrenching away is second nature. The wild look in Tillie Jean's eyes—half *what just happened* and half *yes, please*—sets my teeth on edge and my pulse flying higher than it can handle.

"I said shut up," I rasp out.

I swipe the back of my hand over my mouth, feel the jitters starting in my fingertips, and take off.

I need to be alone.

I need to be alone *right now*.

4

TILLIE JEAN

MAX COLE IS A TERRIBLE KISSER.

Not the part where his lips were warm and delicious. Or the part where he took charge and laid it on me. Or the part where he was a solid wall of growly-bear muscle and touching him was like touching summer in the middle of winter.

But definitely the part where other than initiating the kiss, he didn't work hard at continuing it.

And the part where he jerked back so hard and fast, it was clear he forgot who I was when he decided to kiss me, which I'm pretty sure he did only to make me stop talking.

And also the part where he ran away.

Ran.

I'm talking full-on sprint down Blackbeard Avenue to get away from me.

And now, twelve hours later, I'm exhausted from a restless night of reliving it, and trying to pretend everything's fine. The only thing worse than having an off-day in Shipwreck is having an off-day in Shipwreck when you're supposed to be leading morning boot camp aerobics at the senior center after spilling the coffee that you tell everyone is a protein drink because you were supposed to give up coffee—again—weeks ago.

But if I wasn't supposed to have coffee, it wouldn't be so readily available, now would it?

"Shake that booty, Nana," I call.

Pant, really. Possibly I should do this more than once a week.

Or possibly I'm still reeling from that kiss with Max last night.

"That's right, ladies and gents! Get those legs up and kick!" I stop demonstrating and walk around the class under the guise of making sure everyone else is kicking right.

It has nothing to do with needing a rest myself, or worrying that the kick in my pulse is a reaction to too much caffeine.

And no, I'm not telling the average age of the participants here this morning. Especially since I feel a little older than all of them after tossing and turning all night last night and telling myself lies.

Lie number one: I only liked kissing Max because there are so few other opportunities for kissing in a town this small.

Lie number two: I would totally not kiss him again.

Lie number three: He's not that attractive.

Lie number four: I don't like him like that.

Lie number five: I didn't look out my window to see if he was up and moving around his house sixteen million times overnight and this morning, since my bedroom windows look directly into what I know are his bedroom windows, which have the shades completely drawn, but which aren't so solid that I can't tell when his lights are on.

You get the idea. And let's not talk about *why* I signed up to lead senior aerobics when the vacancy came up a year ago.

It has nothing to do with that article I read about Max doing yoga with the senior residents of his building on his off-days at home during the season.

Nope. Nothing at all.

The timing was pure coincidence.

"Nice punch, Mom. Take out those pirates. Kick! Punch! One, two, three, and squat! How low can you go?

"Is she extra chipper today?" Aunt Bea gasps.

"She's extra *not doing it with us*," Mom replies.

"I already ran four miles today, ladies and gents." More like my body ran four hundred mental laps around analyzing that kiss last night. Technicalities. Doc Adamson will bust my ass if he looks at my FitBit data from the past two days, and not *just* because I've been guzzling coffee like I have a leaking gas tank. "You've got this."

"*Maaaah!*" Sue, my brother Grady's goat, replies.

Yes, a goat.

My mother brought her grand-goat to aerobic boot camp while Grady and Annika are off on their honeymoon.

"You too, Sue." I rub his head. "Kick and punch, little nephew. Kick and punch and squat."

"We need to see you kicking and punching and squatting, Matilda Jean," Nana says.

"Lower on that squat, Nana. You want Pops to think you're going soft? He'll let his parrot walk all over you if you don't keep that booty in good shape."

"Your booty's never been in good shape, Tillie Jean," Cooper calls from the doorway. He's lounging against the frame in his Fireballs track suit, Hydro Flask in hand, his *you love me* grin out in full force.

"Cooper!"

It's like a flash mob. All of my aerobics students abandon their mats and charge him.

I pop my fists to my hips and eyeball his water bottle. Yes, with jealousy. I forgot my own and I'm parched after not sleeping, not working out, and not doing senior aerobics. "Hello, workout people. Those glutes aren't going to shape themselves. And you all saw him just last night."

"But he was talking to the *men* last night," Aunt Bea tells me.

"He spent two hours painting baby Ashes with you."

"*Painting*. Not talking. It's our turn to catch up."

"You saw him at Grady's wedding."

"Psh. He was doing all of his best man duties."

Go away, I mouth to him, remember Max Cole saying the same thing to me a dozen or so times before he finally kissed me and ran away himself, and feel my face heat like the ovens at Crusty Nut, which is where I'm headed for my day shift as soon as senior aerobics is over.

Cooper blows me a kiss.

That's not good.

Does he still have a key to my house?

How long has he been up?

Did he prank me while I was here?

I start to smile. If he got me, I get to get him back.

God, I miss him when he's gone.

Brothers are supposed to be annoying, and Cooper is— Grady too, sometimes—but I don't mind. My brothers are also awesome.

I won the brother lottery, which has become clearer and clearer the further into adulthood we've all gotten.

"Are any of you coming back to work out?" I call to my class.

"Not while you're not working out with us," Mom calls back over the sea shanty music that Nana insists we use every week.

"Don't you have to get to work?" Cooper asks me.

"Aren't you supposed to be running sprints up and down your mountain?"

Yeah, *his* mountain.

Shipwreck isn't hurting economically between the tourism and the side hustles so many of our residents have picked up in the internet age, plus we have a growing segment of people who move here to work from home since we have solid internet and we're basically the best small town to ever exist —and I'm not just biased. We get written up in articles about *The Best Small Towns To Live In Across America* all the time.

But Cooper and his professional baseball salary are a step above. He's been slowly buying all the land on Thorny Rock Mountain as it comes on the market, and at this point, he owns most of it.

Not all—he has a few neighbors, mostly rich and sometimes famous city folks who come out for a few weeks total a year. But if they ever sell, you know he'll be first in line to make an offer.

And he's grinning again. "Wanna join us?"

"Already did my cardio today."

"Lies."

"*Maaaah!*" Sue replies.

"Exactly," I agree. I rub his head again. Goofy boy's missing one horn, and has been since he adopted Grady after the great goat invasion several years back.

"How many more of your teammates are coming?" Aunt Glory asks.

"Are you all going to be running shirtless up and down the street all winter?" Dita Kapinski asks.

"I saw Max Cole come home shirtless last night," Aunt Bea, who lives across the street, says. "Hubba hubba."

"I can hold your feet for you while you do sit-ups," LaShonda Mayberry offers. "And you tell Robinson that Glory might not be available, but I am."

"Does your husband know?" Nana asks her.

"Oh, honey, Robinson's my free pass, and yes, Jason knows it."

I roll up my own mat, toss my Bluetooth speaker in my

messenger bag, and head to the door, watching Cooper's face do the same kind of gymnastics he does with his whole body at second base as the moms and grandmas of Shipwreck pepper him with questions. "Don't keep him too long, ladies, or he won't get his workout in, and then he'll be Cranky Cooper."

"Cooper's never cranky."

"He's a shithead sometimes, but never cranky."

"Check your doors good before you walk in your house, Tillie Jean. We know he owes you for that glitter bomb."

I slip on my jacket, then go up on tiptoe and ruffle his dark hair on my way past. "I hope it's not lame."

He snorts, but his eyes are twinkling. "Ladies. I'm a changed man. I don't pull pranks anymore."

Translation: *I just set up the mother of all revenge plans, and I can't wait to see Tillie Jean's face when she walks head-first into it.*

Time for extra vigilance.

But I'm not expecting to need it *quite* as fast as I do.

I walk out the front door of the senior center and almost run into a very tight baseball ass.

Max is bent over on the sidewalk, dressed in a Fireballs track suit too, petting one of the stray goats that occasionally wander into town. "Who's a good goat? You like shoe laces? Bet you'd like a juicy steak better. Who wants a juicy steak? Who's a good goat?"

And that's my entire problem with Max Cole.

From afar, he's every bit the kind, funny, good guy that I'd want to get to know better.

But up close?

"That's Goatstradamus, and he's the reason we had to install bear-proof trash cans behind Crusty Nut," I say.

Max jerks upright, turns, and his expression goes flat as roadkill.

Up close, he's *that*.

Locked-up, off-limits, and a total stick in the mud. His

jacket is unzipped, and the performance fabric of his white shirt pulls taut over his broad chest, giving me one more view of the muscles I touched last night.

His eyes narrow, which I feel more than see, since I'm still mentally groping his chest.

"Tillie Jean. Didn't see you there."

"Between my invisibility cloak and your lack of eyeballs on your butt, I'm not surprised." I smile.

He doesn't.

"Sleep well?" I ask.

"Great."

"Awesome."

"Yeah."

"Don't leave your doors unlocked or Goatstradamus will pull a Sue on you."

He doesn't blink. Doesn't twitch a facial muscle. Doesn't ask what kind of code that is—it means Sue broke into Grady's house and refused to leave, in case you're wondering —and doesn't answer either.

I sigh and step around him, lifting my messenger bag out of reach of the goat. "Have a good workout. I'm off to work."

"Tillie Jean."

I glance back at him.

He shoves his hands in his pockets and looks down. "Sorry. About last night. Won't happen again."

"Because I'm Cooper's sister, or because I'm that repulsive?"

Good morning, growly bear glare. Been a few hours. I missed you.

"TJ. Quit annoying Max." Cooper pops out of the senior center, Mom on one arm and Dita on the other.

I smile at all of them. "You want me to stop breathing?"

Max flinches.

Cooper's lips twitch.

And Mom gives me a mom look. *"Tillie Jean.* Don't make the poor boy uncomfortable."

The poor boy is towering over all of us and could probably bench press the pirate ship float that Pop rides every summer at our annual Pirate Festival. Rumor has it he's on tap to do a photo shoot for *Arena Insider*'s Bare Naked feature sometime this winter too.

And yes, that's exactly what it sounds like.

He's doing a photoshoot naked.

With all the juicy bits covered once the pictures go to print in the sports magazine, of course, but still naked.

And now *I'm* uncomfortable.

Also, Goatstradamus is trying to eat my messenger bag.

I jerk it out of his reach. "Just heading to work. See you all around."

Probably too soon for some of them.

But that's his problem, not mine.

5

Max

ALL GOOD THINGS MUST COME TO AN END, AND TODAY, apparently, that good thing is me successfully avoiding adding to my list of things I hate about Tillie Jean Rock.

Today, she's having an argument with a parrot right outside my bedroom window.

You heard that right.

She's arguing with a *parrot*.

"Give it *back*, Long Beak Silver."

"*Rawk!* Get your own fucking treasure. *Rawk!*"

It's five-thirty in the morning, and the woman who has been the bane of my existence my entire time with the Fire-balls is once again destroying my calm. I've managed to successfully avoid her for two weeks now—two pretty damn good weeks of settling into a solid routine with my team-mates, getting stronger, staying healthy, maintaining inner peace, doing random acts of kindness by feeding the stray goats and buying lunch at the local pizza joint or the new

Mediterranean grill off the main drag for the locals, all the positive stuff my therapist recommends—but apparently my good luck has run out.

I shove my head under my pillow and try to find the quiet place. *Good air in. Bad air out. Sleep good. You can do it.*

"I swear to Davy Jones, you mangy bird, if you don't give it back, I'm making fried parrot for lunch today."

I'd ask Robinson to trade houses with me, except he's renting out the bedroom over Cooper's parents' garage.

No thanks.

Stafford's in a rental house next to Cooper's grandparents.

Apparently the frisky runs heavy in the Rock genes. Both of my teammates are complaining about the same noises.

Addie Bloom, our batting coach, is out here with us too, renting space above the bowling alley, and Hugo Sanchez, our conditioning coach, is in a spare cottage on a goat farm. Cooper has a couple rental places on the mountain, but they're all booked sporadically through one of those house vacation rental sites, and I'd have to move my crap out every few weeks if I used one.

There are literally no other options in this town unless I want to move into the hotel, which would be even worse. And yeah, I could move back to my own place in the city for the rest of the winter, but other than Tillie Jean, I *like* being here.

I like working out with my teammates.

We're the only ones who know what we're going through, and while there are a bunch of guys still in the city, they're not doing what we're doing here.

They're not being a support group without calling it that. They have their own personal trainers, their own schedules, and their own gyms.

Not like Cooper, Trevor, Robinson, and me. Together. Day in and day out. Like the team we need to be next year.

"Drop it, bird," Tillie Jean hisses.

How a woman can hiss loudly enough to wake the dead is beyond me, but she is, and now, after a couple weeks of not letting her destroy my calm, Tillie Jean is bursting out of that little mental box I store her in.

The one labeled *Her brother is the closest thing I've ever had to a best friend, knows my reputation, and would kill me if I looked at his sister wrong, therefore, it's a good fucking thing she's annoying as hell.*

And then there are days like the glitter bombing day. This morning. The day we met, which I actively refuse to acknowledge for my own sanity, and which has been joined by that stupid kiss on the list of things I pretend I don't think about but which have made my list of things I hate about Tillie Jean Rock grow exponentially.

Concentrate on what you love, not what you hate, my therapist would say.

Fuck him.

He's not here. He doesn't know what it's like.

Sure, Max. Keep telling yourself that. Maybe try to age back up to adulthood sometime today too?

"*Rawk!* Eat shit! *Rawk!*"

"Fine. New tactic. You look lovely today, Long Beak Silver. Your feathers are extra pretty. Who's a good bird? Who's such a good bird who wants to drop it right now?"

"I saw your mama blowing Santa Claus. *Rawk!*"

I roll out of bed, stalk to the window, and open it to a blast of cold air. "Does this town have noise ordinances?"

Tillie Jean shrieks.

"Hide the treasure! It's the po-po!" Long Beak Silver says.

"Go walk the plank, you mangy bird." Tillie Jean lifts a flashlight and aims it at the parrot, who's sitting on her roof with something shiny beside him.

"Middle finger emoji," the bird replies.

Yes, seriously. The bird has learned to say *middle finger emoji*. I watched Cooper teach it the phrase two days ago over lunch at the Korean place that's apparently also relatively new.

Tillie Jean makes one of those *are you kidding me?* noises. Then sighs. "Why do you walk the plank for my brothers but not for me?"

"You're a girl. *RAWK!*"

She swings the flashlight at me, temporarily blinding me on top of all the noise. "Do you see what I have to—*oh my god*, are you naked? Do you *ever* wear clothes? It's thirty degrees out here."

I dig deep to not turn into the cranky asshole I would very much like to be right now. "Why the hell are you arguing with a bird while I'm trying to sleep?"

"He stole my keys."

"Where do you need to go at *five fucking thirty* in the morning?"

"I *was* planning on leaving a present for Grady at his bakery, since he left me a present at Crusty Nut yesterday and this is the only day of the week that he's not there at four in the morning himself, but it appears I'm up early to pluck a parrot featherless instead. *If* I can get my hands on him. And don't tell me this is the universe's way of telling me it's a bad idea to prank Grady. Sometimes the universe wants you to work for it." She tilts her head, and in the span of a blink, she turns back into Cooper Rock's Annoying Little Sister, dropping her voice so it's throaty and full while she bats her lashes at me. "Care to join me? You don't have to put your clothes on."

Four years of being Cooper's teammate.

Four years of Tillie Jean flirting with me.

Four years of my molars getting closer and closer to cracking every time she pushes it.

I've mentioned there are ten million things I hate about this woman, right?

The first time I saw her, I didn't know who she was. I just knew she was in Chance Schwartz's apartment, a dark-haired, flushed-cheek, full-lipped vixen, naked and alone but still enjoying herself in his bed. I couldn't see *everything*, but I could see her full breasts, and I could hear something vibrating under the covers where her legs were clearly spread.

Didn't think much of it, beyond being grateful for the show.

I've had women in my bed too, when my teammates dropped by. Not usually having to get themselves off, but definitely in my bed.

But showing up for lunch with a bunch of the guys on my new team a few hours later and getting introduced to her as Cooper's little sister while Schwartz was slipping his phone number to our server?

She and Schwartz didn't last long after that.

Schwartz didn't last long on the Fireballs either.

Both are my fault, even though any woman deserved better than Chance Schwartz, and Cooper was technically the one who informed management that Schwartz needed to be traded off the team or he'd be calling his agent to make sure he himself was, and even the old management wasn't dumb enough to let Cooper walk.

Also, no, I don't lose any sleep over that. Schwartz was a prick.

If I had a sister, I wouldn't have wanted her dating him either.

And I'm no better than he is when it comes to women—I get around and I don't commit, though unlike my former teammate, I'm upfront about it—and I like having Cooper Rock as one of my friends.

So instead of answering his sister's invitation to join her naked, I slam the window shut, and I take myself back to bed, where I bury my head under two pillows and tell myself I'll be able to get back to sleep.

I don't.

Naturally.

Instead, not three minutes later, I hear the distinct *clink* of a ladder being propped against a roof.

Reason number eight thousand, two hundred fifty-five…

It's dark as a meatball's asshole outside, and she's climbing up onto her roof to chase a bird.

An old, familiar sense of duty pokes me in that damned spot between my shoulder blades, and the next thing I know, I'm pulling on sweatpants and heading out into the chilly night—sun's not up, so *yes*, it's still night—where Cooper's sister is ascending a rickety ladder with nothing but a flashlight and the sound of a parrot's voice to guide her.

And we've added *gets me up at stupid hours of the night* to the list of things about Tillie Jean Rock that I cannot stand.

"*Rawk!* To the left. *Rawk!* To the right. *Rawk!* Dip and grind! Dip and grind!"

"Please just give me back my keys."

"Daddy gives and Daddy takes away. *Rawk!*"

She mutters something she probably learned from the parrot as the dark outline of her reaches the top of the ladder.

I stride to the edge of it and peer up. "What are you doing?"

"Getting my keys. Regardless of what the universe is telling me, *I need my car keys.*"

"This town's four square blocks. *Walk.*"

"It's ten square blocks and growing, and I can't carry Grady's present that far."

"Christ on lasagna," I mutter.

"Aww, you sound just like Luca. That's adorable. Is he

coming to work out with you guys again soon? I miss Henri, and she's not taking texts while she's on a deadline."

Shit.

I *am* cussing like Luca Rossi. Guy hasn't been on the team a full year, and he's already sharing his personality. "Can you please get off the roof before you fall and break your head?"

She twists and plops, and suddenly she's sitting on the edge of her roof, feet dangling, probably staring down at me.

I assume that's what the hairs raising on the back of my neck means, anyway. I can't see her, and my heart's starting that old, heavy rhythm again.

Dammit.

Dammit.

Beautiful morning. Chilly, but clear. Can see stars. She's a grown woman.

Nothing to get riled up about.

My pulse is still inching upward, though, and my lungs are giving me warning signs that this is a complication I cannot afford this morning.

Go home, Max. Go home. She's not your problem.

She sighs loudly. "I sincerely appreciate your concern, but number one, I unfortunately do this all the time, because my grandfather's parrot is an asshole, and number two—"

"*Rawk!* Don't number two on the poop deck, asshole! *Rawk!*"

There's a flutter of wings.

Tillie Jean grunts, and the shadow of her legs flails as the beam off her flashlight flickers and turns wildly. "I swear to the pirate gods, you mangy *aaaaaah!*"

Fuck.

Fuck fuck fuck.

I don't think, I just move, because she's falling off the roof. She's *falling off the roof.*

I shove the ladder and leap to grab her, heart in my throat, lungs shrinking.

Have to cushion her fall.

Stop her neck from snapping.

Stop her head from hitting the ground.

Stop Cooper from killing me for letting his sister dive off the roof on my watch.

I don't know what part of her body connects with me first, but my grand plan to catch her in my arms immediately fails. I'm stumbling backwards, propelled by the weight of a full-grown woman colliding wrong with my shoulder.

Fuck.

My shoulder.

It— "*Oof,*" I grunt.

My ass hits the dirt under a rock.

Specifically, a Tillie Jean Rock, who's sprawled across me and *oof*-ing herself while my palms go clammy and my throat tightens and my heart tries to run a marathon in four-point-two seconds.

Reason number seventy-two million that I hate this woman...

"What are you doing?" she gasps. "You could've hurt yourself, and then what would the Fireballs do? Oh, shit. Are you hurt? Tell me you're not hurt. Max? *Max!*"

There's light in my eyeballs again, and I can't shield my face. She's still on top of my arms, and even if she wasn't, I'm not sure I could breathe.

Dammit.

Fuck.

I'm okay. I'm okay. I'm okay.

"Put that fucking light *away.*" The order comes out on a gasp, but I'm breathing.

Not having an episode.

I'm breathing.

I'm okay. Not dead.

She's not dead.

She's annoying. She can't be annoying if she's dead.

Except it's Tillie Jean. She probably *could* be annoying if she was dead, and *thank fuck*, that does it.

Thinking of TJ as a cranky old ghost yelling at parrots outside of Cooper's window almost has me smiling, which is the weirdest sensation *ever*, and almost smiling has my pulse evening out and my breath coming steadier.

My back is cold and wet. I'm in the grass. Better than concrete. I test my shoulder, then glare at the light. "Are *you* okay?"

"Totally fine. I do this all the time."

Hell.

I think she's telling the truth.

Not gonna help the anxiety here. "You fall off roofs all the time."

"I live with Long Beak Silver. *And* I re-roofed my house myself last summer. It's a short house. I can handle this. Back to you, please. Where does it hurt? Can you move? Can you stand? Can you walk? Cooper's gonna kill me. And not like let Grady's goat into my house to eat my garbage kind of kill me either."

Her fingers are probing me everywhere. My shoulders. My neck. My chest.

And it's causing one very unfortunate reaction south of my belt.

Tillie Jean Rock is *not* supposed to make my body react like this.

I grunt and sit up, shoving her aside. "Stay off roofs."

She makes a low growl.

My dick leaps to full attention.

So I leap too. Right to my feet, carrying me across the yard to my house, where I will go inside, make sure my shoulder's just twinged and not injured, meditate, drink water, and then, if necessary, whack off in the shower while I think about *anyone* besides Tillie Jean.

Reason number eleven thousand that I hate this woman: I

can't jerk off while thinking about her if I don't want to lose the best friend I've ever had.

Not how I wanted to start my day.

But I'm pretty sure this is life in Shipwreck.

Which means I can fight it, I can leave, or I can figure out how to live with it.

6

TILLIE JEAN

BY NOON, IT'S PRETTY OBVIOUS I TWISTED MY ANKLE FALLING OFF my roof this morning.

Not that I'll admit that to anyone.

Nor will I admit what my heart was doing the whole time I was lying on Max in the dirt.

Let's just say I wish I could double-wrap *it* in addition to my ankle. But I can't, and I have to work, so I text my friends Mackenzie and Marisol back in Copper Valley and ask if they know of any single guys who need a winter fling, and then I get on with my day, which is basically a double shift at Crusty Nut.

We're in the middle of our usual lunch rush, which isn't heavy since November's not exactly high tourist season for a pirate town in the mountains, and the retreat center at the edge of town isn't hosting any conferences this week. It's just Dad and me running things, him in the kitchen, me playing hostess, server, bartender, and busser while sneaking regular coffee into my decaf cup. My local besties are all sitting at the bar sharing a basket of gold nuggets—aka fried pickle chips—while waiting for their lunch entrees.

"What's with your dad today?" Georgia, Grady's morning baker at Crow's Nest down the street, asks.

Annika, Grady's wife, chokes on her tea while Sloane, who left the city to come live the small-town life here a few years back, cackles.

She's still waiting for her Hallmark movie romance hero to come and get her.

Me too, Sloane. Me too.

It's the only downside to small-town living. My on-again, off-again boyfriend of five years who agreed to marry me if we were both thirty and single found himself a wife not long after Grady and Annika hooked up, and the pickings are even slimmer around here now.

Especially since the new people moving to town are mostly young married couples looking for a quiet but not boring spot to raise their kids, which is where Shipwreck totally delivers.

I know the right guy will appear when I'm ready for him —the universe works in mysterious ways like that—but some days I wish it would hurry up.

"You didn't hear?" Sloane's dropping her voice while still cackling. "You know how Robinson Simmons is renting that room over their garage? He heard *noises* in the house this morning and—"

"And we don't need to hear the rest of this story," I interrupt as I bend over and straighten the bottle of wine, making sure I don't need to run back to the storeroom and get more before lunch.

Probably not.

There aren't a lot of people who order wine with lunch here.

"*Again?*" Georgia asks. "That poor boy. You'd think he'd learn."

"Grady and Cooper are having a talk with both him and Trevor Stafford later today to offer tips on the best earplugs to use and which noises don't require the senior citizens to be checked on." Annika's eyes are extra twinkly today. They've been twinkly since she told Grady they were expecting a baby right before their wedding a few weeks ago, but this is next-level twinkle. They clearly had a good honeymoon.

"Again?" Georgia repeats.

"They think it might sink in this time. Is it wrong to hope it doesn't?"

I glare at my sister-in-law. She might think it's hilarious that my parents get frisky still, but I don't want to hear about it. "Yes."

"What about you, TJ?" Sloane asks. "Any more excitement with your temporary neighbor?"

"Mr. Growly Bear with a stick up his ass? He's ignoring me when he's not growling at me." And trying to catch me while I fall off my roof.

Holy muscles, Blackbeard. There's knowing a man is large, and there's *feeling* how large a man is for yourself, *again*, and *dammit*.

There goes another hot flash, along with another memory of him kissing me outside The Grog a couple weeks ago. I gulp my coffee to scald my tongue and distract myself.

"You still flirting with him?"

I grin even though I want to fan myself, and also want to kick myself for needing to fan myself. "Incessantly," I lie, since I've hardly seen him. Pretty sure he's avoiding me. "It's the trick in my back pocket that sets Cooper off *every time*."

Annika slides her glass across the bar to me. "I am so glad I don't have brothers."

"You practically grew up with Cooper as your brother, and you have Bailey. She's as much of a handful as they were at her age."

"Or more," Georgia mutters.

We all laugh, but Annika's wincing at the mention of her teenage sister as I refill her water.

There's so much truth to Georgia's statement.

"Has Max retaliated for the glitter bombing?" Sloane asks.

I shake my head. "I don't think he's the prankster type."

"Are you kidding?" Georgia asks. "He was at Crow's Nest yesterday telling Grady about hiding stuffed turtles in Trevor's locker and laughing about that Fiery thong Mackenzie made Brooks wear last season."

"So he's not the prankster type with me. He's not the *acknowledge Tillie Jean is anything other than a pest* type with me either. It's like he's never gotten over—"

I cut myself off.

And my friends lean in.

"Gotten over what?" Annika asks.

"I smell a story," Sloane adds.

Georgia cackles. "Gotten over *how they met*." She's a Ship-wreck native, and so naturally, she heard as much of the story as Cooper knows.

Also, I don't care how muscly Max is, he is *dead* if he ever breathes a word to anyone about the *other* half of what happened.

And I don't mean like the heart attack I was planning to give Grady this morning with delivery boxes of broken plates in retribution for the fake puke he planted in the Crusty Nut fridge last week, which doesn't sound like a bad prank until you find out Grady's been dreaming of replacing all of the plain Crow's Nest plates with custom pottery for over a year, and it's due to arrive any day now.

Definitely not kill Max like *that*.

I mean *tortured for hours and then killed dead* dead.

"Oooh, did you have a one-night stand?" Sloane asks.

Annika's brown eyes light up even more when she smiles. "Or were you hiding in the locker room waiting to prank

Cooper and fell out of the air duct when you saw Max *n-a-k-e-d*?"

I grab a stack of napkins and start rolling silverware. "One, I'm pretty sure Max is *n-a-k-e-d* practically all the time, so no. And two, he found out I was dating Chance Schwartz and told Cooper."

"*Oh my god*, you dated Chance Schwartz? The catcher?" Sloane leans in. "Details. *Details*."

"I hooked up with him for like two nights while Ben and I were in one of our off-again phases, Max found out, told Cooper, Cooper hit the roof, Chance got traded, and now it's common knowledge among the team that I'm off-limits."

"Oh, come on. Hello, double standard. Like Cooper isn't just as much of a horn dog as the rest of them." Sloane shoots a look at the kitchen door and drops her voice. "Your dad *does* know Cooper's a horn dog, right?"

"We all pretend none of the rest of us have sex lives and we all get along better that way." I gesture to Annika. "Artificial insemination and they had to knock Grady out cold to collect his swimmers. That's what I tell myself."

She snorts her water out of her nose.

But Sloane's rolling her eyes. "Cooper should still stay out of your private life. What's the big deal if you hook up with one of his teammates?"

"I could date one of Cooper's friends. Grady's too. They wouldn't be friends with assholes. But a teammate? They're stuck together. Might not pick each other if they weren't. Seriously, how many guys on the team would want Cooper dating *their* sisters? So it's not like I don't get where he was coming from. I just think it's dumb and it makes his teammates either go out of their way to make sure I know they're only being nice because I'm Cooper's sister, or it makes them act like I have cooties."

The doorbells jingle, and the damn parrot flies into my

restaurant a moment before my grandfather strolls in the door.

He's in full pirate regalia today—Pop, I mean, not the parrot, though that's not unheard of either—right down to the eye patch, and the sight both makes me smile and also wish my ancestors could've maybe been medieval knights instead of pirates.

I love my family, but knights wouldn't have parrots for pets. They'd have horses.

The stray goats in town aren't quite the same, though I'll take them, considering they don't curse out passing tourists.

"Ahoy, me lassies." Pop flashes us a wolfish smile and lifts my car keys. "I be finding pirate treasure this morning, and I be in a mood to share. *Arr!*"

"Your parrot is a nuisance, Pop." I try very hard to not limp as I walk out from behind the bar, retrieve my keys, and press a kiss to his weathered cheek. He knew they were mine because you don't live in Shipwreck, with the damn bird around, without learning very quickly to attach a keychain with your name onto your keys. "Look at this place. Practically empty. He scared all the tourists away."

He grunts an old man grunt, just like he does every time we have this argument. "It's all those people heading over for sushi day at that Korean place. You on a pegleg today, girlie?"

Dammit. He's not supposed to notice. Or worry about me. And no, I'm not worried about Crusty Nut losing business to the new restaurants in town. Slow sushi day is normal.

I'd go have sushi lunch myself except one, Dad needs me here so he's not paying for double help, and two, if there's any chance that the guys are headed that way, there's no way I will.

No way I'm giving Max Cole the pleasure of thinking that him calling me a priss for only ordering California rolls led to me branching out and experimenting with a broader variety of items on a sushi menu.

Plus, I really don't want to see him.

I nod to Pops. "Yep. Getting in the spirit early for next year."

"Ye be missing your pirate hat." He pulls his own off and plops it on my head, where it settles so low it almost covers my eyes, smelling like wood smoke and sweat. "There. Now ye be a proper pirate lass. *Arr!*"

"Thanks, Pop. I feel like a real pirate now."

"Ye be a real pirate, Matilda Jean. It's in your blood."

It is. And it probably explains why lately, I've been feeling unsettled.

It's like I need to get out to sea and pillage and plunder or something.

Have a real vacation, since I forgot to do it last year. Sloane and Georgia and I have been talking about a girls' weekend away in New York City forever. We should get it on the calendar, but it seems like there's always something else more important that pops up.

Or possibly I need to crash at Cooper's place for a weekend of playing video games and catching up for real. We haven't had much of a chance yet this off-season between his time with the guys and the increase in endorsement deals he's working through. He's even taking longer to prank me back —with anything good, I mean—which is killing some of my joy in the off-season too.

The bells over the door jingle again, and speak of the devil, there he is.

Cooper walks in, makes eye contact, and starts grinning. "TJ. Long time no see. How's my favorite sister?"

"Meek and humble and not planning any revenge at all for someone replacing my sugar with salt." Which was super lame as far as pranks go, and makes me wonder what else he's planning while he thinks I think that's the worst he'll do.

Or if he's giving me up.

If he's outgrown me now that he plays for a team that wins.

Is this the universe's way of telling me I, too, need to move on? Is that why I'm feeling off lately?

Dammit. Where's my coffee? I need more caffeine to handle thoughts like this.

He shakes his head like he has no idea what I'm talking about. "Grady's really giving you a hard time, isn't he?"

He's not. Not really. I actually wonder if the fake puke was one of my cousins. "Yep. It's all Grady."

Trevor, Robinson, and Max all file in behind my brother.

"Hey, Max." I wink just to annoy him. Again. "Lookin' good today. Take the seat by the window. It's got the best view."

A muscle in his cheek twitches.

Cooper growls.

And I turn and sashay back to the bar.

Or try to.

Stupid ankle.

"That be a damn good pegleg walk," Pop says.

"It's all that pirate in my blood."

My three friends are wearing identical frowns, which is remarkable considering they look nothing alike.

"Order up," Dad calls. "TJ? Where'd you hide the mustard?"

I paste on a smile and get back to work.

My ankle will heal. The guys will get food and go. And tomorrow, Max will continue to pretend he didn't kiss me two weeks ago, that he didn't catch me falling off a roof this morning, and he's never seen me naked.

Just like my overprotective brother wants.

It's what's best for the Fireballs, right?

And that's all that matters.

Dammit.

7

Max

TILLIE JEAN'S LIMPING.

It shouldn't piss me off. What she does isn't my business. But she's limping after she fell off a roof this morning, which means she probably needs to see a doctor, and instead, she's pulling a full shift at a restaurant.

Cooper nudges me hard. "You're not staring at TJ's ass, are you?"

I shake my head automatically and wrench my gaze away from her to look Cooper straight in the eye. "No. Her head. Her hat's a train wreck."

Reason number two. Her ass. She has such a fucking fantastic ass that it was the very second thing to ever go on my list of things I hate about her.

He relaxes back into his seat, his usual grin returning. "It is, isn't it? Pop swears it's been passed down through the family from Thorny Rock himself. Grady's gonna get it one day. Can you imagine? Wearing seven generations of your ancestors' hair grease for forty years?"

Tillie Jean's eyes snap our way, and her blue irises light up like a Bunsen burner while I remind myself he's talking about his sister's hat and not her ass.

"I can imagine your lunch is gonna be decorated with spit if you don't quit irritating your sister," Stafford says.

"Dude, you should lay off the pranks," Robinson agrees. "I like TJ. She's nice. Be good if she stayed nice this winter."

Stafford nods. "Don't want to get caught in the crossfire."

But Cooper's still grinning. "You kidding? She *lives* for the off-season months when I'm home every year. You know how boring this place gets otherwise?"

Stafford, Robinson, and I glance around the restaurant. It's designed to make you feel like you're in the hull of a ship. Plank wood walls. Pirate statue in the corner that looks just like Cooper's grandfather, who supposedly looks just like Thorny Rock, founder of Shipwreck, himself. Pirate treasure maps plastered to the walls between paintings of ships at sea, some with muted colors, some so bright you shouldn't look at them without sunglasses. Barrels holding menus and tourist information stand at either side of the thick wooden door-frame, and more barrels make up the hostess stand. There's a half-wall separating the bar from the rest of the restaurant, and a row of fake parrots sitting on bird swings hanging down above it.

Except for the one real parrot that keeps picking a different swing and insulting the fake birds.

And there's even a mascot for the damn restaurant—a pirate peanut on a pegleg.

"You get bored here." Trevor stares at Cooper like it's the dumbest thing he's ever heard.

"Only so many times you can do glow-in-the-dark pirate putt-putt and tube down a snowed-over waterslide before you've been there, done it all." Cooper shakes his head. "Winter in Shipwreck is a sad, quiet, lonely time."

"Beg to differ," Annika calls from the bar. Cooper's sister-in-law is seated between two other women I've met in passing a time or two in the past few weeks, and I'm starting to remember them all, less from experience and more because Cooper talks a lot.

Annika is the slender brown-haired one and was Grady's best friend in high school despite living in Sarcasm, the next town over, which is officially Shipwreck's enemy town. She moved home to help her mother and sister with their own bakery, and now keeps books for half the businesses in both Sarcasm and Shipwreck. Rumor has it she's expecting, though I'll be the last person to bring it up in conversation with her not showing at all.

Georgia works for Grady at Crow's Nest bakery and runs an Etsy shop selling soaps and candles, and it took me a minute to place her. She cut off her cornrows since last week, and now her tight black curls are cropped close to her skull.

Sloane is the redheaded nurse who moved to Shipwreck after falling in love with it during a destination wedding here. She works for Georgia's grandpa, who's the town doctor, and basically every unmarried guy between the ages of eighteen and fifty regularly fights for her attention. All seven of them.

Pretty sure Georgia's about to give her a run for her money though.

In short—everyone's connected to everyone else here, and they're all tight as family, or they want to make the people here their family.

"You haven't been home long enough to know how very boring it gets," Cooper tells Annika.

"I've been home a couple years. If you get bored, you're doing it wrong."

"Hush, both of you." Tillie Jean slides three plates onto the bar, putting one in front of each of her friends. "We're not starting the Shipwreck-Sarcasm wars again."

"Sarcasm-Shipwreck wars," Annika mutters loudly.

Cooper rolls his eyes.

Tillie Jean rolls her eyes.

Mr. Rock pops out from the kitchen just to roll his eyes, spots us, and waves. "Morning, boys. Good workout today?"

"We kicked ass," Cooper calls to his dad.

"Good. Watch your language around the bird."

My shoulders bunch.

Not because of the bird, or the warning about language, but because three generations of Rock men are all grinning at each other now.

I know it's wrong to hate Cooper Rock for having everything I ever wanted growing up, but the anger and frustration still hit me sometimes.

He grew up playing pirate. It's family tradition.

I grew up learning how to roll my old man onto his side after he drank too much so he wouldn't suffocate in his own vomit since he didn't know how else to handle the demons haunting him.

"TJ," Mr. Rock says, "you get these boys drinks yet?"

"What do you boys want to drink?" she calls to us.

"*Tillie Jean.* Walk your butt over there and take their orders."

"Cooper smells like a dog wash."

"She's got a point, Mr. Rock," Robinson calls. "TJ, can I get some of your sweet tea?"

"Water for me," Stafford adds.

"Plain tea," I say without looking at her.

"Coming right up," she says, cutting Cooper off before he can ask for a drink.

But he's not offended.

Not Cooper.

He's grinning.

Probably planning on egging her car later.

And when my eyes wander over to the bar, where she's flipping empty glasses onto the counter beside two sweating pitchers of tea, she's also smiling.

Cooper and Tillie Jean aren't just brother and sister. They're friends.

A weird kind of friends, but still friends.

"I can't believe I miss him too when he's gone," Georgia says, barely loud enough for us to hear.

"Sarcasm would chew him up and spit him out," Annika replies.

"We might need that by the first of December. He's extra...*Cooper* this year."

"That means extra fabulous," Cooper translates.

My shoulders twitch again, but I roll them back and remind myself I knew what I was signing up for when I came here for the winter.

"How's PT?" I ask Stafford, forcing myself to look away from where TJ's taking a massive gulp off a huge coffee cup and muttering something about *decaf* to Annika.

Not my business.

Working out and keeping up with Trevor?

Completely my business.

While I'm doing strength training and conditioning with the coaches, he's in physical therapy for his agitated shoulder. Again. He's been a reliever for the Fireballs longer than I've been on the team, and no one's talking about if he'll be able to rehab enough to come back in the spring after irritating it all over again in our last game.

Or if management will sign his contract extension.

Not like any other teams are knocking for him.

He ignores my question and looks at Cooper. "You really go down the waterslide when it's snowed over?"

"Hell, yeah. On inner tubes. But only in the middle of the night. Here's my plan—we're gonna get all the guys from the team who stayed in Copper Valley to come out right before the first big snowfall of winter, and then we're having a midnight snowpark party. We'll do all those videos they put on the scoreboard between innings. Debating who has the best form at the bottom, talking about DJ Darren Greene's questionable choice in music, scoring each other on our lazy river performance. Hitting balls off the top of the water treehouse. The whole deal."

"Coach Bloom'll bust your balls if you break your leg falling off a waterslide, man," Robinson mutters.

Can't say it too loudly or she'll hear.

And it doesn't matter that she's not in the restaurant.

She hears all. Swear she does.

But Cooper's shaking his head. "That's why we put the trampoline cover over the landing pool. I'll talk to management. They have the best video equipment."

"Cooper, come get your friends' drinks," Tillie Jean calls. "And bring me their orders when you come this way."

"No service, no tip," he calls back.

"Seriously, man, she's gonna spit in all our food," Robinson mutters.

Stafford shakes his head. "No, she won't. She'll get him back by blowing a bullhorn through his window at two AM. And he'll deserve it."

TJ has four glasses sitting on a tray on the bar, and she's eyeballing them like batters tend to eyeball me when I've struck them out twice already in a single game.

Cooper doesn't move to get the drinks.

But then, he probably doesn't know she fell off her damn roof a few hours ago, and he probably didn't notice her limping, or if he did, he thought it was her actual pegleg impersonation.

Dammit.

I shove up out of my chair and stalk to the bar to grab the tray. My quads cuss at me. Today was leg day at the gym and that's what they do on leg day. Feel like jelly until you sit, then they get angry when you try to move again.

But it means I'm alive, and I'm kicking ass at getting in top shape for next year, so I'll take it.

Tillie Jean shifts that wary gaze my way as I stop across from her and reach for the tray. "Two parrot burgers, a grilled chicken salad, and whatever Cooper hates most," I tell her.

"We don't serve parrot burgers."

"But you want to." I glance at her grandfather and Long Beak Silver, who are entertaining her friends now.

"Go sit down. I can bring those over."

"Yeah, limping and carrying a tray full of drinks go great together."

"I'm not limping."

I tilt a brow.

She ducks her head and grabs an order pad. "Two hamburgers, a grilled chicken salad, and the gristle leftover from the smoked pork butt for Cooper. Got it. What kind of dressing, and how do you want those burgers cooked?"

"Twist your ankle?"

"Vinaigrette because it's what you always have, medium for one burger and well-done for the other."

"Or is it your knee?"

"What's wrong with your knee, TJ?" Sloane spins on her stool and glances between us.

Tillie Jean doesn't blink. "Banged it on my footboard again."

"Before or after you fell off the roof?" I ask.

"You fell off the roof?"

Silence descends, but only for a minute.

Annika's the first one to talk. *"Again?"*

"What do you mean, *again*?" Cooper yelps.

"Get up on the bar and pull your pant leg up," Sloane orders. "Let me look."

But Tillie Jean waves her away. "It's *fine*. I twisted my ankle a little, and I'm in that stupid ankle brace just to be safe. If it still hurts tomorrow, I'll make an appointment with Doc, okay? It's tweaked. It's not injured."

"You can't be walking around on a twisted ankle." Cooper's next to me now, peering over the bar like he can see his sister's injury through the wood.

"And who'll serve your food if I don't?"

"If you'd told me *you were hurt*, I would've come over here and gotten my own damn drink."

"I'm not hurt. I'm *irritated*."

Okay, that's funny. Cooper's used that line every time he's been put on the injured list since I joined the Fireballs.

Not that it happens often, but a guy can't dive for every baseball the way he does at second base and *not* get injured a time or two.

He shoves me. "How'd you know she was hurt?"

"Live next door to a person long enough, they'll eventually wake you up cussing at a parrot and falling off a roof at five in the morning."

Mr. Rock pokes his head out of the kitchen again. He's in a pirate hat over his hairnet too, though his doesn't have mostly dead feathers like Tillie Jean's does. "Were you chasing that damn parrot again?"

"He stole my keys."

"Pop." Mr. Rock puts his hands on his hips and glares at his own father. "If that bird doesn't quit causing trouble, we'll have to retire him."

"*Rawk!* Eat shit and die. *Rawk!*"

Robinson grunts behind us. So does Trevor.

All of us made the mistake of sitting down after working out, and they're rising to join Cooper and me at the bar.

"We can sit over here," Robinson says, pulling up a stool next to Georgia.

"I'm *fine*," Tillie Jean insists once more. "Who's having the hamburgers? You two again? Fruit on the side, Robinson? Trevor, you want to upgrade your side to a salad with just vinegar because you're insane, right? Go sit. Quit fussing."

"The cussing's a serious problem with tourist season, Dad," Mr. Rock grumbles.

"It's only a problem because people are afraid of words. What can words do? Not a damn thing."

"*Rawk!* I'm gonna eat your pussy! *Rawk!*"

All of us turn and stare at the bird.

Pop Rock shifts in his seat and goes red in the face. "I didn't teach him that," he says gruffly.

"That's not what Nana says," Tillie Jean mutters under her breath.

The things I did *not* need to hear.

"Brain bleach," Trevor says.

Robinson's grimacing next to him. "I think I just lost my appetite."

"Pop, Dad's right." Cooper grabs a tea off the tray, takes a sip, makes a face, and hands it to Robinson. "That one's yours. Back to the parrot. He needs remedial training or he'll start scaring the tourists away. *Gah.* That's *really* sweet tea." He sticks his tongue out and waggles it around like that'll get the taste out of his mouth, then grabs another cup of tea and takes a big gulp.

And promptly sputters and chokes on it. "What the *hell*? Are these all sweet?"

Tillie Jean beams at him. "Yep."

And then she does the most Tillie Jean thing possible and winks at me with another of her saucy grins. "Don't worry. I would've warned you. I like you better. Hold on two seconds and I'll get you the fresh stuff. No sugar and two lemons, just the way you like it."

I'm twitching.

She's flirting with me merely to annoy her brother, and I know it, and I'm still twitching. "We have to quit coming here," I mutter to Cooper. "She's gonna break both of us."

He laughs. "Speak for yourself, man. The fun's just getting started. But if she gets to be too much, let me know. I'll make her stop."

Right.

I need someone else to tell a woman to stop flirting with me.

I'd ask what's wrong with me, except I already know.

It's Tillie Jean. Tillie Jean is wrong with me, and she has been from the moment we met.

8

TILLIE JEAN

THERE'S EXACTLY ONE CURE FOR A LONG DAY, AND IT'S AUNT Glory's whiskey sour, but replace the whiskey with fresh dark roast coffee and the sour with a little splash of Bailey's Irish Cream, and then add more coffee, which is exactly what she does before serving it in my stein. She knows my mother worries about my caffeine consumption but also that I need a cure for a long day.

Probably I shouldn't be on my second already, especially considering my dinner was a side salad—spend all day delivering greasy fried food to people, and it loses its appeal after a while—but the beautiful thing about Ship-wreck is that I can walk home with one leg tied behind my back.

Preferably the leg with the achy ankle, but it'll be fine tomorrow.

I swear. It's only cranky because it's tired, not because it's anything more than tweaked. And I'm not drunk. I'm buzzed. Caffeine buzzes aren't illegal, no matter what laws the town council tries to pass to get me to cut back when I fall off the wagon and back into the latte pool.

Buzzkills.

Sloane looks up from her phone and shakes her head at me. "You missed the dart board."

"You wouldn't know. You weren't looking."

She flashes her phone screen at me. "You're trending in Shipwreck's Facebook group. Dakota's counting how many darts you get stuck in the wall."

I glance over my shoulder at Dita's son, Dakota, who's out for a night with his wife while Grandma Dita babysits their four-year-old twins.

He lifts a beer. "Keep going, TJ. I got five bucks riding on you not hitting the board at all."

"No cheating," Vinnie Carpelli, a middle-aged electrician who's been everyone's favorite person at some point in the last few years, calls from across The Grog. "I got ten on her finishing out the night with a bull's-eye."

"Aunt Glory, TJ's next drink's on me," Dakota hollers.

"Make it water," Vinnie orders.

I turn back to the wall and launch the last dart in my hand.

It bounces off the side of the board and clatters to the floor near my seat.

Possibly I'd hit the board better if I were standing up, but I like lounging on one chair with my foot propped up on the other.

The jittery hands most likely aren't helping either.

Aunt Glory makes seriously good coffee. It's like she sprinkles it with magic mocha dust or something, whereas my coffee grinder hasn't been the same since Cooper left those roasted goat turds in it last winter.

No, I did *not* brew goat turds. And yes, it took me off coffee for at least three months, which he swears was his only intention, and the reason my coffee grinder hasn't been the same is that I got a new one and haven't found the right setting yet.

"Anyone who wants to make money off my very bad dart game better get over here and pick up the darts for me," I call.

Sloane grins and shakes her head.

"Game over," Dakota crows.

"Not if I get my ass off this stool and pick up her darts," Vinnie replies.

A shadow moves behind me. All the hairs on the back of my neck stand up, and not just because that's a semi-normal reaction to two of Aunt Glory's not-whiskey-sours at nine at night.

Max is here.

When did Max get here?

Whenever it was, he apparently came without a coat. Actually, I haven't seen him in a coat all week. Did he lose it? I didn't ruin it too when I spilled all that paint water on him, did I?

Or does Max Cole merely like being naked?

Oof.

That was a whole-body shiver. Yum.

More coffee. Definitely time for more coffee.

Sloane smiles at him. "Hey, Max. Cooper coming?"

"You slept with him!" I abandon my plans for coffee, sit straight up and drop my leg off the chair, wincing when my heel bounces on the floor.

She tilts an amused look my way. "Not sure which *him* you're talking about, but no. That said, I am *highly* entertained by your brother's attempts to charm me, and you're talking more to the dart board than you are to me, so..."

"So you *haven't* slept with him?" It's been a running question every winter since Sloane moved to town, and every winter, she tells me the same. I'm pretty sure she means it. She saw him naked after one of my own pranks gone wrong —long story—and she slapped his ass with a wooden spoon last Thanksgiving. Those two instances didn't turn either of them into hornballs who had to climb all over each other, so I figure they really don't like each other like that. Plus, Cooper morphed into a whiny baby when Mom let Sloane have her last piece of Grady and Annika's leftover wedding cake a couple days after the wedding.

Is there anything more unattractive?

But Cooper is Cooper, and Sloane is basically the hottest single woman who's not related to half the town—Georgia being the hottest single woman who *is* related to the half of the town that I'm not related to—so it's a legit question.

She laughs though. "Sisters before misters. Oh, look, Vinnie sent you another drink. Like you're going to finish the second, much less a third."

"Are you calling me a lightweight?"

"Yes."

I grin. "I would've made an awful pirate." Only partially because I'll take an espresso over rum any day of the week.

Aunt Glory hands me my glitter tumbler that Luca Rossi's girlfriend, Henri, gave me—so *this* is where it's been—then smiles at Max. "Wings and a beer, hon?"

"Burger and fries and an iced tea, please, ma'am."

"What?" I gasp in mock horror. "A *burger* will touch those lips? Say it isn't so."

He takes the seat my foot just vacated, frowning at me. "Are you drunk?"

"Nope. Just happy. But I'm always happy. The jitters make me *extra* happy. What makes you happy, Growly Bear?"

"Not being called Growly Bear."

"But you don't like it when I call you sexy beast either."

He props an ankle over his knee. "Why do you flirt with me?"

"That's a bull's-eye question."

He bends, snags a dart off the cement floor, and flings it at the wall without looking.

The dart makes a dull thump that says it hit the board.

There's no way it was a bull's-eye, but you know what?

I'm feeling generous. And I really don't want to fight with Max.

Joke with him? Yes. I joke with all the guys on the team. Why should he be any different?

Because he's hot, he's seen you more than just naked, he's kissed you, you like how his skin and muscles feel, you're both single, and he acts repulsed by you, which is the best challenge you've ever had, my nipples whisper.

Whoops. I'm at nipple-talking caffeine-high stage. That usually only happens when I'm exceptionally tired and *only* propped up by the caffeine.

I should go home and go to bed, which is code for *I need to go home and paint until I can fall asleep since there's no way I'm sleeping until my first coffee of the night has worn off.*

Instead, I crook a finger at him. "You want to know?"

He doesn't lean in for the secret, but he does drum his fingers over his calf like he's waiting.

I wish he was in shorts. I love muscular calves. Especially hairy muscular calves. Why is it that he wears short sleeves everywhere in pre-winter, but he doesn't wear shorts too? "At first, it was so Cooper would get *you* traded too," I whisper loudly.

Sloane darts to her feet. "Bathroom."

"Want me to come?" I ask her. "That's not exactly a secret. And if it was a secret, it didn't need to be."

She gives me a look that's a little fuzzy.

Uh-oh. She's not fuzzy.

My eyes are fuzzy.

That's a bad sign, and I should definitely stop drinking coffee *right now.*

But I don't *want* to.

"I'm leaving because I want plausible deniability in whatever you say next," she informs me. "I won't sleep with your brother, but that doesn't mean he can't trick knowledge out of me. I want no knowledge of what you're about to say. Text me if you need me to help you keep your clothes on though."

"No, no, come back," I say to her retreating backside. "Make me stop talking."

"You gonna throw a dart, TJ?" Vinnie calls.

Max bends and grabs another dart from the floor and hands it to me. "Go on. Throw it. Then tell me why you flirt with me *now*."

I take the dart with jittery fingers and toss it at the wall, where it bounces off and clatters to the floor again. "Whoops."

His long arms once again extend to the floor, and the next thing I know, I have seven darts in my hand.

Or eight.

Or two.

The fuzzy-buzzy is getting real. I should go home and eat a grilled cheese sandwich.

Instead, I aim a very sharp dart at a very solid wall and throw.

It thuds.

"*Yeah*, TJ!" Dakota yells.

"Did I bull's-eye?"

"No. You stuck it in the picture of the 2005 pirate crew above the board."

I shoot out of my seat to look, swaying and grabbing Max's shoulder for support, because it's the nearest solid object.

Hello, Max's muscles. Why am I not immune to you?

I've been around baseball players my entire life, because Cooper's been a baseball god *his* entire life, and the thing you do when your older brother is good at something is trail along after him while he does that thing he's good at for your entire childhood until he leaves for college and then the minors. You know that falling for a baseball player means coming second to the game every time, and you know that he's gone half the year, and you know that one day, he'll hang it up and come home and not know who you are since you've grown apart in the years that he was putting baseball first.

And I wouldn't date a hockey player, football player, soccer player, *you name it* player for the same reason.

And I've never *wanted* to.

But Max?

I *want* to get to know this man who's been getting under my skin for four years now. I want to know if we can be friends. I want to know if I do other things to offend him, or if he's just an asshole and I have a complex where I'm attracted to assholes and I need to go back to therapy to work through this.

Supporting people is good.

Trying to fix people is bad.

Can't fix an asshole that doesn't want to be fixed, and even if he wants to be fixed, he's the one who has to do the hard work.

I open my mouth to ask him if he really hates me so much because I flirt with him all the time, consider that he'll be entirely too honest for me to handle, and also that if I was supposed to know the answer to that question, the universe would've let me in on the secret a long time ago.

So instead, I get a grip on my over-caffeinated self, jerking my hand away and looking up at my dart, which is impaled in a poster-size print of an old Pirate Fest crew picture.

"Oooh, I got Long Beak Silver!" I shake my booty and roll my shoulders. "Take that, you bad, bad parrot."

I try to flip the bird off, but I'm not very good with my middle fingers since I use them relatively seldomly, and I think I give it the pinky instead.

Max glowers at me. "Do you need to go home?"

This is what I do. I piss him off, and he glowers, and *why* can't I be attracted to guys who *like* me instead of guys who are impossible to please?

Fuck you, Max Cole. "Aunt Glory, can I have a grilled cheese sandwich?"

"You got it, sweet cheeks," she calls back.

"Yay, chair." I smile at Max as I sink into it, almost miss with half my butt cheek, and wiggle back onto it, my temper igniting in time with the java juice flowing through my veins. "Now you have to tell me why you flirt with me."

His eyes close, and his chest rises and falls in one of those massive sighs that my parents never really made with me, but that Aunt Glory makes over her kids all the time.

My parents are *awesome*.

"Never mind," Max says.

He starts to rise, but I fling my arm out to stop him.

I'm mad at him.

I want to make him mad too. "I flirt with you because it obviously annoys you, and it annoys me that it annoys you, because I am not your sister. You are not supposed to be in the circle of annoyed."

"Why not?"

"Because I'm a very nice person, and I'm a good person to be friends with, and I get along with every other person on your team, but not you. *Never* you. I don't think it would've mattered how we met. I think you'd be bound and determined to not like me no matter what."

His Adam's apple bobs and something flickers in his eyes, highlighting the flecks of caramel amidst the dark chocolate in them, and I realize I've struck a nerve.

He doesn't *want* to like me.

He *actively* works at not liking me.

I fling another dart at the wall. I'm frustrated and mad and suddenly very, very sad.

"Cooper said you were valedictorian of your graduating class."

My shoulders hitch. Apparently he knows how to hit nerves too. "School came easy to me and I like working hard. Cooper's not the only winner in the family."

He glances around The Grog like he's asking what the hell I've done with my life since, and it's like being back with Ben Woods, my former on-again, off-again boyfriend that I thought I'd marry when I turned thirty, despite the fact that he really should've been permanently off from the first time we broke up two weeks after our first date, since he kept pushing me to be something I'm not.

Go sell your paintings in Copper Valley, Tillie Jean. Make something of yourself. You're smart, you're talented, and you want to waste away in this little pirate town for the rest of your life? Go back to college. Be a doctor. Be a lawyer. Be an engineer.

I curl my fingers around the rest of the darts in my hand.

Max's gaze lands back on me, and he holds me captive with that growly glare. "Everything comes easy to you, doesn't it?"

It feels like a slap in the face, and I don't know why. "So you don't like me because you think I'm a spoiled princess."

My voice cracks on the last word.

Crap.

Crap crap *crap*.

Should *not* have come out tonight. So what if he thinks I'm spoiled? Who the hell is he?

Nobody.

That's who he is.

He's nobody to me.

Someday, my somebody will come. And when my somebody comes, I'll be ready for him.

But Max Cole is not my somebody.

He's my nobody.

And I need to remember that.

I bolt straight upright again. "Aunt Glory, forget the

grilled cheese. I gotta get home. Put everything on my tab, yeah?"

Max rises too. "Tillie Jean—"

"Don't worry, Maxy-poo. I won't flirt with you anymore. You don't like me. I get it, okay? *I get it.* Enjoy your burger." I reach for my glittery tumbler that usually makes me so happy but feels like a false front right now, and I knock it over.

Max snags it like it's a line drive hammered straight at him on the mound. "I don't—"

"Like me. I know." I snatch the mug. "Thank you. Enjoy eating alone. I'm done here tonight."

Tonight, and as far as I'm concerned with Max Cole, forever.

9

Max

I DON'T LIKE BEING A FUCK-UP, BUT I CAN'T SEEM TO HELP myself around Tillie Jean. And now I feel like I need to fix it.

Because I have *so much practice* fixing shit with women.

Reason number eighteen million...

Except I don't hate her for me screwing this up.

And I do need to fix it.

She's Cooper's little sister, she's well-loved in this town, and clearly, I stepped over some invisible line that's left me feeling like a thirteen-year-old kid who wasn't supposed to tell my coach that I was late to practice because my old man couldn't drive, because my old man didn't want anyone knowing that his preferred therapy for the depression he didn't talk about was vodka.

Difference is, I know now it wasn't my fault when I was thirteen.

This? Tonight?

Yeah. This is probably my fault.

I shouldn't have stopped to talk to her.

Doesn't matter that all I wanted was to see if we could clear the air and get past all the shit that's made it so fucking hard to be around her the past couple weeks. I knew better.

I don't wait for my burger, but I still stuff a hundred in the tip jar on my way out the door, chasing Tillie Jean, her coat in hand.

Crazy woman left without it.

She's not on the street, which means she's either hiding in a side alley, she took off at a run, or she flagged down a friend driving past and got a ride the three blocks home.

All three are equally likely around here.

Two goats trot along behind me as I march through the cold night to the little house I'm calling home these days. Stars are shining overhead. Moon's not up yet. I don't have any extra food in my pockets to give to the goats like I usually do, since I don't usually see the goats this late at night.

When I hit my block, the lights are on in Tillie Jean's house.

She's home. She's safe. I could go straight to my own house.

Pretend this didn't happen.

But there's an anxious feeling roiling my gut and telling me I need to apologize, if only so Cooper doesn't get pissed at me for picking on his sister.

So I man up and knock on her door.

She flings it open with an expression igniting in her eyes like maybe I should call *her* Growly Bear tonight. "So you were the lookout man so Cooper could get his revenge, hm? Nice. Well-played. Congrats. You win."

She slams the door in my face.

And now *I'm* pissed. I don't get involved in her stupid pranks.

I bang on the door again.

She yanks it open, snags her coat, snaps out, "Thank you," and shuts the door again.

But this time, I get a shoulder in the way. "I'm sorry."

I don't *sound* sorry. I sound pissed and I know it.

"Congratulations. Never too late to learn new words, and you just did it. You can leave now."

Reason number two hundred billion... "Can we please call a truce?"

"That would sound so much more sincere if you weren't yelling it at me."

"I'm not yelling."

"You're not sounding very contrite either."

My hands ball into fists. "I'm not good at this, okay?"

She eyeballs me with one bloodshot blue eye while the other scrunches closed, but this is no saucy wink.

If anything, this is probably an attempt to make it look like there's just one of me.

Hell.

I'm negotiating with a drunk.

You'd think I'd know better.

She flings the door open. "Fine. You can come in and undo what Cooper did, and then we can discuss if we can call a truce. *If* I'm still awake."

Despite the sinking feeling in my gut that this is a terrible idea, I follow her inside, expecting much of the same as I get in my roughly-same-shaped house next door. Small living room, kitchen and dining room combo, two bedrooms, a powder room, and a main bath between the two bedrooms, with utilitarian but clean furniture that *is* from this decade, upgraded with family pictures here since they're all tight and that's what people tight with family do.

They show off their family pictures.

Sometimes on blankets and pillows even.

Instead, I walk into an art gallery.

There's no television in Tillie Jean's living room. Only bright paintings on the muted gray walls. Her couch is a low modular thing that looks more like a pile of ivory cushions than furniture, and the only family portrait in the room is a large digital frame flashing candid shots of her brothers, parents, friends, and extended family on a white end table that looks like it, too, belongs in a museum instead of inside a small two-bedroom house in a dinky mountain town.

I should add this to the list of things about Tillie Jean Rock that drive me up a wall—*well-rounded in unexpected ways*—but I can't.

I should also keep up before she catches me gawking, as she's headed through the doorway at the back of the room that I expect leads to the kitchen. Unfortunately, I get stuck looking at a painting that seems like it's a woman peering around a tree, except the tree is made of a complex pattern of stripes in bright colors that shouldn't go together.

It's oddly soothing. And peaceful. And the woman—she has as much mischief in her bright lavender eyes as Tillie Jean has in her—

"That's not what Cooper did."

Caught.

I jerk my head away from the painting and follow TJ into the kitchen, where the first thing I see is—wait.

What *are* those?

Tillie Jean grabs a handful of her own face and yanks.

Towels.

Holy shit.

Cooper papered half her kitchen with tea towels with her face on them.

And it's quite the face she's making on the towels too. One eye shut—much like she was staring at me at the front door, except her other eyeball is half-rolled into her head, with her mouth twisted open and her tongue showing.

For the first time since I left the guys up at Cooper's house, telling their funniest family memories that left me unsettled and in need of a break from people who grew up with the kind of normalcy I thought was a lie, I'm smiling.

"Cooper was with me the whole day." It comes out automatically. I've had teammates I would've fed to the wolves at the first opportunity, but I've owed Cooper Rock more than my life for most of the time I've known him, and it's second nature to defend him.

Even to his little sister.

Okay, *especially* to his little sister.

"Start pulling them off or go away. And don't damage my paint."

I turn to the wall and gently pry off the nearest towel printed with her face. It's attached with a thumb tack. She'll probably have to spackle and repaint her whole wall. "He *was*. He couldn't have done this."

"News flash, Cole. We have teenage cousins who'll do anything for gas money."

I get one tea towel off the wall while my stomach grumbles a protest that I'm missing my cheat day hamburger, but when I turn to toss it on her table, food is the last thing on my mind.

Her cabinet doors are even more interesting than her living room. They're also painted.

I think.

They sparkle over swishes and swirls of gold, blue, and black. It's almost like staring at the universe on a clear, dark night, except they're *her cabinets*. Her countertops are white marble, the perfect complement to the cabinets. The floor is wide-planked gray wood, and the backsplash is a soft aqua green glass reflecting the designer coffee maker and planter of three succulents on the otherwise clean counter.

I glance at Tillie Jean. "Your kitchen—"

"Is none of your business." She's scowling, which both feels wrong but also inspires a naughty teacher fantasy that makes my cock leap to attention.

If her hair weren't tied up in a bun and she wasn't in a Crusty Nut blouse with the top two buttons undone and giving me a peek at her cleavage, I swear my cock would be behaving itself.

I turn back to the wall and grab another Tillie Jean Face Towel and make a hesitant attempt at peace. "I thought you liked it when Cooper pranked you."

"When he pranks me *good*. This is lame. It's the tea towel incident revisited except not at all funny. Even if he put these all over town, it's like…it's been *done*."

"Tea towel incident?"

"People on my shit list don't get that story from me." She frowns at me, a one-eyed, squinty frown. "Your burger's ready."

I blink. "What?"

"Go back and eat your burger." She pries another towel off the wall, revealing more white paint that I'm positive is a design choice and not the path of least resistance in getting her kitchen finished.

She also completely ignores me, which makes me mad. Again.

"Did you get a text?"

"Thirty-seven years in food service. I know when a burger's ready, dude. Yours is up."

"You're not thirty-seven years old."

"But I feel like it tonight."

Any other day, she'd probably accompany that statement with a wide Tillie Jean smile—*number four hundred twelve*—and top it with a *but you're welcome to make me feel young again, big guy* wink.

Tonight, she doesn't.

And right now, I miss the happy-go-lucky, freckles-in-summer, mischief-in-winter, big-hearted woman that she is around every other person on the planet.

Every other person who's not me.

She stifles a yawn. "Seriously, Max, go get your burger. I don't need help. I forgive you for being an ass, okay? We can be friends. No biggie. If you can't leave for your burger, leave for your fries. They're no good after they're—*oh!*"

Gone is the cranky, tired woman ready to give up on fighting for the night, and in her place is a firecracker with pink rising in her cheeks and horror making her mouth go round.

"TJ?"

She ignores me and dashes out of the kitchen.

I glance around her kitchen one more time, then set aside the towel in my hand and follow her.

And immediately wish I hadn't.

Not just because she's in her bedroom, climbing onto her four-poster bed, but because her bedroom has charcoal walls broken up with wispy ivory and pink sketches of rose buds, and her bed is draped with twisted black sheets and wrapped with soft pink gauzy stuff hanging between the posts, and now I'm thinking about fuzzy handcuffs and feather boas and leather.

My mouth is dry.

My gut is quaking.

My dick wants out to play.

And this is *Cooper's sister.*

His baby sister.

His very, very off-limits baby sister who's standing in the middle of her bed, reaching a hand up to the ceiling fan blades, making her shirt lift and exposing a slice of skin that reminds me of a ripe summer peach.

If ever there was a recipe for a panic attack, it's the idea of getting caught in *this* bedroom with *this* woman with my dick straining in my pants.

I have to swallow three times before I remember how to form words. "What are you *doing?*"

"A-*ha!* Hand me the vacuum, Growly Bear. Someone sprinkled glitter on my ceiling fan blades." It's like she flipped a switch and all of her mad disappeared, which is also something I've seen before, and one more reason I dislike Tillie Jean. How does she get over being mad so easily?

"Get. Down."

"I knew it couldn't be so obvious that he'd stop with just papering my walls with tea towels." She teeters over her bed.

I reach for her hips to steady her, pretend I'm grabbing one of the damn mascots that management had competing to be the team's new primary mascot all season, and don't pull it off.

I am definitely grabbing Tillie Jean Rock by her very shapely hips, right here, next to her bed, and my body knows it.

"Vacuum?" she repeats. And then she does the last thing in the world that she has any business doing.

She runs her fingers through my hair. "Oh, look at that. You still have glitter. I didn't mean to do that, you know. I really didn't. Every time I see you, I think, *Bad Tillie Jean. All that glitter wasted. It could've been ruining Cooper's chances at endorsement deals instead.*"

"Tillie Jean."

"You shouldn't growl my name like that. I like it, and I don't want to. I wasn't dating Chance Schwartz seriously, you know. At first I was excited that he was into me, then it was like, this rush to sleep with him, especially since I was off-again with Ben at the time, except he wasn't very good—which you probably figured out—and he was really into himself. Like, *way* into himself. I knew what I was involved with."

"Please stop talking." One, because I don't want to know.

Two, because she could just as easily be describing me.

She turns, and now I have a face full of Tillie Jean boob while my hands are still gripping her hips.

If Cooper walked in here right now, I would be a dead man.

I would be *such* a dead man.

"What would it take for us to be friends like I'm friends with Luca and Emilio and Trevor and Robinson?" She's still running her fingers through my hair, and my scalp is in heaven.

I don't like people touching me.

Not as a general rule.

Tillie Jean could give me a scalp rub all night, and my scalp—and my skin, and my hair, and my face, and my whole damn body—wouldn't mind a bit.

I jerk back out of reach. "Get down. You can clean the glitter tomorrow."

"Why are you so—" A car door slams outside, cutting her off, but only for a second. "*Oh!* Aunt Glory must've sent a delivery."

She bends, plants her hands on my shoulders like she's planning to use them as a vault, and freezes.

Our faces are inches apart.

Not even.

I can see the darker blue ring around her irises, the brush strokes of lighter blue fanning out from her summer sky irises, and I can't look away from the way her eyes are dilating as her breath gets heavier.

The tiniest threads of pink in the whites of her eyes.

The hint of coffee on her breath.

The quiver of her nostrils.

The heat of her fingers on my shoulders and the firm muscle in her ass. I'm not trying to grab her ass, but my hands are big, and they've been sitting on her hips, and my fingers naturally go all the way back to those sweet round globes.

"I'm getting down," she whispers. "Your hamburger is here."

I suddenly don't give a damn about my cheat burger.

Kissing Tillie Jean to shut her up a few weeks ago wasn't a fluke.

It's what I've wanted to do for weeks. Months.

Years.

I don't have ten million reasons I hate Tillie Jean Rock.

I have ten million reasons that I hate that I like her.

"Get back, you mangy goats," someone says distantly, and I realize who I am, where I am, and what I need to do.

"Get down," I say again, except this time, I grip her hips tighter, lift her off the bed, and set her on her feet.

And then I retreat.

Tillie Jean Rock is my teammate's sister. She's off-limits.

She's—she's—

You know what?

She might as well be *my* sister. And that's how it'll be.

Yes.

Yes.

This is the perfect plan.

As far as I'm concerned, Tillie Jean Rock is now my sister, and therefore, disgusting and repulsive to my body.

That's my truth now.

Just as soon as I get this boner from hell under control.

10

Tillie Jean

"Let's call a truce, Tillie Jean," I mutter to myself while a whole-body shiver dances from my scalp to my toenails approximately two seconds after I walk out of my front door two mornings later. *"Let's be friends. Let's put the past behind us."*

A concrete garden gnome snickers, and another one moons me.

No, I'm not kidding.

There's a freaking terrifying mutant garden gnome holding his pudgy concrete hand over his mouth while his eyes twinkle with the light of hell and another one right next to him peering over his shoulder while he holds his pants down, exposing two round concrete butt cheeks, and two dozen more garden gnomes are lined up alongside them right at the property line between my house, handed down to me by my great-aunt Matilda, and Max Cole's winter house, which he's renting from my great-uncle Homer.

My brother can't pull off a decent prank to save his life

this winter, but Mr. Two-Faced Growly Bear is sending a freaking *garden gnome army* after me.

How do I know Max set them up?

Because I know Uncle Homer put them in his basement a few years back after the sight of them made me take out his mailbox with my car, which I *don't think about*. When I think about an army of garden gnomes in the basement of the house next door, I can't sleep, but having them stored and forgotten in the basement is so much better than having them running around next to my property line.

Also, Cooper wouldn't prank me with garden gnomes.

He just wouldn't.

I shudder again.

"Dead," I say, pointing to each and every one of them. "You are all *dead* to me."

I swear to god, one actually makes noise, and that's all it takes to make me shriek and dive for my car.

Unfortunately, the four-block drive to Crusty Nut doesn't relieve the shivers.

Or the images from my brain.

Neither does an eight-hour shift.

And when I get home, Max's Mercedes SUV isn't in his driveway, but the gnomes are still there.

"There are freaking *rules of engagement*, Max Cole," I mutter to myself.

And then I march inside, brew myself a very, *very* strong, very large afternoon latte, and pull up my big girl panties.

There's vengeance to be had.

"I'd ask what you're doing, except then I wouldn't have plausible deniability," Annika says from somewhere behind me thirty minutes later.

I straighten and turn to face her.

She's not alone, and the sight of my older brother walking his goat with his pregnant wife makes me smile. "Hey, it's my favorite people."

Sue bleats out a greeting, so I bleat back at him.

"Are you torturing your neighbor, or the garden gnomes?" Grady asks.

I lean over and move one more gnome into formation in the middle of Max's yard.

With gloved hands, for the record.

Gloves that I'll be burning as soon as I'm done here.*They touched garden gnomes*.

I shudder and almost dry-heave, but I'm nearly done, so I grab the last gnome and put him in place.

"Aren't you the one who had nightmares after Cooper made us watch that old *Gnomeo and Juliet* trailer on YouTube last year?" Annika says.

I tilt my head to the side, clamp my teeth around the bite valve connected to the tube sticking out of my small day pack and hanging over my shoulder, and suck. Warm mocha latte floods my mouth, and I sigh in relief. "Don't wanna talk about it," I say as the liquid courage reassures me that I can, in fact, finish this job.

Grady looks at me, then at Max's house, then at the gnomes, then back to me, and I swear he pauses with a significant glance at my day pack along the way. "What, exactly, did Max Cole do to you to make you brave enough to touch *garden gnomes* in the name of retribution?"

"*He* set them up along the property line. This is *not* my doing."

My oldest brother starts to grin. "Tillie Jean, do I need to have a talk with your neighbor about how we court ladies in this town?"

"Shut up and move that last concrete *thing*, please."

Annika tilts her head. "Did you really put them in the shape of a middle finger?"

"They didn't put themselves in that shape." I suck on my hydration bladder of coffee again, ignore that voice whispering that *hydration bladders are for carrying water on long hikes, not coffee in the front yard,* and say a prayer of thanks that garden gnomes *cannot,* in fact, line themselves up, and that even if they could, I'm deadly with a tire iron.

Which I'll be sleeping with under my pillow until these fucking gnomes are gone.

Uncle Homer swore they didn't move, but I heard Pop talking about animatronic garden gnomes, and between that one garden gnome *moving*—and yes, that's why I took out the mailbox—and the thing that we don't talk about that happened when I was four, *I. Hate. Garden. Gnomes.*

"That's really impressively creative," my sister-in-law says. "Especially the part where the top of the middle finger is the one mooning you."

"Can we please stop talking about them like they're real?"

Grady hands me Sue's leash and takes the last garden gnome.

Without gloves.

"I wouldn't let him touch you for like three weeks if I were you," I tell Annika. "That's how long it'll take all the cooties to come off his skin."

She laughs while Sue rubs against my leg. I peel off my own gloves, making sure to not accidentally touch the parts of them that were touching garden gnomes, to rub his goofy one-horned head. He has the funniest smile ever, and he loves Annika more than he loves my brother, and I'm okay with that.

"How's your ankle?" Grady asks after finishing my dirty work for me, but not before I realize Max Cole has once again made me stretch outside my comfort zone.

Dammit. "Completely back to normal. Can you hold Sue again? I need to do a little B and E."

Grady takes his pet back, but he's staring at me like I've lost my mind. Annika's choking on her own spit.

She's really adorable when she's choking on her own spit. I can totally see why Grady married her.

"B and E? What, exactly, are you doing?" she asks me.

"B and E. Braiding and erasing my memories." And if they believe that's what B and E stands for, then I'm very worried for their offspring.

"*Tillie Jean!* You're breaking into Max's house."

"Uncle Homer asked me to check on something."

"I'm not watching this," Grady mutters.

So he says.

But he and Annika and Sue are still standing on the sidewalk, more or less playing lookout to make sure my cousin Chester, the sheriff's deputy, doesn't catch me, after I've slipped into Max's side window and done what I needed to do in his house with the *other* item inside my daytime hiking backpack, which is something I'd intended to put in Cooper's house, but not anymore.

Now, Max Cole is in the circle of people who will lose at winter prank wars.

"Yep," I announce as I slide back out the side window. "The windows *do* open without squeaking. I'll report back to Uncle Homer."

Annika's squinting at me, her dark eyes suspicious. "You like him, don't you?"

"Uncle Homer? He's a good guy, even if he can't remember us half the time anymore. But he lets me have his chocolate pudding anytime I go visit him at the nursing home. Were you around the summer he bought that tractor with the trailer bed because he wanted to be a farmer pirate and also Shipwreck's original trolley? He swore he was going to transport people up and down Blackbeard Avenue on the trailer like they were having hay rides."

Grady squints at me like he's wondering if I've had too much coffee again today.

Hello. Of *course* I've had too much coffee. But I'd rather talk about Uncle Homer. "I was never sure if he was extra fun, or if he never got over that bump on his head that Mom and Dad used to whisper about from time to time."

"Let's go with extra fun," Grady says.

I nod. "I like that better too."

Annika bumps shoulders with Grady. "You're going to let her distract you?"

He grins. "She's not ready to face the truth yet."

Her entire face melts into sappy cartoon hearts. "Ah. And you *would* know a thing or two about that?"

When Annika came home two years ago, I was in my last phase of off-again with Ben and quite happy without all the drama Grady was going through.

I was also trying to kick the coffee habit and loving the freedom that came with being done with getting my associate's degree from the local community college so I had more time to paint and travel into the city for drinks with Cooper's teammates' wives and girlfriends, and other friends who moved there.

Now?

Now, I'm doing the same thing, without being in that off-again part of a relationship, which is the last time I was in anything resembling a relationship. Sometimes when I head into the city, I'll use an app to find a hook-up, but that doesn't always go well.

Okay, that *rarely* goes well. The theory of random hook-ups is a lot better than the actuality of it for me. And other than Grady and a random cousin here or there, my friends are still single too.

So why am I suddenly cranky at seeing my brother and his wife—who's been his soulmate basically since they met in high school—happy and teasing each other?

Because when you tease guys you like, they turn into growly bears, my brain helpfully reminds me.

"I don't like Max," I announce, completely unnecessarily, which makes me want to snag the words back out of the air.

Who randomly announces things like that?

Liars. That's who.

"You flirt with guys to annoy them," Grady points out.

I gasp and pretend to be offended. "Are you saying I'm annoying?"

"You flirt with *our cousins*."

"It's practice in case someone single that we're not related to ever moves to town. The universe *will* provide one day, and I need to be ready when it does. I also flirt with *plenty* of guys anytime I head into the city. *Practice*."

"You don't flirt with Robinson or Trevor," Annika says.

"Robinson's barely old enough to drink, and Trevor would probably think I meant it, but he's got a lot of stuff to work through before he'd be real relationship material."

"Or maybe he'd like having someone to work through it with."

"Do you want to be around Cooper the day he discovers his body doesn't want him to play baseball anymore?" Yes, I'm whispering.

I like Trevor. He's a good guy. A lot like one of my brothers, though older. Gives good hugs. And he's struggling to accept what the rest of us can see.

His best pitching years are behind him.

Poor guy.

"You don't want to be the person warming him up at night to take his mind off it?" Grady wiggles his brows, making Annika laugh.

I pull a *no* face. "You know I'll be the first person taking him a cheesecake and a handle of Jack if he figures it out while he's here, but he's a friend. Period."

The sound of a distant car motor gets louder, and we all glance at the corner as it comes into view.

It's not Max's Mercedes SUV, but it's still a car I recognize. "Oh, *yay!*"

More Fireballs. Though not Fireballs that I'll be flirting with. Brooks Elliott is *very* much taken.

It's his wife I'm more excited to see, and that's her unmistakable car.

"Did he seriously ride out here from the city in the passenger seat of a Mini?" Grady mutters.

Mackenzie Elliott parks the Fireball-mobile in front of my house, leaps out, and circles the small vehicle to tackle me in a hug. Where her car is custom-painted in an ode to the Fireballs and Fiery the Dragon, the team's original mascot, she's in jeans, hella awesome boots, and a fluffy black jacket over a vintage Fireballs T-shirt. The only thing different about her is that her smile is bigger than ever. "Tillie Jean! I missed you."

"Mackenzie! I missed you more. How was your honeymoon?"

"Oh my god, we swung by the Baseball Hall of Fame and I got all tongue-tied, which *someone* found hilarious, but I got over it. How are you? Are you going to Marisol's wedding? Are the guys behaving here? Do you have to work all the time, or can we hang out at your mom's adorable coffee shop sometime this weekend? I need to hear all about this glitter bomb you exploded on Max. We're staying up on the mountain and *I miss you.*"

Mackenzie's long-time BFF married Beck Ryder, the former boy band guy-slash-underwear model from Copper Valley who owns a house down the street from Cooper's—that's one of the rich weekender properties Cooper hasn't snagged up—and she's been visiting Shipwreck longer than Brooks has played for the team. I knew her back when she used to get too nervous to talk whenever Cooper was around.

"Game room time?" I ask her. Beck's basement man cave is legendary.

She squeals and hugs me again, and I get a mouthful of blond hair. "You know it. I have to introduce Brooks to getting his ass spanked in ping pong."

"What's with the gnomes?" Brooks asks. Mackenzie's husband was a new acquisition this past year, and his bat is half the reason the Fireballs made it to the post-season. He's a lot less cranky now than he was when he first arrived, and I think it has less to do with the dog he's letting out of the car, and more to do with Mackenzie. "And are those—are they— those gnomes are giving someone the finger?"

"What a coincidence. That's what I'd like to do to Max for launching a garden gnome army and trying to take over my yard. Not that I had anything to do with *this*. I don't touch gnomes. They freak me out."

Annika stifles another laugh behind a cough.

Grady sighs.

"What? I *hate* garden gnomes."

Brooks and Mackenzie share a look.

"Max did this?" Mackenzie says.

"Unless Cooper's trying to make me think Max did it, and really, how likely is that?"

Brooks winces. *He* knows Max's reputation, and he knows Cooper's reputation, and he also has a sister of his own that he's overprotective of, just like Cooper and Grady are over-protective of me.

Mackenzie's nose wrinkles. "Max paid you back for the glitter bomb?"

Either that, or he's trying to demonstrate how horrified he was of kissing me and touching me and getting close to me by planting evil garden gnomes in my yard. "Looks like. So, I apparently need to up my prank game. Seems there are *two* fools in town who have no idea the beast they've unleashed." I flex my muscles, grin, and then take another hit off my coffee backpack.

"Tillie Jean."

I roll my eyes at Grady's older-brother frown. "Would you rather I was pranking the assholes over in Sarcasm?"

"I would, but my wife wouldn't. Gotta keep the missus happy."

"Sue, eat Grady's shoe," Annika orders.

The goat looks at both of them, then flops to the ground.

Coco Puff, Brooks and Mackenzie's not-quite-one-year-old, adorable, curly-brown-furred Cavapoo, barks, and his collar translates. "I love Ash the Baby Dragon best!"

I lock eyes with Grady. "Long Beak Silver," we say together.

"Your grandpa's parrot?" Mackenzie asks.

"Where'd you get that collar?" I point to Coco Puff. "We need one for Pop's parrot. He's getting worse."

"Can it give an electric shock every time he cusses?" Grady adds. "Just until we've re-trained him to only say normal pirate things again."

"Seriously. He's a nuisance. I won't repeat what he said at lunch today, but no one wanted to eat after that. And we don't want enough volts to fry him. I'm joking when I say I want to serve parrot burgers."

"No, you're not."

"Whatever, Mr. Fondant Parrots for Therapy. I *know* you bite the parrot heads off first and smile while you're doing it."

"Stop." Annika's waving both hands in front of her face like she's overheating as she laughs. "Dammit. Tillie Jean, I need your bathroom."

I turn and make the *it's all yours* gesture, and catch sight of a Mercedes SUV turning the corner as I do. "Oh, crap."

"Busted," Grady mutters while Annika dashes for the house. She's only a few months pregnant, not showing yet, but I know she's drinking a ton of water and hormones are crazy things.

"Is that Max?" Mackenzie claps her hands. "He's not throwing too much, is he? He needs to rest that arm."

"He's got this, Kenz. Not his first off-season." Brooks grins at her, then waves as Max passes us and turns into the driveway next door.

He climbs out of his SUV, his eyes flickering over the gnomes, landing on me for a split second before switching his attention to Brooks and Mackenzie.

But that split second?

That split-second glance had a big ol' dollop of amusement sparkling in it.

Not a single ounce of growly bear.

Nope.

It was all *so you think you can rearrange the gnomes and that counts as winning, do you? Lame.*

It definitely wasn't *this is better than almost kissing you again.*

Nope.

Wasn't that.

I refuse to admit there might've been *any* smolder in his sparkle.

How could there be?

They don't go together *at all.*

Mackenzie slips to my side, giving Coco Puff enough leash to say hi to Sue without losing control of the puppy. "Did Max just *smile* at you?" she whispers.

"Nope. Had to be a trick of the light."

She is so not buying it. "*Tillie Jean.* I thought you two just liked to annoy each other. We really do have a lot of catching up to do, don't we?"

I sigh and angle closer to her, dropping my voice low. "Remember Chance Schwartz?"

Mackenzie came out of the womb a die-hard Fireballs fan. I used to think Cooper was the ultimate Fireballs fan—his life goal from the time he could walk was basically to play for the Fireballs and lead them to World Series rings—but he has *nothing* on Mackenzie. Of course she knows who Chance Schwartz is.

"He had potential, but that's pretty much every player to play for the team for the last fifty years," she murmurs back, clearly confused about where I'm going.

"The reason I annoy Max at every opportunity is that he found out I was flinging with Chance and told Cooper, who had him traded, and so I've been trying for four years to get Cooper to get Max traded too."

She gasps.

The men all turn and glance at us.

And because she's Mackenzie, and she's come *so* far from the days when she couldn't even blink in the presence of baseball players, she immediately dials up a grin. "I didn't think it was true, but Max, your hair really does sparkle. And pink looks so good on you."

"Flip my wife off and die," Brooks says before Max can react.

But the weirdest thing happens.

Max smiles.

He *smiles*. An actual, full-faced, happy-eyed, no-questions-asked smile.

It's aimed at Mackenzie, but it's still a smile. "Only the best *sparkle*."

And *oh my god*, is he sparkling.

Growly Bear Max?

Adorable in a resistible way.

Smiling Max?

I'm in so much trouble.

The men huddle back up. Mackenzie grabs my hand and squeezes. "But now you don't want him to get traded," she whispers.

"There is *nothing* going on here," I whisper back. "Absolutely *nothing*. He's only smiling to try to annoy *me* now."

"He's the best pitcher we have. The team isn't trading him, no matter what Cooper thinks about anything. I won't let them. No matter what you do or don't do with Max."

She's dead serious.

It should be funny. There's no way anyone—even Mackenzie—can tell the Fireballs' management what to do.

Except if anyone could, it's Mackenzie. She made quite the name for herself with her support for the team this past year. The national news covered some of her antics. She's not *a* superfan. She's *the* superfan.

"This is *nothing*," I repeat.

It's not. It's a silly practical joke that I totally deserved— aside from the fact that he used *garden gnomes*—and I've paid him back, and that's that.

We'll now go back to being a woman who flirts incessantly with a guy who hates it, and everything will be completely normal, and Max won't smile at me again, and my ovaries won't melt again, and the team will have nothing to worry about.

I think.

I hope.

I gulp and look at Mackenzie. "But if it's ever not nothing and I need help or I accidentally break his game, you'll be my first call."

11

Max

"DUDE, YOUR BALLS *DO* GLOW IN THE DARK." I GRIN AT COOPER over the first hole at Scuttle Putt, Shipwreck's miniature golf course, where we've broken in to play a round while Brooks is in town.

Doesn't hurt that we just came from The Grog. Between settling into the post-season routine, having more teammates in town for a few days, and deciding that I can adopt Tillie Jean as my sister two days ago, I'm feeling relaxed and steady and on top of the damn world for the first time since before the play-offs.

"My balls don't just glow." Brooks pumps his hips. "They fucking *sing*."

I snicker.

Cooper snickers.

Brooks snickers.

Robinson snickers.

Trevor doesn't snicker, because he's an old man and he went home to sleep and isn't here, so he doesn't know about

Cooper's glowing balls and Brooks's singing balls, which sucks for him.

"*Rawk!* Keep your pants on! *Rawk!*"

Brooks bends over and moons the bird, so we all follow suit.

Jesus, this feels good.

And it's not the buzz coming off my first couple beers in months either. It's being with the guys. Having fun. Not thinking about the season coming up.

Fuck.

No, no, no. *Do not* think about the season.

"Thousand bucks says I can sink this in one shot," Brooks announces.

"Your dog can sink it in one shot," Robinson replies.

"Fuck yeah. My dog is *awesome*. My dog can eat your dog for *breakfast*."

"That's because Robby's dog is *imaginary*." Cooper bends over and puts his glow-in-the-dark ball on the mat at the first hole. "Your dog can eat his dog for breakfast and *both dogs can still exist*."

I frown.

Brooks and Robinson look at each other.

"Whoa," we all mutter.

"That's deep, man." Brooks slaps Cooper on the shoulder as Cooper swings his club, making Cooper's first shot bounce off the spinning pirate wheel blocking the entrance to the little pirate tavern that the ball needs to get through.

Cooper shoves Brooks. "Foul!"

"There's no foul balls in golf."

"There's foul balls in Scuttle Putt. House rules. You take three extra strokes."

"Three strokes is all he needs," I mutter to Robinson, who cracks up.

Brooks turns and stares me down. "For the record, I can last *five*."

Cooper trips over his own two feet.

Brooks cracks up.

And then Robinson and I both go down too.

Fuck, I miss this. *All* of the guys. The whole team.

"You remember when you all dragged me and Rossi into that curse-breaking ritual in spring training?" Brooks says.

"What happens at the shack stays at the shack, dumbass. Don't go talking shit and break the un-cursing."

"I'm glad it was with you guys."

"Is he getting sappy now that he's getting laid on the regular?" Robinson whispers.

"Happens, man. Look at Rossi too."

"Huh." He reaches into his jacket and pulls a beer can out of an inner pocket. "I could go for a chick that would make me sappy like that."

"Are we golfing with our glow-in-the-dark balls, or are we sapping it up?" Cooper asks. "Not that I mind either way. I just wanna know before I pull out all my tricks to start my game over *without* interference."

"That's your cue, rookie," I mutter to Robinson. "Go blow in his ear next time he tries to take a shot."

"I heard that, Gnome Man," Cooper says. "Elliott. *You* go next. And I got a grand on you taking at least *five strokes* to sink this one."

Brooks snorts with laughter. "You're so on."

Brooks misses. Robinson misses. I miss. Cooper misses again.

"Fuck this, man." Robby picks up his ball. "Let's play hole three. I like hole three. It has *wenches*."

"Oh, sweet, are we picking holes?" Brooks asks. "Dibs on the cannon hole."

I trip over the edge of another miniature golf hole's green, and I go down with a snort. "What's a cannon hole, man?"

"They are seriously toasted, aren't they?" a new voice says.

It's women.

There are *women* on our golf course.

"Off with you, wenches," Cooper calls.

"Yeah," Brooks agrees. "We're taken. Us and our glow-balls."

"Sweetie, I think you're the only *taken* one in the bunch," Mackenzie says. "Unless I missed something. Robinson? You dating someone? Max, who's your special lady friend?"

"No way," Robinson says.

"I only sleep around," I call.

"I'm single, Mackenzie," Cooper says.

"The entire country is aware, Stinky Booty," another woman replies.

My balls perk up—and I don't mean the glow-in-the-dark balls—and I mentally slap myself with a raw steak before I remember that Tillie Jean is my sister now.

"TJ! My sister-girl!"

Eighty-four sets of eyeballs swivel in my direction.

Or maybe just like six or seven. Plus the parrot.

What was in that beer?

"Sister-girl?" Tillie Jean repeats.

Clearly I need to learn a little about being a brother. Like what to call the woman I'm now claiming as my sister. I step around Mackenzie to swing an arm around Tillie Jean's shoulders. "Yep. Congratulations. You hung your picture on my shower curtain. That makes us related."

She did.

It matches the picture of her on her towels.

And I'm not talking to you about the heart attack I didn't have when I walked into my bathroom a few hours ago.

Or about how that's what drove me to drink.

Heh. Just kidding.

I think.

But now that I'm here, and happy, and with friends, and with *my sister*, life is fucking *awesome*.

Cooper eyes me like I've lost my marbles. And my balls. "Tillie Jean. Did you break into Max's house?"

"That's what sisters do, right?" I interject.

Tillie Jean peers up at me, the moonlight catching her bright eyes and the shadows making her lips look even fuller. "Have you been drinking?"

Don't kiss your sister, Max. Don't kiss your sister. I grin, then boop her nose. "Yes, but I'm *fine*."

"Yeah, you are, baby." She winks.

My dick springs to life. He's forgotten that we're sisters. Brothers.

Brosters and sibyl-ings.

Huh.

I'm funny in my brain too when I'm tipsy.

But not drunk.

Never drunk.

Cooper wrenches us apart. "TJ. *Quit flirting.* Jesus. Max, dude, you okay?"

"I always wanted a normal family." Good god. Who *am* I? Did I just say that out loud?

"Are you cracking?" he mutters to me.

Am I? Probably. "You—" I poke him in the shoulder with a finger, or maybe two fingers "—are my *broster*. And that makes your sither my sither."

He tilts his head. "Is this like that time in San Francisco when you did two shots and demonstrated that you have the tolerance of a thirteen-year-old girl?"

"I wouldn't challenge some of the thirteen-year-old girls I know," Tillie Jean mutters.

I giggle. "I challenge you."

What's a cat that prowls good in the moonlight? That's what TJ is. She's like a cat. A sexy, sleek, prowly cat who's sneaking up on my good intentions with that amused smile that makes her look like one of those super porny drawings of women in short skirts with big boobs and open blouses.

Tillie Jean—my *sister* by way of making my dick behave—crosses her arms. "I accept. Coffee-drinking challenge, coming right up."

"To a *hole*."

"Did you slip him an edible?" Mackenzie whispers to Brooks. "He's as funny as you on magic brownies."

Cooper hands Tillie Jean a glowing ball and mutters something to her.

She shoves him away. "Ha. You just don't want to get beat by your baby sister."

"You're *my* baby sister." I try to lift a finger but it's full of golf club, which means I lift the club and almost take out a shrubbery. *Shrubbery.* Heh. That's a good word. "Annoying. And younger. And annoying. And younger. And hot. Because I'm hot. So my sister's hot."

Cooper claps me on the back. "Pick your hole, man. You're gonna kick TJ's ass. I can feel it."

"I'm hot."

"You usually are," Tillie Jean mutters.

Fuck.

Fuuuuuuck. I'm *really* hot. This shirt is hot. Pants too.

"Here we go," Brooks says.

"Hey, Max, bud, we have some decency laws here in Shipwreck." The other woman—oh, it's Georgia, Grady's baker—holds my shirt out to me.

I look down, and I grin. No wonder I feel better. Shirt's all gone. "Ooh, daddy looks *good*." I pump one pec, then the other, making my chest dance.

Robinson cracks up. Brooks is howling. So I reach for the button on my jeans.

Tillie Jean grabs my hand. "C'mon, Max. I have a hole you'll *love*."

"I don't like your holes, Tillie Jean. You're my *sister*."

"Right? I don't like your holes either."

She's still holding my hand—gripping it, really—and her

hand is warm and soft and strong and everything a good hand should be. I stumble over the flat ground, and that's *bad*, Max.

Bad Max.

Can't wipe out Tillie Jean.

But she's like a tree.

Deep roots.

Steadies me. Peers up at me. Her hands on my skin. "You're only pretty because I'm hot," I tell her. "Good genes runses in the familieses."

She smiles. "You're a mess."

"You're a mess," I mimic.

Her face twists comically.

I grin. "Heh. Made you tongue-tied. Three hamburgers and a garden gnome say I can get a hole in one on this hole."

I point, and I have no idea if I'm actually pointing at a hole.

Probably not, considering she doubles over laughing.

No, that's a hole.

"You think you can get a hole-in-one on the *hurricane* hole?" she asks.

"I'm a winner, baby. Sister. Baby sister."

"You are seriously in some kind of mood tonight, aren't you?"

I poke her shirt. It's a good shirt. I like it.

It has *Fearlessly Me* scrawled across her boobage under her jacket that's hanging open.

I like her boobage. Good boobage clearly runs in my family.

"I," I tell her, "am *also* meerlessly fee."

"Is someone recording this?" Georgia whispers behind me.

"Hurricane me to the point," I order.

Tillie Jean grips me by the shoulders, turns, and gives me a gentle shove, and whoa.

Look at that.

I was already at the hurricane hole.

"How much did he have to drink?" she whispers to Cooper.

"Two beers," he whispers back.

"And a tot of shequila," Robinson adds.

"*Shequila!*" I crow.

God, that's funny. Robby's a funny kid. I'm a funny kid. I kick ass at minigolf. Tillie Jean has an awesome ass.

"Okay, Growly Bear," TJ says. "Take your shot."

"You got it, Trouble Jean. I'mma gonna kick your booty to there and back." I swing my club, hit my ball, and I miss.

Wait.

What? "Why do I have two balls?"

"Because only real men have three," Brooks replies.

I snicker.

Cooper and Robinson snicker.

Tillie Jean grabs me by the hand and guides me to aim at the other ball, and huh.

That one connects.

But it doesn't go very far.

"Are you sure you want to play me?" she asks.

"Oh, yeah, baby. Baby *shister*. I'm gonna play you *so good*."

She lines up and takes aim with her glow-in-the-dark pink ball—heh, just like her favorite glitter, and her bedroom. I like her pink bedroom.

I whack off while I'm thinking about her pink bedroom.

Shh.

Don't tell sober Max I admitted that.

Ping.

Her fuzzy pink ball sails into the shipwrecked ship, shoots out the other side, bounces off the wall, dips into the swirly whirly of death, shoots out onto the lower level, bounces around the corner, and then *plops* right into the hole.

"What the *fuck*?" Cooper yelps while Georgia and

Mackenzie explode in cheers. "Tillie Jean. Are you *sharking* us? You out here all summer practicing? *Not. Fair.*"

"Not fair," she mimics back to him with a grin.

"Foul," I call.

"Holes in one are not fouls, *big brother*. But nice try."

"Yep. And now you have to do her laundry for a week for trying to cheat," Georgia adds, like Shipwreck has rules about punishments for cheating.

"He is *not* touching her laundry," Cooper growls.

"Oh, please." Georgia gives him a playful shove. "Get over yourself, Rock."

"No one touches my sister's underwear."

Tillie Jean laughs. "You are such an ass when you're drunk."

My whole body goes stiff.

Not loose. Not happy. Not anything other than *drunk ass.* She's right. Cooper's drunk.

But more—I'm drunk.

I'm *drunk.* And acting like a fool.

Like an *ass.*

I drop my club. Need to get home.

Now.

And throw up.

Alone.

"Max?" Tillie Jean calls.

She was right there, but now I'm moving, and she's not there, and what the *fuck* is this pirate ship doing in my way?

"This way, dude." Cooper grabs my arm, and I don't want it to be a lifeline, but it is.

It fucking *is.*

Because he's Cooper. And he knows. He knows *everything.* And he's still here.

He was here when I went full-on, can't-breathe, catatonic with a panic attack the night I pitched my first no-hitter not long after I got to Copper Valley—*Jesus*, the questions—*you here to turn the Fireballs around, Max? Max, you carrying the team out of this pit of loserdom all by yourself? How's it feel to get the biggest win Copper Valley's ever seen, Mr. Cole?*—and he was here when I passed out and he was here when I woke up in the trainer's room, and he was the guy who drove me to my first therapy appointment with nothing more than a *dude, if it was your ankle, you'd go to a doctor. No shame in doing the same for your brain.*

I don't hate Cooper Rock.

I want to *be* Cooper Rock.

But I never will.

TILLIE JEAN

AN ODE TO COFFEE ON A BRIGHT SATURDAY MORNING:

COFFEE MOCHA LATTE
  Espresso yum yum yum
  Give me hazelnut and French vanilla
  To get me through this run

"COME ON, DITA, YOU'VE GOT THIS," I PANT AS I JOG MOSTLY IN place and backwards with Dita and Vinnie, who are walking slower than snails for the last quarter mile of Shipwreck's annual Scurvy Run.

Yes, the *Scurvy Run*.

We run a 5K the Saturday before Thanksgiving every year so we remember to eat our vegetables and not get scurvy. I know. It's dorky.

It's also fun, and we tend to raise a lot of money for charity, plus, we follow it up with a food cart vendor feast in the park.

Usually Cooper and Grady would be with me, but Cooper's MIA after last night's drunken glow-in-the-dark putt-putt game that he and Max abruptly left early, and Grady didn't want to leave Annika early this morning, since she's apparently having a morning sickness day. I'd put a hundred bucks down that he shows up to serve Crow's Nest donuts and muffins, but that he doesn't hang out at the park any longer than about half an hour, except I know literally no one who would take that bet.

My parents, grandparents, friends, aunts, uncles, cousins, and the Fireballs players who showed up to participate this morning—Trevor, Robinson, Brooks, and Luca Rossi, who drove in from the city early this morning with his girlfriend—have all crossed the finish line.

Mackenzie and Henri walked the race, and they finished twenty minutes ago too.

I'm starting to think Dita and Vinnie are trying to see how long I can jog with them before I drop dead of exhaustion.

Heh.

Like I'd show up for the Scurvy Run without beefing up on coffee first. I could do this all day.

Though I'll hurt like Captain America's stuntman tomorrow.

And no, I don't want to talk about why I like to keep up with the back of the pack.

It has nothing to do with seeing Max running backwards and encouraging the slowest pitchers during warm-ups a couple years back when I was in the city for a ball game and got into Duggan Field early, for family hours, before they opened the doors to fans for the day.

Nothing at all.

That would be like admitting *my brother* has influenced me over the years.

Hmph.

Brother. Whatever.

"She's evil," Vinnie pants.

"I know," Dita agrees on a gasp. "I hate her."

We're about two inches from my driveway, which means we're two inches and the width of my front yard from Max's house. "Join the club, my friends. Get those knees up! You can do it. We're not letting you give up when we're this close."

"Can you imagine—" gasp pant "—what would happen —" pant pant "—if TJ and LBS—" gasp groan "—had a love parrot?"

"*Dita Angelina Kapinski!*" I gasp in mock outrage. "Hush your mouth. Even if Long Beak Silver were a shape-shifting parrot, he would *never* be my type."

Max's front door opens, and Cooper sticks his head out. His hair's standing at all angles like he slept over, and he rubs his face like he's not sure what he's seeing.

"Hey, Sleeping Beauty," I call. "So nice of you to show your face for the Scurvy Run. You wanna come help me motivate these two so we can get to the food?"

"Did you just say you want to sleep with Long Beak Silver?" he calls back.

I flip him off.

And again, since I have basically zero experience doing it even if I can line up garden gnomes—*shudder*—in the shape of a fisted hand with a middle finger up, I end up showing him a pinky on one hand and my index finger on the other.

"I got your back, TJ," Vinnie says. He flips Cooper the double bird.

"Good man, Vinnie. Good man. Now *lift those knees* and let's get going. Can you smell those donuts? If you don't move it, they'll be gone before we get there. You know Grady's gone as soon as his food is."

Cooper disappears back into the house.

And finally—*finally*—Dita and Vinnie and I make it to the park.

Dita collapses dramatically onto a park bench at the edge of the festivities.

I might collapse dramatically next to her. This is what I get for my pride refusing to admit I need to exercise more before I run a 5K at half a mile an hour in forty-degree weather.

"I can't feel my legs," she gasps.

"Like *I need a doctor* can't feel my legs, or like *wow, that's good, I always wanted jelly for legs* can't feel my legs?" I ask.

Which is a massive mouthful when I'm panting like this too, for the record.

"The second. And I still hate you. But I also love you. Don't ever change."

That's a relief. "You kicked booty, Dita. Way to go." I try to lift a finger to signal Grady to bring one of his donuts over, but I can't lift my hand, so I try a Jedi mind trick.

It doesn't work.

Instead, Cooper shows up next to us, bottles of orange juice in hand. "Drink up, me hearties. Yo ho ho."

"How—" Vinnie bends over and pants too "—the fuck did —" and now he's wheezing "—you get here first?"

"Dude." Cooper bends over to peer into his face. "Your pulse okay? You gonna pass out? Drink something. I walked and I got here before you. Jesus. Don't do the 5K if the 5K's gonna do you up the ass instead, you get me?"

"Fuck off, Rock." Vinnie glugs the orange juice, then plops onto the bench on Dita's other side.

"Tillie Jean," Dita pants, "he stinks and I can't move. Make him move."

"Cooper," I pant. "Make him move."

He pins me with a glare, looking so un-Cooper-like that I stop panting.

"How much coffee have you had today?" he demands.

"Enough to clean me out before my run. You're more or

less dead to me for Jell-O-ing my toilets, by the way. I expect a gift certificate for Sienna Bordner's housecleaning service for Christmas. *Weekly*, Stinky Booty. I want *weekly* maid service."

He doesn't smile.

And now I'm *seriously* concerned.

I down the orange juice in one long gulp, then give Dita a shoulder bump. "Stay here. I'll bring you a donut. Or the next best thing."

And then I join my brother and smother him with a hug, since it's not often *I'm* the sweaty, stinky one. "Aww, my favorite brother," I say. "Right behind Grady *and Max*."

"Don't start, Tillie Jean."

"What? I have the best brothers in the world. Why wouldn't I want more?"

He untangles himself from my grip and looks up at the overcast sky as he turns and heads toward the food tables. "I'm not telling you this," he mutters.

"Clearly."

"Look, Max grew up…"

"With a shitty home life," I prompt.

His face dances in irritation. "Right. You read *all* the articles about him."

"I read all of the articles about *all* of you." Mostly so I have a reason for reading all of the articles on Max. But I didn't just tell you that. "Go on. Quiz me. I can even tell you what Darren had to bring home from the ballpark for Tanesha every night when she was pregnant and why Francisco keeps an Easter egg in his locker."

"Wait, you know about that? He's never told us why he keeps that egg in there."

I smile mysteriously.

He shakes his head. "Not the point. Point is, I need you to quit flirting with Max. You're not…helping."

"I'm not flirting with him anymore." Final decision. Right now. Mostly because I was possibly offended that he thinks of me as a sister after he kissed me once and tried again. But I'm also rapidly figuring out that no good comes from me getting any closer to Max Cole.

I fuck with his head. I don't know why, or how, but I know I do, and I know that having their brains fucked with isn't good for anyone on the team, and therefore, it's not good for the team as a whole.

"That got old since he's next door every day," I add.

Uh-oh.

Cooper's giving me the flat, *I don't believe you* glare. "Nothing ever gets old with you."

"Not true. I outgrew my addiction to Lucky Charms."

"After you ate too much of it while you had a stomach bug."

"Maybe I flirted with Max while I had a stomach bug and now the thought of him makes me turn green too."

"Tillie Jean, do *not* fuck with him. This isn't a normal off-season. Last year? Last year, we had nothing to prove. Yeah, we knew things would be different since the new manage-ment would care and want us to win, but nobody expected us to make the play-offs. We just had to win a few more games, which was almost a given with fans coming back and us knowing we'd all get fired and the team moved to Vegas if we couldn't pull it off. And you know what? We're professional athletes. *We like winning.* Of course we were gonna win more. This year? This year, there's pressure. Like *we need to win it all* pressure. And *nobody* feels it like the pitchers. Lay off, okay? Be a friend, not a pain in the butt."

"Do you know what relieves pressure?"

My brother glares down at me with that *do not sleep with my teammates* glare that he's worn since we were all old enough to understand what *sleeping with* was.

I roll my eyes. "*Fun*, Cooper. *Fun* relieves pressure. I would be happy to have *fun* with Max, and after the stupid *garden gnomes*, despite the fact that he did it with *garden gnomes*, I thought he was having fun back. And weren't we having fun at Scuttle Putt last night? *He* was having fun. *He* called me his sister. *He* challenged me to the hurricane hole, and you know as well as I do that it was pure luck that I sank that shot, but he couldn't handle losing to—"

"*Just lay off*, okay?"

"*Rawk!* Land ahoy, motherfuckers! *Rawk!*"

We both glance up at Long Beak Silver, who's sitting on a lamppost.

"Go walk the plank, you miserable old bird," Cooper snaps.

"*Rawk!* I hate you and your mother's left tit too!" The parrot lifts one leg, falls off the lamppost, plummets toward the ground, but catches himself and swoops away before he turns himself into a colorful splat on the ground.

"I seriously hate that talking chicken," I mutter. "Why won't he walk the plank for me?"

"Probably because you call him a talking chicken. And also because you break into people's houses and replace their shower curtains with giant ugly pictures of yourself."

"That was for you, for the record. I wouldn't have done it if he hadn't pulled out the garden gnomes. The *garden gnomes,* Cooper."

We reach the tables, and Yiannis Florakis, who owns the Mediterranean deli, Port of Athena, near the spa, flags us down. "Cooper, I made your special baklava. And dolma! Grape leaves cure any hangover."

Yiannis finishes his pitch with a grin.

He's been in Shipwreck for two years and is still impressed with Cooper. I've assured him many times he'll get tired of my brother, but a lot of the newcomers haven't yet.

I attribute that to Cooper not being here as often as the rest of us.

Until a few years ago, our family—aunts, uncles, and cousins—owned most of the town. But more and more people from the city have moved out here to work remotely or try a slower-paced life, which means our little town is expanding with new residents enamored with our local celebrities.

And by *local celebrities*, I unfortunately mostly mean just my brother, whom I elbow out of the way to get a sample of the dolma before his appetite wreaks havoc on what's left here. "Oh my god, Yiannis, this is *delicious*."

He gives me the stink eye. "I was saving that for *Cooper*."

I smile at him. "Guess Cooper'll have to come into the deli this week to try them for himself. Again."

"Bring all the baseball players," Yiannis tells him. "And you tell me if you're having a party. Free food for a picture."

Cooper snags the baklava before I can get to that too. "Thanks, Yiannis. Will do." He nudges me down the row. "I need you to invite Max to stay for Thanksgiving and promise him you'll behave yourself."

"Right. If I do that, he'll think I'm plotting special ingredients in the gravy."

"The laxative kind of special ingredient?"

"The pot kind of special ingredient."

He gives me the side eye of *don't*. "Not funny, TJ."

That would've been funny any other year. Especially since he snuck pot into the cranberry sauce last year and got Nana high as a kite, which was basically the best entertainment we've had in Shipwreck since the loose goats interrupted that destination wedding here a few years ago.

It's also why the town council voted to ask all the restaurants on Blackbeard Avenue to open for a progressive dinner for Thanksgiving this year.

So we can *all* enjoy drunk, high Nana if it happens again.

And probably also so that we're making sure we include as many new people in town as possible.

I nudge Cooper. "So spill. What's got you so worried about Max? Trevor's the one everyone else is freaking out over." Can't blame them. Trevor's looking at his career being over.

His jaw clenches and he looks quickly around the park like he's afraid of who's listening to us.

"*What?*" I press.

"You remember Mr. Atherton?"

"High school geometry?"

"Yeah."

I don't think there's anyone who went to school with us who doesn't. Mr. Atherton took a leave of absence midway through my freshman year—Cooper's junior year, when Grady had already left home for culinary school—for what was rumored to be a nervous breakdown. No one said *depression* back then. "You think Max is gonna be like Mr. Atherton?"

"I think there's a lot that you never know about another person, and you need to lighten the fuck up on Max, okay?"

We get to the next table, and I spot the man in question himself hanging out under a barren oak tree at the end of the next row. He's angled away from me, but not enough that I can't see his face, and not enough that I can't see that he's sneaking a piece of Anchovies pizza to Goatstradamus too.

He was so funny last night.

Relaxed. Happy.

Attractive.

And if Cooper's trying to tell me that Max is dealing with a mental heath struggle, then yeah, I need to lighten up. "I've been trying to annoy both of you for *years.*"

"A few times a season when the stakes weren't so high. Not every day. Just lay off, okay?"

Heat creeps into my chest.

No, not heat.

Embarrassment. Shame. Guilt.

"He laughs when Marisol or Tanesha tease him," I grumble.

Cooper's jaw ticks again.

Comparing myself to Marisol and Tanesha isn't fair. Marisol's engaged to the Fireballs' right fielder, and Tanesha's married to the Fireballs' left fielder. They're spoken for.

They're *safe*.

But any of the single guys on the team who flirt with me have to pass the Cooper test.

And if anyone knows first-hand what Cooper's willing to do if he feels like I'm in danger, regardless of the variety of danger, it's Max.

"You know it's ridiculous to pretend I'm some wallflower who has to be saved from ruining herself, right?" I tell him. "I knew what I was doing with Chance."

"Okay, Mrs. Ben Woods."

My entire body twitches. Our parents give us the space we need to make our own mistakes, and they don't weaponize guilt, but they're *excellent* at *Tillie Jean, we hate seeing you upset, and this on-again, off-again thing you have with Ben doesn't seem to be making you happy. What can we do?* when one of us has been dumb for too long.

And no, I haven't dated anyone seriously since.

I haven't even followed through with hooking up with any of the guys I've tried to meet on dating apps when I'm in the city.

It just never feels *right*. There's something wrong with each of them.

Definitely the universe telling me not to waste my time. "You are so lucky I barely have the energy to walk right now, much less kick your ass."

"One, he was a shitty catcher and needed to go anyway. Two, I'm not trying to rule your life, TJ. But I know you, and I know them, and yeah, I have opinions, and yeah, they impact my job. Quit making Max uncomfortable. Nothing good comes at the end, okay?"

I sigh.

He's not pulling the *I'm worldly now that I live in a big city and travel for my cool job and just come to little ol' Shipwreck in the off-season* card.

He's pulling the *people have demons you don't know about and I don't want you or anyone else to get hurt if I can give you a little more information* card.

And the truth is, Cooper wouldn't interfere with my personal life if he wasn't worried. He's watched me make enough questionable choices in life without comment for me to know that he's not just being an ass right now.

Chance Schwartz was a womanizer. I was well aware that if we lasted more than two days, he would've slept with other women on the road while sleeping with me when he was home.

And I was fooling myself in thinking I'd be okay with that.

I wasn't.

But I wanted *something*. Something I couldn't get in Shipwreck, something I couldn't get from my relationship with Ben, something I couldn't get from my family and friends, no matter how much I love them and take joy in being with them.

We pause at Mom's table, and she hands Cooper a steaming mug of hot chocolate. "Oh, here, honey, take another to Max. Poor thing looks tired."

I reach for a coffee.

She lifts a brow, and I take the water bottle she hands me instead.

"Tillie Jean!" Mackenzie waves, and Coco Puff barks, sending an echo of his collar's translated "*I love big sloppy kisses and hugs!*" around the park.

Cooper slides me a look.

"Best behavior." I lift a pinky. "Promise."

"It's not all you, TJ. I know it's not. But it's…"

"Complicated," I finish for him.

"Yeah."

"Then really, there are far worse things that I could be than *like a sister* to him, hm?"

Cooper twitches, but he also nods. "Far worse."

We reach the spot at the edge of the park that we dig up every summer, looking for pirate treasure during the pirate festival, and I attack Henri with a hug. "Hey, you. Did you get your next book turned in? How was your book signing?"

We chat for a few minutes, and when I look up, Max is gone.

I don't like that.

So several hours later, when I get home after hanging out with my friends all day, I head to his house and knock on the door.

He doesn't answer.

I knock again.

Still no answer.

Could he be out with Cooper and the guys? Of course.

Any one of them could've given him a ride, and they would've had to, since his SUV is still in the drive. Or he could've walked somewhere.

But the three goats lounging in his front yard, munching on cabbage and asparagus spears, suggests he's at least been home to toss out food for the strays.

So I head to his side window.

The one I crawled through yesterday.

And I peer inside.

Huh. Look at that. Max is hanging out in his living room.

I rap on the window.

He leaps sixty-five feet in the air, then turns a glare on me.

A woman who didn't grow up with Grady and Cooper might take the hint. But I'm not that woman, so instead, I pop the screen out and press on the glass *just right* to make the window lift from the outside.

Max's glare gets glarier. "Go. The fuck. Away."

"I wasn't just valedictorian of my high school class. I was also Miss Shipwreck my sophomore year, which was basically unheard of for anyone younger than a junior since Nana pulled off the same feat like three hundred years ago." Yes, Nana will forgive me for the exaggeration. "And I was Homecoming Queen and Prom Queen and voted most likely to succeed *and* best hair in my senior yearbook. Plus, my banana pudding won best in fair when I was fourteen, and while I'm not at Grady's level, I can pretty much guarantee I'll get a blue ribbon in desserts anytime I enter."

"I'm calling the sheriff."

"My cousin Chester will probably answer the call. Won't be the first time he's ticketed me. Probably not the last either. I was sometimes a spoiled shit when I was little, and I probably deserve it. But my point isn't that I'm perfect. My point is, I left home to start college at Virginia Tech, where I intended to become a graphic designer, and not just *any* graphic designer, but a world-famous, make-a-billion-dollars graphic designer wanted by every company in the world. I like art, even if I don't like computers, and who cares if you do a job you hate for eight hours a day if it means you can do whatever you want the rest of the time, right?"

"Stop talking."

"But two weeks into the semester, I overdosed on espresso shots and ended up in the emergency room with an irregular heartbeat that nearly put me into shock and scared the ever-loving *fuck* out of my roommates. I dropped out, came home, and spent the next month basically melting down since I was a complete and total failure for the first time in my life, and not because I OD'd on caffeine—I mean, let's be real, *who does that?*—but because I didn't even last two weeks at college, which meant I didn't give it a fair shot and I was a chicken, right?"

I pause.

He's still giving me the growly bear look, but he's not telling me to shut up and go away anymore.

"And then I started dating Ben Woods while working at Crusty Nut to *find myself*, and I was safe here, and I moved in with my Great-Aunt Matilda to help watch over her so she could stay home longer while her body was giving out on her, and I didn't need anything because my family really has owned this town forever and it means certain comforts get passed down generation to generation, and I was on this path to being my parents, and my parents are pretty damn awesome, so that was great too."

He rolls his eyes.

"Except for the part where I felt like everyone was whispering about me. I was valedictorian and Queen Everything and I could paint and still do a handstand and basically everything I touched turned to gold, so *obviously* I should go off and be this big important person who did big important things and was super successful and rich and perfect forever instead of staying in Shipwreck and working for a family business, because really, what kind of mark was that to leave on the world when I had all these brains and talents?"

"You are exceptionally annoying."

"Hush. If you're going to be my big brother, you need to know my big secret."

"Which is?"

"I ended up going to see a therapist in Sarcasm—do *not* tell my family I went to Sarcasm—because the weight of everyone's expectations was utterly crushing me, and I felt guilty for *liking* working for my dad. Like I was a failure for not trying to find what else would make me happy when there was nothing holding me back from opportunity. Like I was hiding from the world in a safe place instead of getting out and experiencing what else there is. But it turns out, Crusty Nut and Shipwreck and my family *do* make me happy. I don't have to have a big title or a big job or make a ton of money to leave my mark on the world. I don't have to marry the guy who's conveniently there but not all that attractive to me down deep in the pit of my soul. I can travel—and I do—but I love coming home, and this is where I *choose* to stay, happily. Some day that might change, and if it does, I'll know I can trust myself to take a leap."

Max isn't growly-bearing me anymore, but he's not smiling either. "If you're trying to tell me you know pressure—"

"I know *my* kind of pressure, Max. I don't know yours. I know what makes *me* happy. And I don't have to apologize for it or live up to anyone else's expectations. And I *won't* apologize for it. Neither should anyone. I mean, provided it's not illegal or immoral, you know? But I still slide backwards sometimes and have to consciously remind myself that I define my happiness, not anyone else, which is why I got so irritated with you at the bar the other night when you asked about the valedictorian thing. That was *my* problem. Not yours. I'm not perfect. I'm irrationally freaked out by garden gnomes. I feel completely inconsequential and worthless every time I hear Cooper made a huge donation to his favorite charity, since I can't afford to do the same, even though I know it's an irrational reaction. I got offered a painting commission once by a bigwig in Copper Valley, and I turned it down because I was afraid that I couldn't live up to expectations. And I started the paint night at The Grog when Dita recommended a book club and I couldn't bear the thought of reading the classics and pretending I really *got* them, so I distracted everyone with something that put me in charge instead."

I pause and look at him again.

He's just lounging on his couch, in a T-shirt and jeans, watching me with those fascinating brown eyes, his facial tics telling me I'm hitting a nerve but he's not going to call me on it.

"Anyway," I say, "I just wanted you to know that I'm not perfect, and if you need anything, I'm next door."

His gaze drops to the floor for a second before he lifts his eyes back to mine. "I didn't leave last night because you got a hole in one."

"Why not? Cooper has before." I smile.

He doesn't. "I don't get drunk."

Warning alarms go off in my head. Did I call him drunk? He *was* drunk.

Wasn't he?

And he was funny and relatable and irritating with the way he kept insisting that I was his sister, but also exactly what I've wished he'd be around me for longer than I can admit even to myself.

I don't mind self-reflection.

But it's interesting to realize I've been missing my own signals for so long.

"That was my old man." He looks past me, or maybe at the wall next to me. "He had demons. Fought 'em with booze. The only reason I'm here is because he was a warning of what not to be. I worked my ass off to get out of his house and *never* be like him."

And here I am, with an awesome family and everything handed to me on a silver platter.

It's not that I've never struggled or had to work hard. But I definitely had a head start. So much makes sense now. "Does baseball make you happy?"

I get the most honest *what the fuck is wrong with you?* face he's ever sent my way. "I fucking *love* baseball."

It's hard not to smile, and not because he's funny, but because I'm getting warm and glowy in my chest at seeing what I suspect is raw, unfiltered Max. "Just checking."

He leans back and looks away again. "But I didn't know if it loved me," he mutters.

"How so?"

Max Cole has his own demons. I think I've always known it, but it's never quite as clear as it is when watching him silently wrestle with himself.

And the man is *definitely* wrestling with himself. He opens his mouth. Snaps it shut with his growly bear face. Shakes his head a little like he's lecturing himself on whatever it is he's thinking of doing. Shoots me a side eye. Mutters to himself.

And finally pulls himself off the couch, stalks across the room like he's a tiger and I'm a gazelle and he's going to have a nice little snack of Tillie Jean that'll leave him sated and ready to lay out in the forty-five-degree weather, getting a tan. The man *never* wears long sleeves more than three minutes.

At least, in my experience.

And right now, his biceps are bulging under a faded gray T-shirt that says *Pet My Rock,* which feels weird given that I *am* a Rock, but really, there are more important things at play here.

Like the fact that he's now squatting two inches from my face so that we're nearly nose-to-nose, and he smells like Luca Rossi, but better, like the patchouli and sage in the shampoo they both use blend in better with Max's natural heady scent.

I swallow hard and try to not lean in to sniff him more.

He didn't smell this good last night. Which means he took a shower. And now I'm picturing him naked behind that shower curtain with my face on it, and I wonder if seeing my face turned him on.

He leans even closer and lowers his voice. "I had a panic attack that put me in the hospital after my first no-hitter for the Fireballs. Cooper took me to the ER. Helped me find a doc. Someone to talk to with a prescription pad. Never judged. Always has my back. I'm not fucking that up. *Ever.* No matter how much I might want to. Okay?"

Oh, shit.

My heart squeezes. Was *not* expecting that.

So I slowly nod. "Okay. Got it."

He nods back, then rises, puts a hand to my forehead, gives me a shove, and the next thing I know, I'm staring at the glass.

And I don't like it.

I don't want a damn barrier between me and Max. Not when I feel like he just hit a button to open a secret door and let me in.

He doesn't want to ruin his friendship with Cooper.

I get it.

And there's the whole *don't fuck with the team* element too.

Also get that.

But who doesn't need one more friend? I can be a friend. I can be the best damn friend he's ever had.

I knock on the glass one more time. "You can still prank me," I call. "I'm still your little sister. And I give good prank back."

There you go, Max.

I caught your pitch. I lobbed it back.

Let's see what you want to do with it now.

13

Max

Fucking snow.

Fucking snow on a fucking holiday in a fucking town that's fucking perfect.

Except it's not, Max, Tillie Jean's voice whispers in my head. *Come to dinner. It's just dinner. Just people. Except more food and more people.*

And that's exactly why I need to go to the city.

Lots and *lots* more people, but none of them will give a shit if I don't show up for someone else's idea of a good time.

For the record—there's no snow in the city.

Copper Valley is *lovely* today. A little chilly, but *not snowy.* Or even wet.

But can I get there?

Not until I shovel ten damn inches off my driveway. And even then, there's no telling if or when the streets will get plowed.

But I'm still out on my driveway, shoveling snow, at seven AM.

Just in case.

Maybe I can shovel the street too.

If I can't get out of town, I'll have to explain to Mr. and Mrs. Rock why I don't want to join them for the Thanksgiving thing they've been making such a big fuss over, and *I don't want to look Tillie Jean in the eye after everything I confessed to her Saturday afternoon* won't cut it.

Holidays suck, thanks for asking isn't something you say to people who've been nothing but kind to you for years.

Don't want to bring you down when I inevitably get stuck obsessing over how it's all just for show probably won't go over so well with the Rocks either. They seem legitimately tight without a lot of dysfunction, and knowing Tillie Jean's talked to at least one professional too?

They might be the real deal.

They might be the one normal, healthy family in the world. The anomaly.

The *fucking perfect* example for the rest of us.

Trevor left yesterday.

Robinson flew out Sunday.

Elliott and Rossi and their ladies didn't stick around past the weekend either.

I should've left last night, but I was tired after pushing myself too hard at the gym. Plus, I kept telling myself I'd go talk to Tillie Jean and ask her to not say anything about everything I told her, when really, it would've been an excuse to see if she looked at me any differently, and I know it.

And on top of my physical and mental issues, we were only supposed to get half an inch of snow.

"Not to tell you how to shovel, but most people wear clothes while they're doing it," Tillie Jean herself calls.

I straighten and glare at her even though she's fucking gorgeous leaning out her own window this morning and the mere sight of her makes me want to drop my shovel and dive into her house with her.

Reason number forty thousand this woman gets under my skin.
"It's hot."

"You're hot." She grins, then stops and sighs. "Sorry. Habit. I'm stopping, I swear. But seriously, you can't expect a woman to not react to a guy in his boxers shoveling three feet of snow."

It's not three feet, but it's the heavy, thick, wet kind of snow that sticks together, as opposed to the light and fluffy, airy stuff that you could sweep away with a broom, so I don't correct her.

Mostly. "I'm wearing boots too."

"Ooh, I love boots. Are they lined?"

I grunt and start counting shovels of snow by the fours, which is a pretty decent indication that I should be inside, accepting my fate of being stuck here for the weekend and finding something more productive to do with my time instead of being out here, counting by fours.

Like maybe calling my doc and asking if it's okay to double up on anxiety meds through the holidays.

The next step in shoveling snow this morning is getting upset that she interrupts me at—

"Cooper's stuck up on the mountain. We're probably pushing the progressive dinner to tonight," Tillie Jean continues. "Or at least later this afternoon. Gotta have time to digest before bed and the world opening up again tomorrow, right? Not that I'm telling you that because I don't respect your decision about whether or not you want to come. It's more that I know you guys are tight and if you wanted someone to commiserate with about interrupted plans, he'll have extra time today. And I think Uncle Homer probably has snowshoes in your basement if you want to hike the mountain. Not like he'll be using them."

Three.

I didn't make it all the way to four.

Go inside, Max. Go. Inside.

I hate holidays.

I hate holidays more than I hate knowing that Tillie Jean talked me out of my darkest secrets. I hate holidays more than I've ever hated Tillie Jean. And I hate holidays more than I hate knowing that I don't hate Tillie Jean, not even close, but *she's still fucking off-limits*, which might be what I hate most of all.

Right behind *she somehow isn't making me feel like a loser-failure for having a meltdown on the driveway over not being able to leave town for Thanksgiving when all I really need to do is barricade myself inside the house.*

How does she do that?

How does she talk and talk and talk and then say the exact right thing that should be the wrong thing, since she's the one saying it, but it isn't?

There's another noise next door, and I slide my eyes just enough that way to see a leg come out a window.

It's dressed, albeit in bright pants that are most likely pajama pants.

In a boot of its own.

And it's followed by the woman who haunts my sleep now shimmying out of her window in a coat.

I stop shoveling. "What are you doing?"

She reaches back inside the house and pulls out a shovel. "My front door won't open. I'm gonna go free it."

"I'll get your door."

"Aww, that's sweet of you to offer, but I love shoveling snow. The *first* time it snows, anyway. I manage to forget over the summer how much I hated it the last time I did it last winter."

She's completely serious.

And she very much needs to be none of my business, so I go back to my own shoveling.

One scoop. Two scoops. Three scoops. Four scoops.

One scoop. Two scoops. Three—

"Did it snow a lot where you grew up? I forgot where that was."

"Some." One scoop. Two—

"Like Alaska some, or like you lived in Texas and occasionally had weather that shut the whole state down?"

I straighten and start to glare at her, but she's not wiggling her eyebrows at me, tugging up her pants to show me her ankles, winking, making duck lips, or doing anything beyond attempting to walk through snow that almost reaches halfway up her calf.

Actually, the snow's deep enough that she's taking comically large steps, her arms extended, one holding the shovel, balancing so she's not dragging her boots through it.

She's only leaving footprints.

No shuffle marks.

The other thing she's not doing?

Shooting me covert looks to see if I'm *mentally stable* today.

Of all the days to check, today would be that day.

Fuck, I like her.

And *I can't*.

"What do the goats do when it snows?" I ask.

"Pop has a barn that he opens up so they can hide in there. Plus, everyone donates to the wild goat fund at the Pirate Festival every summer, so there's goat food stocked in there year-round too."

I lean on my shovel. Wind's not so great when you're in nothing but boxers and boots and standing still. Didn't notice while I was shoveling. But I'd still rather be out here without any more layers. My body runs hot enough as it is. "So they don't need everyone in town to feed them."

"Nope, but if it makes your heart happy to take care of an animal, then take care of an animal. You could adopt one like Grady did. Goatstradamus really seems to like you. And if he's anything like Grady's goat, once you let him inside, he's yours forever."

"I'm not taking a goat back to the city. Who the fuck would feed him while I'm—"

She smiles, and it's a warm, crinkly-eyed, tooth-showing, pretty kind of smile that reminds me exactly why Cooper feels the need to tell the rookies and new guys every year that his sister's off-limits.

She's fun. She's smart without being a know-it-all. She's entertaining without being a ham. And she's gorgeous.

Cocky too, but I hurl fastballs near a hundred miles an hour for a living and know I'm a god on the mound. I'm not one to judge cocky. And if I'd grown up knowing I fit, that I was where I belonged, and that people around me loved me enough for me to be myself, yeah, I'd be the Rock kind of cocky as well.

I shake my head. "Right. You're joking."

"*That*, I won't promise anyone I won't do. Sorry, Mr. Cole. There's only so much of my personality I'll suppress for any one person."

Mr. Cole usually makes me twitch. *Mr. Cole* is my father, and I abhor being called *Mr. Cole*.

But when Tillie Jean says it, I get images of her in leather and lace, offering me handcuffs in that pink and black bedroom of hers, and telling me it's time to punish her for being a very, very bad girl.

I grunt and go back to shoveling. If I don't, I'll have a very visible problem here very soon, and it'll be a much bigger problem than counting to fours.

My shovel scrapes the concrete driveway, and then another scrape joins it in the cloudy morning.

Tillie Jean's shoveling too.

I slide another glance at her. The temperature's right at freezing, and she's in a light coat over her pajamas.

I wonder if she's wearing a bra, then promptly give myself a mental head slap.

Bad enough I'm also wondering how much she can lift.

She's slender, but curvy, and I know she has solid definition in her arms and legs.

She glances over and catches me watching her, so I duck my head and shovel another scoop.

But I'm not counting anymore.

"What do you usually do for Thanksgiving?" she calls.

"Whatever I want."

"Such as?"

"Eat. Scratch myself. Sleep. Whatever."

"Don't lie, Max Cole. I know you're perusing those shopping ads and hitting the stores as soon as they open to buy presents for orphans and widows."

I jolt and whip my face up to look at her as my entire body flushes, and it's not like I can hide *that* in this weather.

Her mouth goes round. "Oh my god. You do."

"Incorrect."

"Which part's incorrect? The part where you send presents to people in need, or the part where you shop for good sales to do it?"

My agent sent me a proposed four-year contract extension with the Fireballs yesterday. It starts with a bigger number than I could count to the first time I held a baseball, and ends with enough zeroes to guarantee I never have to lift a finger again in my lifetime once my career's over.

My current contract is nothing to shake a stick at, and I could live on the few endorsement deals I have alone. I'd have to live somewhere like Shipwreck, but still.

I could do it.

I don't need to look for good sales on anything, and I don't want to talk about it anymore. "Do the weathermen always get it this wrong out here?"

"Avoiding the question. So you do shop for sales, but it's only habit because your neighbor Mrs. Bradford used to pay you a penny for every dollar you saved her when you shopped for her groceries using the weekly coupons?"

"What the hell are you talking about?"

"It's best to just answer the questions, or I'll make up my own version of the truth. Ask Aunt Glory sometime about her broken ankle. Hint: it wasn't broken, but people came out to help fix her porch in droves anyway. Also, everyone knew it wasn't really broken, but that she wouldn't ask for help on her own, and we very much wanted her to not fall through the porch."

She smiles.

Dammit.

We can be semi-friendly, but not today, and not if she smiles at me.

She goes back to shoveling her own porch in front of her door. "I know, it's a little messed up, but if you knew Aunt Glory when she was younger, you'd understand. People are weird sometimes."

"People are weird all the time."

She laughs. "Also true."

Tillie Jean's being nice to me, and I don't know if it's because of this weekend, or if it's that we've gotten more used to each other since I came to Shipwreck for the winter, or if it—if it's—

Fuck.

I don't care, and I'm tired of fighting this, and I suddenly have an overwhelming urge to lob a snowball at her.

I'm bending over and packing snow into a ball before I let myself stop and think, and then I lob it in the air, and in that moment, I'm about six years old again, playing in the yard, with no cares, no worries, and no idea what the rest of my childhood would bring.

I miss that kid.

I miss *being* that kid.

And when my snowball lands directly on its intended target—the door three inches to the left of Tillie Jean's face—I smile as broadly as I would if she were Cooper.

But that is *not* Cooper swiveling to face me.

Nope.

It's his sister. His off-limits, unfortunately sexy, even when she's talking—possibly *especially* when she's talking—sister.

Not *my* sister, no matter how much I've tried to convince myself she could be.

"Did you just throw a snowball at me?"

"If I threw a snowball at you, it would've hit you."

"Are you supposed to be throwing right now? I thought you had to take a couple months off to let your arm recover from the season."

I bend, pack another snowball, and lob this one straight at her.

She shrieks and dives, and comes up with a snowball of her own.

I probably should've put clothes on.

But then, I didn't expect to be dodging snowballs and flinging them right back when I got too hot shoveling and stripped out of my shirt.

Also, it's probably a sign I shouldn't be out here at all that I didn't stop to put on pants before heading out to shovel snow.

That's the kind of *get the hell out of here as fast as possible* fog I was in when I woke up to the sun reflecting off of ten inches of snow on Thanksgiving morning.

I lob another snowball at her, and it lands square on her chest.

She fires one back that splatters hard against *my* chest. I stare down at the snow, still packed over my left nipple. "Holy hell."

She smirks. "Cooper's not the only one in the family with an arm. Do you surrender, or are we doing this to the death?"

"I will *never* surrender."

I'm smiling.

It's Thanksgiving, I'm trapped here, and I'm *smiling*, just like I smiled when I decided to put those garden gnomes from the basement out along her property line and like I was smiling after I got over the initial jolt of terror of seeing her gigantic face on my shower curtain.

"You've sealed your fate, Captain Cole! Prepare to die!"

We both dive for the snow again, packing and flinging snowballs at each other until she gets me in the face.

"*Oh my god*, I'm so sorry!"

I sputter and wipe it off, and when I blink my eyes open again, Tillie Jean's right in front of me. She attacks my face too, wiping more snow away from my cheeks. "Are you okay? Can you see? Do I need to call Doc? Blink twice if you can hear me."

I don't know who I am today, but the question makes me crack up. "My ears are *fine*, Trouble Jean."

"Thank god. I know they're what you throw with."

She's so completely serious that I laugh again.

She doesn't.

Instead, her eyes go dark, her lips part, and her tongue darts out to swipe at her lower lip.

And suddenly all I can think of is her lying in Chance Schwartz's bed, her bare breasts peeking out from beneath the sheet, head thrown back in ecstasy, very clearly pleasuring herself.

I shouldn't have been in his apartment at all, except I'd misplaced my phone, and that was the last place I remembered having it. He'd forgotten his gym bag, but also had a meeting with management, so I offered to get both.

And instead, I got a show.

I pretended I didn't see a thing. You don't screw around with your teammates' girlfriends, and if she was in his apartment alone, she was clearly involved with him somehow.

But when she showed up again a few hours later at Duggan Field, pretended she didn't see him and gave Cooper a hug, I asked if she was sleeping with everyone on the team.

And that's when everything went to hell. When I discovered the wet dream from Schwartz's apartment was off-limits for so many more reasons than I thought.

But forgetting how she looked writhing under those sheets?

Hard as I try, I can never quite do it.

And living next door to her? Seeing her almost every day, aware of her coming and going even when I don't think she realizes I'm close by?

Hearing people talk about her and all the little things she does every day to spread some happiness here in Shipwreck?

Reminding myself of all those reasons I hate her?

I can't do it anymore. I don't *want* to do it anymore.

Fuck, I wish she wasn't Cooper's sister.

"You shouldn't smile at me like that," she whispers.

"I shouldn't." Hell, my voice is hoarse, and it's not the cold air causing it.

"We can only be friends if you don't smile at me."

"Then we can only be friends if you go back to being annoying."

She smiles, and I want to kiss her. I want to kiss her again, this time in the snow. I want to feel the heat of her lips contrasting with the ice of the world around us, stroke her skin, embrace her curves, taste her mouth, make her moan, and soak in that feeling of being around the simple joy that is Tillie Jean.

I know it's a bad idea, but I don't care.

I feel *happy*.

Cold and alive and *happy*.

I want to be happy.

What was it she said the other day? *I had to find what made me happy, not what other people thought would make me happy.*

I've been avoiding what I think would make other people unhappy. Like, I can't be the kind of man who deserves a woman like Tillie Jean, even if Cooper *could* forgive me for trying.

I'm not the kind of man who'll ever deserve *any* woman.

Not long-term.

But *god*, it would make me happy right now.

I dip my head. Angle in. Watch her quick intake of breath.

Feel her hand still on my face.

I'm doing this.

I'm kissing Tillie Jean.

Consequences be damned.

But just before my lips brush hers, she ducks.

I blink.

And more snow rains down on my head.

"Ooh, gotcha!" Tillie Jean calls, but she's not backpedaling like a woman afraid of revenge.

She's backpedaling like a woman afraid of what we almost just did.

Again.

I should thank her.

Instead, I turn around, trip over my shovel, recover, and head inside.

Must not kiss Tillie Jean Rock.

It's a rule.

And I need to remember it.

14

TILLIE JEAN

MAX ALMOST KISSED ME.

Again.

And I almost let him.

Again.

And since I can't stop thinking about the way he was looking at me, like he'd just emerged from living in an Armageddon bunker for thirty years to discover there's still sunshine and flowers and snow and mountains, I'm not paying attention to the massive pot of sweet potatoes in Dad's kitchen at Crusty Nut.

"I think you got them all, hon," Dad says behind me.

I jump, then look down at the pot.

Our sweet potato casserole is never lumpy, but I do believe I've taken smooth to the next level here. Have I induced decomposition? Are they runny now? *Gah.* "Getting my exercise in with the potato masher," I tell him. "I'm earning all of that turkey I'm planning on eating later."

"I thought you did that with a snowball fight in your front yard."

The kitchen's always hot, but not usually face-flaming hot. "Meh. It wasn't the best snowball fight. My yard still has untouched snow. You know that wouldn't have happened if Cooper and Grady were there. We would've used all the snow on the entire block before calling a truce."

He grins at me.

It's a classic Dad grin. The *someone has a crush and I'm going to tease you incessantly about it* grin.

I frown at him the same way he used to frown at me when he caught me after I'd tell him I cleaned my room but actually shoved everything on my floor into my closet. "Dad. He's Cooper's teammate. Winning before sinning, okay?"

He laughs, but it's an awkward, wincing kind of laugh. "*Sinning?* Tillie Jean. I don't want to know what you do on a date, but I don't want you to feel ashamed of yourself either. Some things are, ah, natural, and, ah—"

"Dad, I know grown-up activities aren't a sin. But interfering with the team's vibe is."

More wincing, which better not be the theme of this year's Thanksgiving. "I suppose I can see that."

Mom pops into the kitchen. "How're the turkeys coming?"

"Right on schedule."

"Good. Glory's on track too, Grady's reporting he's ready, and Pop's been working with Vinnie to get the roads cleared."

That's worth smiling about. We've never done a progressive dinner for Thanksgiving before, but considering how tight we all are, it makes sense, and I'm excited.

And so, *so* glad for the distraction from thinking about Max.

We'll have turkey and sweet potato casserole here at Crusty Nut. Salad and green bean casserole at Anchovies, the local pizza joint. Grady's covering dinner rolls at Crow's

Nest, Aunt Glory has the stuffing—dressing, whatever you call it—and cranberry sauce, and Mom's café, The Muted Parrot—and yes, we all *do* wish Long Beak Silver would stop talking so much—is handling pie.

Anyone without other plans in town is invited to start wherever they want along Blackbeard Avenue and enjoy Thanksgiving dinner on us.

And I'm tied up in knots hoping Max shows up.

So I need to not think about him. Enjoy the day. See all of my favorite people and play peek-a-boo with the babies and talk strategy with my teammates on our summer softball team—never too early to start planning to win against Sarcasm's team—and help run the cookie decorating tables that Mom's setting up at each location to keep any of the kids, teenagers, and adults busy if they don't want to watch football or plot shopping trips in the city.

"How was your snowball fight with Max this morning, sweetie?" Mom asks.

Argh. "He bowed out of battle after realizing that even his pitcher's arm is no match for me with a snowball in hand." I sigh dramatically and put my hand to my forehead, *alas*-style. "Woe is me—I'll never find a worthy snowball fight competitor."

"Probably would've helped if he'd been wearing clothes," Dad says.

"Oh my god, *right?* I asked him why he was shoveling practically naked and he said he *got hot.* Probably Doc should check him to see if he has a fever."

"Oh, I don't know." Mom leans in next to me and peers at the sweet potatoes as I dump in brown sugar and cinnamon and start whipping it all together. "Cooper's always hot too. I think it's all that muscle mass. It just keeps a body warmer."

I know she's talking scientifically, but *I'm* getting warmer thinking about Max's muscles.

Hi, I'm Tillie Jean, and I'm into buff athletes.

"You're really mad at those potatoes today, aren't you, hon?" Dad says.

The potatoes aren't the problem.

A limited dating pool and a guy who's not supposed to be as attractive as he's always been is the problem.

And knowing how much he's overcome to be the man he is today? And that he likes me, but doesn't want to mess up his friendship with my brother, which I *totally* understand?

Also knowing he probably has hang-ups about relationships that *I can't solve*, because he has to do that work himself if it's going to stick?

But I still want to make him smile. I still want to joke around with him. I want to spend time around the uninhibited, funny Max that he was at Scuttle Putt, but I don't know if that's the *real* Max Cole.

"Tillie Jean?" Mom says.

I jump.

Crap. Did it again. Disappeared into my own head.

Or my own libido.

Whatever.

"Shh. Grady talks to his dough, but I use telekinesis to communicate with the potatoes."

"Telepathy?" Dad corrects.

Dammit. Now I'm mixing my words and not the potatoes. "Shh."

"Yoohoo, did someone order a lonely former city girl to help in the kitchens?" Sloane calls.

And I'm saved. "*Yoohoo?*" I call back.

She leans over the bar and peers in the kitchen door at us with a grin. "Do you know how long I've been waiting to be a city girl turned country girl who calls *yoohoo*?"

"Tillie Jean, let the girl yoohoo if she wants to yoohoo." Mom waves Sloane back. "Put on a hairnet and come help with the sweet potato casserole. Tillie Jean's turning it into a murder scene."

"Ah. Didn't get enough snowball fight with your naked neighbor?"

"*Gah.*" I shove the spoon at Mom. "You finish. I'm gonna go climb the mountain and have a real snowball fight with Cooper."

"No can do, little sister." Cooper swings in the back door, stomps his boots off, and grins at me. "But if you'd care to join me in the square, we'll have a snowball fight to work up an appetite."

"Cooper! You made it." Mom switches course in hugging Sloane to cross the kitchen and attack her baby.

"How's the snowmobile?" Dad asks. "She start on the first try?"

They talk man-toy maintenance while Sloane joins me at the sweet potato pot. "Neighbor trouble?" she whispers.

"If he weren't you-know-what with you-know-who, and I was visiting the city for a weekend, we would *so* have a fling," I whisper back.

"We're talking about him being teammates with SB, right?"

I assume SB means Stinky Booty, aka Cooper, so I nod.

"So pretend he's not off-limits and see what happens."

"Nope. Not a chance."

"You like him. He likes you. How often does that happen?"

I almost drop the sweet potato pot as I'm lifting it to dump it into the industrial-size casserole dish.

And yeah, I'm completely blaming it on the pot being heavy and not on Sloane suggesting Max Cole *likes me.*

"He does *not* like me," I mutter as she grips the other handle on the pan and helps me tip it over.

"He tries too hard to not like you because he knows what *someone* will do, given his reputation. But you know what's interesting? He's *aware* of his reputation, and he's aware of the potential consequences to him, you, and his position if he misreads the situation and you end up wanting something more than a casual fling. Which means that if he's willing to risk it, he thinks you're worth the potential shit that would come if he fucks up."

Crap.

If she can see that, who else can?

I shoot a look at my family.

Cooper's saying something that has Dad laughing, and Mom's shaking her head like she'd bop him with a wooden spoon for giving her a heart attack, which means he probably almost wiped out riding his snowmobile down off the mountain.

"I'd let them *all* down, Sloane," I whisper.

Somehow, my parents have managed that magic trick of morphing from parental overlords to friends. Crusty Nut isn't just the restaurant where I slave away my days, it's part of my family too. Grady's awesome and just down the street, and him marrying Annika brought another layer of fabulous to town. Cooper's still one of my best friends, and it's not only the prank wars that make me happy to see him when he comes home for the winter.

And then there's everyone else. Old-timers and newcomers alike.

We're family.

We're safe.

We're happy.

And I work my ass off to make sure we stay that way. If I treated Yiannis like competition instead of like a neighbor, one, I never would've had the joy of being able to have his dolma any day of the week, and two, the magic of Shipwreck would break under the tension the rivalry would bring in.

Rivalry with Sarcasm? Yes. Rivalry within Shipwreck itself? No.

If I was here out of obligation instead of joy, my parents would know they were holding me back, and they'd feel bad, and we'd have a level of resentment to our relationship that I don't want, and neither do they.

So when I say I'd let my family down?

That's not guilt or obligation. That's real fear that the people I love would be hurt by my actions.

If Max and I had an actual future? Yeah. My family would rally.

But he's not the settling down type, and he clearly has walls up keeping him from winning over whatever demons he's fighting. I don't have a magic vagina, the world's best personality, or whatever else it is that would convince a playboy pitcher like Max to quit hooking up with one-night stands in the city, and honestly?

I'm not ready to settle down either. I still have more things I want to do first. Things I need to quit pushing off, honestly. It just always feels like it's not the right time.

Oh my god.

Am I standing in my own way too?

Sloane shakes her head. "I suppose I get it, but..."

I tilt my eyebrows up. "But there isn't a good *but*."

"Maybe Cooper can convince some of the single hockey players in town to do their summer training out here."

I burst out laughing.

She does too.

And then Dita and LaShonda show up with offers to help, and Annika's mom, her boyfriend, and little sister pop by, and the day slips away with good food and laughter and hugs and stories and bets over football games and plans for who's heading into Copper Valley for shopping trips with whom.

The next thing I know, I'm stuffed, the sun's long gone, and the kitchen at Crusty Nut is clean and ready for tomorrow morning, when we'll open early with a reinforced wifi signal for everyone who wants to start their holiday shopping online over eggs benedict and mountain man breakfasts.

Max didn't come out for the festivities.

The roads are finally clear, so I have no idea if he's still in Shipwreck—Cooper didn't say anything about him, and I didn't ask—but I still pack up a box of leftovers when I kill the lights at Crusty Nut, lock up, and head home.

Max's SUV is in his driveway, and there's light flickering in the front and side windows, suggesting he's watching TV.

A wave of melancholy hits me, both in the heart and in the gut. I don't know a lot about his past beyond the basic, no-details run-down he gave me the other day, but I imagine holidays aren't for him what they are for me.

I also know odds are high at least a half-dozen people from the block would've knocked on his door to invite him to join us for our progressive dinner today.

I'm probably not the first person to think to leave a box of leftovers on his porch, and given his usual strict diet, I don't even know if he'll touch most of the food.

But I leave it on his porch anyway, ring the doorbell, and retreat back to my own house before he can answer the door.

A guy doesn't stay locked inside his house in Shipwreck on a holiday unless he *wants* to be alone. It's not my place to make him do anything else.

But at least he'll know we were thinking about him.

And that, I'd do for anyone.

Not just Max Cole.

But the one thing I do for him that I wouldn't do for anyone else?

I think about him long, *long* after I should.

And for the first time in my life, I wish he wasn't a pitcher for the Fireballs.

15

Max

MY FAVORITE PART OF BASEBALL HAS ALWAYS BEEN THE WAY IT makes me feel like one of the guys, like a normal person with normal relationships, and today I'm seeing a few more teammates for the first time since our post-season run ended, and it's good.

It's *really* good.

We're all up at Cooper's place—like a dozen of us—plus a camera crew, testing a new card game management had developed to highlight the mascot wars that went down last season at Duggan Field.

They're technically over, with Ash the Baby Dragon hatching in a surprise reveal after management got the fans all riled up over retiring Fiery the Dragon, the Fireballs' much-beloved mascot from their losing decades, but management also declared that the four terrible options for replacement mascots were staying on at Duggan Field until they, quote, *can find new jobs.*

The firefly and the duck have half a chance, but the *meatball*? No way. And definitely not the echidna either.

No one outside of Australia even knew what an echidna was until the new Fireballs owners insisted on making it a mascot option.

But they knew what they were doing all along. Case in point—the news is still covering Ash's antics as she travels all over Copper Valley visiting schools and fire stations and the other local pro sports teams' venues, and all the baby dragon merchandise keeps selling out online.

And the Ashes we painted last month with Tillie Jean just sold for ungodly sums of money for Robinson's family's favorite charity.

Ah, hell.

There I go.

Thinking about Tillie Jean again.

It's been two weeks since she left me a box of Thanksgiving food, and other than putting a glow-in-the-dark golf ball in the box, along with a note that she's always happy to show her *friends and siblings* how to get better at Scuttle Putt, she hasn't tried to get revenge for me throwing snowballs at her, nor has she treated me any differently than Robinson, Cooper, and Trevor the two times we've gone into Crusty Nut for lunch while she was working.

She's more or less leaving me alone, and it's making everything worse. She's *supposed* to flirt with me.

"Just play a card, dude," Robinson says to Cooper. I'm at the dining room table with the two of them, plus Luca. We're surrounded by video lights and camera people, with half the rest of the team watching our game from behind the scattered cameras until it's their turn to play. All of us are wearing our team jerseys under orders from the marketing director, drinking out of Fireballs-branded water bottles, each holding a single card in our hand until it's our turn to draw one more from the deck and pick which card to play, and yeah, it feels good to be in uniform again, even if it's only my shirt.

I don't love a lot of things, but I love baseball.

It's Cooper's turn. He's been studying his two cards for what feels like an hour, even though a round of this game should be done in about the amount of time it takes for a commercial break between innings.

"It's not that complicated," Rossi says. He and his girl-friend are crashing at the inn in town for a week or so, and she's busy hanging out with the rest of the Lady Fireballs booster club. "You need me to pick? Here. Play that one."

He flicks a card.

Cooper leaps back like Luca's trying to steal it from him. "Hands off the cards, Rossi. You can pick when it's your turn."

He throws down the other card—Meaty the Meatball, the worst possible mascot choice from last season's contest, even without the pirate costume he's wearing on this card—and mutters something as we all read the instructions on the card.

"What?" Robinson almost shoots out of his seat. "*No.* I hate that card. Why'd you play *that* card? Take it back. Play the other one."

"I *can't* play the other one," Cooper snaps back.

I snicker. I'm holding a crap card—the damn Firequacker the Duck card—and I'm more than happy to follow instructions on the card Cooper played and pass Firequacker to Rossi on my left. "Pass your hands, suckers."

Cooper snarls too as he hands me the Ash the Baby Dragon card.

Heh.

Winning card if I can hold onto it until the draw pile's gone in another two rounds. Cooper's right. He couldn't play that card. He had to play Meaty, or else he would've lost.

And based on Robinson's reaction to passing the cards,

I'm betting Cooper has Fiery now, since it's the second-highest points card in the deck.

This game's both hilarious and easy, and the deck's small—only fifteen cards or so—which means the game does go quick when you're not playing with Cooper. I have zero doubt that Brooks Elliott's wife will be carrying a pack or three around in her purse to challenge random strangers to games all the time.

And since none of us like to lose, we have side bets going, and we're all keeping track of who's winning the most rounds.

House rules?

Hell, yeah.

We're implementing them next time we play. Like when the cameras aren't following us.

I could challenge Tillie Jean to Strip Go, Ash, Go.

And I'm back to needing to slap myself with a raw steak. *Do not think of Tillie Jean naked.*

Belatedly, I realize I shouldn't involve a baby dragon in sex games.

And now I'm thinking of Tillie Jean naked again.

"I'm kicking your butt next game," Cooper mutters to me.

"Good luck with that." I grin like I'm not about to pop a boner over the thought of his sister, and I draw a card to start my turn, then groan.

It's the Uncle Thrusty card. I either have to discard Ash—and lose the game, since that's what happens if I play Ash—or play Uncle Thrusty, mascot for Copper Valley's hockey team who sometimes visits Duggan Field for mascot shenanigans, and gather everyone's cards, including my own, shuffle, and deal them back out without looking.

So much for holding onto Ash.

I toss down Thrusty, and both Luca and Robinson pump their fists in the air. Cooper snickers too.

I'd flip them all off, but the cameras are watching.

"You have Ash, don't you?" Luca says to me.

"Not telling."

Cooper punches me lightly in the arm as I shuffle the four cards. "That's *my* Ash."

"Kiss my Ash," I retort.

I re-deal, end up with Fiery the Daddy Dragon, and watch my teammates closely to try to figure out who's holding on to Ash.

Not Luca. He draws, snickers, and throws down Firequacker.

"*Quaaaaack*," Cooper groans.

And I crack up.

Quack up, even.

Not because I don't hate the Firequacker card—I do, to the depths of my soul—but it's nice to see someone else upset that we're only allowed to speak in quack until the start of Luca's next turn, or be eliminated from the game.

Dumbest fucking card *ever*.

How do you play when all you can say is *quack*?

Not even kidding. That's the first card getting modified with house rules the minute the cameras are off.

Something pokes me from behind, and I glance up to see Ash peering over my shoulder.

Yeah.

Ash. The baby dragon in the flesh.

I grin at the mascot. "Hey, baby girl. You wanna walk around the table and flash me a thumbs-up when you see yourself on a card?"

She shakes her head.

Shakes her whole body, really.

And then she rubs her hand all over my head and hugs me.

Robinson clucks his tongue. "No cheating, Maxy-pants."

"You wanna sit, Ash? Come help Uncle Cooper play."

Cooper scoots his chair away from mine. "Lopez, grab Ash a chair."

Luca shoots to his feet. "*Quack!* Yeah, baby! You losers lost first!"

Robinson groans.

I groan.

Cooper gapes. "What? No. That's not—*mother quacker*."

Luca twerks for the camera, then does some move his grandma made famous on TikTok.

Dammit.

He's right.

All three of the rest of us talked instead of quacking, since a cute baby dragon distracted us. And that means Luca—the last man left quacking—just won the round.

"Rematch," I declare. "Stupid Firequacker card. I hate that card."

Ash covers her mouth and mimics laughing.

I cover my heart and play wounded. "Ash, did you set us up?"

She nods.

We all groan again, and the guys on the sidelines crack up.

"Deal me in. Cooper. You're out." Brooks edges in with Spike the Echidna mascot tiptoeing between the cameras behind him, and Francisco Lopez and Emilio Torres pile in too, trailed by Firequacker the Duck and Glow the Firefly.

Luca takes one look at Glow and grimaces. "Yeah. Take my spot."

"Darren, get in here for Max," Cooper calls.

I rise, and Ash hugs me. She's not quite my height, unlike the other mascots, who are about seven feet tall each. "You gonna play a round?" I ask her.

She giggles.

I freeze.

I know that giggle.

I'm *drawn* to that giggle.

I start to smile, then realize Cooper heard it too and is turning a glare that could melt granite my way, which means my only other option is to jerk back out of her grasp.

Unfortunately, Spike's right behind me, and I topple into him and we go down.

"Mascot fight!" Luca yells.

He grabs a cup of poker chips that we debated using to keep score and tosses them in the air, then turns and fake-punches Firequacker the Duck.

Glow spins and knocks Luca with his giant ass-ball, making me wonder if it's Tanesha or Marisol under there. Henri wouldn't torture Luca with the giant ass-ball. She's a softie like that.

Meaty lumbers through between two cameras and bumps into everyone in his path, then sweeps the table, sending cards flying.

Undoubtedly Mackenzie.

She has experience playing Meaty.

"Clear the benches!" Cooper yells.

The cameras back up as the rest of the team comes darting in.

Ash tries to hug me again. "You have to save Ash, Max," Tillie Jean says inside the costume. "You *have* to."

"You are a royal pain in the ass." *God*, she's funny. And bright. And funny. And sexy. And yeah, I said *funny* twice.

She is.

So funny.

"True, but also, you really need to save Ash before Fiery kicks your ass."

She's right, of course. I have to save Ash, and it has nothing to do with the old mascot getting mad if I don't. Let's be real. Worst he'll do is call me out on his Instagram.

More important—the fans love the new mascot as much as they love the team. Above all else, I can't disappoint the fans.

But does *she* have to be the one inside Ash? Has she been to mascot school? Or—oh, *hell*.

Did Mackenzie steal the mascots again? Does management know about this?

Doesn't matter.

What matters is playing hero to the baby dragon.

Bonus that I get to sweep Tillie Jean off her feet with justification.

You wanna know how hard it is to scoop a mascot with a giant-ass stubby baby dinosaur tail off her feet?

It's awkward as hell.

But I do it. I sweep the mascot off her feet, and I dash her to the relative safety of the living room while my teammates and the failed mascot contenders make a disaster of Cooper's dining room.

Would I dash her to a bedroom instead?

Yes.

Yes, I would.

But *fuck*, carrying a mascot is awkward. I'd probably smash her into the wall and ruin the mascot head before I got Tillie Jean exactly where I want her.

"My hero," she sighs as I set her down.

I look down at the baby dragon face.

Legit—I can't see TJ in there *at all*—and suddenly I'm cracking up. "Jesus, you drive me insane," I mutter.

"That's what little sisters are supposed to do."

I squeeze my eyes shut.

I'm not having this conversation with her while she's dressed up like a baby dragon. In a diaper.

Makes me feel like a total perv.

"Have you won any rounds?" Tillie Jean asks. "Cooper wouldn't let me play the game with him last night, but Mackenzie brought extra copies so we got to try it out too. I'm gonna burn that Firequacker card the next time I'm at a bonfire. Did you know Henri has an evil cackle? I did *not* see that coming. But it's really fitting that Luca just won with the Firequacker card too. It's like they're soulmates even when they don't know what the other is doing. She's Meaty, by the way. You would've thought Mackenzie would go for Meaty, but nope. She let Henri have Meaty."

I leap in front of her as Spike, the echidna, comes darting her way. "Back, Spike. Nobody touches Ash on my watch."

"Swoon," Tillie Jean sighs.

My dick leaps to attention.

Unfortunately, at the exact same moment, Addie Bloom walks in from the foyer. She's our batting coach, and she's one of the staff out here this winter helping us train. She's about my age, grew up with brothers, and doesn't put up with any of our shit.

Can't.

Not if she wants to make it long-term as a coach in the big leagues.

And don't let the smirk in her eyes fool you. She might be amused, but she won't let any of us get away with anything.

Probably.

She's fingering a whistle around her neck, but she's not blowing it yet.

"I'm so glad you're all out here," Tillie Jean says inside the Ash costume, finishing on a sigh that hits me between my shoulder blades in that spot I can never reach. "Makes me feel like I'm part of the team too. But without all that god-awful exercise."

I choke on a laugh. "You have a coffee IV inside that costume, don't you?"

"You know it, baby." She slaps my ass.

Cooper's throwing bananas and Nerf balls at the mascots and doesn't notice, but there's a camera aimed my way, so I turn and glare at her. "Ash. What would your father say?"

She wiggles her tail and feigns giggling.

And once again, I want to pick her up and carry her somewhere else.

Somewhere private.

Ask her more about dropping out of school. If she's the one who did the painting of Duggan Field in Cooper's man cave downstairs. Why the lights in her spare bedroom are always on at midnight.

I don't *talk* with women.

I flirt, I screw, I walk away. But I want to know more about Tillie Jean.

And not because I'm pretending she's my sister.

"You should go help remove the problem mascots from the house," she says.

I glance over at my teammates.

Robinson and Francisco are dragging Meaty by the arms, taking the flaming meatball—management's answer to the Thrusters hockey team's bratwurst mascot—out of harm's way.

Darren and Luca are tag-teaming to throw a Fireballs blanket over Glow's head.

Brooks starts a fake fist fight with Spike, proving once again that he's not afraid of the crazy Australian anteater things.

And Firequacker the Duck is shaking his butt at everyone else, swinging a foam pool noodle like a sword.

Don't ask why management put a duck in the potential mascot lineup.

You don't want to know.

But TJ's right.

My teammates and the mascots are all having fun while I'm standing here on the sidelines.

Is that what I'm doing in all of my life?

Standing on the sidelines?

Playing it safe?

Getting involved just enough to feel like I fit without stretching to where it might hurt?

Screw this.

I'm going back into the fun.

But as soon as I take a single step, Addie blows her whistle.

I wince and clap my hands over my ears.

"Fuck, Coach." Cooper winces, covers his ears, and glares at her while the rest of the team snaps to attention.

She doesn't crack a smile. Not that any of us expect her to. "Keep brawling, and you're all doing burpees all day tomorrow."

Firequacker drops to the floor, does a push-up, leaps back to his feet, jumps with his hands up, and drops back down to the ground.

"She is such a badass," Tillie Jean whispers.

I have no idea who's in that mascot outfit, but I don't care.

What I do care about?

Fun.

I'm in a friggin' pirate town in the mountains, with my teammates, a woman who intrigues me, and hardly any responsibilities.

It's time to have fun.

TILLIE JEAN

SATURDAYS WITH EXTRA FRIENDS IN TOWN ARE THE BEST, AND I didn't realize how much I missed *all* of my Lady Fireballs friends until they arrived in Shipwreck this morning with their significant others—aka half the team. We Lady Fireballs don't play ball. At least, not all the time. We get in the occasional softball or baseball game for fun. But overall, we support the team with fundraisers and booster club activities and community service.

I'm the only member not married to or dating a Fireball, and I joined because I love getting into the city at every opportunity, but hate being there alone.

Also possibly because sometime in the season before last, I came to town for a weekend game, hit the locker room with Tanesha afterwards, and started organizing everyone for heading out to a bar, at which point Max walked past, muttered how nice it was that I did so much for the team and community, and it made me feel so much like a worthless party animal that when the new management re-started the booster club this past season, I was third on the list to sign up, right behind Tanesha and Marisol.

Not that I'll tell Max that.

Mostly, I tell people I'm there because Cooper takes a lot of ribbing over having his sister on the Lady Fireballs as his *significant other*.

Plus, we get to hang out more often when I go to him during the very, very long baseball season, so it's a win on lots of levels, regardless of my inspiration.

After crashing the guys' Fireballs card game with the mascots, we spend the afternoon at my mom's coffee shop, The Muted Parrot, which is the most aptly named shop in all of Shipwreck.

Annika and Grady are hanging out with her family in Sarcasm today, which means Georgia's covering Crow's Nest. Sloane is volunteering at a flu shot clinic at the county health department. So it's just my city friends with me, drinking coffee and tea and catching up on all the fun that's been going on everywhere, from me and my pranks here in Shipwreck to Darren's wife Tanesha's latest stories about the baby to Luca's girlfriend Henri's stories about a book signing she did at an adorable bookshop in the city that Levi Wilson unexpectedly crashed. He's one of the hottest pop stars in the world and also brother of the Fireballs' owner, who are both former Bro Code boy band members.

Once the guys are done at Cooper's house, they gradually work their way off the mountain and back down into town, claiming their wives and girlfriends one by one. When the last of them have left, I head home to change into my Grog clothes.

Boots, jeans, and a fitted sweater.

But as I pull into my driveway, pointedly *not* looking at Max's SUV in the drive next door, I remember the mountain of laundry in my closet. Do I even have clean jeans?

Huh.

Guess it'll either be what I'm wearing—sweatpants and a paint-stained Blue Lagoon County High hoodie—or I need to call Georgia or Sloane and ask to borrow something.

My eyes drift next door again, and I wonder if Max is home, or if he's out with the guys.

Him picking me up while I was in the Ash costume? And then *talking* to me?

Not so helpful for this crush problem.

And since the Scurvy 5K day and the Thanksgiving snowball fight?

This crush really couldn't get worse. He nods to me without growling anytime we happen to cross paths. He put the glow-in-the-dark golf ball that I stuck in his Thanksgiving leftover box in my mailbox with a note attached that said *Help! I can't see in the light!* And he holds eye contact and says *thank you* now after I serve him whenever he and the guys come into Crusty Nut for their weekly lunch.

He's not necessarily *smiley* Max—at least, not until earlier today at Cooper's place—but he's not Growly Bear Max either.

It's different enough that I don't know if we're finally moving past the way I've tried to irritate him for the past four years, or if this new way of talking to each other is polite distance on his part without the intention of making me obsess over him.

All I really know, though, is that I want to see him smile at me again.

I hardcore want to see him smile at me.

And to what end? It's not like we'll get involved. Not when it would put a wrench in the team's dynamics.

If ever there was a sign from the universe that Max is off-limits, it's the team. They worked too hard this past year and need too much to stay tight next year to make all of Cooper's dreams come true.

I slip in my back door and dial Sloane as I turn down the hallway to my bedroom. "Hey. You done for the day?"

"Yep." She yawns. "Down time. I'm catching up on that show about the American football coach trying to turn around a British soccer—*football*—team. It's my *favorite*. Want to come over?"

"The Lady Fireballs are in town. We're hitting The Grog. You should come."

"Whoa. Seriously?"

I squint at the phone. "Why wouldn't I be serious?"

"Is Luca bringing his girlfriend?"

She's a little breathless and asks the question quickly, and I start grinning as I dig into sorting my clothes. I really should've done laundry three days ago. "Sloane! You've read her books? I didn't know that."

"Spend your teenage years having to hide your romance novels from your family, you learn not to talk about it. I've been reading Nora Dawn for—*oh my god*, do I get to call her Henri? Is that weird? Will it be weird if I ask her to sign my autograph book? I don't have paper copies of books anymore."

Dammit. My favorite sweater's dirty. Favorite jeans too.

What can I say? I hate doing laundry. "No. That's not weird. She told me someone passed her a book under a bathroom stall once at what was supposed to be her wedding reception after one of her previous fiancés dumped her. I guess his aunt was a fan? So I'm sure signing an autograph book is in the normal range."

We're both silent for a moment, and I'm no longer contemplating how I should do laundry more than once a month.

"You're going to say it's weird to have an autograph book, aren't you?" she asks.

"Nope."

"But you're thinking it."

"Never."

"Tillie Jean. Don't lie to me."

"When Cooper was little, he used to wear the same socks every time we went into the city for a Fireballs game. He called them his future lucky socks. So you having an autograph book is *not* the weirdest thing I've ever heard of."

More silence.

"Who else is in it?" I ask. I can't help myself. I need to live vicariously through my friends, and I know for a fact that when she was working at a hospital in Copper Valley, she met a celebrity or two, though she's never told us which ones.

She sighs. "Not talking to you."

"But I'm your best friend."

"Georgia's my current best friend. She brought me Nutella donuts when she got off work this afternoon."

"Good. You work hard. You deserve them. But can you really be bought off with donuts?"

"Yep. Who's going tonight? Will I have to put up with your brother flirting with me again?"

"No. I'm going to call Mackenzie to get those Meaty the Flaming Meatball stress balls that I know she's still hiding from Fireballs management, and then I'll glue them to his hands and he'll be otherwise occupied with... Huh."

She laughs. "I take it he retaliated for whatever it was you did last to him?"

"No, he hasn't."

"That's really sad."

"It is. He's either biding his time to do something seriously big, or he's growing out of all of this. His pranks have been weirdly lame this year. Even the Jell-O in the toilet—he's done that one before. It's like he's not even trying. Be honest. Are we being childish with pranking each other?"

"Tillie Jean." She clucks her tongue like she's chewing me out with just my name. "Do not ever—I repeat, *ever*—feel like you've gotten too old for fun. Which would you rather be, sixty-three and telling your grandkids that you used to play pranks on your brother but that you *grew out of it*, or ninety and hanging with your great-grandkids while you all plant fake bugs in his flour?"

"Clearly, *I want to be Nana* is the correct answer. Okay. Next phase in the prank wars it is."

"Good. Except I'm calling a no-go on gluing stress balls to his hands. Sorry, but he needs his hands to play, and to lift weights until the season starts again, unfortunately. What if you painted a sheet with a giant Meaty and hung it over his bed?"

"I don't think I have enough room to paint a sheet that big, and Cooper's bedroom is massive, but also too small for how large of a Meaty I'd want to use."

"Glue his furniture to the ceiling?"

"Grady tried that once a few years ago and almost gave himself a concussion when a chair fell on him."

"Oreo his car?"

"Say what?"

"Take Oreos apart and stick them all over his car. The cream acts like glue, though it's better in summer when it melts."

"That might be a waste of good Oreos. Maybe. Maybe not. I could stock up the holiday colors and save them for summer..." I heft my laundry basket up and carry it around the corner to my itty bitty laundry room, my phone tucked between my ear and shoulder while I dump the first load into the washing machine. "Except I don't want to distract him in the summer. Or ruin his car. There's this line, you know? Push too far, and one of us will never speak to the other again."

"Decorate his hairbrush with Vaseline?"

"That would be better for Luca Rossi. All that good hair, right? But I'm not going to prank Luca. He promised to get us all samples of the new bath bombs from the shampoo company he models for. Do you have a sweater I can borrow tonight? Maybe that burgundy one? With the low cut?"

"It's dirty. Just like your thoughts about Max Cole..."

"Those are only semi-dirty and involve flinging mud pies, not getting naked."

She laughs. "Thank you. If you're playing with mud pies, I feel much less embarrassed about my autograph book."

"Did you get all the guys to sign it? Because if not, *don't*. The egos. *Oh*, the egos..."

"Darren signed it. He's such a nice guy, though."

"He is. Oh, he and Tanesha and the baby are coming tonight." My clothes don't all fit in my washer, and I'm having to pull some back out. If I don't, it'll clog and back up and I'll have to wait a week for our resident appliance repair person to fit me into his schedule while mopping up gallons of water off my floor.

Why, yes, that *is* experience talking. I mentioned I hate laundry, right?

"Is Max coming?" Sloane's looking through her closet. I can tell by the sound of hangers sliding on metal.

And I'm really glad she can't see my face right now. It would totally give me away.

"I don't know." I grab my laundry detergent and measure a cup to pour in.

"*Tillie Jean.*"

"*What?*"

"I know that voice. That's your *I have a crush* voice. I mean, I suspected as much after watching you try to annoy him for years on end, but that's the same voice you used last year when you were flirting with Deacon Gunderson during softball season."

"It is *not*."

"Yes, it is."

"Even if it *was* that voice, it's irrelevant. You should've seen his face when he realized I was in the Ash costume for the video shoot today. It was like someone fed his last steak to Grady's goat." It was so not like that. It was like, *Oh, it's Tillie*

Jean! My eyes are going to light up for that split second before I remember she's Cooper's sister and therefore off-limits.

So I *wish* he'd glared at me like I fed his last steak to Grady's goat.

"Maybe you're trying too hard," Sloane says.

"Or maybe he almost kissed me during our snowball fight and now we're in this weird place where maybe I don't annoy him and maybe I can't stop thinking about him smiling at me, which is basically the worst thing *ever*. Cooper would have a shit fit. He knows I can take care of myself, but *it's the rule*. You don't screw around with his teammates. Especially the teammates who have reputations, and *especially* when expectations are so high for next year, and especially when—just *especially*, okay?"

"Tillie Jean."

"Don't *Tillie Jean* me. This isn't superstition. It's emotional reality."

"So you and Max hook up, it doesn't go anywhere, maybe one of you is a little hurt, and then *everyone gets over it*. Cooper can shove it. He can't protect you from getting hurt, you won't die from a little heartbreak or relationship disappointment, and I would be more than happy to tell him so. Or *maybe* you and Max hook up, you both find something in each other that you didn't even know you were looking for, and you're the key to helping him pitch better than ever next year. There's something to be said for being happy in your home life."

"You *do* read Henri's books."

"Don't *oh, it's just the romance novels talking* me. Look at Grady. Look at Brooks Elliott. Look at Darren. You know what? Look at Robinson. He's *single*, but he's happy in his personal life, and he shines. Max Cole shines, but I get the feeling he's missing something. If that something's you, Tillie Jean—"

"Enough about Mr. Growly Bear next door. Are you busy in ten? Because—*AAAAAaaaaaahhhh!*"

Spike is in my house.

Spike the Echidna mascot is *in my house*, and he's standing in my laundry room doorway, arms crossed, and *mascots are not supposed to be in my house*

I don't stop to think past that, because *demon mascot.*

I just act, dropping my phone, grabbing my detergent jug, and flinging it at him. "*Dammit, Cooper, you are DEAD!*"

He ducks.

I charge.

And that's mistake number two. The lid flew off my soap and there's slick detergent coating the floor, which wouldn't be a problem if I hadn't pulled out all of my carpet last year and replaced it with tile in here.

Instead, I take two steps toward my soon-to-be-dead brother, slip, and go down.

My arms flail. My hand connects with the wall, and my ass tries to dent the floor.

"Shit," Spike mutters, and everything inside me freezes.

That is *not* Cooper.

"Tillie Jean?" Sloane calls from somewhere inside the washing machine. "TJ? You there? *Tillie Jean?* I'm on my way, so whoever's there with you better be ready for a fucking takedown, because *we don't do this shit in Shipwreck.*"

Spike squats to the floor with me, not slipping at all in the carnage. He's coated with laundry detergent too.

Fireballs management won't be happy. There's one more mascot costume they'll have to replace.

"Fuck. Dammit. Are you okay?" Spike says.

My tailbone's cranky and my arm is probably bruised, but it's the shock of realizing *Max Cole pranked me* that has me staring at the giant echidna in stupefied silence.

And not just pranked me a little.

He got me *good.*

His giant mascot paw reaches for my foot. "Did you twist your ankle again?"

I jerk out of reach and scurry back into the laundry room. *"I could've been naked!"*

Yep.

That's the first thing that comes to mind.

Followed immediately by *what would he have done if I were naked?*

He makes another noise. *"You broke into my house,* so I thought this was fair game."

"And you couldn't call out and announce your presence?"

"I would've if I thought you could hear me over yourself."

"Did you just tell me I talk too much? Did you *really* just tell me I talk too much?" I'm arguing with a person inside a giant foam spiny anteater, and *oh my god,* I love it.

"You—you—*you glitter bombed me* and you replaced my shower curtain with a gigantic image of your ugly face."

"And I've been nothing but nice to you since, and also, *I respect the hell out of prank-backs,* so why are we arguing? You don't have to justify pranking me, but you *do* have to justify telling me I talk too much. There's a line, Max. *There's a line."*

"I don't know what the lines are."

Oh, god.

He doesn't.

And he sounds so horrified and frustrated and upset by it that I suddenly want to hug him. "Would you take that costume off and talk to me like a regular human being?"

"Maybe *I'm* naked."

Hello, nipples on full alert, mouth going dry, and desperate yearning in my pussy. It's been a while.

Like maybe two weeks or so.

You know. Since the snowball fight and near-kiss.

Also?

The odds that he's naked under that costume are very, *very* high. He's *always* naked. He's like—he's like my diamond in the buff.

I hope he can see as well out of Spike as I could see out of Ash earlier—which is to say, not necessarily all that great—because if I'm visibly drooling over the idea of him naked, I'd prefer he didn't know it.

Or would I?

He mutters something that sounds suspiciously like *Cooper's gonna kill me*, but it's muffled behind the costume.

"Max. Take the mascot off." My voice is breathy and hungry, and I suddenly need to know what makes Max Cole tick.

I need to know *all* of what makes Max Cole tick.

He doesn't obey.

Instead, he shoots to his feet, turns, and scurries down the hall. My front door clicks shut a moment later.

"*Tillie Jean!*" Sloane yells from inside the washing machine.

I need to answer her.

Let her know I'm okay.

But I'm not okay.

Physically, I'm fine.

Emotionally, though? Emotionally, I'm a mixed wreck of guilt that Max feels guilty, worry that he thinks I'm mad, and also horny as hell.

He pranked me back.

I know it's weird, but it's like…it's like he sees me.

For the first time in four years, I know without a doubt that Max Cole sees me.

Max

THERE'S SOMETHING WRONG WITH ME.

Scratch that.

There are *many* things wrong with me.

One, my dick went hard as steel inside the echidna costume, and now I feel like I violated the damn mascot.

Two, there's a high likelihood that international incidents have nothing on the war I've just sparked with Tillie Jean Rock.

And three, I can't fucking wait for round two.

The beast has been awakened.

She's going down.

Christ.

Now I'm picturing her sucking my cock, and this is *not* how I want to head into a bar where her brother's waiting.

Think about losing. Think about Cooper smashing my face in. Think about Luca's dance moves.

I think about overhearing TJ telling whoever she was

talking to on the phone that she wanted to kiss me. Or whatever it was she said.

All I know is, Tillie Jean wants to get naked with me.

That's my takeaway from her conversation.

She wants to do me. And I want to do her. And I *cannot* cross that line and risk losing Cooper as a friend. Some of the other guys on the team know I take meds for anxiety, but they don't know the rest of it.

They weren't there when I thought I was going to die.

They didn't pick me up without judgment, tell me it was okay, and help me get help.

Friends like that don't come around every day.

Even if they did, I wouldn't trust them, because I wouldn't let myself.

Fuck.

"Max, over here, bro."

The Grog's door shuts behind me, and I wave at Emilio, who's at a table along the far wall with a bunch of the guys.

If Tillie Jean were Luca's sister, or Robinson's sister, or anyone else's sister, this would be okay.

But not only is Cooper Rock the closest thing I've ever had to a best friend, he's the heart and soul of the Fireballs, and there's no denying it.

Guy has lived and breathed this team since he could walk. Rumor has it *Duggan Field* was his first word. He still has a ratty old stuffed Fiery the Dragon that he slept with supposedly through high school. And I completely believe the story Tillie Jean was telling her friend on the phone, that he kept every pair of socks he ever wore to a Fireballs game as a kid.

Screwing around with Cooper's sister would be like asking to be traded away from the team.

And I don't want that.

So I man up, walk across the bar, and sit down next to him at the long row of pushed-together tables near the dart board. "I pranked your sister. Again."

He grins. "Good. Make her think I've forgotten and you're taking over. For the record, she hates clowns as much as she hates garden gnomes."

Good to know. Unfortunately, I hate clowns too. "I put on the Spike costume and broke into her house and scared the shit out of her."

That sounds bad when I say it out loud.

But Cooper's still grinning. "That's next-level."

"She's gonna kick your ass," Francisco tells me. "TJ gets bored out here. She spends eight months of the year plotting for prank wars. You're basically a dead man."

"Don't leave your door unlocked," Darren agrees.

His wife, Tanesha, cackles. She *cackles*. "Like a locked door could stop her."

"I know. She can open my windows from the outside, and they don't have locks." My pulse is kicking up. Not sure that's a bad thing. "You're not pissed?" I ask Cooper.

"Sleep with her and I'll kill you. Distract her so she's not sprinkling sprinkles all over the ceiling fan in my bedroom? I'm good with that."

"Sprinkles on your ceiling fan?"

"Worse than glitter, man. Sweat a little at night and you wake up sticky as hell."

I rub a hand through my hair, which is still glittering. "At least you can eventually wash it off."

"You'd think, wouldn't you?" He frowns. "This isn't foreplay, is it? I'm serious. Don't touch my sister."

"I'm not touching your sister." Fuck, I want to touch his sister.

"Aw, Cooper, go easy on him," Luca's girlfriend, Henri, says from down the table. "Every playboy can be redeemed by the right woman."

"He can redeem his own fucking self if he wants to go near my sister."

Mackenzie leans around Brooks to peer at us too. "Would you let Francisco date your sister?"

He makes a face like he's thinking about it. "Probably."

"What the fuck?" *Shut up, Cole. Shut. Up.* "He's no Boy Scout either."

"Yeah, but I've seen how he treats his mom. He'd shape up for TJ."

Luca throws a napkin down the table at us. "Don't be a dick, Cooper."

He rolls his eyes. "Or maybe I'm protecting Max from Tillie Jean. Ever think of that?"

Now I want to throw something at him. "I don't need protecting from your sister."

He glances around, then pinches the bridge of his nose. "Look, I'm not saying this, because my sister is fucking awesome, but TJ...she's like, queen of the on-again, off-again thing. You two would fuck with each other's heads. Okay?"

Dammit.

Dammit.

I'm sweating again, and on the verge of wanting to throw him out the window.

He doesn't usually use my weaknesses against me.

"Where *is* TJ?" Cooper asks.

Looking for something to wear is probably not the right answer. "Sloane's car was at her house when I left."

He frowns. "Don't sleep with her either. She's like, long-term material, and you two don't go."

"I know some single women in Sarcasm if you get lonely," Annika says as she and Grady join us.

Cooper tilts his head. "Yeah, I'm okay with that. You can sleep with anyone in Sarcasm. *Except* Annika's sister. Or her mom."

I recoil. Annika's sister is in high school, and her mom's in her fifties and dating someone.

"You're being a dick again, Cooper," Darren calls.

"Yeah, but it was worth it to see that look on his face. Who's up for a game of darts? I feel an ass-kicking coming on."

Cooper slaps me on the back as he rises. Robinson hops up too, and Trevor slides into Cooper's vacant seat. "Tell me you're not being an idiot."

"Four years, Stafford. I've been on this team for *four years*. You think I'm gonna suddenly be interested in somebody's sister?"

He frowns. "Yeah."

"Not happening." It is *so* happening.

"Fuck Cooper, man. I'm not worried about him. I'm worried about you."

I jerk my head toward him. "Grown man here. I think I can handle living next door to a single woman without any danger to my heart."

He grimaces.

And I realize he might not be talking about me at all. This is my first time spending an off-season here, but it's not Trevor's. "Holy shit. You hooked up with her last year, when you were out here for off-season with Cooper, didn't you?"

"No."

"But you wanted to." And now I want to put my fist through a wall.

She's a damn Siren. She's getting all of us.

He shakes his head, but it's not a denial. "I'm about washed up, and I have been for longer than I want to admit. Put me in a house next to a pretty woman who smiles and waves and drops off leftovers after her shift for four solid months, and yeah, it's hard to not feel like you found a place to belong."

"She brought you leftovers *every night*?" Forget the wall. I want to punch Stafford.

"Yeah. *I'm nice to her*. Try it sometime. And don't let anyone tell you her banana pudding is where the magic is. It's the blondies. With the walnuts and ice cream and maple sauce." He wipes his mouth. "I'm drooling, aren't I?"

I signal the server and order a beer. If I don't, I'm gonna get pissed.

Jesus.

I'm turning to *one beer* to distract myself.

This is a bad sign.

I also cut a glance at the door. Where *is* Tillie Jean?

And how good are the locks on my house? And why am I on the verge of raising my flagpole again at the idea that she'll crawl through my windows and get revenge while I'm gone?

"Why do you get dessert and I get pranks?" I ask Stafford.

"I'm not a dick."

"She's a dick."

He grins. "She is not. And you wonder why you don't get desserts. But Cooper's wrong. TJ's not the queen of on-again, off-again. That was *one* guy. Not every guy she's ever dated. For the record. Not that I won't kick your ass myself if you do something dumb, but I'm not going to lie to you about why."

Groans and cheers explode at the end of the table, and we both lean in to check it out.

Darren, Tanesha, Luca, and Henri are playing the Go, Ash, Go card game again. Based on the way Henri's dancing in her seat, I'm guessing she just won.

"Rematch," Tanesha says. "We played *three cards*."

Henri's still dancing. Her short, curly hair's grown out since this summer, and it's not quite as crazy as when it was sticking up like devil horns when we first met her. "Who's a winner? I'm a winner!"

Luca's grumbling, but he's smiling at her too.

Brooks and Mackenzie are leaning over a tablet with Emilio and Marisol, probably looking at honeymoon pictures or talking about weddings.

Francisco's at the bar chatting up Georgia.

Grady and Annika are making eyes at each other over a basket of fried mushrooms.

And I'm sitting here wondering where my annoying neighbor is, and if she hurt her tailbone or twisted her ankle again, and if I'll wake up to Lego pieces all over my bedroom floor tomorrow.

And how I should pay her back if I do.

The server returns with my beer, and I climb to my feet as soon as I've had a gulp. "Pool?" I ask Trevor.

"Aw, I thought you'd never ask."

Team first. Team second. Pranks a distant third.

More boners for Tillie Jean, never.

That's the plan.

We'll see if it works.

18

TILLIE JEAN

Sloane and I walk into The Grog like two cowboys swinging into an old west saloon, except for the part where my ass hurts a little every time I step with my left foot, there's no saloon music, and if I called out *Giddyup, cowboy!*, my grandfather's parrot, who's flitting around the room from perch to perch, would probably laugh at me and tell me to fuck off because this is a pirate town.

But we're still trying for swagger.

"Oh my gosh, she's even more adorable in person than on the picture on her website," Sloane breathes.

It takes me a minute to remember who *she* is, since my eyes have immediately gone to the pool table, where Max and Trevor are engaged in a game that has both of them appearing relaxed and happy, which is dangerous territory.

They're both drinking out of traditional Grog steins, though I'd bet hard money Max's drink is plain tea. And then I wonder if he's having a hamburger tonight. I've heard through the grapevine that he stops by once a week and orders one. His one indulgence after eating clean and working out hard all week to stay in top shape the other six and two-thirds days of the week.

I can't do *one* indulgence a week.

I need one of Grady's donuts at least two mornings a week, plus Korean barbecue any opportunity I get, and I'm no slouch in the kitchen *or* on the grill.

It's why I have to do aerobics at the senior center and participate in the town's 5k runs.

And now I'm wondering if Max would ever do aerobics at the senior center like Cooper does on occasion.

"I can't do it, TJ," Sloane whispers.

"What? You stop by boot camp all the time."

She gives me a weird look.

I give her a weird look right back, realize I was lost in my head and boot camp has *nothing* to do with what she's talking about, and straighten with a hot-cheeked smile. "Oh. Right. Henri. C'mon. She's awesome, and you'll make her night if you ask her to sign your autograph book."

One eye crinkles. "Why were you thinking about boot camp?"

"The brain works in mysterious ways. And right now, my brain says you need to meet Henri."

"Can we do it in the ladies' room though? I don't want the rest of the team to see."

"So long as I give her a heads-up first. If it's a planned bathroom ambush, that's okay. If it's unplanned, it's awkward."

"Tillie Jean!" Marisol rises and waves at me, and the group bent over a card game at the end of the pushed-together tables all look up too. "Come show Emilio the picture of your painting that you showed me earlier."

And now I'm blushing even worse.

I shoot one last unintentional look at the pool table, catch

Max watching me, and duck my head and cross the bar to the group, waving at other friends as I go.

Sloane's previously met a bunch of the team here tonight, since Cooper's teammates aren't usually strangers to Shipwreck. But she was visiting a friend up in DC the last weekend Luca and Henri were here. I introduce her to everyone, and the minute Sloane gets flustered over *I've read your books*, Henri leaps up, hugs her, and orders her to sit and play a round of Go, Ash, Go so they can be friends.

"TJ." Marisol nudges me. "The painting."

I pull my phone out, scroll through to find the picture of the painting she made a fuss over at coffee this afternoon, and hand it to Emilio.

He's grinning while he takes it, but the grin quickly morphs into a furrowed brow and a *whoa* face. "Dude."

I snatch the phone back. "It's not weird. I did one for almost everyone on the team. Wait. Maybe that *is* weird."

"You have one for Brooks?" Mackenzie leans over the table and holds out a hand, making the *gimme* gesture.

She'd left the coffee shop before Marisol asked if I'd painted anything new recently, and missed the whole story. But I did do one of Brooks, so I pull my phone out again and flip through for the picture. "Don't tell Cooper, but I was working on paintings of all three of us to give to Mom and Dad for their anniversary, and right after I finished his, he had this six-game streak where he was just *hot*, you know? So I was like, *I wonder what happens if I paint someone else on the team?*, and then—"

"*Oh my god*, you were painting our luck?" Mackenzie squeals.

If ever there was a human born who appreciates baseball superstitions, it's Mackenzie.

But I shake my head. "It didn't work." No need to go into details. Nobody needs to know that I painted Trevor, and the day I finished it, he gave up a two-run lead in the bottom of the ninth. No one ever remembers when the relief pitchers *save* a game. They only remember when the relief pitchers lose it. "But I felt weird having two guys on the team painted and shoved in my closet, so I started doing everyone. I thought—okay, it's silly, but I thought if management wanted to use them—"

"Or *buy them from you because it's art?*" Marisol says pointedly.

I wave a hand. "It's a hobby."

"Show Mackenzie your painting of Max."

Hello, bad idea. "It's not done yet."

"It's a masterpiece."

"It is not."

She leans back in her chair and glances at the dart board, where Cooper's battling Robinson in a Cooper-style game of darts, with both of them throwing darts over their shoulders, with their eyes closed, between their legs, and whatever other weird ways they can think of to toss darts. "Cooper, your sister's doubting her artistic ability."

"It must be Saturday," he calls back.

"Or Friday," Aunt Glory adds.

"Sometimes Wednesday," LaShonda calls from the bar.

Max slides me a look that I pretend I don't see, because otherwise, I'll wonder if he's wondering when I paint. If he's noticed the lights on in my house late at night. If he ever looks at my house at all.

Stop thinking about Max, Tillie Jean. He's off-limits.

"Wait, what art?" Henri asks. "Tillie Jean, I didn't know you made art."

"She paints," Sloane announces.

"Like fruit paints, or like people paints, or like does that weird pouring and spinning thing?" Luca asks.

"Those videos are *so* mesmerizing." Henri smiles at him, all joy and love and happiness, and he smiles back, and my heart does that thing where it aches with the kind of longing I pretend I don't understand.

It'll happen when it's supposed to happen, Matilda Jean. Trust the universe.

I'm only twenty-six. It's not like my eggs are drying up.

But they *are* very curious about what Max thinks of this entire conversation.

I have a problem.

I very clearly have a problem.

"Like people and places paints." Sloane pulls out her own phone, dashes her fingers over the screen, and hands it to him. "You didn't hear about the night we all painted Ashes? Tillie Jean taught us. And here. She painted this picture of one of her cousins. It's hanging in her living room."

I'm not embarrassed by my hobby. I *like* my hobby.

But everyone tells me I should take commissions or try to sell something to an art gallery in the city, and I don't want to.

See again, *do what makes you happy.*

Here, I paint when I want, there's no pressure, and if someone wants to hang one of my paintings in their house or business, it's just a thing where I made something they like, and I'm flattered, and it's win-win.

If I tried to sell my art, to sell my hobby, strangers would get to pick apart every wrong brushstroke, and take all the joy out of it.

Been there, done that. I'd rather keep loving my art and keep it to myself and the people who love me than let the world tear it apart in the hopes of making money from it.

"Tillie Jean!" Henri looks up from Sloane's phone. "This is amazing."

I flap my hands. "I mean, yeah, I can paint circles around a seven-year-old, but it's just a thing."

"Say *thank you*, Tillie Jean," Cooper calls as he nails a bull's-eye while blindfolded.

"Is that Pop's trick see-through blindfold?" I call back.

"What?" Robinson looks between us, then shoves Cooper. "Let me see that thing. Aw, man. You *cheat*."

"Have you *met* my brother?" I call to Robinson, and everyone cracks up.

Even Max, though he glances away the minute our eyes connect.

Robinson lifts a dart and squints at it in the soft light. "Do these things have homing sensors? Did you microchip them? Is that why you're playing with your *lucky set*?"

With my paintings forgotten, I relax into the evening, only occasionally stealing a glance at Max.

He is in a black T-shirt and tight jeans, staying on the one half of the bar and oozing confidence and some kind of magical aura that makes me want to be closer to him.

I keep to the other half of the bar, as I'm practicing resisting temptation.

Until Cooper challenges me to a round of pool.

Mr. Professional Athlete thinks *he's* the winner in the family, but he's not the only one with a competitive streak.

And he's going down.

He racks the balls.

I inspect them.

We go five rounds of rock-paper-scissors to determine who goes first, and Grady finally calls it when Cooper demands seven rounds after losing the initial five.

Grady's such an oldest kid.

But it means I break.

And it's a glorious, beautiful, perfect break that sends the nine ball into the corner pocket.

"Scratch," Cooper says.

"In your dreams, Stinky Booty."

"Your left boob touched the edge of the table."

"That's not against the rules."

"House rules. You can't put your boobs on Aunt Glory's table."

I'm grinning while I eyeball the table to decide how I want to play my next shot. "House rules. You lose a turn for making up stupid house rules."

"Agreed," Grady calls.

"*Rawk!* Eat shit and sniff my armpit. *Rawk!*"

Cooper points at Long Beak Silver, who's flitting around unsupervised. Pop must have left the window open for him again. "That means he's taking my side. We need a tie-breaker."

"Are they always like this?" Henri whispers to Luca. Everyone's gathered around to watch. The locals because they know we're going to be utterly ridiculous, and the team because the locals gathered.

I assume.

Possibly Cooper's planted people in the crowd to distract me and throw me off my game.

"I took a glitter bomb meant for Cooper," Max tells her dryly. "Pretty sure they're always like this."

"Oh my gosh, I wondered if you knew your hair sparkles a little when you turn just right."

"Been saving it to share with Luca."

"Get your glitter hair away from me, dude. I've got a commercial shoot next week."

"Tillie Jean's turn," Aunt Glory calls. "You're rusty on dreaming up dumb rules, Cooper."

"*Rawk!* Girls smell like fart powder! *Rawk!*"

I lean over the table. "Eleven in the side pocket. Also, I get seventy-five Shipwreck points if I manage to take the bird out with a ball shot off the table."

"You get three thousand Shipwreck points if you take the bird out with a scratch," Annika corrects.

"Babe," Grady says.

"I said what I said. That parrot needs remedial training."

"But three thousand Shipwreck points means she'll get the trophy even if she poisons everyone at the Pirate Festival."

"Worth it."

"*Rawk!* You wet the bed and your mother reads Chuck Tingle! *Rawk!*"

I ignore the bird and take my shot, but just as my stick's about to connect with the cue ball, Max speaks up. "Manners, you mangy bird."

And I scratch.

I freaking *scratch*.

Cooper starts to hoot, but then—

"*Rawk!* Sorry, King Growly Bear, ruler of all the land. *Rawk!*"

The entire bar goes silent, and all of us turn to stare.

Half of us gawk at the bird.

The other half of us—me included—gawk at Max.

"What did he just call you?" I ask.

Max doesn't look at me. He's having a stare-down with the bird, who's sitting on a pirate boat steering wheel mounted to the wall.

Also?

His cheeks are going ruddy under the thick stubble he's been growing out this week, and the bar's soft lighting can't hide it.

"Long Beak Silver." Grady steps between them. "Go swab the deck."

"*Rawk!* Asshole."

The parrot fluffs his bright feathers, then takes off from the wheel and flies to the perch set up just for him over the door.

Vinnie reaches over and opens it, and he departs into the night.

I look back at Max. Our eyes meet for a split second before he drops his gaze to his stein.

My heart flutters.

I don't know *why* it flutters, but it freaking *flutters*. I feel thirteen again, wearing braces, my biggest worry that my acne medicine won't work in time for my skin to be clear before the very first dance of my life where the boy I was crushing on would probably be there.

Long Beak Silver hasn't ever called anyone *king* of anything before. And *King Growly Bear*?

I call Max growly bear.

Pretty sure no one else does.

Did *I* accidentally teach Long Beak Silver to say that?

Or did he?

"Asshole parrot," Grady mutters, snapping my attention back to the game. "Cooper. Your turn."

Cooper props his hip on the table, slides his stick behind him, and takes aim at the cue ball. "Four in the corner pocket."

I shake my head, which is still living in Max-land. "Do I even have to remind you that you just tried to make it illegal for me to put my boobs on the table, and now you're sitting on it?"

"We don't both have boobs, but we both have butts. You can sit on the table too. That's fair."

"That is *not*—"

"Agreed," Grady interrupts. "You both have butts. That house rule can stand."

I point to my eyes, then use my fingers to point at Cooper. "Don't try anything else cute. I've got my eye on you."

"Did you know he could play pool?" Robinson mutters to someone behind me.

I say *someone* because I can't afford the distraction of acknowledging who that someone is.

Not if I want to win.

Cooper won our final game last winter before leaving for spring training. I owe him payback.

"Yes," Max answers Robinson. "That's why none of us play him when we're out."

Cooper taps the cue ball, shooting from behind, and it rolls smoothly across the table, cracks against the four, which ricochets off the side of the table and sails directly into the corner pocket.

"Is Tillie Jean any good?" Robinson whispers.

I look back at him. "You wanna play me next?"

His eyes go comically wide, and you can practically see him debating with himself if he wants to lose to me, or if he can live with himself—and Cooper—if he beats me.

"I can take losing," I tell him.

Max smirks. "I'll play you."

"Three in the side pocket," Cooper says, saving me from answering Max.

I wonder if Max knows any trick shots. Or if he cheats. If he'd insist on playing again if he lost, or if I'd be the one demanding a rematch.

If I'd let *him* win.

What would I bet Max Cole if we were playing pool?

Probably my underwear.

And if we were anywhere else, and I were related to anyone else, he might take that bet.

The balls crack together on the table, and I jolt back to reality as Cooper puts the three ball in the side pocket.

He grins at me over the table. "Should I go easy on you?"

"Never."

"Remember, you asked for it."

"Famous last words, Stinky Booty."

I'm eating my own words, watching as he sinks the two, six, five, and seven balls as well, ignoring my attempts to distract him or make up new house rules until he has one solid ball and the eight ball left.

He squats next to the table, examining the layout. It's not looking good for him—I have five balls clearly between him and his precious one that he needs to sink without hitting any of my balls first, plus, he's in a better position to sink the eight ball and lose outright—but I don't ever, *ever* count Cooper out.

"You ever play?" Brooks asks Grady.

Our big brother shakes his head. "Not against the two of them."

"I won't think less of you if you call it a pass and walk away," I tell Cooper.

He snorts.

It's so predictable that I smile bigger.

"Off the top, around the corner pocket, one in the side," he announces.

"One-armed and blindfolded?" I ask.

His eyes meet mine, and he starts to grin. "If I hit that shot, you're doing my laundry for the next month."

"And if you miss, you'll pose with Long Beak Silver for next year's Pirate Festival flyers."

"Done."

"In Pop's costume. Stinky Thorny Rock pirate hat and all."

"Hells, yeah. Robinson! Bring me that blindfold."

I turn to watch Robinson dash over to the dart board, but instead, I catch Max looking at my ass.

And he doesn't realize I'm watching him watch me, so I roll my hips.

His brown eyes go the color of midnight, and his Adam's apple bobs, which makes my skin tingle and my nipples tighten.

As if he can feel my body's response, he lifts his eyes, catches me catching him, and steps back, right into Aunt Glory, who's carrying a full tray of beer.

Was carrying a full tray of beer, I should say.

The pint glasses mostly bounce as Aunt Glory wobbles and loses her balance, beer spraying everywhere, the people around us scattering to get out of the way of the blast zone.

Max spins and grabs Aunt Glory, who's tumbling into him. "Fuck. Shit. Sorry. Sorry."

"Party foul," Vinnie calls.

"Drinks on Max," someone else yells.

"Free drinks! Free drinks!"

"Calm your tits, Albert." Cooper's leapt up onto the edge of the pool table. "You didn't pay for drinks when you crashed the whole liquor shelf three years ago."

"Didn't replace the shelf either," Grady adds.

"Oooh, snap," Vinnie crows. "They've got you there."

I squat and start grabbing the larger pieces of broken beer mugs off the floor while everyone debates if Max has to pay for a round of drinks. "Ignore them," I tell him. "They make up house rules as much as Cooper does."

He shoots me a look that I can't interpret.

It could be *thank you for helping*.

Or it could be *I wasn't looking at your ass*.

Or possibly it's *I'm a grown fucking man with a bank account the size of a mountain and I can pay for making your aunt drop a keg's worth of beer on the floor. Shut up and let me be a growly bear*.

And there's not a single option that doesn't make me want to grab him by the collar and haul him out the back door.

Possibly to tell him to quit being so grouchy.

But more likely because I want to kiss him.

Are *my* eyes going dark?

Considering I can't quite catch my breath or look away from him and my mouth is suddenly dry and a familiar ache is pooling between my legs, I'd bet yes.

Yes, my pupils are probably dilating and oh, crap, I'm licking my lips.

I'm licking my lips and holding eye contact with Max over spilled beer and broken pint glasses and I want to haul him up by his collar and shove him against the wall and kiss him until I can't breathe.

Bad idea, a voice that sounds like Long Beak Silver whispers deep inside my brain.

One corner of Max's lips tilts up, and my uterus faints dead away in a swoon. "Fucking town," he mutters before he drops his gaze to the ground and gets back to grabbing larger pieces of broken glass to set on Aunt Glory's tray.

I gulp hard and do the same.

Not the part about muttering about the fucking town.

I love this town.

But the part about picking up.

Luca and Henri and Sloane squat and help us while Aunt Glory's server appears with a mop, and Sloane is shooting me looks the whole time.

Yeah.

She knows.

I couldn't stop this crush on Max any more than I could stop a cannonball.

It's not five minutes before it's like the beer was never spilled at all.

Cooper misses his trick shot, but he still beats me in the game. Sloane leaps in and challenges Trevor to a game before I have to decline a rematch from my brother, and I realize Max is gone.

Brooks and Mackenzie have headed out. So have Darren and Tanesha. Half the locals.

Grady and Annika are slipping on coats too.

Cooper flings an arm around me. "Need me to buy you a consolation prize, TJ?"

"I let you have that one to build up your confidence."

"You're a giver."

"I am."

We both crack up.

"Thanks for the entertainment. Again." Annika stops and hugs us both. Cooper and Grady do their man-hug before Grady smothers me in a hug too.

"If Cooper's being an ass and keeping you from what you want, let me know," Grady whispers. "I'll keep him distracted."

I love my brothers. Both of them. "Shut up. Winners before sinners."

He snorts in laughter. "Now you're being ridiculous."

"Go on, go home with your wife to your goat."

"Just saying, TJ. Regrets are hard and opportunities are rare." He ruffles my hair and turns to pull Annika away from Cooper, who's trying to steal her for a dance on the non-existent dance floor.

"Rematch, Cooper?" Robinson flashes three darts at us.

"You're on, dude."

And here it is.

My opportunity to sneak out into the night.

Head home.

See if Max's lights are on.

Do something bad.

Or possibly really, really good.

Is this what I've been waiting for the universe to deliver?

Or am I misreading everything merely because I want to?

Either way, I know what I want to do.

And tonight, I'm doing it.

Max

ANXIETY HAS BEEN A PART OF MY LIFE SINCE BEFORE I KNEW THE word for it. But tonight's anxiety is a different kind of anxious.

I'm counting my steps by four. Doing four sets. Turning ninety degrees. Counting four sets of four until I turn again as I pace around the statue and fountain—dry for the winter—in the center of this little garden behind the shops on Blackbeard Avenue.

I think the pizza place is close by. Maybe the inn. I don't know.

I just know I can't stay in the bar, and I don't want to go back to my place.

I don't want to be alone, but I don't want to be with my teammates.

One. Two. Three. Four.

One. Two. Three. Four.

"*Rawk!* If you're gonna jump, just jump, motherfucker! *Rawk!*"

The parrot flies from one corner post of the iron fence lining the garden on two sides to another, then to the buildings bracketing the other two sides, pacing with me.

I stop and glare at it. "What's that, Long Beak Silver? Timmy fell down the well?"

He tilts his head and goes silent.

"Your father was a studmuffin and your mother smells of Kangapoo." I don't know. I'm making it up. I just want the damn bird to quit with the cussing. He's annoying the fuck out of me.

And don't *at* me about my language. I don't *fuck* in front of the kids, okay?

"*Rawk!* Kangapoo gives your down under a shine! *Rawk!*"

So the bird's seen the commercials for the shampoo Luca shills.

Awesome.

I shake my head and start walking again. One. Two. Three. Four.

"Max?"

"*Jesus.*"

"No, just Tillie Jean." She tilts her head just like the damn parrot did a minute ago, not outright flirting, not leaving either. Tonight, she remembered her coat on the way out of the bar. I almost ask why she's out alone, then remember we're in Shipwreck. It's not the same as wandering city streets alone near midnight.

Still, my pulse rachets up to *game on the line* levels, and I can't find my breathing rhythm to get it under control.

She takes two steps into the garden, lit only by a weak spotlight in the corner. "Are you okay?"

I thrust my hands through my hair. "Yeah."

"Are you sure?"

No, I'm not sure. She's temptation in this happy package of curvy hips, perfect breasts, full lips, bright blue eyes, and the confidence that comes with belonging, though it's not something she takes for granted or hasn't worked to accept. She's also completely off-limits because she's my teammate's sister, not nearly as annoying since she quit flirting with me, which is annoying all by itself, but not as annoying as wanting to kiss her and knowing I can't.

Scratch that.

I *can*.

But I shouldn't.

And the line between can and shouldn't is the same line between fitting on the team that's the closest thing to family I've ever had, and being all alone, on my own, with nothing but the cold, hard comfort of victory and money to keep me company.

Eighteen-year-old me thought victory and money would be enough.

I want to go back to that kid, hug him, tell him he was a fucking rock star for getting as far as he had already more or less on his own, and that he should make a few friends instead.

But I also wouldn't listen if fifty-year-old me suddenly appeared and told me the same thing about myself today.

Just *fuck*.

One. Two. Three. Four.

One. Two. Three. Four.

"Max."

"Why do you have to be too damn pretty?"

"I ask myself that every morning, and I still don't have an answer."

I jerk my gaze to her.

She smiles, and it's like staring at Cooper.

All the way from her blue-eyed, cheerful smile right down to her cheeky answer.

Except she's *nothing* like Cooper.

She's Tillie Jean.

And she's fucking perfect just as she is.

I blow out a hard breath, and it hangs in the air, a white puff of visible irritation in the night.

"We should screw around," she says.

My dick leaps to attention, but the rest of me breaks out in a sweat. "No."

"Why not?"

Jesus. "Because."

"I'm a grown-ass woman who knows better than to think one night of fun means we have to get married, and you seem like you could go for blowing off some steam. Worst case? It's awful for both of us and we never want to do it again."

"That would be *best case*."

She smiles again, which is not helping the blood flow to the brain. "I mean, best case would be that we didn't want to do this at all."

"I don't want to do this."

"You kissed me. You threw snowballs at me. You tried to kiss me again. You pranked me back. Max Cole, your problem isn't that you don't want to do this. Your problem is that you don't want to want this, but you can't help yourself."

She's right.

Fuck me with a rusty spoon. She's right. "You're off-limits."

"That's the stupidest thing you've ever said."

"No, it's not." She's north and I'm a compass. The steel to my magnet. And for every step I order myself to take away from her, this invisible connection carries me two steps closer instead. "You're family and happiness and belonging. You're where you're supposed to be. Doing what you're supposed to do. I'm just passing through. Not here to disrupt anything or break anything. You're off-limits."

"I'm not a fragile flower, Max." She's not cross. Not yelling. Not sarcastic.

Not Tillie Jean.

She's swaying her hips back and forth to music I can't

hear over the sound of her soft, hypnotic, Siren's voice. "You can't break me."

"I break everything."

"What, like three pint glasses? Half the town's descended from pirates. We get drunk and break glasses all the time. Sometimes we break plates. Once we broke a whole parade float, but that was a freak accident."

"*People*. I break people."

"Who?" She plants her palms on my chest and peers up at me. She's not short, but I still have at least six inches on her.

And no, that wasn't a dick joke.

Fuck, I wish it was.

"Who have you broken, Max?"

"Me."

Her eyes flare wide.

Fuck.

Fuck.

I didn't mean to say that out loud.

"Na," I add. "Meena. Some chick I met at—"

Tillie Jean's finger lands on my lips, and I cut myself off with a sharp breath.

"Let's play a game," she whispers. "We're going to pretend we just bumped into each other in a park in the city, and I'm not related to anyone you know, and you're not famous in sports circles, and we're just two people who think the other is attractive."

My brain short-circuits.

Okay, it doesn't.

It flashes back to walking into Schwartz's apartment, which was supposed to be empty, and hearing noises in the bedroom that turned out to be a topless Tillie Jean doing something to herself under those sheets that I very much wanted to be doing for her.

That's about the same as short-circuiting.

Especially with her fingertips trailing down to stroke my jaw.

I lick my lips and stare down at her. "I don't do pretend."

"No? You've been doing a pretty good job of pretending you don't like me."

"Self-preservation and pretend aren't the same thing."

"The Fireballs aren't going to trade you if you do something Cooper's being a neanderthal about, and even if they do, you'll kick ass wherever you go."

"You don't know that."

"You don't know that I don't know that."

I can't track what that means, but I *can* track that she smells like French fries and apple pie, that I'm warmer just for being next to her—in the good way—and that I want to kiss her.

I want her happiness. I want her spirit. I want her fun. I want *her*.

"One night," she whispers. "One night, Max, and then we see where we go from there. Cooper won't find out. We'll get this out of our systems. You'll go back to being Mr. Growly Bear, I'll go back to flirting with you, and everything will go back to normal. I'll even pretend to be your sister if that's what you need."

"It doesn't work like that."

"Sometimes we tell ourselves the easy lies to convince ourselves not to take the chances worth taking." There's that smile again. That smile is so damn addictive.

"I'm not good for you, Tillie Jean."

"Your objections have been noted."

Her fingers drift into my hair, her nails teasing my scalp, my nerve endings leaping up and partying like we're at a rave, and I can't do it anymore.

I can't resist.

I can't remember why I *should* resist.

She's here.

She's willing.

She's *eager*.

She's not asking for commitment or promises or a fairy tale.

And I want her.

I want her.

So I crash my mouth against hers, lift her by the backs of her thighs until she's wrapping her legs around my waist, turn us against the side of the nearest building, and I kiss her.

I'm possessed.

That's the only explanation.

Or possibly her lush lips and the way she tastes like sea salt and rum, the way she's wrapped around my body like a shield from all the bad to ever exist, the way she's teasing my ears and scalp and neck with those magical fingers, heating the world around us with those soft noises coming from the back of her throat as she kisses me back—possibly, she's every inch the kind of woman I like kissing and stroking and screwing around with.

It's game time, and I'm on the mound. Ready to do what I do best.

Play ball.

Focus.

Achieve.

Win.

Slip my hands under her jacket, beneath her shirt, feel her silky skin quiver and her hips buck into my rock-hard boner while I stroke higher, looking for—

Lace.

She's wearing a lace bra.

The texture against my fingers sets my skin on fire. I don't know what it is about a woman in lace lingerie that does it for me, but *fuck*, I love the lace.

I scrape my thumbs over it, feel the hard nubs of her nipples beneath it, and I nearly come in my pants.

"Oh my god," she gasps in my mouth, jerking her hips against me.

"We have to stop," my mouth says.

It's not me talking.

I don't want to stop.

I want to yank her clothes off, lick her from head to toe, suck on her nipples, eat her pussy, drive into her, and make her scream until everyone in the whole entire damn county knows that Tillie Jean Rock has had the orgasm of her life.

And I've seen her masturbating.

I know what a Tillie Jean orgasm looks like.

I want to top it.

Her eyes are pinched and her lips are parted, sending puffs of crystallized pleasure into the air between us, and she's riding my hard-on like it's a life raft while I squeeze her breasts—*god*, that lace—and kiss her again.

I need to keep my mouth occupied before the demon possessing me says we need to stop again.

Fuck that demon.

That demon isn't making Tillie Jean moan and whimper in sheer pleasure right now, is he?

And what's more important than making a woman feel good?

Staying employed, that fucking demon whispers.

I kick him out of my brain and into outer space, then pinch Tillie Jean's nipples through her lace bra—is it pink? Ivory? Red? Black? Fuck, I hope it's black—and her legs tighten around me, her whole body going stiff while she moans into my mouth.

I want to come.

I want to come *so fucking bad*, and she's squeezing me so hard, holding so still, I know she's coming.

Tillie Jean rock is coming against my cock and I can't feel it and *I want to fucking feel it*.

I want to feel her come around me. I want to know what

it's like to be inside her. I want to know how hard her pussy's clenching. I want to know if she feels empty without my cock inside her.

I want to know if she wants to come home with me.

Sleep in my bed.

Shower with me.

Laugh at that absurd shower curtain I still haven't taken down.

Flip pancakes in nothing but one of my shirts while I fry bacon next to her.

Blow me before I leave for the gym.

Let me eat her for dessert.

"*Rawk!* Eat her pussy! *Rawk!* Eat her pussy!"

She breaks away and smacks her head on the brick wall. "Oh, shit," she whispers.

And then I hear it.

Voices.

Trevor. Sloane.

Cooper.

Tillie Jean and I make eye contact. Even in the dim light, I can tell her cheeks are flushed, and her breath is still coming in fast white puffs. "Stay," she whispers. "Pace again. Whatever."

She shimmies down the wall, straightens her coat, leaps up on a bench, and swings over the iron fence as a goat bleats behind me.

Swings over the iron fence.

What is she, Spiderman?

Holy nutballs. That was fucking *hot*.

And the woman who fell off her roof? The woman who slipped in laundry detergent a few hours ago?

Not a sign of her.

This woman could be an Olympic gymnast, and that ache in my junk gets so thick I might have to throw up. She's—she's—*fuck*, she's sexy.

"Whazzup, Goatstradamus?" Cooper calls.

Pace.

Right.

Pace.

Fuck.

I can't count. I can't remember how. My dick is harder than steel and my balls are bluer than the Mediterranean Sea. I try to pace and my legs don't work, because they forgot what they're used for.

I gave Tillie Jean an orgasm and now my body doesn't remember how to do anything else.

I'm a sex machine.

Nothing else matters.

"Whoa, Max. Dude. Whatcha doin'?"

Cooper pauses next to the open gate into the garden and grins at me.

"Meditating," I blurt.

He nods. "Good job, my friend. Carry on." He salutes me with a stein from The Grog and keeps walking.

"Isn't your house the other way?" I call to him.

"Goin' to see my *seester*," he replies. "She owes me a rematch."

Fuck. Shit. Tillie Jean's not home. "You beat her, asshole. Let her lick her wounds in private and go to *you* for a rematch."

He walks backwards until he's back in view, tripping over the goat on his way. "That makes logistical reason."

"*Maaa!*" Goatstradamus agrees.

"*Rawk!* Pussy-licker. *Rawk!*"

In my dreams, Long Beak Silver. In my hot, wet, horny dreams.

"To pussy!" Cooper cries.

"You're seriously drunk, man." Trevor stops beside him, giggles, and then trips over Goatstradamus too.

"You're *both* drunk," Sloane corrects.

She slides me a look, does a double-take, and then grins.

Grins *big*.

Like she knows.

Fuck.

"Hamburgers," I sputter. "They need hamburgers."

She's still grinning. "Sure. C'mon, boys. My place. Hamburgers."

"I want *pizza*," Cooper declares.

"I want *pho*," Trevor says.

"*Pho* you," Cooper retorts, and they both crack up.

Sloane grins at me one more time, grabs each man by a collar, and steers them around, heading away from Tillie Jean's house two blocks away—and mine too.

I sink to the bench in the park.

That was close.

And it can't happen again.

No matter how much I want it to.

Guys like me don't get the girl when she's my teammate's sister.

Guys like me don't get the girl *period*.

End of story.

TILLIE JEAN

I'M PULLING A LATE AFTERNOON SHIFT AT CRUSTY NUT THREE
days after the Spike incident—yes, the Spike laundry incident, not the bar incident or the kissing incident—when Max
walks in alone in jeans, sneakers, and a zipped-up Fireballs
windbreaker, which makes for a safe bet that he's not doing
well.

He's _never_ in a zipped-up coat.

Either he's sick, or it's colder out there than I thought
it was.

His dark hair, which still glitters a little when he turns his
head the right way, looks like he's been running his fingers
through it, and his jaw looks extra chiseled, like he's
clenching it since he knows he has to see me if he walks into
my dad's restaurant, and he doesn't know what to do about
that.

I don't know if he's been actively avoiding me or if I've
been actively avoiding him, but we haven't crossed paths

since I vaulted out of Thorny Rock's garden behind Anchovies after he gave me the fully-clothed orgasm of my life.

And here I go, getting wet in the panties just from looking at him.

But I keep it as normal as I can despite my pulse picking up and my nipples asking if he'd like to play with them a little more back behind the restaurant. "Sweet tea, banana pudding, and a chaser of pirate swords, right?"

He doesn't give me the usual brow twitch of irritation, but instead, flashes a small smile before glancing down and settling at the bar across from me. "Yeah. You guessed it. All the crap food. Great for training."

Despite sitting, he's towering high on the seat. My brothers are both right at six feet, and I'm somewhere between average and tall for a woman, but it's remarkable what Max's few extra inches do to make him even larger.

"Want me to add on a milkshake, cheesy pirate boats, and a double whiskey sour too?"

Finally, he shudders. "Alright. I'll call uncle. None of the junk. How's your butt?"

Dad leans out of the kitchen, eyebrows furrowed at me. "Something wrong with your bottom, sweetie?"

Twenty-six years old, and my father still asks about my *bottom*. Given the way his eyes are twinkling, though, he probably both knows why Max is asking and he's also trying to get my goat.

So to speak.

He better not know about what happened in the gardens though.

"I had a run-in with a rodent," I tell Dad. "Startled me. I fell. I'm fine."

He frowns. "You're falling an awful lot these days. Might want to see Doc Adamson and have him check your ears. Make sure it's not a balance issue."

It's a balance issue.

It's an *I lose my balance around Max Cole* issue, and I thought that was just mentally, but apparently it's physically too.

Probably a good thing I didn't trip and fall on my way over the fence the other night. "It's almost four. School's out soon."

"Yep. Back to chopping onions. Don't mind the old crying guy back here. Better me than my daughter being tortured." He disappears into the kitchen.

I turn back to Max. "Unsweet tea?"

He nods. No *yes, please*. No *thank you, Tillie Jean*. Just a regular old nod while he watches me with those fascinating brown eyes.

That sort of response annoyed the crap out of me a week ago.

Today?

Today, I want to know why he works so hard to stay aloof. And I can't figure out if I'm irritated with him, or if I'm intrigued at whatever it is that he's holding onto to make him go so far out of his way to act like he doesn't like me.

After all of our encounters since he arrived, you can't tell me he doesn't like me.

And after the few personal details he's let slip, I'm starting to get a picture of him that I very much want to fill in.

Does he avoid me *only* because of Cooper?

Or does he avoid me because he has some kind of inferiority complex?

"Tillie Jean?" Dad calls. "Have you seen my favorite skillet?"

"Drying rack," I call back.

"Ah, got it. Thank you."

I dump ice in a tall glass, then reach for the pitcher of tea.

Max leans forward and snags me by the wrist.

My skin reacts like I'm a lightning rod and he's a thunderstorm. Everything's electric. Humming. Buzzing. Eager.

Did he jerk off in the shower after I left him in the garden the other night?

Would I have liked to watch?

Or help?

Sweet baby Thorny Rock, it is *hot* in here.

"Unsweet." His voice penetrates the haze of lust making my breasts heavy and my lady bits ache, and it takes me a minute to realize what he's saying.

I force a smile when what I'd really like to do is lean across the bar and kiss him. "Relax, Growly Bear. Unless my brother's next to you in a magic invisible suit, you're safe here. We like to keep paying customers happy. It's unsweet." I wink. "But I can't promise I won't replace the tea in your fridge at home while you're not looking."

He looks down, seems to realize he's still holding me, and snatches his hand back like my wrist is burning him.

But I don't think I'm his problem.

Not exactly.

"How's training?" I ask as I hand him the tea.

He takes a hesitant sip, then a bigger gulp before answering me. "Fine."

"Phew. For a minute there, I was worried it might've been *good*. Or even *great*. Fine is so much better."

His eye twitches.

I should ask if he wants his usual, but as soon as I take his order, I'll have to make sure Dad gets it, and then I'll need to get the dining room prepped for the after-school crowd, and then it'll be drink orders and the pre-dinner rush, and it's Tuesday, which means Pirate Festival committee meeting, which means Pop will be having a pre-meeting in the corner with Aunt Glory and a few other people before I know it, and then Max will be gone.

I don't want him to leave, so I lean on the bar, pushing my boobs together. Not like I'm showing cleavage—there was a huge dust-up a few years back when Dad announced he was going to have his staff wear wench and pirate costumes, since that's The Grog's thing and we're already pushing limits for family peace by also having a bar—and yes, family peace is different from welcoming outsiders peace—so we updated Crusty Nut's uniform to branded blouses and jeans instead.

I just want to get a *little* closer to Max. "You want some lit cannons? Also known as jalapeño poppers. Our appetizer menu is pirate-themed, which you probably would've picked up on by now if you ever looked at the menu instead of ordering the same thing every time. And really, the gold nuggets—aka fried pickle chips—are where it's at."

"Grilled chicken salad."

I arch a brow, and not because I didn't know that's what he'd want.

"Vinaigrette on the side," he adds.

"Walk on the wild side, Max. Get a few oars to go with it."

I'd bet you a thousand dollars he won't take the breadsticks, but that wouldn't be very kind of me to take your money on a sucker's bet.

"Just the salad," he says.

"Okay, okay, just the salad. But maybe next time you put a little *please* on the side, hm?"

I turn away without waiting for him to answer, because the door bells are jingling. "Hey, Aunt Bea. Pick a seat anywhere. Margarita time? Or you want a Diet Coke today?"

My dad's sister-in-law smiles at me. "Lay that margarita on me, sweetheart."

"Rough day?"

"Long Beak Silver got into Cannon Bowl and terrorized a group of kids who came for a field trip."

I wince.

Pretty sure Dad's wincing back in the kitchen too.

Probably Grady down the street as well. His bakery's right next to the bowling alley, so he's undoubtedly already heard.

"Maybe we should ship him up to Sarcasm for a couple weeks."

Aunt Bea gasps. "Tillie Jean. *Watch your mouth.*"

"Would you rather he tell a bunch of school kids to fuck off, or would you rather he says *nice throw* when one of their balls goes in a gutter?"

"She's got a point, Bea," Dad calls. "I'll talk to Annika's mom. See if she knows anyone good with parrots over that way."

"Grilled chicken salad with vinaigrette on the side for Mr. Predictable," I tell Dad.

"Don't call customers names, Tillie Jean."

"It's on his driver's license. Middle name. I checked. Make sure you put the red pepper *under* the sliced chicken. He likes it best that way."

"Ignore her," Dad says to Max.

"He usually does," I answer for him. "And look at that. School's out and the bus dropped off all the kiddos. Here we go."

A flood of teenagers pass the front door, and five of them stop and come inside. They take over three tables in the center of the dining room once a week to play *Dungeons & Dragons*, usually cobbling together dollar bills and coins to afford sodas and nothing else, and we spoil them with swords and cannonballs—also known as french fries and fried mushrooms.

Pretty soon, at least two of them will be old enough to work here part-time, and I can't wait. Our other help left us for college, so it's mostly been Dad, me, and our night and weekend people.

Between the kids and the early dinner crowd, I'm busy nonstop for the next few hours.

Max stays the whole time, taking refills on his tea and playing on his phone after he's done with his dinner, making my body painfully aware that he's hanging out without having to do a thing beyond breathing.

No one from the team joins him.

No teammates. No training staff. No mascots.

Just Max.

All alone.

Occasionally answering questions and being friendly with the locals, always ignoring me.

But still hanging out.

Looking lonely and a little out of place.

He's still on the same stool when the dinner crowd thins out. I don't know if he's been listening in as I catch up with my friends and neighbors about who took a trip where and who's having surgery next week and who's going to be grandparents soon, but he hasn't moved.

"Dessert?" I ask him as I cruise past him behind the bar with a tray full of dirty dishes. "Sugar rush in a bowl? Dad made homemade cinnamon ice cream to go with the apple pie. I can slap a slice of cheddar on it and call it second dinner. Protein and calcium, right?"

"Where'd you get all the paintings in your house?"

"Hold on. I need to catch this tray before I drop it. Are you talking to me? Are we having a conversation?"

He gives me a look that he never gives anyone else. The one that says *don't be cute, you're annoying me.*

And it's so normal that I smile. If he can be annoyed by me, then he's probably also suppressing being turned on by me.

At least, that's the theory I've been working on since he keeps catching himself kissing me—and more—all over town.

I slide the tray up on the bar and lean my forearms next to it. "I did them."

"All of them?"

"All of them."

"And these?" He hooks a thumb toward the far wall.

"Half of them. Pop's Aunt Thelma did the faded seascapes and pirate ships. I did the rest, the ones with bright colors."

"Even the ones with people?"

"Especially the ones with people," Dad calls from the kitchen. "She has a gift."

I wave a hand. "Bah. I have fun and I get to make Shipwreck a little more colorful."

"Pretty sure that's what you have that bird for." Max's gaze hasn't wavered off me, and it's making me warmer than hefting around trays full of food all night.

And I don't want to talk about me.

I want to talk about him. "What's with the lone wolf routine tonight? The guys ditch you? Or should I be very, very cautious when entering my car and my house after my shift? Are you Cooper's lookout man again? Is my ketchup getting replaced with hot sauce? Are my sheets getting swapped out for sandpaper? Will my car look like a pirate ship when I get home?"

"Cooper's having a sleepover."

"Ew."

He laughs, and teenage Tillie Jean makes moon-eyes at the sexy sound.

I have it bad.

I have it so, so bad.

"What about Trevor and Robinson?"

"Shopping."

"Grocery shopping?"

"Christmas shopping. Robinson's sister's into unicorns, and—"

I put a finger to his lips. "Say no more if you want to live," I whisper.

You don't say *unicorn* in Shipwreck. It's against the rules ever since Sarcasm started having a unicorn festival the same week that we do our pirate festival.

And I'm doing my best to keep thinking about Sarcasm and Shipwreck and our town rivalries. If I don't think about something other than Max holding my gaze while I keep my finger touching his soft lips and the scratchy scruff around his mouth, I'll start thinking about what happened in the garden the other night, and then I'll want to do it again.

I keep trying to convince myself that a guy who'll tell me he's not good for me really isn't good for me, because I want a man who loves himself first and foremost and doesn't need me to save him, but there's something about Max that gets under my skin.

He makes me question why I'm on this earth if not to help my fellow human beings.

He's a fellow human being.

He clearly has some issues he needs to work through.

And he's here tonight. Alone. Watching me work my shift like he has nothing better to do.

Which means he's either a stalker, or he's a guy who doesn't know how to ask for what he wants.

Or possibly he needed a change of scenery and felt comfortable enough to take it here.

Gah.

I need to get out of my own head.

"Max got something on his face, TJ?" Dad asks.

I straighten and jerk my hand back, then rub it over my apron like that can remove the feel of him off my skin. "He said the u-word," I stage-whisper.

Dad lifts his brows like I've lost my marbles.

I jerk my head at the corner table, where Nana is still eating banana pudding with Aunt Glory, then mouth *unicorn* to Dad.

"Oo-ee-oh?" he asks like he can't read lips.

Max coughs one of those *I'm not going to get caught laughing* coughs, which makes him even more irresistible.

Dad grins. "You looking for artwork, Max? Tillie Jean can paint about anything, and Cooper mentioned you spend time in galleries in the city sometimes. Maybe she can make you something similar to things you like."

"*Dad*. I don't forge art."

"No, honey, you *improve* it. Whoops. Your mom's calling. I think I was supposed to send her a pork chop an hour ago."

He disappears into the kitchen again as two late stragglers push through the door. "Still got pie, Tillie Jean?" my cousin Ray asks. He's nineteen and seriously in love with Georgia's little brother, Jacob, who's completely clueless about Ray's affections.

Georgia and I can't decide if he's *actually* clueless, or if he plays clueless since he doesn't want to ruin a good friendship, but I lean toward clueless.

This could go either way for poor Ray if he ever tells Jacob how he feels, and it makes me nervous for him too.

"Just one piece left," I tell him.

"We can share," Jacob says. "I mean, if that's cool with you, Ray?"

Seriously, I have no idea how he doesn't catch on, but he seems to entirely miss the googoo eyes Ray makes at the suggestion, which makes me cringe.

Poor Ray.

But he's lit up brighter than the Christmas wreaths hanging up and down Blackbeard Avenue. "Yeah. Cool. I mean, if it's good with you, it's good with me. It's always good with me."

"Cinnamon ice cream?" I ask them.

"No!" Ray barks. "Jacob's allergic. Don't kill him. Jesus, Tillie Jean."

Max slides a look my way that makes me wonder if he knows that there are two full pies in the kitchen and that

I'm very well aware of Jacob's cinnamon allergy. I grin at him.

He looks back at the two young men, then shakes his head at me. "Trouble Jean," he mutters.

"It's the pirate blood. Can't help myself."

It only takes me a minute to get the dirty dishes back to the kitchen and emerge with Ray's pie, but Max is pulling on his coat when I get back.

Disappointment washes over me harder than a surprise spring rain.

"Beauty rest time?" I ask him as I step out from behind the bar with the pie.

"Something like that."

"Is it like, minus seventy-five degrees outside? You're wearing a coat."

"Feeling chilly today."

"Might want to check your temperature."

"Okay, *sis*."

He doesn't ask how late I'm working or what I'm doing later or if he can stop by and see my paintings again.

I don't offer any of the same. "Careful getting home. The goats get frisky with the full moon."

"They really do," Ray agrees. "One stood in the middle of the road yelling at all the cars half the day today down by the inn."

Dad pops out of the kitchen. "Taking off, Max? Travel safe. I hear the Caymans are amazing this time of year."

I look between the two men, my stomach dropping harder than it has any right to. "You're traveling for the holidays?" I ask Max.

My voice doesn't wobble. Nope. No way.

That's all a figment of my imagination.

He nods.

No eye contact.

It's all zip-up-the-windbreaker-and-don't-say-a-word.

"Well. Have fun. Get a tan for the rest of us."

I'm being ridiculous.

He's been here all of—what? Six weeks?

And I'm acting like he would've been living in that house next door forever.

Of course he won't. He reports to spring training mid-February, just like Cooper does every year.

But I don't know if he'll be back next off-season.

Or who'd move into the house next door for the winter.

Or if Uncle Homer's kids would sell the house to someone in the meantime.

Max lifts his fathomless brown eyes to mine. "Thanks for dinner."

And then he's gone.

"Really nice that Cooper's helping him out this year, isn't it?" Dad says as the door jingles shut behind Max.

"Yeah," I murmur absently.

Ray laughs too loudly at something Jacob says, and Nana and Aunt Glory shoot him indulgent grins.

The entire *town* is pulling for poor Ray, even without knowing what Jacob wants.

Is that what I'm doing with Max?

Am I making it up that he's into me?

Or is he into me and resisting it for some unknown reason like everyone hopes Jacob is?

"You wanna take off early, hon?" Dad asks behind me. "Been here all day. I can clean up the last few dishes."

I should tell him no.

That I've got this, and *he* should head home early.

But he knows what he's doing.

I know what he's doing.

And I can send him home early tomorrow.

I'm untying my waist apron before I think better of it. "You know what? Yeah. I'm tired. Thank you."

He squeezes me in a one-armed hug as I make my way past him to grab my coat out of the back.

I don't stop to think about what the hug means.

Dad hugs me all the time. I hug him all the time. Mom, Cooper, and Grady too.

We're huggers.

Just because I think my father knows what I'm about to do doesn't mean this hug suddenly has meaning.

But if it does, I'm glad to know my dad's in my corner.

Max

I'VE BARELY STRIPPED OUT OF MY T-SHIRT ON MY WAY TO BED when someone knocks on my door.

Ignoring it is an easy option.

But it's my back door.

Someone who doesn't want to be seen by the neighbors.

"Don't answer it," I tell my reflection in the ornate mirror over the bed.

And then I ignore myself and pad through the house to the kitchen, barefoot, in just my jeans, and answer it, letting in a blast of cold air around a woman whose dark hair and pale skin is lit by the light of the full moon, shining like a candle in the dead of winter.

Tillie Jean opens her mouth, drops her eyes, and sucks in a breath. Her tongue darts out to swipe over her lower lip, and my cock goes straight back to the garden the other night.

But then she shakes her head and scowls at my face. "You're *leaving*?"

Tell her to go away, a sinister little voice in the back of my head orders.

I ignore that too and step aside so she can come in. "Holidays suck. The beach doesn't."

"You weren't going to say goodbye."

"I'm not supposed to say anything to you." Especially not *I'm leaving because I can't handle the temptation of you next door. Or if I don't go, I'll accept your family's invitation to Christmas, and then I'll start to get ideas that I cannot afford to have.*

Or *Yeah, I'm leaving, but I can't wait to get back, since you aren't at the beach.*

Her gaze drops to my pecs again as she stops in the middle of my small kitchen. "You're a dick, you know that? It's all *I want to kiss you* one night and *you're a problem* the next. Decide, Max. Pick one. We can be friends. We can screw around and have fun. Or you can be a dick. But you don't get to waffle."

"You're—"

"I swear to Thorny Rock's ghost, if you say *Cooper's sister,* I'm going to beat you with that banana on your counter."

I swallow the words *Cooper's sister,* take in her flushed cheeks and flashing eyes and rigid posture, and remind myself that *this* is why I don't do relationships.

One-night stands on the road?

Yep.

Hook-ups at the bar that end with me getting a hotel room for the night instead of taking a woman back to my place?

That too.

Relationships that last more than twenty-four hours?

No.

But Tillie Jean's under my skin. She's a part of my life whether I like it or not, but unlike anyone else's sisters or female friends, she *gets* to me.

I always thought it was because she has no idea how

lucky she is to have such a great family, that she treated them like crap and took them for granted, except I was wrong.

She doesn't just prank Cooper. She drives up the mountain and drops off his favorite soup the one day a week that Mr. Rock makes it, and she smiles when he pranks her back. She doesn't just make jokes about Grady's goat. She also slips the animal treats and texts her brother funny baker memes. She hugs her grandparents. She has Sunday lunch with her parents every week and stays after to play board games even when her brothers don't. She tells her friends when they walk out of the bathroom with toilet paper stuck to their shoes and she slows down to run at the back of the pack, offering encouragement and company to the slowpokes during local 5k races. She pays attention to what's going on around her. She listens. She cares.

She knows who she is. She knows where she fits.

She doesn't irritate me because she doesn't appreciate what she has.

She irritates me because she has everything I never did.

And right now, she's standing in my kitchen, breasts rising and falling under her Crusty Nut T-shirt and puffy coat, her breath quick, glaring at me since to her, apparently I'm a friend.

The kind who's supposed to mention when I'll be gone so she doesn't worry.

Or maybe the kind who's supposed to mention when I'll be gone since she'll miss me.

I can't offer her any of that in return. I don't know how and the idea of someone expecting that of me ramps up my blood pressure and sends my anxiety into overdrive.

But I also can't stop myself from what I'm about to do next.

"Well?" she says. "What are we?"

I take one step toward her.

Then another.

She doesn't back away, but instead flares her shoulders back, lifts her face to watch me, and widens her stance like she's getting ready for me to step between her legs.

Fuck.

How's a guy supposed to resist this?

"We're fucking complicated," I tell her.

She loops one arm around my neck. "I can live with that."

And then she's up on tiptoe, kissing me, wrapping one leg around my hips, thrusting her tongue into my mouth and her fingers into my hair.

I don't know why she keeps coming back, but thank fuck she does.

I push her coat off her shoulders and tug her shirt out of her jeans so I can feel the hot, soft skin of her belly and sides.

More.

More Tillie Jean.

More skin.

More glorious breasts, and *yes*, more lace.

The door's locked. The light's low. No one knows she's here.

So you're damn right I'm pulling out of the kiss to unbutton her shirt and find out what color lace she's wearing tonight.

"Pink," I groan. "Fucking pink."

With black ribbons, but I can't force that many syllables out of my mouth.

She starts to talk, but stops with a gasp when I lick the line of her cleavage down to the rough material holding them in place.

I love breasts.

I love breasts in lace.

I love women gasping my name when I lick their breasts in lace.

She fumbles with yanking her shirt all the way off, then grips my head and holds me to her chest while I lick and suck and nibble my way around the edges of her bra. My thumbs are teasing her hard nipples, my dick so hard it could knock a fastball out of the park, and it's not enough.

I want more Tillie Jean.

I want *all* of Tillie Jean.

My fingers slide around her back and flick her bra clasp open, and her nipples peek out from behind the edge of the lace as the fabric slips down her arms.

"Oh, god, *Max*," she gasps as I suck one sweet nipple into my mouth, rolling my tongue around the tight nub.

Fuck, I love breasts.

And she has a glorious pair.

She grips my hair hard. "Need—closer. Touch me."

I didn't know I was the following instructions type until my hand instinctively goes between her legs to cradle her pussy. Her jeans are soaked, and the scent of her arousal tickles my nose, reminding me what else I love on a woman.

"Off," I order as I slide my mouth to suck on her other nipple.

She yanks at her button. I push her jeans down over her hips, and *yes*.

Pink lace panties.

No, a pink lace *thong*. With little black bows on either side of the little patch of lace.

This woman is gonna kill me.

I lift her in one smooth motion and set her at the edge of the rickety old table under the lone window in the kitchen. Her eyes are midnight blue and hungry, her parted lips moist, her cheeks stained rose.

"Back out now if you don't want to do this," I tell her.

"I wouldn't be here if I didn't want to do this."

"One time only."

"If you say so."

"One time *only*."

"Then you better make it good."

That mouth of hers makes my dick strain even harder.

Walk away, dumbass, that snide fuckwad in my brain hisses.

I mentally flip it off, then grab Tillie Jean's hands and brace them behind her. "Stay."

"Bossy." She pushes her breasts out, and this time, when I bend to worship them, I stroke the wet lace between her thighs with my knuckles too.

She replies with a garbled moan that I take as encouragement, especially when her hips buck against my hand.

Heaven.

And it's all mine.

One time only.

I lick a path between her breasts, down her belly, swirl my tongue over her tight little belly button, and lower.

She spreads her legs wider.

I slip my finger under the fabric and feel her hot, wet, silky skin, the delicate folds, that tight bud of her clitoris, and *yes.*

Just *yes.*

Her hips jerk in my hand as I thumb that magic button. "Don't stop, Max. *God*, don't stop."

The table creaks under her thrusting hips. I push the lace to the side, lean in, and lick her seam, but it's not enough.

Not with her pressing her most intimate parts into my mouth, gasping my name, fisting my hair in one hand while she braces herself with the other.

I don't want to lick and savor.

I want to devour.

Claim.

Conquer.

This pussy?

Mine.

So long as she's on this table, her legs wrapped around my head, pumping into my face, she's *mine.*

I haven't shaved in two days, but she seems to love the

feel of my rough whiskers on her delicate skin, so I'm not gentle.

I'm *hungry*.

I'm desperate.

I want Tillie Jean to come all over my face and feel me imprinted on herself every time she takes her panties off for the next week.

"Oh, god, Max, *more*," she pants.

I can barely hear her with her thighs clamped around my ears, but I hear enough, and it's driving me fucking wild.

I'm so hard diamonds would feel like cotton balls next to my cock. I want inside her.

I want inside her *now*.

But she comes first. She *always* comes first.

I'm selfish a lot of places. But in the bedroom—or the shower, the couch, in front of the fireplace, on the beach at midnight, on my kitchen table, behind the stadium, in a broom closet, wherever—I'm a goddamn fucking gentleman.

Tillie Jean's thighs clamp around my head and she muffles a scream as she grips my hair so tight I feel it all the way in my balls. "Oh god, *yes yes yes*."

Her breathy orgasm moan makes my cock weep, and the taste of her climax on my lips gives me a euphoric high.

Fuck, yeah, I did that.

And I lick and lap at her until her thighs fall open and she collapses back on the table, which squeaks, sputters, and then gives up the ghost.

"*Aah!*"

"Fuck!"

Her hands and legs flail as the whole table tips sideways.

I grab her around the waist and shoot to my feet, except they've lost all feeling, and I sway backwards across the kitchen until my ass collides with something furry.

Furry?

"*Maaaa!*" a goat bleats.

"What the *fuck*?" I spin, still holding Tillie Jean, who squeaks as we trip over a massive furry goat with just one horn.

"*Oh my god*, the door." She squirms. "Turn around. *Turn around!*"

"*Maaa!*" the goat bleats again.

"Sue?" a voice calls in the night.

Tillie Jean squeaks harder.

"*Maa maaa MAAAAAAAA!*" the goat yells.

"Dammit, Sue, where are you?" someone answers.

Grady.

Tillie Jean's brother is out looking for his goat, who's *standing in my kitchen*, right on top of Tillie Jean's pants.

"Bad Sue," TJ hisses. She finally gets herself disentangled and hides behind me as I realize it's chilly in here, and anyone can see us if they happen to be strolling along the alley behind the house. "Go away. *Go!* Shoo."

Sue eyeballs her, then dips his head—yes, *his* head—grabs one of her shoes, and turns away.

She starts to dart after him, looks down at her own bare breasts and her crooked thong, gasps again, and does the lady squat, attempting to cover all of her naked parts while penguin-walking after the goat. "*Sue!*"

I lunge for the goat myself, and it breaks into a jog while Grady calls its name again.

Running with the hard-on from hell?

Not awesome.

In case you were wondering.

Also not awesome?

Suspecting that my own fist is the only thing that'll be giving me relief tonight.

Again.

I turn the corner of the house and am halfway to the sidewalk when Sue drops Tillie Jean's sneaker at Grady's feet in my front yard.

Grady looks down at the shoe, then up at me. He has the same sly grin that Cooper wears when he's being an ass, but it's not quite as hard as it should be. "Is that TJ's?"

"No idea," I lie. "He broke into my back door with it in his mouth. Not mine. That's all I know."

Grady stares me down.

I stare right back.

If he asks what's up with my boner, I'll tell him I was watching porn and invite him in.

Swear to god, I will.

Jesus.

I need to get out of this town.

"Heard you're abandoning us for the holidays," Grady says.

"Miss real sunshine."

"Gonna miss Tillie Jean's Christmas log too."

That should not sound the least bit erotic, but my cock still twitches like he wants to hear more. "Mojitos and steel drums top Christmas logs every time."

He's still grinning. "Suit yourself, dude."

I start to reach for the shoe the same time he does, realize I probably smell like his sister's pussy, and back off.

What the fuck am I gonna do, tell him I'll take it back into my house for her?

"You seen Tillie Jean?" he asks.

"No."

Shit. *Shit.* That was such a bad lie.

He glances at my junk.

I scowl at him like he's Anthony Bryant digging in at home plate with the tying run on first. Don't ask how many times that fucker's hit a home run off me when we've played Milwaukee. I don't want to talk about it.

Just want to throw better so he can't do it again next year.

"Sure you haven't seen TJ?" Grady asks.

"Not since dinner."

He doesn't believe me, but I stay stone-faced. I won't crack. I won't.

He lifts the shoe. "Guess I'll leave this in her mailbox. Thanks for finding my goat. Enjoy the tropics."

I grunt.

Another goat bleats somewhere in the distance.

Sue answers.

A third goat *maaa*s from another direction.

Grady takes Tillie Jean's shoe, crosses the yard to her mailbox, taps the damn box, then whistles as he continues down the street, his goat trotting along with him.

And when I turn back to my own house, I catch sight of a Tillie-Jean-sized figure darting half-clothed in the moonlight back to her own place.

Fuck.

Not how that was supposed to go.

Not at *all* how that was supposed to go.

But it's probably for the best.

Maybe she'll get a boyfriend for Christmas, and then I can legitimately wipe her off the list of eligible women around here.

At least, a guy can hope.

22

TILLIE JEAN

ABSENCE DOES NOT MAKE THE HEART GROW FONDER.

In my case, it makes the heart obsess, cringe, re-imagine a different ending—no, I don't want to talk about sneaking out of Max's house while he was talking to Grady, because even I know I'm lying when I say I didn't want word to get back to Cooper that I was there—question why I can't stop thinking about him, get irritated all over again since I don't even have his phone number, start to ask my friends a million times over the holidays if I'm being ridiculous, realize yes, I'm very much being ridiculous if I have to ask and then stop myself this many times.

Max Cole is a freaking *drug*.

He's a hot-mouthed, hard-bodied, sometimes broody, sometimes happy, sometimes funny, well-equipped—oh, yes, I felt that—growly bear drug.

It's been three weeks since he left, and I haven't heard a peep from him *or* about him. Cooper's not saying a word.

Trevor and Robinson left for shorter holidays and came back and haven't said a word either.

Not that I've seen them much.

I even made a couple trips into the city to see my Fireballs girlfriends, and they didn't mention him either.

And now I'm standing in my studio at home, paint-brushes in hand, glaring at the painting I was working on last night after my shift at Crusty Nut.

It's a bear.

It's a freaking *bear* with Max's eyes and Max's smirk, which doesn't fit at all with the blues and greens and purples of his fur.

He's a technicolor hippie bear hiding dark secrets in his beautiful brown eyes.

I groan and toss my brush down, wipe my hands on my smock, and grab my phone.

Seventeen missed calls and four texts.

That's weird.

It rings silently in my hand again as I'm swiping it open. "Hello?"

"I waffled on whether or not to tell you this," Georgia says, "but basically every horny woman and gay man in the county is gathering at Sunrise Ridge, because…well, you know that sports magazine that does those naked athlete shoots, and how Sunrise Ridge overlooks—"

"*Oh my god*, tell me everyone isn't gawking at Cooper. Ew. *Ew*. Gross. Why would they do that?"

"Tillie Jean. It's not Cooper. It's *Max*."

My mouth goes dry, my knees buzz, and my nipples tingle, making the skin across my chest shiver as goose bumps erupt across my breasts. "What? No. He's not back. I'd know if he was back."

I march to the window and peer through the blinds.

No car at Max's house.

Duh, Tillie Jean. Not if he's at Sunrise Ridge.

But I would've heard his car. I would've heard him coming and going.

Unless he moved so he doesn't have to live next to me for the rest of the post-season.

My stomach drops.

Georgia's talking again. "—your Aunt Bea told my mom that the photographers are staying at the inn, and that she'd heard from Dita, who heard from Vinnie, who heard from Yiannis, who served a gyro to a very talkative stranger who's apparently in the know, that they were doing a naked shoot with Max at the ball fields at the high school, and they had to do it *today* since it's the only day there aren't any extracurriculars going on, and—"

"Are you there?" I have my keys in hand and am headed to my car without thinking about taking off my paint clothes, and I don't know if it's because I want to see Max totally naked, throwing a ball around, or if it's because I want to tell my friends and neighbors to *stop gawking at a naked Max.*

Definitely the second.

I mean, the first too, but *no.* Not like this.

"No," she groans. "I'm at work today."

"Would you be there if you weren't at work?"

"I don't know." She heaves a sigh. "I mean, they're not going to show his ba-dingle-do in the pictures, so it's like, my only—"

"*Georgia.*"

"What? I'm *not* there, and it's like forty degrees, so it probably wouldn't even look all that impressive." I can hear her grinning. "But you should go. Sloane and I counted the number of times you looked out the window at his house and sighed dramatically last week at movie martini night. She tried to take a drink every time but realized she'd be wasted before we got through the opening credits, and gave up. So either *you* want to see his ba-dingle-do, or you're about to chew out the half of Shipwreck who are up on the ridge with binoculars. *No, Grady, I'm not talking about your ba-dingle-do. Go back to being disgusting with your donut dough.* Jesus. Your brothers. I swear."

"I know. They're such guys. Back to Max—"

"Customers. Have to go."

She hangs up, and I dive into my car.

Twenty minutes later, I'm pulling up behind a line of cars at the hook in the road for the Sunrise Ridge viewing area. I should've worn my boots, but I didn't, so I tromp along the dirty, snowy edges of the road to where a dozen women from Shipwreck are all leaning over the fence, most of them with binoculars. "What are you doing?"

"Tillie Jean." Nana makes a *come here* gesture. "Come look. Are all the kids these days packing packages like this?"

"*Nana. Give him privacy.* He signed up to do a photo shoot, *not* to have half of Shipwreck gawking at him from—"

"Whoa, TJ, we have permission." Aunt Glory steps back from the railing and lets her binoculars dangle from their strap around her neck. "We bought tickets."

"You bought tickets." Right. "From who?"

"Cooper and Max. Hundred bucks a pop, and all the money's going to Robinson's niece's charity. Except Max's ten percent cut. He and Cooper rock-paper-scissored it out until Max agreed to take a cut. Cooper insisted."

My jaw flaps open.

"Wait a minute." Ray turns from peering down in the valley too. "Tillie Jean, are *you* allowed to be up here? Where's your ticket? Did you sign the waiver?"

"*Tickets?*" It's all I can manage.

"I got you covered, TJ." Nana flashes me a wide grin. "You know Cooper'll take late payment for a ticket, but you have to promise me you'll sign the waiver too. No pictures. If we take pictures, that magazine paying Max to strip down will get really mad at us and probably never sign Cooper up to do the same. Put your phone in your car and come have a looky-loo."

"They did *not* sell tickets. Also, please don't ever mention Cooper doing a naked photo shoot again."

Aunt Bea reaches into her back pocket and waves something at me without looking away from the ballfield in the valley below. "They did sell tickets. You really think we'd be up here ogling a naked visitor to town without his permission otherwise? Also, if that's what he looks like with shrinkage from the cold, can you imagine what he looks like when—"

"*Aunt Bea.*" I glare at her even though I *very* much want to know what his package looks like.

I've felt it.

I know it has to be glorious.

Even in forty-degree weather.

Possibly *especially* in forty-degree weather.

Oh, crap. Was he showing his package to someone else the past three weeks? Did he hook up with a beach bunny? Has some other woman had her hands on what half of my town currently has their eyes on?

It's not like he's mine. I have no right to be jealous.

But I am.

I'm jealous of the beach bunny in my head who got to hook up with Max Cole.

And now I'm also jealous that *my family bought tickets to see him naked,* and I didn't even know he was back in town.

I whip out my phone and text Georgia. THEY SOLD TICKETS?

Her reply is nearly instantaneous. *I started to try to tell you, but you were on such a roll, I figured it was best to let you figure it out on your own.*

I pocket my phone and glower at my family. "You paid for a peep show!"

Total honesty here—I'm not mad that Max is comfortable

228

enough in his own skin to fleece my family in the name of charity.

I'm mad that they got the option of buying a ticket and I didn't even know he was back.

Ray shoots me a glance and goes wide-eyed next to his mom. "Uh-oh. Prude police."

I can see figures on the ball diamond behind the Blue Lagoon County High School, and I can see skin on one of those figures, but I can't see anything else clearly.

Not on the field.

The sheriffs' cars with lights flashing blocking the entrance to the school and a few other streets?

Yeah.

I can see those clearly down in the valley.

But I can't see any portion of Max's anatomy, other than enough to be able to tell that there's a man, possibly with a tan, down there on the pitcher's mound, and one or two clearly dressed people with equipment around the field, which is still littered with snow over the brown grass in the outfield.

Does he have a tan?

Does he have tan lines?

Was he sun-bathing nude in paradise for the past three weeks?

Am I sweating?

Yep. Definitely sweating.

And don't ask about the state of my panties.

I shake my head and point to one of the cars with flashing lights around the roads to the high school. "No, I don't want a ticket. And you guys shouldn't have bought any either."

Aunt Bea squints at me. "Tillie Jean, the man was shoveling snow naked here not that long ago, and throwing snowballs with you at the same time to boot. You really think he's not comfortable in his body?"

"But you're—this feels so—"

"You'd deprive an old lady of a thrill?" Nana demands.

"You and Pop watch porn every Tuesday night. You get your thrills."

"Not in person."

I step up to the railing and hold out a hand. "The binoculars, Nana. Aunt Bea. Ray. Aunt Glory. Dita. All of you. Put them down or hand them over." I am such a stick in the mud.

"Holy shit," Ray breathes. "The muscles on that guy are like...this isn't fair. Women can get turned on and nobody knows, and here I am, popping—"

"*Gah*. Enough." Aunt Bea snatches his binoculars with one hand and waves him away with the other. "I don't care who you pop for, but you don't do it in front of your mother."

"I don't mind if you pop it in front of me," Nana tells him. "Here, sweetie. Have a candy. Tillie Jean, fetch my purse and get that boy a peppermint."

"*Rawk!* Big dick growly bear! *Rawk!*"

I fan myself. He certainly is a big-dicked growly bear, and I would *very* much like to look.

Especially since Ray's talking about his muscles.

And *he sold tickets*.

Max throwing a ball on the mound fully-dressed in his uniform is catnip for this Max Cole-obsessed kitty cat.

Seeing how his muscles bunch and flex under his bare skin while he's hurling a fastball?

It's an erotic dream.

Stop it, Tillie Jean. He's not into you.

I shake my head again and frown at my grandmother. "Nana, that bird's going to get arrested for his mouth."

She shoves her binoculars at me. "That man should get arrested for having a body that hot and hard. Your pop was a good-looking man in his day, but even he wasn't that glorious. And he got a new tattoo."

"Pop?"

"Max. *Hoo*, it's a beaut."

I'm holding binoculars.

I was basically naked in his kitchen three weeks ago while he ate me out like a beast, and I have zero doubt I would've gotten the full close-up view of a hard-on blessed by the gods if Grady's freaking goat hadn't broken in.

He *sold tickets*. He's okay with people looking. "Did he put a restriction on who could buy tickets?" I whisper.

Aunt Bea whoops.

"Hundred bucks, TJ," Aunt Glory says. "Cooper kept selling tickets after Max left breakfast. You're good."

Nana shoves a piece of paper at me. "Here. Add your signature to my copy of my waiver. We'll deal with Cooper later."

I shouldn't.

I really shouldn't.

But I scribble my name beneath Nana's on her waiver, and tell myself it's only that I'm curious about his new tattoo.

I'm not going to look at his *ba-dingle-do*.

On purpose.

But, *oh*, sexy Max.

Sexy, chiseled, fully-in-control Max.

He's lifting his bare left knee to his chest as he holds the top of his glove to his chin, staring down the catcher. I can't see the goods. Just the flex and release of his muscles as he pulls his right arm back, ball fisted tight in his fingers, then flings it forward with his left leg stepping down and his right leg lifting high in the air behind him as he releases.

It's a gorgeous pitch made even better by being able to see every last inch of his sun-kissed skin—he was *totally* sun-bathing nude on vacation—and the new sea turtle tattoo on his shoulder and the heavy weight of his package between his thighs.

My thighs clench and everything inside me gets warm and tingly.

I should stop watching.

I should really stop—

A police siren cuts through my thoughts, and I drop the binoculars with a shriek. They tumble down the side of the mountain.

"Tillie Jean!" Nana gapes at me. "Those were my favorite pair."

Busted.

I am so busted.

My lips flap for a minute before I find words for Nana. "Sorry. Sorry sorry. I'll buy you a new set."

"Ladies," my cousin Chester says as he pulls himself out of the sheriff's car. "Ray. What're we doing up here?"

"Bird-watching," Nana says.

"*Rawk!* Big dick growly bear! *Rawk!*"

"I'm gonna shoot that parrot," Dita mutters to me. "But isn't he hot? I finished hot flashes two years ago and here I am, forcing them on myself again and about to get arrested. *Worth it.*"

"Y'all ain't standing here looking at a naked man down there having a photo shoot, are you?" Chester asks, eyeballing Ray's crotch.

"Go away, you turd," Ray snaps. "We have permission to be here."

"Don't be disrespecting the law, little brother."

Dita waves her waiver. "You *are* a turd, Chester, and we *do* have permission to be here. Plus, we're keeping any other onlookers from watching if they don't have tickets. But you know what you really need to do? You need to get over *there*." She hooks a thumb over her shoulder. "I saw a flash of light on *that* mountain. And you know if it's over there, it's those assholes from Sarcasm, and they *definitely* don't have permission."

Chester hooks one thumb in his waistband and rocks on his heels. "It's against state law to buy tickets for a peep show."

"Chester Rock, you're not planning on taking your granny to the station in handcuffs, are you?" Nana asks. "If you are, I might have to call your grandfather. You know he loves it when I get cuffed."

Chester winces.

The rest of us wince too.

Some days I really wish I didn't know Doc Adamson kept little blue pills in stock just for my grandparents.

"I'm gonna have to cite all of you," Chester tells us.

Dita gasps. "What? We were just standing here looking at the pretty mountains."

Chester looks at me. "And using binoculars to spy on a private photo shoot."

I lift my hands. "I don't have binoculars."

"Tillie Jean, I got a dash cam. Don't go being cute. The rest of these fine ladies have an argument to be made, but you're red-handed, cuz."

"And you haven't actually paid for your ticket yet," Aunt Glory side-whispers to me.

I gasp. "I wasn't—it's not—but I—*you know I'm good for it.*"

"Gonna have to ask the fine gentlemen down in the valley if they want to press charges."

Now he's playing dirty. "Do *not* make me tell the story about you on your fourteenth birthday."

"Threatening an officer of the law…"

"Chester, we all know this is about her chocolate cake taking top honors at the fair three years ago." Nana clucks her tongue. "You need to let that go, sweetheart. It was a losing proposition to start with, and we told you so."

"Nana. She was staring down in the valley with her binoculars and I got it on my dash cam. Can't help that. The law's the law."

"You gonna call her parents too?" Ray scoffs. "Quit being a dick, Chester. We all know the dash cam can malfunction."

"It's fine," I tell Ray. "Let him cite me. Whatever. He's the one with the birthday coming up."

"And the bachelor party," Aunt Bea agrees.

"And the wedding," Nana muses.

"What do you think his bride would say about him citing Tillie Jean for bird-watching?" Dita murmurs.

Chester mutters something he probably shouldn't say in uniform.

I hold my hands out. "Go on. Arrest me. I can take it."

Some time in the slammer might cool my attraction to Max. That wouldn't be a bad thing, would it?

He's scowling as he pulls out his citation pad and scribbles something on it. "I'm just doing my job."

And I'm totally busted.

You don't get a citation from Chester without the news of your indiscretion making it all over Shipwreck in three-point-two seconds. Aunt Bea already has her phone out.

Probably texting my mom.

"Tracy knows I'm just doing my job," he tells me as he hands me the citation. "Now go on. All of you. Get out of here before I have to cite you all for loitering."

Ray grins at me as he heads for his car. "But it was worth it, right, TJ?"

"Don't worry, sugarplum," Nana says. "We'll get you drunk at The Grog and help work out your defense. It'll all be okay. And I'm gonna pay for your ticket. The one to Cooper, I mean. And I'm gonna tell him I made you. You might be on your own with Chester though. Your grandfather wants me to quit baiting him."

It's not the citation that bothers me.

It's knowing that Max will find out I was willing to pay to see him naked.

Three weeks without a peep after he went to town on my lady bits like he needed to teach me how a real man gives a woman the big O.

After informing me he's a one-night-stand kind of guy, and after I freaked and ran away because it *was* the best orgasm of my life, and I didn't want to let myself get attached to a guy who doesn't do attachment.

Plus, Grady almost caught us, which would've meant Cooper found out, and then Max's life would be hell.

And now, I'm no longer the woman who flirts with him to annoy him.

I'm officially a citation-holding stalker.

And I need to get over Max Cole.

Pronto.

"The Grog sounds great," I tell Nana. "It's not too early to start now, is it?"

"Don't make me come back for a drunk and disorderly." Chester's face is pained like he knows Dad's going to overcook his steaks and Mom will get his coffee order wrong and Grady will only serve him ugly baked goods already for the next forever just for citing me for using binoculars on an overlook, and he really doesn't want to get on anyone else's bad side.

But I also know he wouldn't have cited me at all if he wasn't still holding a grudge about the chocolate cake incident at the fair.

Still, I smile at him. "Start the day the way you intend to finish it, Chester. It's a life rule."

I don't look back over the valley at Max throwing naked down below as I head back to my own car, citation in hand.

But I want to.

I very, very much want to.

And that's the whole problem, isn't it?

23

Max

BEING BACK IN SHIPWRECK IS WEIRD.

Wasn't sure I wanted to come back after three weeks on the beach, but I miss working out with the guys, and if I'd rescheduled today's photo shoot, it wouldn't have happened at all.

Do the Bare Naked feature for Arena Insider, Max, my agent said. *You want the big endorsement deals, people need to know who you are.*

Strip down physically?

Yeah. I can do that. Made almost two grand for charity selling tickets too.

Can't argue with that.

It's the mental shit that fucks with me though. Watching families. Lifelong friends. Wanting to fit in.

Not trusting they'd still want me around if they knew all of me, but starting to want to try anyway.

What's the worst that happens?

I sleep with Tillie Jean, Cooper finds out, and gets me traded so I don't have to get closer to anyone here?

Fine.

Fine.

I almost didn't come back to Shipwreck because I want to sleep with Tillie Jean Rock, and once will *not* be enough, which became glaringly clear when I couldn't look at another woman the entire time I was gone. All I could think of was TJ and her magic pussy and how much I want another chance to hear her scream my name.

Happy now?

Is that enough honesty for one day?

Jesus.

I have issues.

I shrug off the thoughts as I pull into Cooper's driveway. I can act normal. Laugh. Shoot the shit. Plan for spring training next month. Talk about doing today's photo shoot and interview on school grounds with my junk hanging out like that's not the creepiest possible thing a guy could do.

While knowing a bunch of women were watching with binoculars from the ridge above.

The guys get it. Our lives aren't normal.

There's a bunch of cars here at his mountain mansion already, which doesn't matter when my phone dings with a message from my agent.

Good shoot today. Got a call already. They want a more in-depth interview. You said the A-word. Ready to strip all the way down and talk about your anxiety?

I roll my shoulders back on the way to the front door.

Am I?

Do I want to put it all out there? Talk about the ghost haunting me twenty-four-seven? About growing up with a depressed father who self-medicated with vodka? Relying on virtual strangers to get me to baseball practice and buy my gear for me?

Nope.

Not really. As far I'm concerned, every athlete has some level of anxiety, and that's that.

I rap my fist on Cooper's door and wait for him to open the door and let me in.

Learned that lesson once. I don't need to learn it again.

He looks equal parts cross and amused when he yanks the door open. "Dude. You can just come in."

"Nope."

"She's in massage chair number three, and she's toasted. She's not pulling shit on you today. And she swears she was only up there on the ridge to tell everyone else to give you your privacy and didn't know we sold tickets. Whatever." He pulls the door open wider. "You coming in? Trevor's having a day too. Pulled something in his shoulder at the bowling alley last night. Pretty sure he's done. Done-done, you know? Like, finally accepting that his contract isn't getting renewed and he doesn't know what he wants to be when he grows up, and when he grows up is *today*."

Fuck.

I angle into the house, walking through the foyer like a glitter bomb might jump out at me at any minute.

And when we turn into the living room—high ceiling, plank walls, massive top-of-the-line television set-up on one side, stone fireplace on another—there's Tillie Jean and Trevor, both of them in their own massage chairs, since Cooper has four in here.

I've never asked why.

Don't want to know.

"I was bird-watching, not looking at you naked," Tillie Jean says directly to me. Her hair's piled in a messy bun on top of her head, and she's wearing paint-splattered jeans, an oversize Fireballs hoodie, and has bare feet.

Fucking gorgeous, which is not what I need to be thinking about her.

Trevor giggles. He has his arm wrapped in a sling, which means he probably shouldn't be sitting in a massage chair. Rubbing injuries wrong can fuck them up. "Your nana wasn't."

Tillie Jean almost drops the coffee mug she's trying to grab out of the vibrating cup holder attached to the chair. "Don't talk shit about my Nana!"

"Not shit if it's true."

"Cooper, he's talking shit about Nana."

Cooper scrubs a hand over his face and shoots me a sideways glance, still cringing. "I can't believe I actually regret using you to make money for charity."

"I broke Nana's binolu—bidonkular—bi-whatevers," Tillie Jean says.

She giggles.

Trevor giggles. "An' you got *arrested*."

"Asshole cousin."

"To asshole cousins!"

They clink glasses. Trevor flinches, hunching in on his slinged-up arm.

No small part of me wants to hug the guy, and I'm not a hugger.

Cooper sighs again, his face telling me he's trying not to think about Trevor too as he looks at Tillie Jean. "She didn't get arrested. She just got a citation, and she showed up here and shoved five hundred bucks at me to pay for her peep show ticket with late fees. I'll get you your cut later."

I snort. "I don't want her money."

He eyeballs his sister once more. "This was funnier a few years back when it was Chester citing her for indecent exposure. He didn't like that her shirt said *My cake kicks your cake's ass.* Especially the part where she fought it and demanded a court date to tell her side."

"Did it hold up?" I ask.

His brows twist and flex the same way his whole body

does when he's diving for a line drive at second base. "Are you serious?"

I shrug.

Seeing her after spending the last three weeks trying to forget the sound of her screaming my name, the taste of her lingering in my mouth, the feel of her skin, and then jacking off to thoughts of her several times a day when I couldn't forget—this should be awkward.

It's never awkward with other women I screw around with. I mostly don't see them again, and when I do, I'm voluntarily a dick so they stay away.

I'm used to being a dick, therefore, not awkward.

But right now?

I want to pull her onto my lap and ask what she thought of me pitching naked.

If it turned her on.

If she'll get it if I tell her that I'm breaking my one-time-only rule just this once since I still want to feel my cock inside her. That last time was a half, and I want to cash in on the other half of our deal.

Yep.

I'm working on getting my ass traded. Because I very much want to fuck around with Cooper Rock's little sister.

And?

Not awkward.

Uncomfortable, yeah, but only physically.

Emotionally?

I don't want to talk about how fucking good it is to see her mere feet away from me, and how thirty seconds here with the woman who only annoys me because I don't want to want her is settling something deep in my soul.

She brought me Thanksgiving leftovers.

Old news.

But it's what keeps sticking with me.

"Did it?" I repeat. "Did it hold up in court?"

He finally cracks a grin. "Yeah. She got Judge Namasaki on her court date."

"He hard?"

"His wife submits a peach cobbler to the county fair every year, and every year Tillie Jean's apple strudels beat it, and Mrs. N swears TJ cheats by having Grady make them for her, except Grady was off at his fancy cooking school a lot of those years when TJ won, which also pissed them off. So the judge was inclined to take a stand against profanity on T-shirts too, especially when those T-shirts were smack-talking his wife. Just in case she was having Grady mail her apple strudels."

"That's sixty-five levels of fucked-up."

"She had to do two hours of community service trying to teach Long Beak Silver not to cuss."

"And that mother-beaker taught me a few new cuss words," Tillie Jean proclaims proudly.

"To wuss curds!" Trevor cries.

They clink again.

He flinches again, I flinch for him again, Cooper winces again.

This is the hard part of the game.

Watching teammates face what we'll all face eventually.

And what will you do then? that voice whispers in my head.

Three or four years might be all I have left. This contract I just signed? I know it's my last.

Some pitchers make it to their late thirties, but that's assuming no injuries. No accidents. No freak twists of the world throwing a curve ball at my plans.

No getting *tired*.

I don't want to stay in until my late thirties. I don't want to leave baseball broken and cranky and sore and needing constant painkillers on top of my anti-anxiety meds. I want to leave while I'm still in good shape so I can enjoy the rest of my life in relative comfort.

And *what then?*

I shrug out of the light jacket I'm wearing and toss it onto the back of a chair, because *what then?* always makes me break out in a sweat.

Plus, it's three or four years away.

Practically a lifetime.

And I'm not looking at Tillie Jean while all this shit is rolling through my head.

Swear to god, I'm not.

Fine.

Fine.

I don't want to be looking at Tillie Jean, but she's so fucking comfortable and confident that it's hard not to trust that everything will be okay when she's around.

I don't know how that happened, but it did.

Cooper shoots a glance at my jacket. "You're seriously hot in here too?"

"I'm always hot."

Tillie Jean finishes off her drink and leaps up, swaying for a second before getting her footing. "I was *only* looking at your new tattoo," she tells me. "Also, you have pretty good form for a guy who hasn't balled a thrown in *hic!* months."

"Thank you."

She twirls in the center of the room, dancing to some music only she can hear.

Cooper's making a career out of grimacing today.

Trevor's working on the giggles more.

And Tillie Jean keeps talking. "Did you know Thorny Rock kept a pet sea turtle? He named him Bob and tried to bring him with when he moved to Shipwreck before it was Shipwreck. Bob's buried with Thorny Rock's treasure."

"No, he didn't," Cooper mutters.

"Yep. He did. I know because my paintbrush told me."

"I need a beer. Max, want one?"

I'm not driving. My shoulders aren't hitching at the sight

of Tillie Jean. I'm feeling weird and warm and unusual, but not anxious, and I'll stop at one. "Sure."

Cooper heads to the kitchen that lines one corner of the massive open room.

Tillie Jean stops twirling as she gets close to the empty fireplace, and looks me dead in the eye. "How do you just get *naked* in front of the whole world?"

I almost reach for my T-shirt hem to show her, except I still have a single shred of common sense keeping me from being a total idiot. "I work hard and look good."

She licks her lips and winks at me. "Yeah, baby."

"Knock it *off*, TJ."

She rolls her eyes at her moody brother, and yes, Cooper is definitely in a mood.

Not normal.

Makes me wonder what else is going on with him.

"For realsies," Tillie Jean says, swirling closer to me now. "How do you not think, *Maxy Max, everyone and their mama's gonna see your junk hanging out and compare it to every other junk they've ever seen, and it might not measure up, and they might tell you so?*"

"No more alcohol," Cooper says.

"No, top her off again," I say. She's funny right now. I don't know who I am and what I did with the old *Maxy Max*, but tipsy TJ is unexpectedly amusing the hell out of me.

In all the years I've known her, I've never seen her drunk.

Over-caffeinated like that night at The Grog, yes. Lightly buzzed, occasionally.

But not drunk.

She doesn't make a habit of this.

She's not my father. "And to answer your question, Trouble Jean, I know my junk looks good."

She squints at me, but only with one eye. Wonder if she's seeing two of me. "I've seen a lot of junk," she starts, but

Cooper cuts her off with a noise that's somewhere between a grunt and a coyote howl.

"Don't make me call Mom," he says.

She blows a raspberry, then whips her phone out of her pocket, loses her grip, and sends it scattering across the floor. "Sham." Her nose wrinkles. "Dit. Sham. Shap. Doot. *Gah*. I can't say cuss words!"

Trevor giggles again, and next thing I know, I'm snickering as I retrieve her phone. "Try *fuck*."

"Do *not* say *fuck* around my sister," Cooper growls.

"Duck!" Tillie Jean cries. "Shoop! Kama-chameleon!"

"Llama-ka-leemons!" Trevor agrees.

They both explode in a fit of laughter. I'm grinning as I take the beer glass Cooper hands me. "What's with the bad mood?" I ask him.

"Nothing."

Right. Like *nothing* ever puts Cooper Rock, smiley-happy-annoying one, in a bad mood. "Accidentally hook up with a cousin or something?"

He shudders. "No."

"Fireballs aren't trading you, are they?"

"*No*. Fuck, no. Where'd you hear that?"

"Didn't. Just don't know what else would put you in a bad mood."

He shoots a look at his sister, who's now sitting on the arm of Trevor's chair and whispering something to him.

Okay, yeah.

I can see how that would put him in a bad mood.

It's putting me in a bad mood.

Cooper can't threaten Trevor with anything if he touches Tillie Jean.

Not if Trevor's *done*.

And honestly?

He's a good dude. If I had a sister, I'd let him date her.

Fuck. Now I'm scowling too. "Where's Robinson?"

Cooper hooks a thumb over his shoulder. "Hot tub."

"With three of our cousins," Tillie Jean adds. She hiccups. Then laughs. Then hiccups again. "You should go join him, Growly Bear. Steal all of our cousins away. Make Cooper blow steam out his nostrils. He could stand in for a mascot when Addie's done chewing him up and spitting him out. *Without* a costume. He'd be the mascot Cooper Chewed-Up Rock."

One, I'm twitching at the idea of flirting with *any* of Cooper's cousins, but not with Tillie Jean.

Two— "Coach Addie's giving you shit?"

"She says his swing needs work." Trevor snorts. "No one *ever* tells Cooper his swing needs work unless they're trying to get under his skin."

Tillie Jean nods. "Well, he *did* hook up with her baby sister…"

"I did *not*. Jesus. Does she even have a baby sister? I thought she only had brothers."

Trevor and TJ both crack up so hard that TJ almost falls off the side of the chair.

Cooper makes his annoyed noise again. "I'm gonna dunk both of you in the hot tub and not feel bad when you drown."

"She really say your swing's shit?" I ask.

"She said I have *room for improvement* and that I don't *trust myself enough*. Maybe she wants to show me how to tag a runner out at second next? Maybe how to do a few somersaults? Some flips?"

Huh. I'm laughing. Again. "You gonna get her traded too?"

Tillie Jean snort-laughs. Trevor tilts his head, moves, winces, and leans back again. "You can't get a coach traded. We get a new catcher yet?"

Cooper grunts.

I grunt in return.

We need a catcher. Heard rumors management was

looking at some guys in our minor league affiliate team, but we haven't heard anything else since Jarvis got traded for a draft pick after the season. People think pitchers are the most valuable part of a team, but we go to shit fast if our catcher isn't worth a damn.

And Cooper needs a good catcher too, since he's the one snagging throws from home when runners try to steal second.

"We should consult the mascot cards," Tillie Jean announces. She lunges for a set of Go, Ash, Go cards on an end table and holds the deck to her forehead. "Meaty the Meatball, tell us who will be the catcher to Max's naked pitching? *Ooooohhhhm... Oooooohhhhmmmm... Ooooohhhmmm...*"

"She's usually so funny," Cooper mutters.

"She's *very* funny," I tell him. Weird, since drunk people normally annoy me.

"Meaty the Meatball says we must play three rounds of Go, Ash, Go, then do a bat spin race, and he will not tell us who the next Fireballs' catcher is, but he *will* tell us we're doofuses. *Hic!*"

Her cheeks are flushed pink, and her eyes are the kind of glassy that often puts me on edge, except she's also smiling.

She's smiling so bright and happy, like instead of alcohol turning her into an asshole, it's turning her into a brighter, happier version of herself.

Magnifying what's already there.

And what's already there is already fucking spectacular.

I eyeball the beer that I have yet to take a sip of and wonder what too much of it would say about me.

Probably that you're a fuck-up who would only dim her light, the beer suggests.

Officially decided—I'm not drinking that shit today.

I set it on an end table and hold out a hand to Tillie Jean. "C'mon, then. Let's see if you're right. Hundred bucks says I kick your ass in this game."

"*Two* hundred. And a back rub." She winks. "You're

gonna make me empty my *entire* piggy bank today, Max Cole."

Cooper growls.

I snort and dig deep for what I hope is a convincing, "Dude. You think I'm gonna touch your sister?"

He gestures to her. "She's the best you're gonna get here, so *yeah*."

"Not true." TJ's dancing again as she slides out of yet another chair. "Dita's a tiger in the sheets. Which you'd know. *Mrow*."

I wouldn't put it past Cooper to be into one of the older ladies around here, but the way he spits his beer out in horror makes it pretty clear he's never considered that as an option. "I'm calling Mom."

"Good. She'll tell you to quit being a ninny."

"Last time she got drunk, she streaked through Sarcasm and left boob prints on all the dusty cars on the street," Cooper mutters to me.

"Oh my god, I was *nineteen* when I did that. And *you* were egging me on."

And I'm suddenly incredibly uncomfortable in my jeans. "Were you naked too?" I ask Cooper.

"Yes," Tillie Jean stage-whispers.

He glares at her. "*No*."

"He *was*, but he can't tell the baseball gods that, because he's afraid they'll go back in time and *hic!* take away his dream." TJ pats my chest with the cards. "Play me, Max. Play me for dinner."

"Can't. Signed a contract. I owe Cooper backrubs if I play you for dinner."

"*Ew*."

"Exactly."

We grin at each other.

"But I can play you for the joy of kicking your ass," I tell her.

"Trophy! Stinky Butt, get one of your old Little League trophies. We need a prize!"

Trevor snores.

Cooper's eyes both visibly twitch.

And Robinson knocks on the back sliding door in nothing but wet swim trunks. "Hey, can we get a towel out here?"

Cooper looks at me.

Then at Tillie Jean.

Back to me.

I lift my hands in surrender. "We won't start without you, dude." And then I crack a grin. "Strip Go, Ash, Go is way more fun when you have to watch me get naked."

Am I pushing it?

Yes.

But for the first time in years, tossing shit like this makes me feel normal.

Home.

Like I might have found a place I truly belong.

TILLIE JEAN

I DON'T KNOW WHO'S KNOCKING ON MY DOOR, BUT WHOEVER IT is will die.

Dead die.

Monday can die too. I hate Mondays.

Or possibly I hate hangovers.

Is today Monday?

I don't know. It's Blursday. Let's leave it at that.

No, wait. It's Sunday. Day off. Thank goodness.

But someone's still banging on my door.

I lift one corner of my sleep mask and cautiously pry open a single eyeball. My brain's not swishing around in my head, which is a good thing, but the soft light peeking through my curtains stabs my eyeballs and makes me mutter a curse that I shouldn't say in Long Beak Silver's presence if I want him to not repeat it in front of a bunch of preschoolers.

"C'mon, Sleeping Beauty," a voice that is definitely inside my house and definitely male and which definitely does not belong to one of my brothers calls. "I have to give Cooper proof of life or he's coming down off his mountain to splash you with cold water."

Am I dressed?

Do I care?

Would seeing me naked render Max helpless to resist my body and make him determined to cure my headache with a few dozen orgasms like the one he left me with before going off to get that delicious no-tan-line tan?

Could I handle moving my head enough to enjoy sex right now?

Am I mad at him for leaving after that orgasm? Do I have any right to be?

Do I care?

Maybe I want to be mad.

But probably not.

"Mmfllbub," I say.

"I'm coming in, and I'm not looking at you other than the proof-of-life picture, and I'm bringing aspirin and water and a country loaf from Grady."

When did I get home last night?

Did I call Chester and tell him that I know he gets his magic potluck macaroni salad from the grocery store?

And why do I keep picturing Cooper riding Ash, the dragon mascot, while Luca Rossi slaps Glow the Firefly's ass?

Right.

Too many rounds of Go, Ash, Go.

"Fresh bread?" I croak.

"Came out of the oven an hour ago. He was going to shove it in your mailbox. I offered to keep it warm." Something shuffles in the room, and I peer out from under my sleep mask again in time to see Max setting a plate and a glass on my nightstand beyond the gauzy pink curtains.

I mumble something else that probably sounds like *oh my god I love you*, but then Max lifts his phone. "Smile."

The flash pierces my skull and murders me in my bed.

Okay, not really.

But it hurts like hell, and I can't see the aspirin or the bread.

Miracle bread.

Beautiful, delicious, stomach-healing bread.

My brothers are sometimes the best.

"You're a disaster, aren't you?" Max says.

I grunt something in response and try to fling my arm just right to grab the bread.

Bread first.

Yeasty, nutty, delicious yummy bread.

Miss.

Miss again.

I whimper.

Risk opening my eyes one more time to try a puppy dog face at Max.

He's not growly today. It's weird.

If anything, he's relaxed and happy and looking at me as if we're friends.

What the *hell* happened yesterday? I know I didn't black out, even if I had weird dreams after getting home last night.

With a ride from Georgia, thank you very much. *Not* a ride from Max.

I remember that part.

"Need help?" he asks.

He very much needs to not give me that half-smile and aim kind eyes my way.

"Please?" I whimper. I try to add *coffee*, but my words don't work like that.

My mouth.

I mean my mouth doesn't work like that.

Not right now.

He grins a little more as he hands me a slice of the bread. I chomp into the crusty part and sigh in utter heaven, letting my eyes drift shut again while the yeasty deliciousness floods my mouth with something much better tasting than whatever died in there last night.

"Grady makes the best bread," I say.

Maybe.

I'm still gnawing on the bread, and I think my words come out sounding like something a neanderthal woman would've said to her husband when he left his rock tools hanging out all over the cave.

"Were you honestly that upset at getting a citation that you had to get plastered yesterday?" Max asks.

Oh. Right.

My cousin gave me a citation yesterday. I swallow, and I form real English syllables. "Nuh-uh. Didn't want Trevor to drink alone. Poor Trevor. He gives good hugs."

Max makes a noise.

I slide a glance at him. "You give good other things." What the hell do I have to lose?

Other than him being nice to me like we could be friends for the first time in my entire life?

He ignores my comment, and I let my eyes drift shut again.

But only for a moment.

The him being quiet part, I mean.

"You're a funny drunk," he says softly.

"Thank you?"

He hesitates. I don't see it so much as I feel the weight of the air shifting around me. I lift one eyelid again.

He's sitting against my closet door, and he meets my gaze for half a second, then drops it. "My old man...wasn't."

I picked up on that right before Thanksgiving, and I've read enough articles about the team to know that people compare him to Luca Rossi all the time, but where Luca's father is a shithead former athlete who pops up whenever Luca does something awesome, and *only* then, in the hopes of getting accolades himself, Max's dad is nearly always quoted as being an absent figure in his life, but not before the articles mention that his mom died young in a car crash.

It's like the reporters are saying *there's a deeper story here, folks, and we're gonna find it.*

"Are you worried you'll be like him?" *Smooth, Tillie Jean. Smooth.* Hit the guy in the gut when he brings you bread and aspirin.

And I don't think I'd be holding back if he'd brought me coffee either.

But Max doesn't flinch. He just shakes his head. "Got my own problems. Being him isn't one."

"What are your problems?"

Those deep brown eyes shift up at me again. "Are you still drunk?"

"If I say yes, will you spill all your secrets?"

"If you say yes, I'm getting all of *your* secrets."

"Who are you, and what did you do with Max Cole?" I gasp and sit straight up in bed, even though it makes my head feel like someone took a meat cleaver to it. "*Oh my god.* You're Max's secret evil twin. Except possibly his secret angelic twin? What's your real name, and what did you do with my growly bear next door?"

He stares at me for a second, then ducks his head with a rough laugh. "You're like this all the time, aren't you?"

"Fabulous?" I croak as I realize my head needs me to hold it together before it splits open. I press my hands to my head just above my ears and try to push it back together, but this isn't helping.

He cracks a snicker again. "Yes. Completely uninhibited."

"Fearlessly me." I snag another piece of bread and slowly lower my head back to my pillow. "You should try it."

"Being fearlessly you? No thank you."

"Who would you be if you weren't afraid of who you think you are?"

His eyes snap to mine like it's the most profound question he's ever been asked.

I get it.

It's the same question my therapist asked me seven years ago, and yeah, it rocked my world too.

His Adam's apple bobs, and after a moment of holding my gaze, he rubs his chin. "I'd be a guy who'd risk asking a woman out for something more than a one-time-only thing."

Good morning, nipples. Lovely to see you made it through yesterday's drunken escapades. You too, Ms. Clit. "Why's that a risk?"

"You know why."

"You're not Chance Schwartz, Max. You're Max Fucking Cole, and you wouldn't be here if Cooper didn't think you were a decent guy."

"He invited the whole team."

"And you don't think he would've figured out how to subtly suggest somewhere else for you to go, with or without the help of other people, if he didn't want you here?"

"Your brother. Cooper Rock. The guy who went out of his way to ask Darren and Luca to sign a ball for a dude he hated more than life itself in high school, and not because the guy was dying or because his life imploded or for any reason other than that it made it through the grapevine that the asshole wanted a signed ball?"

He has a point.

Cooper wouldn't have tried to keep Max from coming out here any more than he would've tried to keep any other guy on the team from coming out for team workouts. He has this belief that all people are inherently good, even if they're annoying from time to time, and as someone who's been fortunate in every aspect of his life, he owes a karmic debt of kindness to the world.

He was the guy who came home in late October slobber-crying in Mom's kitchen. It wasn't that he was broken over the Fireballs getting eliminated from the play-offs.

Nope.

Those tears were because he was so overjoyed that he'd been a part of making his lovable losers get as far as they did.

"*Fine*. But you're still Max Fucking Cole."

Ah, there's the growly bear stare.

It's so familiar and perfect, I can't resist smiling. "Take me to breakfast."

"Absolutely not."

"Then let me take you to breakfast."

"No."

"In Sarcasm. It'll make everyone talk. *So* much gossip. But you haven't lived until you've had a bubble waffle with ice cream for breakfast to get over a hangover, and Annika's family's bakery makes the best bubble waffle sundaes *ever*."

"I'm not hungover."

"That's okay. I'm hungover enough for both of us."

He goes quiet again, and I mentally cringe, which makes my head ache a little more.

Is he sensitive about other people drinking? No one's making him go out to The Grog, and I know he goes out to bars while the guys are on the road during the season. I've seen the pictures and heard the stories. So I don't think he's hung up over watching other people enjoy alcohol responsibly, but what do I *really* know about him?

I'm lost in my head wondering what's going on in his when he speaks again. "Coffee?"

I wink. It's habit, I swear. "Are you asking me out for coffee?"

"Yes."

"Seriously?"

"Yes."

"In public?"

"Yes."

"Are you pretending you're my sister again?"

"Backwards, TJ. I'm no one's sister. But no. I'm not pretending I'm your brother. I'm asking you out to coffee because I know it'll make you feel better, Ms. Coffeeholic."

Okay.

Did *not* see that coming.

"Can I go dressed like this?"

"Wrapped in a sheet with hair that looks like you fought a rabid Shar-pei and lost last night?"

"Yes."

"I don't care. But do you want your cousin to give you another citation for disturbing the peace by looking like that?"

Be still my heart.

Max Cole is *fitting in*. Here. In Shipwreck. *With me*. Joking about Shipwreck things. Understanding how we work.

And—*liking* it?

I'm listening, Universe. I swear I'm listening.

I push myself up to sitting again, fling back the covers, and don't bother trying to hide that I'm only wearing a threadbare T-shirt and lace panties.

His eyes go dark and he visibly swallows again, but he doesn't move from his spot against my closet door.

Nor does he move when I slide off the edge of my bed and stand on unsteady legs, putting my crotch more or less at eye level and only a foot or so from him.

But he's looking.

He is *definitely* looking.

And not running. Or trying to hide that he's looking.

Max Cole is checking me out and asking me out for coffee.

I don't know what game it is he's playing now, but I am *in*. "Give me five minutes to shapeshift back into a human. And then you're gonna get the coffee date of your life."

Max

ONE...TWO...THREE...

No.

No.

This is *just coffee*. In a bright, seashell-themed coffeehouse on Blackbeard Avenue owned by Tillie Jean and Cooper's mother, who's not here, but her barista is giving me a knowing look.

I tell myself it's because Tillie Jean's wearing oversize sunglasses and her hair still looks like she might have an echidna nest hiding in it, and while she put on clothes, her sweatpants are close to falling off and I'm nearly positive she doesn't have a bra on under her hoodie.

Not that anyone who wears a black hoodie with bright, sparkly purple letters spelling out *FABULOUS* across her chest needs a bra.

The hoodie speaks for itself.

"Oh my god, this coffee is the best," she moans after downing the whole cup in one gulp.

My cock leaps to attention and asks if it, too, can have some of what she's having.

Preferably with her.

I lean back, hook my ankle over my knee to hide it, and signal the barista. "Can she get another one of those, but decaf?"

TJ gasps in horror.

And it's so Tillie Jean, and exactly what I thought she'd do, that I'm suddenly laughing, and there's no amount of holding my own mug to my face that'll hide it.

"*You.*" She points at me, eyes still as round as her pretty pink lips. "You are *pranking* me before the sun's up on a Sunday morning."

"It's eleven AM, Trouble Jean. Sun's been up for hours."

She gasps. "And now you're depriving me of my fantasies. For shame, Max Cole. *For. Shame.*"

I am not flirting with Tillie Jean.

I'm not flirting with Tillie Jean. I don't have a death wish, and flirting with her in broad daylight, here in Cooper's mother's coffee shop, would be a death wish.

I'm being her *friend*.

At least, if anyone asks, that's what I'm telling them.

The truth?

The truth's hairier.

The truth is, I'm taking Tillie Jean on a date. In her mother's coffee shop. Where Cooper will hear about it.

You don't do that if you're not serious about treating your teammate's sister right.

"TJ, you want another full-octane caramel macchiato?" the barista calls.

"Two, please." She winces like the sound of her own voice is hurting her head. "This is why I don't drink," she mutters to me.

"Alcohol turns you into a grandma sloth?"

She pulls her sunglasses down just enough to peer at me

with bloodshot eyes. "Have you been saving that one all morning?"

"Nah. Came up with it on the spot. I'm quick like that."

I'm not touching her, but I want to be. I want to rub her temples and feed her more bread and hand her a coffee mug full of water to see if she'd drink it or if her palate will *only* tolerate coffee.

I fucking missed her. She snuck in the cracks between all the reasons I've sworn I've hated her forever, and *I fucking missed her*.

"You paint this?" I gesture around the room.

She nods, then winces as she leans back in her chair, sunglasses back in place. "I was thirteen the first time Mom remodeled. Now, we freshen it up every three or four years. She'll shut down for a weekend over the winter and Grady and Cooper and Dad stop by and offer exceptionally unhelpful ideas, like *you should put an octopus eating a crab on that wall, Tillie Jean,* but Cooper always gets us take-out for all of our meals, and Grady bakes us cookies, and all three of them move the tables around while we fight over which music to listen to. It's glorious."

"You know how lucky you are to like everyone in your family?"

A smile touches her lips. "I do. But you know, family comes in all flavors. I've never seen the team as tight as you guys seem to have been this year. You're a family all your own."

"Still can't pick them all ourselves though. If only we'd get rid of that Cooper guy. His feet stink."

"That's the lucky socks." She frowns. "What's your lucky charm?"

"Hard work."

"That's it?"

"Can't change luck, but you can change yourself."

"Just when I think you can't possibly get any sexier," she murmurs.

It's not the casual, annoying flirting she used to do. There's too much sincerity in her words, and it makes every spare drop of blood in my body—and some that are definitely not spare—surge to my dick. "So spying on me naked didn't do it, but hearing I work hard did?"

She grins. "It's stair steps. Whatever will you do tomorrow?"

I lean back, put my hands behind my head, and casually flex my triceps. "I'll think of something."

"I am so dead if my brother walks in that door," she whispers.

"Because a friend who saw you needed a helping hand took you for coffee?"

"That is *not* what this is, and you know it."

I do.

But it's nice to hear she agrees.

It's also probably a very good thing I can't see her eyeballs. If I could, they'd probably be very obviously stripping me out of my clothes and humping me against the windows of the sun porch in here.

Much like I'm mentally stripping her and bending her over the counter between the cake plate holding scones and the tip jar. "You know that photo shoot I did yesterday?"

"Yes. You were in the way of the birds I was watching."

I wait for my brain to tell me to shut up.

It doesn't. "They want a longer interview. Want me to talk about playing with anxiety."

Her lips purse for a second before she gulps more coffee. "Do you want to?"

"I don't know."

"Because you'd have to bare your soul, or because you think there are better guys in the league to open up and talk about the stuff that nobody talks about?"

I jerk in my seat and look at her closer.

One corner of her mouth hitches up. "You guys live out of hotels four to six months a year and get asked to do things like star naked in shampoo commercials and strip down for photo shoots on baseball diamonds in January. There's pressure to always get better. You never know when an injury might derail you or when your contract won't get picked up or when you'll hit a rough patch. You're born to win, but you can't win every day. You are *not* the only guy in the league to battle demons, Max. So, do you want to be one more of the few guys talking about it to make other guys feel normal and know it's okay to struggle, or do you want to be the guy waiting for someone else to talk about it to make *you* feel better?"

I reach for my green tea. "Are you sure you're hungover?"

She grimaces, then grabs her head. "Very much so. I've also been around professional athletes for almost a decade, and it drives me freaking *batty* that you men are always like, *I can handle my problems on my own. I don't need to talk to anyone. Grunt. Sniff. Scratch. Grunt.* Oh my god. *Just talk to someone.*"

I shouldn't be smiling, but she's fucking adorable.

And right.

"I do talk to someone."

"High five, studmuffin. You get a gold star."

She holds out a palm, and I hit it with mine. "Thanks."

"So. You gonna do it? Gonna spill your guts in a national magazine to match all those buff pictures of that new tattoo you still haven't told me about?"

"Tillie Jean." Mrs. Rock—the elder Mrs. Rock that all the kids in town call Nana—bursts through the door before I can answer. "Are you grilling that young man on what kind of oil he put on his body to make it all sparkly and defined and pretty yesterday?"

She plops down at our table without an invitation, which is only awkward since it's a two-person table and I don't leap up fast enough to help her drag over the wooden chair, considering if I do, I'll show off a very impressive boner.

Being naked on a baseball field at a high school? Sure.

Flashing the whole town what I'm packing while I'm having coffee with Cooper's little sister?

Make your own luck, and don't sign your own death warrant.

Max Cole's rules of life right there.

"No, Nana," Tillie Jean replies with a smile. "I would *never* talk to Cooper's teammate about his naked body. That's against the rules."

"Psh. Cooper can eat *my* lucky socks. If you can score with a hottie, score with a hottie. You only live once. I wish I'd scored with that curling player when I was seventeen. Who knew I'd never see him again? Not that I'd trade your grandfather for anything, but all of us could use a few more good memories, right?" She turns a frown on me. "You're not the type who thinks you're too good for my granddaughter, are you?"

"No, ma'am. Quite the opposite."

Mrs. Rock leans on the table, peers into Tillie Jean's empty coffee cup, then makes a face. "So. What was it? Coconut oil? Or some kind of magic photographer grease?"

I'm saved from answering by the sound of a coffee machine screaming to life to foam TJ's milk.

She cringes and covers her ears.

I shove a plate of bread toward her. No one blinked when she walked in here with Grady's sourdough under her arm, and she's munching on it still.

Mrs. Rock stares at me expectantly all through the whirring and frothing. I point to my cup and lift my brows at her, a silent *get you something to drink?*, but when the noise stops, she lifts *her* brows. "So? What kind of oil was that?"

"It was sweat, Nana. Pure, testosterone-fueled *sweat*," Tillie Jean replies for me.

"And how do you know, missy?"

"I licked him while I was drunk yesterday."

Fuck me, this boner hurts.

Also, *no she didn't.*

I'd remember that.

Mrs. Rock frowns. "He didn't taste like coconut?"

"No, he tasted like *it's none of our business what he does when he's naked.*"

"I heard he's doing an in-depth interview about the pressure of being a professional athlete."

I jerk in my seat again, but then Tillie Jean's talking.

Again. "I heard he signed a contract to be a backup dancer in the next *Magic Mike* movie."

Nana's eyes narrow. "I heard he's posing for *Playgirl.*"

Tillie Jean leans closer to her grandmother. "I heard he's opening a male strip club."

"I heard he's doing a naked cowboy movie."

My dick has whiplash. Tillie Jean makes up something ridiculous about me being naked, and my hard-on surges. Her grandmother tops her, and my balls shrink into my body.

And this might be the most fun I've had since the after-party when we made it to the play-offs.

"I heard he's starting a commune and only naked people can join," I interject.

"Ooh, can I join?" Mrs. Rock bolts to her feet and rips off her sweater. The barista drops her tray, and Tillie Jean's two lattes crash to the ground, the mugs landing with a shattering smack.

Just as Cooper walks in the door.

"*Aaah,*" he groans, turning around and walking back out.

TJ leaps to her feet, shoving the tablecloth at her grandmother and making everything fall off *our* table in the process too. "*Nana.* Oh my god. I love your bra, but *put your sweater back on.*"

"What? My nips aren't showing."

Good news?

The boner situation is taken care of, so I can get up and help clean up the coffee on the floor.

Bad news?

Pretty sure all of Shipwreck will hear about this before eleven-thirty.

The door cracks open. "Are you seducing my *grandmother*?" Cooper demands without looking inside. "And is she dressed now?"

"She's hot," I call back. "Fight me."

"*Gah.*" He makes a face like he got sweet tea when he wanted tequila, turns, and stomps out again.

"At least you'll inherit all my money when she leaves your grandfather for me and then kills me with sex," I yell after him.

He flips me off through the window.

And I grin.

Fuck, this feels good.

"Max Cole, are you fighting for me?" Tillie Jean whispers as she squats—wincing—to also help pick up the broken pieces of aqua-colored coffee mug.

I meet her eyes.

Well, her sunglasses.

Pretty sure I'm getting the general area for her eyes right. "Work hard. Play hard. Take a chance."

She looks back at the door. Cooper's not there anymore, but I have zero doubt he'll be back.

Can't blame him.

I'm playing with fire here. If I fuck up—even if this is temporary fun and Tillie Jean and I both know it—next year could be ugly.

Or, clearing the air, taking a chance, and working on being a better me—on the inside, not just the outside—might be exactly what the team needs.

"You're a grown-up. I'm a grown-up. We know the score,"

I add when the barista slips out of hearing range again, Nana following on her heels, looking for a muffin.

Tillie Jean doesn't answer.

It's not a no.

It's not a yes either.

"Ball's in your court, Trouble Jean." I rise and stroll to the counter. "Got a mop?" I ask the barista.

"You don't have to—"

"If my options are cleaning the floor while you make Tillie Jean *another* coffee, or making her wait for her caffeine, I'll clean the floor."

Yep.

That'll get back to Cooper too.

Ball's not just in Tillie Jean's court. It's in his too.

Let's see what they both do with it.

TILLIE JEAN

FOR ALL THAT I LOVE MY BROTHER, HE'S ANNOYING THE CRAP
out of me today.

We've been at Mom and Dad's place for two hours, had a
late lunch, played sixteen rounds of Go, Ash, Go, and now
he's demanding a seventeenth round because I'm up six
games to his five. Annika and Dad split the other five rounds
while Mom and Grady sat on the sidelines debating which of
us would get violent first over that stupid Firequacker card.

I hope Cooper dreams in *quack*, since he's the one who
keeps making the rest of us quack through various rounds.

But Meaty?

I'm starting to really like him. All because his cards
always upend the game in the most interesting ways.

"I'm *done*," I repeat to Cooper. "Mom can sit in, but my
head hurts and I'm going home."

"You're going to hang out with Max."

"One, I have no idea where Max even is, and two, *so what
if we hang out?* Do you know what your problem is? You talk

big about team and family, but you also want everyone to follow *your* rules without considering what's good for anyone else. Grady gets to be friends with your teammates. Why shouldn't I?"

"Max isn't the settling down type."

"Maybe *I'm* not the settling down type. Maybe *I* want to travel to thirty cities every year and sleep with a different guy in every one."

He rears back, horrified, while Annika snorts in laughter. "She's got you there, Cooper. Don't have double-standards. Dick move."

He growls and stomps out of the house.

"Maybe don't tell us if you go on a thirty-city dick tour?" Dad says. "I won't tell you how to live your life, but…"

"Jesus." Grady leaps to his feet and leaves too.

Mom clears her throat and goes back to the refrigerator, where she pulls out the leftover cheesecake and dives in without cutting herself a slice. "Mmph?" she asks Annika, holding out the fork.

"No, thank you, Libby." Her eyes are dancing in amusement. "I think you need it more than I do."

The dishes are done. Food's put away. Except for Mom's half of a cheesecake, of course.

I could stay and play Mom and Dad in Scrabble or Clue or Yahtzee, but instead, I reach for my coat on the back of my chair too. "I'm in the middle of painting something, so…"

"Sure," Dad says quickly.

Mom mumbles something around her cheesecake again.

"Oh my god, I'm serious. I'm going home *to paint*. And I don't want the trouble of finding worthy dick in thirty different cities, okay? It's hard enough to find it in *one*. Mom, I'll see you at aerobics tomorrow morning. Dad, I'll see you after. Annika—"

"I'll walk with you." She hugs my parents. "Thank you for lunch and the entertainment."

"Be honest," I say when the two of us slip out the front door. "Am I being ridiculous, or are they?"

She glances at her phone, which I'm nearly certain has a text from Grady saying he's chasing after Cooper to commiserate about the fact that their baby sister has a sex life. "Oh, they are. Completely. But if you *are* planning on sleeping with Max—"

"Team dynamics, blah blah blah," I mutter.

"Actually, I was going to say, my phone's always open if you need to talk or if you need someone to run interference with Cooper. Grady and I are both in. I'd offer my door being open, but—"

"But you're still a honeymooner and I wouldn't touch that offer with a ten-foot pole."

She laughs.

And I smile.

But only for a minute. "It would be a short-term fling," I say quietly. "He has his own issues, but he's hot, and he's next door, and he's leaving in another month. You can put an end date on a fling, right? That's a thing?"

Yes, I *am* asking as someone who's only had one serious relationship in her life.

"Some people can. Some people can't. Only way to know if you're one of them is to try."

"What if I really do fuck up his game?" I whisper.

"Then that's on him," she replies firmly. "You can't manage other people's feelings and you can't be responsible for them lying to themselves. You *can* be responsible for being upfront and honest with him about expecting things to end when he leaves for spring training, and you'll probably want to consider how much you want to stay involved with the Lady Fireballs if it's awkward afterwards, but he has to decide for himself if you're worth the risk to his game."

I'm twenty-six.

I love my life, even on days when I fight with my brothers and have the hangover from hell.

But I also know sometimes you have to leap. You have to pay attention to the signs.

Even if you leap wrong, you learn something from it.

And I don't want to leap with a one-night thing in the city with a guy I found on a hook-up app.

I want to see where things go with Max.

I think I've wanted to see where things could go with Max since the minute he showed up at the ballpark after I chased him out of Chance Schwartz's apartment.

There's always been something about him that screams *I'm a good time, but I'm more if you can get past my barriers.*

And I very, *very* much want to get past his barriers.

Not to win. Not because it's a contest.

More because over the past four years, he's snuck past mine.

He doesn't know it.

But he has.

Sometime during that season when we met, I wrinkled my nose in passing when someone suggested Thai food for dinner before a club after a game, and Max gave me this *look*—no, this *sneer*, the one that said, *whatever, small-town princess,* and I've been on a mission to try new foods ever since in a way I'd never considered before.

When the team had their parents' weekends last year and Henri went out of her way to find Max's old T-ball coach, I tracked her down and asked her what she knew.

He told me he started arranging his own rides to baseball practice after his first coach realized he wouldn't show up without help and picked him up the first two years he played ball.

She'd added he also said if she told anyone he'd kill her in her sleep, which she didn't believe. Henri is the best kind of optimist.

But it was one more little poke.

Your parents made sure you wanted for nothing important, Tillie Jean. Get out there and help some other kids.

So now we have D&D afternoon at the restaurant for a bunch of kids who'd otherwise go home to empty houses, and I organized a sign-up to match retirees with kids whose families need a little extra help so they can get to extracurricular stuff like ball games and play practice and dance lessons.

I joined the Lady Fireballs because of him.

I volunteered to run senior aerobics because of him.

I tried sushi for the first time because of him.

Just the *idea* of Max has been pushing me to do better, without me actively acknowledging that's what he was doing to me.

What happens if I let him in all the way?

What happens if I *embrace* all the little ways he steers me on a path to expand my horizon and look beyond my own little world?

His SUV is in his driveway when we hit my street, but I don't go straight to his house.

Instead, I do something I've been dying to do since the last time I saw Henri.

I draw a bath and drop in one of the bath bombs she brought me. Luca stars in all the commercials for Kangapoo, and they apparently send him product samples all the time.

And after a citation, a hangover, a date with Max—*oh my god*, a date with Max, where we talked about *real* things and he flirted with me *and* my grandmother—and then Cooper turning into *Cooper*, I want some me time.

But not five minutes after I crack my bathroom window for steam control and climb into the tub, someone's knocking on my door.

I roll my eyes, reach for my phone, and text my brother.

I'm in the bath.

He replies with a side eye emoji.

Fine, I type back. *Come on in and see for yourself.*

There's a muffled click beyond my bathroom, and then I hear *two* voices.

"You're on your own if you walk back to her bedroom," Grady says.

"Chicken," Cooper shoots back.

"*Whoa.* Tillie Jean. Holy shit, your kitchen cabinets are awesome. When did you do that?"

Grady's still yelling from the front of my house. Good thing it's small. "Six months ago," I yell back. "Maybe you should come visit more often."

"I don't visit single people. They might be naked."

"You can always call first."

"Then I *know* you'll be naked. *Shudder.*"

"Did you *seriously* just say *shudder* out loud?"

"Trying to stay hip for when I'm a dad."

I laugh out loud, but the distinctive creak of my bedroom floor makes me shut up and rip the shower curtain mostly closed around my tub. "Are you *seriously* coming in here to make sure I'm alone?" I ask, and no, I'm not talking to Grady anymore.

"Yes," Cooper replies.

"Get ready for an eyeful. Arlo, Sven, and Ricky are in here with me."

His face appears in the doorway, eyes mostly elevated, like he's hoping his peripheral vision will pick up wherever anyone else might be hiding in my little bathroom. I can just see him through the crack between the curtain and the shower wall.

"I'm not trying to be a dick," he says gruffly. "But there are things—"

"Did I say a single word when you hooked up with our night manager two winters ago?"

"I didn't know she was the night manager."

"But *she* did. And you *should've.*"

"I wasn't a dick to her. It ended...very nicely."

"Cooper, *you* might think it ended nicely, but that does *not* mean it wasn't awkward as hell and *not nice* for everyone else."

"You flirting with Max is—"

"If you say completely different, I fully support her climbing out of that tub and naked wrestling you into her dirty bathwater for a swirly," Grady interrupts. I can't see him, but he's closer than he was before. He whistles softly. "Jesus, TJ. How long has your bedroom looked like this?"

"*Quit talking about her bedroom,*" Cooper snaps.

Grady ignores him. "If this Crusty Nut thing doesn't work out, you could be an interior designer for the young and horny."

"You are *not* seriously getting turned on by *Tillie Jean's* bedroom."

"Nah, man, I'm not young anymore. Horny, sure. But not young."

"Love you, Grady," I call. "Favorite brother. You get the trophy."

"Hot damn. I never win trophies over Cooper. And to think—all it took was a few kind words and minding my own business."

"Would you two *knock it off?*" Cooper snorts, which is both amusing and a big warning sign.

He doesn't do mad well.

Not a lot of practice.

I peek out from behind the shower curtain, and *uh-oh.*

That's the same face he wore when he got sent home early from summer baseball camp for raiding the kitchen for a late-night party to celebrate one of the kids who got his first home run *ever* despite not usually connecting with the ball at all.

His heart was in the right place, and he got punished for it.

"You're going to have to spell this out for me *very clearly,*"

I tell him. "What's your issue with me being friends with Max?"

He grunts, which is also un-Cooper-like.

He only grunts when he can't fix something and he knows he's being an idiot.

At least, that's how I see it.

"You hear about the three dozen women Max has loved and left since he got here in November?" Grady says conversationally.

I almost bolt out of the tub, except *no*. I haven't.

And that's the point.

I could wait until two in the morning to sneak over to Max's house, climb in the window, and seduce the hell out of him, and I'd get away with it for one night.

Maybe even a full week.

But absolutely no more than that.

This is Shipwreck, and *someone* will catch us.

Probably.

I *also* know Shipwreck.

I could finagle this. I could make it work and keep it a secret.

But Max seeing someone on his own?

Nope. We'd all know.

"He's not fucking around with anyone," Cooper mutters.

And I believe him. We would've heard about it if he was.

At least, all except those three weeks he was gone.

And if he slept with someone while he was on the beach?

It's not like we were in any kind of committed relationship. That's his right.

Except I don't think he did.

He didn't come back acting like a guy who spent three weeks hooking up with women. He came back acting like a guy who'd had a lot of time for self-reflection and made a big decision.

"Huh." I don't have to see Grady to know he's rubbing his

chin like he's pondering the magnitude of that statement, and also because he knows rubbing his chin like he's pondering something will piss off Cooper. "Don't you all fuck around basically every road trip and home series? Like you can't play if your dick doesn't get some action or something?"

"It's the off-season."

"All that free time. Playtime. Have women in from the city time with all that privacy you have up on the mountain... Or is it like, you have to be celibate in the off-season? Do you like, masturbate more to gear up for making it through sex-with-strangers season too?"

I snicker, then clap a hand over my mouth and hide behind the shower curtain when Cooper shifts a glare at me.

"No," he snaps. "We don't *train our dicks* for sex with groupies all season. *Jesus.* Why are we discussing this?"

"Because you're being an overprotective wanker?" I offer.

"Wanker," Grady says on a snort. "Nice one, TJ. Fist bump."

"Fist bump," I call back.

Cooper growls again. "You know what? *Fine.* Go fucking sleep with Max. But I swear to the baseball gods, Tillie Jean, if you fuck up his game by fucking with his head or promising him things you can't deliver, *you* will be at *every single fucking game* sacrificing live chickens and making out with the damn meatball and doing *whatever the fuck it takes* to get his head back on. *Got it?*"

I peek out from behind the curtain one more time. "You know I wouldn't ever do anything to hurt your team, right?"

"Sure. Right. Whatever."

"Cooper. You've wanted to win a World Series with the Fireballs since before I was born. You get ten, maybe fifteen chances—"

"*Twenty,*" he growls.

"Fine. You get *twenty* chances at that, and you're through like seven or eight of them already, and it's only going to get harder. It's easy to suck but it's hard to win and now you're the team to beat. *I respect that.* I'm not going to do anything to fuck up your chances. I want you to win. I want your dreams to come true. Could you maybe find a way to freaking *trust me* here? And maybe have some respect for your teammate at the same time?"

He stares at me.

I stare back.

I'm not compromising on this one. If he doesn't know I support his dreams, he needs to. And if he can't respect his teammates' abilities to leave their private lives off the field, he needs to do that too.

Even with Max.

Especially with Max.

A guy who grew up figuring out how to get himself to baseball practice on his own before he was out of grade school—a guy who grew up to *be a pitcher* while getting himself to practice on his own—isn't the kind of guy who'll throw away winning or his career for a woman.

"He's a fucking professional, Cooper. He could have a foursome with me, Georgia, and Sloane, and you could quit talking to him entirely because you had your panties in a twist over the other adults in your life being consenting adults, he'd still strike out more batters than he lets on base next year, and *you know it.*"

Cooper shoves away from the doorway, retreating into my bedroom with a muttered, *"Fine."*

"Not just *fine,*" I call after him. *"Good.* Trust is *good,* Cooper. And you know you can trust us."

I don't have to see him to know he's twitching at my use of *us* instead of *me.*

Maybe I should be twitching at it myself.

Except it feels right to be in this *together* with Max.

Not that he has any clue we're in anything together beyond a coffee date this morning that had more than a few smoldering looks from him making me feel completely naked.

Okay.

Yeah.

He probably knows we're in this together.

If coffee meant he's willing to risk pissing off Cooper to have a little off-season fling with me.

And I should probably examine what it means that I feel like I'm lying to myself about something here, but I don't want to.

Cooper suddenly sucks in a breath and charges back into the bathroom. "*Fuck*," he gasps.

"*What?*" I gape at him.

"*You're pranking me.*"

I freeze.

I'm not, but if he'll *lay off*, I would absolutely let him think this is another phase in our winter prank war.

In fact, that's a *brilliant* idea.

Let him think it's a prank until either I can prove to him that this was a good idea, or until it's over and Max and I go our separate ways.

I don't even know if it's a good idea yet. But I know that if Cooper gets it in his head to interfere, even *after* our talk here, that everything with Max will be over regardless of what it could've been otherwise.

I smile at my brother. Surefire way to make him believe he has nothing to worry about. "Am I?"

"And we're done here." Grady appears in the doorway long enough to grab Cooper by the arm and haul him away. "Enjoy your bath, Tillie Jean."

"Thank you, favorite brother," I call back.

Yes, fine, I shouldn't bait Cooper even more right now.

But he'll snap out of it.

Max and I will do whatever it is we do.

The Fireballs will rock this season.

Cooper won't freak out about Max and me, which would make Max freak out too.

And everything will be fine.

The door clicks shut again. I drift lower in the tub. Think about Max.

Think about Max sitting on my bedroom floor asking me to coffee.

Think about Max adjusting himself at Muted Parrot when he thought I wasn't noticing what was happening south of the belt.

And then I decide I might've had enough of bath time, except I still need to sit in this water for *at least* thirty more minutes to make sure Cooper's not coming right back.

Okay.

Plotting time.

I'm distracting myself from thinking about Max naked by plotting more pranks on Cooper.

Or trying to, at least, when a knock at my bathroom window startles me.

I shriek, slip, and grab the sides of the tub. "*Hello?*"

And then a sexy, smooth, rich-as-chocolate voice sneaks into the room. "Room in there for one more?"

27

Max

I AM THE WORST KIND OF PERV.

But in my defense, I've resisted wanting to have sex with Tillie Jean for years. So I'm a perv with self-control.

Until now.

Now, I'm a perv who's run out of self-control and who just listened in while she told her brother to *trust us*.

Pretty sure that wasn't just to piss him off either, no matter how he interpreted it.

"There is *no way* you'll fit in this tub," Tillie Jean whispers. She's peering at me from her bathtub, her skin wet, her breasts hanging heavy and disappearing behind the side of the tub before I can see those gorgeous nipples again, her eyes dark and intrigued and hungry like she's trying to imagine me naked. "Or through that window. The back door's unlocked. I'll meet you—"

"Stay."

She starts to grin, and oh, *fuck me*, is that a promising grin. "I'm not getting dressed if that's what you're afraid of."

"You use a bath bomb?" The wrapper's still on her sink.

"Max Cole, are you addicted to Kangapoo bath bombs too?" When she drops her voice low and throaty like that, it doesn't matter what she says. My brain short-circuits and I want her.

I want her.

But I need to focus. *Focus, Cole. Focus.*

Bath bombs. We're talking about bath bombs. "No, I hate those things. They have glitter in the middle. *Shudder.*"

She squeaks, looks down, and then her gaze flies to me again.

I grin.

Yeah, I'm quoting her brother, so she should figure out pretty quick I listened in on *everything*. Also, if that bath bomb had glitter in it, she'd be all sparkly now, and she's not.

God, she's sexy.

"You are seriously hot when you tease me." She crooks a finger and makes me wish I could fit through this tiny window over her toilet, and she sits straighter in the tub, but not straight enough for me to see her nipples. "Back door. Quick. Someone's probably already spotted you, so flip the lock and shove a chair under it before Grady sends his goat over just for fun."

"Stay," I tell her again.

She slides a hand down her breast and smiles at me. "Like this?"

And if I don't get in her house *right now*, the neighbors calling Cousin Chester to report a peeper will be reporting an engorged pecker too.

It takes me longer than it should to reach her bathroom, but I'm making sure no one gets in through *any* doors. Human, goat, or bird.

I'm also kicking off my shoes and dancing out of my socks as I go so that when I hit her bedroom, all I have left are my T-shirt and jeans and underwear.

The shirt's gone before I skid to the corner to get into her private bath, where she's pulled the shower curtain back and is positioned perfectly in the tub to demonstrate exactly how naked she is while still hiding her nipples and her pussy from view.

"Who's the tease now?" I murmur as my cock surges.

Need to get out of these pants.

Need to get out of them *now*.

She crooks a finger again, and I am powerless to resist.

I trip over to the tub, fumbling with my button as I drop to the floor next to her. "You told Cooper to mind his own business and trust *us*."

"I did." She leans in and bites my lip, and *fuck* again. Why am I still wearing jeans? "I don't think it totally worked, but I don't care. Did it turn you on?"

"You turn me on."

"We need rules, Max." Her wet hand slides over my chest. "I don't want to break your game."

"Rule number one: I won't let you break my game. Happy?"

She laughs, and *fuck*, how did I ever think I hated that laugh?

"I don't think it's that simple, Mr. Growly Bear."

"It's okay for you to be wrong on this one, Trouble Jean." I don't know what she put in that bathwater, but it smells like heaven in here.

Or maybe that's her.

I lean over and press a kiss to her jaw, loving the way her breath hitches, and also the view I get of that deep rosy nipple. "You said I'd strike out batters even if I fucked up with you and your two best girlfriends."

"You will. You'd probably even hit a home run if you wanted to."

I shove my pants down, belatedly remember I have a strip of condoms in my back pocket, retrieve them, and shuck the pants again. "Move over. I'm climbing into this tub and fucking your brains out."

Her hungry eyes rake over my raging cock, and she reaches for it like it's instinct, stroking me and squeezing and licking her lips. "Oh my god, you're—wait. Rules."

She drops my hard-on, which isn't a strong enough word for what I'm sporting.

I whimper.

She starts to reach for my dick again, but grabs the side of the tub instead and leans into my face. "My life's here, Max. When you leave for spring training, that's it. Which is all the more reason to not tell Cooper. Just in case. Because I plan for us to stay friends, but if we can't..."

"Mm-hmm." *Touch my cock. Let me in the bathtub. Ride me like you'll never get dick again after I leave tonight.*

She grips my cheeks instead of my furious boner. "And there's no acting weird because we've seen each other naked."

"Everyone's seen me naked."

"Oh, god, that should *not* turn me on like it does." Her cheeks are flushed and her chest is rising and falling rapidly, and I don't know how she's staying in that tub if she's half as turned on as I am right now.

She believes in me. "I've been hard as a rock since—"

Her fingers land on my lips. "Steel. Don't use rock."

That shouldn't be funny, but it is.

And *fuck.*

I feel light as a damn feather. Not my cock, but my body. My spirit.

My damn *soul.* "I've been hard as steel since I walked in your front door this morning."

Her finger trails down my chin, my neck, leaving a cool, wet path in its wake. "Whatever am I going to do about that?"

"Fuck first. Talk later." I kick the rest of the way out of my jeans and swing a leg over into the tub.

Water sloshes everywhere, but *yes*.

Yes.

Naked Tillie Jean. Her breasts. Her belly. Her legs.

That sweet, sweet pussy that I would drown to devour right now.

"*Oh my god*, Max, we don't fit," she gasps on a laugh.

"Want. You. Now."

"Okay, Growly Bear." She pushes my chest to reverse my direction, and it doesn't matter that she uses no more force than a snowflake would.

I'd let her do whatever she wants.

Except when I resist to capture her mouth, she doesn't resist.

She surrenders.

I surrender.

God, her mouth. Her tongue. She's my one salted caramel hot chocolate of the year. A cinnamon vanilla latte made with real cream. Bacon dipped in Nutella.

And those noises coming from the back of her throat— those desperate, needy whimpers and aroused moans that get deeper and faster when she tugs me to my feet, pulling me into the tub with her, the warm water coming up to my calves while I push her against the shower wall.

"Don't slip," she gasps.

"I got you." I fumble one hand to the faucet and crank the bathwater on. Her skin's pebbling in the cool air.

And then I'm kissing her again, stroking up her thighs, over her belly and breasts, back down again while she hooks one leg behind my hips.

"Protection," she gasps.

I could tell her I'm clean—and I am—but the subtle reminder that I do this *all the fucking time* makes me wince.

Why?

Why do I do this all the fucking time when it doesn't mean anything?

She ducks out of my reach, grabs the strip of condoms on the edge of the tub, and flips the knob to switch the water flow to the showerhead.

Scalding water flies out on us, but then she's kissing me again, reaching between us, rolling a condom over my length, and *fuck me*, if all she ever did was stroke my cock, I'd die a happy man.

"I should take you to a bed," I try to say against her lips as I stroke between her legs, completely helpless to keep my hands to myself when it comes to her body.

"You should fuck me hard against this wall." She tilts her pelvis into my hand, and her eyes roll back in her head. "Oh, god, Max, more. Right there. *Right. There.*"

Is this why I've resisted?

Because I didn't want to know she was uninhibited and hungry and liked sex?

Does it matter?

She grips my ass and squeezes while she wraps her other leg around my hips again, riding my hand while I stroke her pussy and slip two fingers up inside her, and nothing else matters.

Just this.

Tillie Jean.

Hot water.

Hot pussy.

Hot kisses.

Desperate noises.

Eager body.

And then she's coming all over my hand, squeezing my fingers with her inner walls, head back, lids heavy, one lip caught in her teeth, her body flushed, her nipples so pert and tight and gorgeous. "Fuck, Max," she gasps.

More.

I want more Tillie Jean. I want *all* of Tillie Jean.

I pull my hand away, reposition her, and I thrust into her tight pussy.

"*Oh my god.*"

"Want. You. So bad," I grunt.

I know I should slow down. Take it easy. Make this last.

But she fists my hair, pulling my face back to hers, and thrusts her tongue into my mouth while her hips buck against mine.

She's so tight. So wet.

So mine.

I pump in and out, and she squeezes me harder with those glorious thighs, riding me, meeting me halfway, even pressed against a wall, and *holy fuck.*

Holy fuck and a half.

She's coming again, a groan ripping out of her throat while she fucks my mouth with her tongue, or maybe she never stopped coming, but she's squeezing my cock with her pussy and *fuck fuck fuuuuuck.*

Tillie Jean Rock's pussy is a drug, and I'm high on it.

No control.

No smooth moves.

Just my hips jerking erratically as I come so hard my vision blurs and lightning streaks through my chest and my head floats away off my neck. "Oh, *fuck*, no," I groan while I shoot my load.

"Oh, god, oh, god, *yes*," she gasps in my mouth. "Yes. No? Yes?"

Her pelvis grinds hard against mine, holding me inside her while she squeezes and pumps me with her inner muscles, her thighs a steel vise locked around my hips, my orgasm ripping through me like I'll never have another in my life.

"Want—to last," I grunt.

"Oh my god, I see stars."

"More, TJ. *More*."

"Growly Bear. Magic Max. *Oh my god*."

I don't want this to end.

I want to die still having this orgasm fifty years from now, with scalding water pounding down on me and Tillie Jean's pussy coaxing my dick and my feet buried in lukewarm water and a slight chilly breeze drifting in to cut through the steam.

"*Max*," she sighs as her body sags and she suddenly becomes dead weight.

"*Fuck*," I mutter again.

My own body's about to give up the ghost.

I'm wound so tight but utterly relaxed and free and *shit shit shit*.

Don't drop the girl.

Don't drop Tillie Jean.

I turn, and somehow I manage to sit, right there in the cooling bathwater, the hot water still pouring down on us, TJ's hair wet and plastered to her face, her legs splaying oddly because this bathtub is fucking small and suddenly my dick's flopping out of her as we try to fit in a space built for a parakeet.

But she doesn't seem to mind.

Not if the way she's collapsing onto my chest is any indication, taking the brunt of the hot water on her back. "Oh my god," she whispers.

I kiss her temple, and that's when I feel it.

Peace.

I'm squished into a bathtub with Tillie Jean splayed across me, one of her knees pressing down on my thigh since there's not enough room for us in here, her other leg twisted in a way that can't possibly be comfortable, one arm around my back, making me arch funny so I don't squish it, and I'm completely one hundred percent at peace.

No counting.

No worries.

No need to move.

Baseball doesn't exist. People don't exist. Stress doesn't exist.

I can breathe.

Tillie Jean settles a hand on my chest. "Have you ever had cinnamon oranges?"

I shake my head.

"When we can move again, I'll make you some."

Home, a little voice whispers deep inside my chest.

I don't fight it.

Not now.

Maybe later.

But not right now.

28

TILLIE JEAN

IT'S THREE AM, AND I HAVE TO BE AT THE SENIOR CENTER FOR aerobics in five hours, but all I want to do is lie here and watch Max sleep.

Unfortunately, that's not going to work.

I poke him gently. "Max. Wake up."

He groans. "I want to, Tillie Jean, but you broke my dick. Five more minutes, okay?"

It was *not* like this the last time I hooked up with a guy. He got his, I got mine, everything about the situation felt weird, and we went our separate ways afterward.

It's not that there's anything wrong with casual sex.

It's more that I haven't figured out how to make it work for me.

But Max has been here since my bath, and he's demonstrated exactly how strong and flexible professional baseball pitchers can be at least three times since, to the benefit of my lady parts every time, and I don't want him to go.

It's in both our best interests if he does, though. "I know.

You broke my vagina too. You need to go home before it's too late."

One brown eye slides open in the dim light. "Can't. Legs go poof."

If he gets any more adorable, my ovaries might *go poof*. "Max. C'mon. Aunt Bea's up at like, four in the morning half the time, and if she sees you leaving my house, she'll tell Cooper, and I know my brother. He needs to come to grips with this on his own time."

He grunts like he knows I'm right.

I grunt back.

And then I giggle, and I grunt again. "This is fun. I should grunt more often."

His lips twitch.

That's all it takes.

One little lip twitch of unabashed amusement at me being a dork face, and everything inside me puddles like candle wax under a flame.

I have it so bad.

And maybe that's why I resisted him for so long. Because I knew this would happen.

I knew I would fall for Max Cole. It's like every time I've tried to annoy him for the past four years, I've been quietly whispering *see me. See me for who I am and like me.*

But is falling for him really a bad thing?

Considering he lives in the city and you live here…

Stupid voice.

What does it know?

"Max." I skim my fingers over his shoulder, pretending my only goal is waking him up and not also shamelessly enjoying touching all that hot flesh over firm muscle. "For real. You need to go."

He grunts again, but he follows it with a big, loud, noisy inhale through his nose that reminds me of my dad waking himself—and half the house—with a snore in the middle of the night in my teenage years before he got his C-PAP machine. "Okay. I'm going."

He doesn't.

Instead, he flings an arm across my midsection and settles his head into the crook of my neck.

For a guy who's always aloof and also too hot, the man likes to snuggle.

One more little facet to him that I wouldn't have guessed but that I am completely smitten with.

"Max," I whisper.

"Shh," he whispers back.

He opens his mouth like he's going to say something, but then he doesn't.

"Are you pretending you're going to answer me so that I quit talking?"

"Mm-hmm."

"You realize I know your tickle spot too?"

His body tenses.

And I suddenly feel like an ass. "Not that I'm going to use it," I add quickly. "But I can't flip a switch and not be myself just because you took me to the top of Mount Max a few dozen times."

"You're going to talk to me until I leave, aren't you?"

"I haven't spent four years annoying you without getting very, very good at it."

He goes still again.

And suddenly I fear I've misread everything, or maybe I assumed too much, or maybe he was just humoring me tonight because he really is a sex god and his pride wouldn't let him not leave me satisfied, or maybe this is why I don't do relationships.

Because I freak men out, or I really am *that* annoying. "Oh. This was that *one time only* thing, wasn't it?" I whisper.

Shit.

Shit shit shit.

Okay.

This is fine. This is okay. This is not the end of the world, and I have a lot of great memories, and—

"No," he says into the darkness, the word sounding almost pained.

"Max. *Oh my god*. You do *not* have to worry about protecting my feelings or anything if you don't want to do this friends-with-benefits things, and—"

"Trouble Jean, would you please give a guy a minute to figure out how to say something he's never said to a woman before?"

I open my mouth to agree, then clamp it shut and nod instead.

My pulse is off like a horse out of the gate at the Kentucky Derby, and given where his hand is resting, he can probably feel it, but I can't squirm away without making it even more obvious that I'm not the cool cucumber I usually am.

Or try to be.

He sighs and turns his head into my shoulder, and I do my best to keep all of my cringing inside.

"I don't want to leave," he mumbles.

"*Oh.*" My racing heart is suddenly swelling thick and warm. "I—oh."

"But if you want me to—"

"No! No, I don't *want* you to go. I just think it'll be easier for everyone else who thinks we're his business if he doesn't have to stress about this too. And by *everyone*—"

"I know who you mean." He presses his lips to my shoulder. My hand shakes like I've had three too many lattes as I stroke his hair.

"I'm not good at this," he says quietly. "I don't know *how*. And I—I'm a little fucked up in a lot of ways."

"Do you eat babies for breakfast?"

"*Tillie Jean.*"

"Life doesn't come with a rule book. The only *this* in my

world is do your best, don't hurt people on purpose, and find what makes you happy." I frown. "Do I make you happy?"

He doesn't answer right away, but I'm realizing it's not that he's hiding some terrible truth.

It's that he needs to think it through.

Find the right words.

And really, it's not terrible to snuggle in bed with Max Cole while he's thinking.

"I've spent four years actively fighting being attracted to you," he finally says.

"I have no idea what that's like."

He lifts his head, and I swear he's giving me a growly bear glare, which makes me crack up even more than the easy sarcasm that just rolled off my tongue.

And then my face is being smothered with a pillow, which makes me laugh harder.

"See, this is *exactly* what I'm talking about." He's not sleepy and snuggly anymore.

Nope.

He's straddling my legs and holding a pillow over my face.

"Uncle," I call as I move my hands to his knees.

Totally his tickle spot.

I'm not tickling him, for the record.

But we both know I can.

The pillow disappears, and then Max is right there, nose to nose with me. "I used to hate the way you never took anything seriously."

"*Used* to?"

"I didn't hate that you never took anything seriously though. I hated that you had that luxury and I didn't."

If Cooper said that to me, I'd point out that he's a multi-millionaire athlete who's never had to play for a winning team to live a very comfortable life.

But Max didn't have the family and community that Cooper has.

I get it.

"I tried Thai food for the first time because of you," I tell him.

I swear he grins, but he's settling in next to me again, his head resting in the crook of my neck, his lips moving just right against my skin so I can't tell if he's trying to kiss me or just tease me. "I have no idea what you're talking about."

"Oh my god, you *do*."

"Reason number four hundred twenty-six that I hated Tillie Jean Rock—she acted worldly and sophisticated but had never tried Thai food until I mocked her for never having tried Thai food."

"You have a *list of reasons you hate me*?"

"A guy's gotta do something with all that pent-up energy."

"Most guys would've just rubbed it out."

"Doesn't always work like it's supposed to."

I squirm out from under him and roll to face him. "Just how many reasons did you have to hate me?"

"As many as I needed."

"Tell me more."

"*Why I hate you* is not first date material."

"*We* aren't first date material. Why else? What else is on your list?"

"And look at that. Aunt Bea's gonna be up any minute now. I better get going."

"*Max.*"

He kisses my forehead, then pushes himself up to sit at the edge of the bed. "Tell me you don't have a list of *ten thousand things I hate about Max Cole*."

"Not really." I push myself up too, watching while he leans over and snags his clothes off the floor. "It mostly all boiled down to you being easy to annoy after all the stuff with *you know who*, and then it became habit."

On goes his shirt.

Dammit.

"You brought the whole team low-sugar cranberry almond cookies the second time I saw you. And then you planted singing *things* in Cooper's locker, and it was easier to say you were distracting us with cookies for your true nefarious plans than it was to acknowledge that he probably deserved it, and that everyone else on the team respected the hell out of you for pulling it off, and also that it was really nice of you to bring sweets that fit into our normal diets."

"You know it's hot when you use big words like *nefarious*?"

He sends me a look over his shoulder.

Definitely growly bear.

So I climb to my knees and crawl across the bed and loop my arms around him from behind, pressing a kiss to his neck. "We're all a little complicated."

"You cried when Joey Ortiz got traded."

"His wife was even sweeter than Henri, which shouldn't be possible, but I swear it's true, and I got to babysit their oldest when the youngest was born. We still text from time to time."

"You *got to babysit*. I would never count that as a bonus, but you do." He leans back against me. "I'm tired of telling myself that you can do stuff like that because you're spoiled, when the truth is, I've spent four years afraid if I let you in, I'd find out I don't deserve all the things you do for your friends." He grunts. "And your brother really is one of the best friends I've ever had, even if he wouldn't say the same about me. You're right. He really wouldn't want to know what we did here tonight. Don't blame him either."

"You know that you don't have to grow up with a good family to understand what makes a family, right?"

"I know how to play baseball and be on a team. Everything else—no. I really don't. But I want to." He sighs. "Sorry. I get too honest when I haven't had enough sleep."

"Honest is good. Honest is *always* good."

He's quiet again.

I like quiet Max. And naked Max. And growly Max.

Basically, all of the Maxes. I like them all.

"You free after ten tonight?" he asks.

"Max Cole, are you asking me over for a booty call?"

"Yep."

"I think I can clear my schedule."

He shifts to turn and kiss me—soft, thorough, and handsy —and then he's gone, slipping through my house and out the back door, back to his own place, where we'll pretend all day long that last night didn't happen.

Until we can do it again.

And that nagging little voice at the back of my head, telling me I'm playing with fire by risking interfering with the Fireballs' team dynamics—that little voice is wrong.

Everything will be *just fine*.

And that's the lie that helps me fall back asleep before I need to be up in a few hours for senior aerobics.

29

Max

I ALWAYS THOUGHT SEX WITH THE SAME WOMAN NIGHT AFTER night would get boring.

That it would get old.

But a few weeks into this thing with Tillie Jean, the only thing getting old is sneaking around. The grumpiness that used to come easily around her takes effort. I don't *want* to be grumpy.

I want to be the guy who keeps smiling after I leave my house in the morning. I want to be the guy who laughs when she cracks a good joke on the days when I have lunch at Crusty Nut with the guys. I want to say yes to heading up to Cooper's place for game night when I know she'll be there.

I want to hold her hand in public.

I want to sneak behind the bar at Crusty Nut and replace the latte in her coffee mug with doctored lemongrass tea to get her back for slipping me flat Diet Coke instead of unsweet tea three days ago.

But mostly, I want to have the courage to ask her why this

has to end when I get on a plane bound for Florida and spring training in mid-February.

Instead, I spend one January weekend in the tropics at Torres's wedding, as planned, with most of the team but *without* Tillie Jean, since her parents are on their annual getaway and she's running Crusty Nut solo, and get back to Shipwreck to a massive snowfall that requires extra planning so I don't leave footprints between my house and her house, which means it's three more nights before I can sneak in her window again.

Neither of us gets any sleep for the next two nights after that.

I've never laughed so much with a woman I'm sleeping with.

I've also never talked so much with a woman I'm sleeping with.

Not about real things.

And every night with Tillie Jean is one more night that makes me feel like maybe—just maybe—I can have more in this lifetime than I ever trusted myself with before.

At the end of January, I head back into Copper Valley for Fireballs Con, a Thursday through Saturday event that management puts on for the fans. Last year, they unveiled the mascot finalists during Fireballs Con.

This year, there aren't any big surprises.

Just fun.

The kind of fun that comes without Tillie Jean again, since we're still ducking Cooper's suspicions and there's no way that I can be in the same city as her without wanting her in my bed when she'd usually stay with her brother.

This fun?

It's a normal kind of fun.

An *old* normal kind of fun.

A *real* normal kind of fun.

My teammates and I sit on panels answering fan questions

and showing our egos when people ask if we're going all the way this season.

We have a dance contest.

We karaoke with fans.

We play trivia.

And I'm weirdly back in my element and completely out of it all at the same time. My condo is exactly how I left it, but I'm not exactly how I left me.

So when I catch myself pacing and counting by fours while checking my phone for texts from TJ every three seconds Friday night, I head out.

Not to catch up with the single guys at a club, but instead, to drop by unannounced on a teammate in what could be a very bad decision.

The little house Luca's renovating is in a solidly middle-class neighborhood, and the lights are still on when I pull up to his curb. I could've called, but I wasn't sure I was planning on stopping until I got here.

Now that I *am* here, I pull out my phone and check it for messages from Tillie Jean again.

You know.

In case my top-of-the-line Bluetooth-enabled stereo system failed to notify me that I had a text from her.

But, there's nothing under the contact labeled *Jenny Smith*.

It's her code name in my phone.

I'm Bob the Backup Plumber in her phone.

And yeah, that was my idea.

I'm still in my SUV, debating if I want to text her and what I want to say—I know she's having a girls' night with Sloane and Georgia and Annika, so I really don't expect her to text me back at all tonight—when movement in my peripheral vision makes me lift my head and look at Luca's house.

Henri's leaning out the front door, squinting at me, her hair tucked back under a bandana and her body wrapped up in sweatpants and a hoodie, which might be her normal work clothes, or it could be her pajamas.

Not much difference with Henri, and yeah, she'll show up at parties dressed like that too.

Talk about owning who you are.

I roll down the passenger window and flip on my interior lights. "Hey, Henri."

"Max? I thought that was you. What are you doing? Wanna come in? We're watching this show that Tillie Jean's friend Sloane told us about. Again. Not that I'm obsessed with it or anything, but I'm kinda obsessed with it. We can start over from the beginning. Luca won't mind."

"Luca will too mind," Luca calls from inside.

"Hush. No, you won't. The first scene will start, and you'll get giddy with excitement at getting to experience it all over again, then you'll tell Max all about how when you retire, you want to go coach a British football team too, since he's a new audience for watching you watch *Ted Lasso* and hasn't heard it a dozen times already." She turns her smile back at me. "I have popcorn."

"So long as you have popcorn," I call back.

I roll the window back up, shut my car off, climb out, and head inside, glancing at the freshly painted walls and the new furniture and pristine wood floor. There's a shelf showcasing all of the books Henri's written as Nora Dawn, plants in the corner, and the massive TV on the wall by the stairs is paused on a scene of a dude with a mustache grinning a goofy grin.

Luca holds out a fist.

I bump. "Nice progress."

"You should see the kitchen," Henri says. "We have a working oven now."

"I thought you had a working oven before the season was over."

"Oh, right. We did. It's the bathroom upstairs that wasn't done yet. But now it is. And it's gorgeous. And you can't see it because I don't remember what I left in there. Sit. I'll go make popcorn. Dogzilla, scoot over. Make room for Max."

Henri's cat is in a soccer uniform—yes, for real, she puts her cat in clothes and costumes—and it doesn't move an inch at her suggestion.

It does open one eye enough to glare at me and silently promise to eat my face off if I dare remove it from the easy chair it's sleeping in.

"Here." Luca reaches over and grabs the cat, setting the furball in his lap. "Her eyeball is worse than her bite. She's too lazy to bite, and her only real objection to you sitting on the chair is that she already put the effort in to hopping up there."

Three months ago, I would've called him whipped.

Tonight, I'm wondering why Tillie Jean doesn't have a cat that she likes to dress up in costumes.

Or why she doesn't have a dog. Or even a fish.

She'd be a great fish mom. That fish would have more fish castles than any fish to come before it.

Fuck.

I should be cranky about not getting laid tonight, and instead, I'm cranky that I'm not in a pet store helping Tillie Jean pick out a fish castle.

I drop into the chair and shove my fingers through my hair.

"You need me to send Henri out to pick up six different kinds of dessert from six different places?" Luca asks.

"I'd do it," she calls from the kitchen, "except he'd probably rather *you* go do the running, sweetie. We all know I'm a better listener."

"Good point. Ice cream? Cheesecake? Cookies? Baked chicken?"

"I have Luca's Nonna's ziti recipe, but we're out of the right kinds of cheese," Henri says. "Not that you want the ziti. It's cursed ziti, but I don't think it's a bad curse. Also, if you want both of us, Max, we can DoorDash something in."

This whole situation is so ridiculously domestic that I should be breaking out in hives.

Instead, I wish Tillie Jean was here with me, and that the four of us were hanging out to watch TV and shoot the shit and maybe play a card game or two.

I shift my head so I can see Luca between my arms, hands still fisted in my hair, then jerk my head toward the kitchen. "How the fuck do you trust yourself to do it?"

He pauses with one hand over the cat, shifts a glance at the kitchen too, then looks back at me, clearly getting exactly what I'm asking.

How do you grow up with shitty role models and decide to take a chance in a relationship anyway?

"Lots and lots of brutal honesty," he finally says.

"With yourself, or with her?"

"Yes."

"Fuck."

He glances at the kitchen again, then slides a look at me and drops his voice. "Does Cooper know?"

"Shut. The fuck. Up."

"Not gonna say a word. And it's not like it's a surprise."

"Is to me," I mutter.

"Relatable." Fucker's grinning.

"She says it's over when I leave for spring training."

He stops grinning. "Why?"

"I don't know. Because that's smart? Because she has a life there? Because I'm gone half the year? Because she's not the settling down type? Because she knows I'm not either?"

He scrubs a hand over his face like there's not enough alcohol, coffee, sugar, or ziti in the world for this, and I don't even fully get the ziti thing. I just guess that's what he's thinking. "Ask her."

"What? No."

"That's how it works, Max. Communication. Ask. Talk. Fight. Make up. Don't just assume. Maybe she's sitting there thinking she's saying what you want to hear. Maybe she's afraid of the same things you are."

If I wanted someone to blow smoke up my ass, I would've gone to talk to one of the single guys.

But Luca—

He grew up with a shitty father and a mother who hated love, and now he's planning a life with a woman who's been engaged so many times she'd only agree to be with him if they could do a relationship without all the fuss of formalities.

If anyone understands fucked-up love, it's him.

"Or maybe she knows I'm not worth it," I mutter.

I'm not looking for someone to pat my back and tell me *oh, honey, of course you are*, which is why I'm glad there's popcorn popping loudly in the kitchen while I pour my heart out to the only guy I know who'd *get* it.

Luca stares at me. "That's not on her, dude. That's on *you*."

"Max Cole, *do not ever* say that about yourself." Henri stalks into the living room, no popcorn in sight, fists planted on her hips, glaring in a way that makes me extremely uncomfortable.

Henri glaring is like the earth rotating backwards.

It doesn't happen.

"Say what?" I ask.

"That you're not worth it. Ah-ah-ah, don't deny it, and don't interrupt. *Listen*. It's easy for people to love people when they've known good love all their lives. But when people who've *craved* love all their lives actively decide to love someone, do you know what happens? *Magic* love. And I don't mean paranormal witches and warlocks love. I mean the kind of love that you feel all the way in your toenails because *you know* what you've missed out on all those years. *You know* how valuable it is. *You know* what it's worth. Your love is a bigger gift than *anything*, and anyone who rejects that is a fool who doesn't deserve you. Do you understand me?"

I open my mouth.

Shoot a glance at Luca, who shrugs. "Don't look at me, man. She's the expert here."

I swallow hard and look back at Henri. "You know that's a lot easier for you to say than it is for any of us to hear, right?"

Her normal big warm smile reappears. "Don't worry. I can email it to you every day until you believe it."

"I will throw this cat at you if you make my girlfriend email you about love every day," Luca says. "I love you, man, but not that much."

"*Luca.*"

He grins at her. "What? I still said I love him."

"You can't use *my cat* as a weapon."

"Oh. That. Yeah, I was exaggerating. I'll just get him with glitter bombs."

They should be annoying, but they're not.

What they have?

That's what I want.

That's what I want *every day* with Tillie Jean.

But no matter what Henri says, I still don't know if I can have it.

TILLIE JEAN

I can't sit still Saturday night, which in theory shouldn't be a problem, considering it's Paint Night at The Grog and there are sixteen ladies here tonight that I'm teaching to paint a tropical beach scene, but I keep getting distracted and checking my watch and looking at the door.

Sometimes mid-sentence.

"It's the coffee," I hear Aunt Bea whisper to Nana. "She ran out of juice."

"I think she's got a secret piece on the side," Nana whispers back.

"She doesn't have a main piece, so how would she have a piece on the side?" Dita hisses.

I clap my hands while Sloane, Annika, and Georgia trade glances in the back row. I might've had one too many caramel macchiatos yesterday and spilled all while we were supposed to be watching some romantic comedy on Netflix. "Ladies, how do your coconuts look? Anyone need help?"

"I wish Jason's coconuts looked like these," LaShonda says with a nod at her canvas.

"*Mom*," Georgia groans.

"What? Gravity happens."

"Your suns!" I shriek. "Let's talk about your suns instead."

I start to circle the room again, glance through the party room door and toward the front door of The Grog, remind myself for the eighty-four-millionth time that *the guys aren't coming back until tomorrow*, and I sigh. "Beautiful, Mom. Dita! Oh my gosh, I love what you did with your tree. And LaShonda, the colors on your sun are *chef's kiss*."

"I like chef's kisses," Annika calls.

"*Ew*," I tease.

"Totally gross," Cooper agrees.

I whip my head to the door so fast I almost trip.

And there he is.

Max is back.

Early.

He's standing behind Cooper, gazing at me with so much smolder that all of the canvases in this room are at risk of bursting into flame. Robinson's angling into the room too, holding the custom beer stein Aunt Glory presented him with early last week, but I barely notice.

Focus, Tillie Jean. "Stinky Booty! Couldn't resist crashing Paint Night, hm?"

"Thought you ladies might need models." He lifts an arm and flexes.

I think.

He's wearing a coat, so I can't say for sure.

Mom, Nana, Annika, Georgia, and Sloane all crack up.

"I'll paint you, Cooper, you studly thing," Robinson says in a fake falsetto, and anyone not laughing before busts a gut now.

Except me.

And Max, who's in a Pirate Festival T-shirt and jeans and

looks like I need to jump his bones in the broom closet *right now*.

I don't even know if The Grog has a broom closet, but I know I need to jump Max's bones.

"Tillie Jean, maybe we should paint Cooper's coconuts," Annika says.

God bless Annika.

That pulls me out of my Max-induced trance like nothing else would.

"I have awesome coconuts," Cooper agrees. "They're mounted in my bedroom."

The weird part?

He really does. Picked them up the last time he was in Hawaii.

"Alright, ladies, if you're done painting, leave your canvases to dry and go fawn all over the guys. I know, I know...it's that time of year."

It takes fourteen centuries, but eventually everyone clears out of the painting room, leaving behind paint water and supplies for me to clean up.

I'm carrying my first cups of water toward the bathroom when someone shouts.

"Damn goats!"

"Who let the mangy animals in?"

"*Dammit*, Goatstradamus, that's my cheeseburger!"

Max appears at my side, grabs the two cups I'm carrying in one hand, takes my elbow with his other hand, and shoves me down the short hallway to the ladies' room.

And as soon as we're in the single-seater room, he flips the lock, tosses the cups in the sink, and shoves me against the door. "Fuck, I missed you."

He barely finishes *you* before I'm flinging my arms around his neck, going up on tiptoe, and pulling him down so I can attack his mouth with mine.

His hands are everywhere—under my shirt, teasing my

nipples, yanking his own pants down, then tugging on my hair to tilt my head and give him better access to move his kisses to my neck.

"The goats," I gasp.

"Distraction. On purpose."

"Oh my god, my hero."

"Five minutes before they notice." He tugs at my jeans, and I help him shove them down too, but they get caught in my boots.

"*Dammit.*"

He spins me away from the wall and pushes me against the sink, facing the mirror, with him behind me so I can see my own flushed cheeks, heaving chest, and tight nipples straining the ivory lace of my bra. "Jesus, you're gorgeous."

He pulls my hair to one side, bends, and bites my neck while sliding his hands down my arms, and I stifle a moan of sheer pleasure.

A condom wrapper wrinkles, and he tugs on my hips, grinding his thick steel shaft against my ass.

My gaze flies to his in the mirror.

His lids are heavy, his eyes a shot of pure dark roast espresso, his lips parted, his cheeks scruffy. I press my ass back into him, and he reaches between us, stroking the wetness between my thighs.

And then his cock pushes into me, and it's such a relief to have him inside me again that my entire body shudders with the pleasure of it. "More," I whisper.

He pumps deeper while I arch back against him, taking him inside me, watching ecstasy and desire flit across my own face as I brace my hands on the sink and he thrusts faster and harder while I chant his name, *yes, more, there.*

I watch him pinch my nipples while he takes me from behind. Watch him bite my neck again, his teeth and the rough texture of his unshaven cheeks setting my already sensitive nerve endings on fire.

And all the while, he's driving into me like he's trying to find home.

Like he needs me, needs to be inside me, needs this reassurance that I'm here, that I want him, that he turns me on and flips me inside out, more than he needs to breathe. "Come, Tillie Jean. Come for me," he pants in my ear.

He nips at my earlobe, drives deep inside me once more, and I clamp my lips shut and rear my head back while I do as he orders, and I come hard and fast and desperate around his cock.

"*Fuck*, yes," he moans tightly, muffling himself against my shoulder. "Oh, *fuck fuck fuck*, Tillie Jean, *fuuuuck*."

He strains into me.

I push back against him, feeling his spasms rocking inside me.

This.

God, I missed this.

Him. I missed *him*.

His arms circle my waist, and he buries his head in my neck as his legs shake enough for me to feel it when he pulls out.

But I can still see myself in the mirror.

And what I'm seeing should scare me.

A woman, mostly naked in a public bathroom, who swore this was a limited-time deal, panting for breath, fully satisfied, wrapping her own arms around her lover's as he clings to her like he, too, would make time stand still if he could.

Someone rattles the bathroom door.

"Shit," I whisper.

Max bends down, yanks my pants up, then his own while I lunge for my shirt.

He's still wearing his.

The condom gets wrapped in toilet paper and shoved in the trash, and it's not more than five seconds since the rattle, which happens again.

He grabs one of my water cups, adds water to it, and dumps it on the floor. "Go," he hisses. "Tell them you made a mess and I'm helping clean it up."

I press a hard kiss to his mouth. "My place. Midnight."

"Trouble Jean, I will *not* last until midnight." He grabs seventeen paper towels from the dispenser and squats to tackle the water he spilled, and I unlock the door and lean out. "I made a—"

"You have about thirty seconds to finish your booty call before Cooper's done with the goats," Sloane says.

Annika appears behind her, shoves her out of the way, and throws more dirty paint water onto the bathroom floor.

"*Oh my god,*" I yelp.

"You really need to be more careful with the paint water, Tillie Jean," Annika says loudly. "Max! Max, come help clean this up."

I gape at her.

Sloane gapes at her.

And inside the bathroom, a low rumbly laugh sets my clit to tingling all over again. "This town is fucking insane," Max mutters.

"You're welcome," Annika replies.

"Go get the rest," Sloane hisses to me. "Is he dressed?"

"*Yes,* he's dressed."

"Go home through the back. We've got you. I'll tell Cooper you spilled water all over yourself. *Again.* And we'll keep Max here for at least another thirty minutes."

"But—"

"Tillie Jean, you walk out of this hallway any way but *out,* and you'll be the talk of Shipwreck in under ten minutes. And that's even *with* Long Beak Silver riding Goatstradamus out there."

I touch my hair.

Remember how I looked in the mirror just a minute or two ago.

And I nod. "Thank you," I whisper.

I don't stop to say anything else to Max.

But I do text him when I'm nearly home. *You really have a way with pipe. And I happen to have some plumbing in desperate need of attention. Again. It must really like the way you handle your tools.*

I get a Growly Bear selfie in return.

His Pirate Festival t-shirt is splattered with paint water, and I can make out Cooper in the background, playing darts with someone, like normal.

And I want to be there.

I want to sit next to Max, laugh with him, tease him, kiss him on the cheek like Annika does to Grady every time *they're* out in public, and for that to all be *normal*.

Except Max is leaving in two weeks.

Heading off to spring training.

And I don't want him to.

I don't want him to stay here either—not for me, and not when he loves playing baseball and is such a great asset to the team.

But am I brave enough to take the leap I'd have to take if this has any chance of lasting past the off-season?

And I don't mean the part where I tell Cooper I've been sleeping with Max.

I mean the part where I'd be signing up to be a full-time baseball girlfriend. Moving away from Shipwreck myself. Finding a new mission when it's not participating in a business that's been in my family since before I was born, in a town where I know everyone, what they all need, and where I fit.

I've been happy with my life here in Shipwreck for almost eight years.

And I've always said I'd take a leap when life handed me an opportunity I couldn't walk away from.

But can I?

Am I ready?

Is this what I really want?

More importantly—is it what *Max* would want?

I don't know.

But I know the only way to find out is to ask him.

And I will.

Soon.

But if there's any chance he'll say we're sticking to the plan—that we're over when he leaves for spring training—then next week or the week after is soon enough.

Max

"Take it you haven't told Cooper yet," Luca says four days later after he and Henri have driven out to Shipwreck to work out with us.

Should've been the other way around this off-season. Cooper, Robinson, Trevor, and I should've been heading into the city to work out with Luca and Brooks and Emilio and Francisco. Makes more sense.

But Shipwreck—it draws you in.

Makes you not want to leave.

Even when you're staying in a place without all the same luxuries you're used to in the city.

I don't bother glaring at him, and not only because I'm concentrating on the weight of the bar I'm benching. "Coach Addie has him in a snit."

"Talk to Tillie Jean yet?"

"Do you *want* me to throw this barbell at you?"

Cooper's not working out with us today. Said he had an appointment in the city. Trevor didn't come back after

311

Emilio's wedding, given the state of his shoulder and lack of contract. Darren's been checking in on him.

Dude's in rough shape, but he'll pull through.

I think.

I hope.

"You giving Max shit?" Robinson asks Luca.

"Yep."

"Is that allowed?"

"I can take him."

Robinson grins and plugs his earbuds back into his ears again, returning to his squats.

I shelve the bar, sit up, and look Luca straight in the eye. "Things are *good*. I don't want to talk to Tillie Jean about it. I don't want to tell Cooper. I want to let things keep being *good*."

"We're leaving for Florida in just over a week. There is no *keep being what it is*. Everything's changing. Hell, even me and Henri have had a couple arguments over spring training, and we both know this is the real deal. But *we talk about it*."

I change the subject and tell him to do his own reps.

Not because he's wrong.

More because the anxiety is creeping in again every time I think about leaving for Florida.

I *want* to go to Florida. I love spring training. Getting back in my groove. Being in the sunshine. Playing ball.

But I've never felt so much like I'm leaving part of myself behind before.

We hit the Korean barbecue joint for lunch, then grill steaks for dinner up at Cooper's place when he gets back from seeing his accountant in the city.

Dude needs to get a virtual one like most of the rest of us have.

He also needs to not talk so much.

I'm about ready to itch out of my own skin by the time it feels safe to say I'm calling it a night and head down off his little mountain so I can sneak in his sister's back door for nooky.

She was pulling a double shift today, which means she's probably tired.

But so long as she hasn't left the *no goats allowed* sign on her back door, I've been told I can come in and jam the door shut.

Any other town on earth, I'd tell her to upgrade her locks. Not like there aren't locks that would keep goats out.

And I can't believe that's a sentence I actually just thought.

There's no sign telling me to get lost, and the light's on in her bathroom, so I sneak in the back door under cover of night. "Tillie Jean?" I call softly. The light's on over her stove, but nothing else is, and her cabinets look extra bright tonight.

Like they're reflecting the Milky Way, but a more colorful version.

"Max?"

Just the sound of her voice quells all the growing panic inside me.

She's here.

We have tonight.

And when she peeks around the corner from the living room, her hair twisted up in a towel, her face coated in green gunk, and her robe gaping open to show off her very splendid cleavage and tease me with what else I know is under there, everything else about the day melts away.

She smiles and gestures to her face. "I swear, I thought I had at least thirty more minutes before Cooper would let you loose."

"Henri wore him out."

She laughs. "Come. You can wait in the bedroom while I wash this all off."

"I can help."

"Yeah?"

"I'm an expert washcloth wielder. Did you get any on your boobs? I can wash those off too."

She pulls me into the house, asking about my day, catching me up on Shipwreck gossip, and she lets me set her on the counter in her bathroom, step between her spread legs, and clean her face mask off.

The window's cracked again, letting in just enough cool air to keep me from overheating in the still-steamy bathroom. Swear she does it on purpose. "I would've showered with you," I tell her as I swipe gentle strokes over her face with a washcloth, revealing soft Tillie Jean skin under all the green stuff.

"I'll need another one soon enough." She loops her arms around my neck and hooks her legs behind my knees while I unwind the towel on her head and grab her comb. "In fact, I'm thinking things *right now* that already have me feeling a little dirty."

"How long are you planning on getting dirtier?" How is it that I've never combed a woman's hair before? And how is it that I can't imagine doing anything else right now?

"At least a couple hours. I mean, if my playmate cooperates." She winks. "But he usually does."

"He must have the proper motivation."

Her fingers stroke the ends of my hair, right at my neck, while her bright blue eyes dance with happiness. "He's my favorite," she whispers.

I am such a goner.

I drop the comb, lower my lips to hers, and *this*.

This is what I've been waiting for all day.

She's the calm to my storm. The joy to my fears. The belief to my doubts.

I push her robe off her shoulders, and she lets it fall, leaving her completely naked and exposed, but she doesn't shy away.

Not Tillie Jean.

She leans deeper into the kiss, and when I lift her, she wraps her legs around me, letting me carry her into the bedroom, settling her onto the center of her bed. She whimpers when I pull back to rip off my shirt and trip out of my pants, her thighs open, her fingers stroking her pussy and driving me completely wild.

"Fuck," I whisper reverently as my cock strains hard and heavy.

"You like to watch," she whispers back.

"Only you."

"I like you watching me."

I have died and gone to erotic heaven.

She crooks a finger on her other hand. "But I like you touching me more."

I don't need a second invitation.

Not to Tillie Jean's bed.

So I take a flying leap, making her shriek with the kind of laughter that she only lets loose when she's completely turned on and laughing while on the edge of orgasm, and when I land on her bed beside her, it's instinct to slide my hand between her legs.

But my hand doesn't make it before there's a loud *pop!*, then a creak, and the entire bed collapses.

"*Oh my go—*" she starts, but a string of *pop! pop! pop!*s interrupts her.

And before I can process that *something is fucking wrong here*, the entire room erupts in glitter.

The.

Entire.

Fucking.

Room.

It shoots out of the floors. The walls. Off the ceiling fan.

"*Oh my god!*" Tillie Jean shrieks.

I can't see her through the glitter.

Gold glitter.

Silver glitter.

Rainbow glitter.

It's everywhere.

It's every-fucking-where.

Raining down.

Floating up.

Swirling like a fucking glitter tornado.

Tillie Jean's making spitting noises.

"Close your eyes," I bark out, snapping my own shut, and I choke on glitter too.

"*Cooper!*" she bellows.

Cooper.

Cooper.

"Fucking fuckity fuckwit," I gasp.

"He is—*bleeeech*—so—eeeehhhhhth!—dead."

He is.

He's fucking dead.

Right fucking now.

"Is it in your eyes?" I blink my own open, see glitter *in my own fucking eyelashes*, and peer at her through the red haze blurring the rest of my vision.

"No. But—" She holds out her arms.

Glitter.

Glitter everywhere.

Glitter on her face. In her hair. Down her arms. Covering her nipples. Piled in her belly button.

Her fucking *belly button* is full of glitter.

Nothing's swirling or falling anymore, nothing shooting up from the floor.

Not a lot, anyway.

Fucker rigged a *glitter blower.*

"Shower," I order.

I'm off the bed, ripping the glitter blower out of the electrical socket behind the bed, then shoving on my own clothes.

"Max?"

"Go. Take. A. Fucking. Shower."

Yeah.

We're busted.

I'm busted.

My glittery ass is *so* busted. I can't walk out of this house without all the evidence of where I've been and what I was doing here.

But you know what?

Cooper Fucking Rock is fucking busted himself.

"Max—" Tillie Jean says again.

I round on her with a glare. "I'm handling this."

I don't bother with a shirt or shoes. Just pants. Just enough that cousin Chester the asshole won't put me in jail if he pulls me over for angry driving on my way up the mountain.

I probably look like a fucking troll doll and I don't care.

It's time.

It's *past* time for me to march into Cooper's house, look him straight in the eye, grab him by the balls, and tell him I'm fucking his sister, and he can go take a goddamn leap if he thinks I'm not good enough for her.

But halfway up the mountain, after rejecting the umpteenth call in a row from Tillie Jean, I realize what I'm doing.

I'm about to go toss the best friend I've ever had off the side of a mountain.

I slam on the brakes in the middle of the road.

Fuck.

Fuck.

If I walk in Cooper's front door and smash his face in, that's it.

We're done.

Spring training will suck. The season will suck. I'll be begging my agent to get me traded before the end of my first regular-season game.

This?

Shipwreck?

Tillie Jean?

It's *not real*.

Luca's right. We don't talk. We just screw. There's no future. This is *fun*.

She has the luxury of fun.

I thought I did too, but I'm sitting here parked in the middle of the fucking road on the side of a mountain with my chest squeezing tight and my throat constricting and it takes me three stabs at the button to make my window roll down.

Can't breathe.

Can't. Fucking. Breathe.

And not because I'm glittering.

But because *good things don't happen to guys like me*.

Head down.

Do your job.

Go home.

Don't get attached.

The rules.

I lifted my head.

I dreamed more.

And now—now—now Cooper's probably going to punch *my* face in for touching his sister.

I can't go back to her.

Can't let her see me like this.

I'm over this shit.

I'm done with the panic.

But *one two three four*, there it is.

One two three four gasp for breath.

One two three four can't find the air.

One two three four it's so fucking hot in here.

Fuck.

Fuck.

"Drive," I order myself on a gasp. "Fucking. Drive."

Driveway.

There's a driveway.
I can make it.
I can get off the road.
Just a little bit more.
And then I'm safe.

3 2

Tillie Jean

Do you know how hard it is to get dressed when your wet body is coated in glitter and you don't want to have to burn your entire house down?

"It's fucking hard," I yell at Cooper an hour later. "*Lines,* Cooper. *Fucking lines.*"

His lips are twitching like he's trying to take me seriously, but the next thing out of my mouth is, "*I will have glitter in my fucking cooter for the rest of my natural life,*" and Luca over in the corner snorts and has to turn away.

Henri tries to give him a stern glare, but even Henri —*Henri*—isn't quite managing.

"You know I'm good for buying you a new bed," Cooper says. "I even made sure I could still get the exact same model."

I shove his shoulder, then swipe my hand over my tongue to try to get more glitter off of it—yes, *glitter on my tongue,* and yes, it's uncomfortable—and then I smear my wet hand all over his face. *"I don't want a new fucking bed. I want to not have to burn my house down to de-glitter it."*

I'm shrieking.

I'm fully aware that I'm shrieking, and it's not that I don't appreciate Cooper pranking me back in a manner that will require me to take out a loan in order for me to get vengeance, because *yes*, there will be helicopters and vats of glue and feathers and ski ramps and manufactured mudslides involved, but *I can't find Max.*

Cooper dodges my glittery slime hand. "C'mon, TJ. Could've been worse. You could've had guests."

"I was banging Max when it happened."

Yep.

That just shrieked right out of me too.

My chest is heaving.

Cooper starts to laugh, but then the worst part happens.

The hot, wet eyeballs and clogged throat.

"Where. Is. He?" I ask.

No one's laughing now.

Cooper's laugh fades into a serious study of my face, his eyeballs wavering between waiting for me to drop the *haha, just kidding*, and barely holding himself back from launching into a tirade of his own if I'm serious.

I clench my fists and fight the damn tears that are threatening to make my voice crack. "Where. Is. Max? Where would he go?"

"No."

"Yes."

"Tillie Jean—"

"I swear to god, if you finish that sentence, I *will* call Mom. And I'll call Nana, and I'll call Aunt Glory, and I'll call Aunt Bea, and I'll call Aunt Matilda's ghost, and I'll call Annika, and I will rain down the hell that is all of the Rock women angry at you all at the same time. *You don't get to decide who I do and don't date."*

Dammit. I'm crying. I swipe the tears, get another bit of glitter in my eyeball, realize I owe Max so much more than I thought for glitter bombing him right after he got here for the inconvenience that is glitter in your eyeballs, and then I look at the door.

If I look at the door, he'll walk through it, right?

And look at that.

The door's swinging open.

I leap toward it, and—

And Grady walks in.

Right.

I called Grady.

His lips twitch as he looks at me, but only for a second before they fade into *which one of you needs your ass kicked?*

He's such an oldest brother.

"Cooper. Sit down. Tillie Jean—" He shakes his head. "Are you mad because he out-pranked you, or are you mad because you weren't alone when he did it?"

"He got Max."

Grady clears his throat. "So you're both starring in the live-action version of *Trolls* when it comes to Copper Valley…"

Luca coughs.

Henri coughs too.

Cooper grunts.

I glare at Cooper.

He glares right back. "There are things you don't know—"

"Are there, Cooper? *Are there?* Or does it bother you that I might know and I might want to date him anyway?"

"I'm just trying—"

"Cooper. Stop talking." Grady steps between us. "Tillie Jean. Do you need to go wash your tongue off?"

Dammit, I'm wiping it again. "I need to know Max is okay. Where is he? Would he be pranking you back, or is he mad?"

Cooper rolls his eyes. "The things you don't—"

Grady gets him in a headlock and clamps a hand over his mouth. "Luca. Where would Max go?"

Luca's green eyes slide my way. "Got a few ideas. I'll go look for him."

"Here, Tillie Jean." Henri squeezes my waist, completely unaffected by the fact that I'm wearing mismatched shoes, sweatpants that are threatening to fall off my hips and have a chocolate ice cream stain in a bad place in the crotch, and a halter top that I might not be wearing correctly because it was the first thing I grabbed.

And glitter. I'm wearing *all* the glitter.

I pull away. "I don't want to glitter you."

"TJ—" Cooper starts from behind Grady's hand.

"Where's Max?" I ask Henri. "He was so mad, and—"

Luca stops next to us. "Trade me phones, angel? He'll answer your number."

Henri swaps phones with him and hugs me again.

Grady lets Cooper go, and he starts to talk, but Henri shushes him like she's talking to a misbehaving twenty-one-year-old.

She's too patient to shush anyone under the legal drinking age that way.

"Let's get you home," she says to me. "Let Cooper stew in thinking about whose lives he can and can't dictate for a while, hm?"

"He shouldn't be alone in case Max is waiting for him to be alone to murder him with mascot bobbleheads."

"I'm sticking around," Grady tells me. "Gonna bake him some *shut-the-fuck-up-cakes*."

"I'm not being an asshole," Cooper snaps. "She looks just like she did when *Ben* used to break up with her too."

I suck in a breath and get glitter caught in the back of my throat, and then I try to cough up both my lungs and part of my spleen.

Henri shoves a water bottle at me, and I almost miss what Grady's saying to Cooper.

Almost, but not quite.

"There's a big difference between a guy who'll date your sister because it's convenient and he's her only option, and a guy who's resisted what he wanted for four fucking years since he knows you'd kick his ass. Why aren't *you* freaking out about no one knowing where Max is?"

Cooper blinks, and suddenly my asshole brother morphs into a wide-eyed dummy who's finally catching on to the fact that there's a bigger problem here than me sleeping with Max.

I scowl at him.

He scrubs his hands through his hair. "This is *exactly* what I was worried about," he mutters.

"Then maybe you should've considered the possibility that Tillie Jean isn't an asshole and that if they'd felt like they could've talked openly with you about what they were doing, then a glitter bomb wouldn't have made Max disappear?" Henri says quietly.

"Can we please go find him?" I ask her.

"As soon as we de-glitter you a little more."

"Tillie Jean—" Cooper starts.

I hold up a hand. "Don't. Not tonight."

Henri insists on driving my car back down off the mountain, chatting the whole way about things that matter and things that don't, while I look this way and that, trying to spot his car, even though I know it's a long shot that he's anywhere in the area right now.

By the time we get back to my house, I'm not angry anymore.

It *was* a good prank. Cooper had me convinced he was too good for pranks, and then he launched the ultimate revenge for everything.

But I'm worried.

"Max was really mad," I whisper to Henri as she pulls into

my driveway. "I've done everything in my power to make him mad at me the past four years, but I've never seen him that mad."

"Dating's hard enough without worrying about all the extra stuff like how it impacts your job and your friendships. Toss in where Max came from..." She twists to face me. "But he's been happy, Tillie Jean. Darren told me during Fireballs Con that he's never seen Max like this, and they've known each other a long time. You're good for him."

Her phone dings, and her face tells me everything before she opens her mouth. "Luca has him. He's—he's okay. Let him sleep it off, okay?"

"He's not okay, is he?"

Her face twists again, which is answer enough.

"Henri—"

"Tillie Jean. He's safe. He's with a friend. And he needs a little space."

"Thinking time," I whisper.

He likes his thinking time.

She squeezes my arm. "You're good for him. And he knows it. Don't panic, okay?"

Don't panic.

Right.

Max is upset. He's not answering my calls. And he told Luca to tell Henri to *give him space.*

"I told him we'd end this when he left for Florida."

"I know."

"But I don't want it to end."

She squeezes my arm again.

Yep.

I'm definitely going to panic.

33

Max

I should've just left.

I should've left and not tried to grab anything from the house, but I didn't, because I wanted my pillow—yes, my damn *pillow*—and now Tillie Jean's sticking her glittered head out of her door and peering at me as I close the tailgate on my SUV. "Hey," she calls.

Fuck.

She's gorgeous. Crazy hair. Glittering everywhere. An old Blue Lagoon County High School T-shirt hanging down to her knees. Bags under her eyes like she slept worse than I did —which isn't possible, for the record, since post-panic-attack sleep sucks elephant balls—and so much worry in those blue eyes that I want to pull her into my arms and promise her I'm not worth it.

So. Fucking. Gorgeous.

Just like that.

I grunt and walk around my SUV on the side where I won't have to look at her.

"*Max*," she calls.

The problem with being six-four is that you're taller than everything, even when you slouch, and I can still see her over the roof of my damn car.

And she's charging barefoot across the frosted grass in twenty-five degree weather like the glitter coating her feet counts as shoes.

I want to sweep her off her feet and carry her back inside her house and warm her up.

But I can't. "Go away, Tillie Jean."

"No."

Okay, yeah, that was dumb. Of course I knew that wouldn't work.

I glare at her. "We're done. Post-season's over. I'm gone. Go. Away."

She freezes on a gasp, hurt streaking so hard and fast over her face that my junk punches itself for me being such a dick.

But I can't do this.

I'm fucking *broken*.

"No," she says again.

It's not a gaspy, desperate, broken-hearted *no*.

It's a *don't be a damn fool* no.

An *I know that's not what you want* no.

An *I refuse to accept that you're being this stupid* no.

"Your rules, remember?" Yeah. I'm an ass.

But she deserves better. All that love shit Henri spouted about me knowing what it was worth for having been denied it for so long?

Total, complete, romance-writer bullshit.

"What are you afraid of?" Tillie Jean demands.

That you won't want me if you know who I really am. "Fucking up my game."

Her eyes narrow and steam slips out her nostrils. "What are you *really* afraid of?"

"I'm asking management to trade me. Can't play with

your brother. It's *over*. Sorry if you can't accept that. Don't come to Copper Valley. I don't want to see you."

Jesus, I'm an ass.

"You don't mean that."

I don't.

Fuck me, I don't.

But I can't be the man she deserves if I'm having panic attacks over worrying more that I'll upset *her brother* than I am at the idea that I'll never see her again. I can't be the man she deserves if I can't promise her that I won't fall apart over other stupid shit later, leaving her to pick up my pieces. And I can't be the man she deserves if I can't pull my own shit together enough to tell her that I love her.

She deserves someone who's already whole.

Not someone who didn't know what whole was until I let her in.

She's whole.

She's always been whole.

And she might be standing there with her hands fisted at her sides, sending daggers my way, but she's also visibly ordering herself to look past the anger.

I can *see* her doing it.

"You can try to be a dick to push me away all you want, but I know this isn't you. And *you* know this isn't you."

"See what you want to. I can't fix that."

I don't wait for her to answer. If I do, she'll talk me into staying. She'll talk me into spilling my guts. Every fear. Every dream. Every worry. Every truth.

And then she'll hate me for real.

I crank my engine, make sure she's not doing anything stupid like leaping behind my car to keep me from leaving, and then I back out of the driveway of my winter house for the very last time.

Shipwreck isn't the real world.

And it's time for me to get back to where I need to be, to do what I need to do, and to live the life I'm supposed to live.

Not this dream.

The thing about dreams?

You wake up.

And last night was definitely a wake-up.

It's time to go.

Max

TIME DOESN'T FLY WHEN YOU'RE MISERABLE.

It fucking crawls.

And no amount of video games, extra workouts, visits with Fireballs management where I chicken out every time on threatening to throw like shit until they trade me makes it go faster.

Movies don't help. Mindlessly scrolling TikTok doesn't help. Sleeping doesn't help. Besides, I *can't* sleep.

Not even getting to Florida helps.

Like last year, management's rented out an entire complex for us to stay at. Together. As a team.

I'm in the pitchers' wing, which is good.

More space between me and anyone who knows firsthand what happened in Shipwreck.

But there are only three other guys with me. Most of our pitching staff are married and staying in the family suites across the complex. Two of the guys are new, and the third has a girlfriend that he's on the phone with all day long when we're not at the ball field practicing.

The team's new catcher is nineteen.

Nineteen.

A fucking *baby* who needs to be broken in, which seems to be amusing the coaching staff to no end.

"No," I yell from the mound on our second day of warm-ups, "if I shake my head on the fastball, *I'm not throwing a fucking fastball.*"

He squats, drops a hand between his thighs, and signals for a fastball again.

I throw my whole glove instead of just the ball.

Fucking catchers.

He pops up from his squat, shoves his mask back, grabs my glove, and runs it out to me, dark eyes shining like a puppy dog's, giant grin spread across his brown face. He was born in the Dominican Republic, moved to Oklahoma sometime in his childhood, spent the past two seasons working his way up the minors with the Fireballs' affiliate teams—yeah, he started when he was *seventeen*—and I swear when God made Cooper Rock, he saved part of the dude's personality to infuse into Diego Estevez.

"Feels good to work out all our issues now," he says. "So we'll rock it in the real season. High five, Fast Max!"

I leave him hanging. "I'm not throwing a goddamn fastball."

He grins bigger. "Why not? Fastballs are fun. You need the practice. And to work out all that anger. Find the zen. Be happy. Throw a curve ball. Hit me in the face. All the pitchers want to. You can be the first. I'll forgive you."

I slide a look at the coaches gathered along the third base-line, all of them sporting massive grins.

"He's great, isn't he, Max?" Tripp Wilson, the team's co-owner, calls, while his wife, Lila, co-owner with the greater power here, hides her mouth behind her hand.

"He's not old enough to drink and he has as much energy as a squirrel."

"My brother has a pet squirrel. For the record, Diego has *more* energy than Skippy does."

Diego grins and taps the bill of my hat. "Slider. Curve ball. Knuckleball. Fastball. All the balls. All the strikes. You'll give up a run or two. I'll miss a catch or two. But we're still gonna be fucking *winners*. Yeah, Fast Max? *Yeah!*"

He trots back to home plate, kicking his feet up—*kicking his fucking feet up*—on the way. "Think I got through, coach?" he calls.

"You nailed it, big D," our catching coach calls back.

"*Yeah!* I fucking love this game!"

I'm being punked. That's the only explanation.

Diego squats.

Signals a fastball.

I throw a fastball and take his fucking glove off. "*That's what I'm talking about!*" Diego yells. He pumps a fist in the air while he throws off his helmet. "You show that glove, Fast Max! You show it!"

"Lay off the Red Bull, Estevez."

"No Red Bull, Fast Max. I'm just living the dream. Hey! Can you wave at my mom? She's taking pictures." He points to the stands. "Hey, Mom!"

I'm twitching by the time I hit the showers after practice.

"Dude's hilarious," someone mutters.

"Fans are gonna love him."

"I got a grand on him having a dance-off with Ash between innings before the end of the first regular-season game."

"And winning."

"No fucking way. You're on."

I strip and stick my head under the shower until they're gone. I don't want to hear it.

I don't want to be here.

I don't want to fucking be here.

And that doesn't get better when I leave the shower and find Cooper leaning next to my locker. "Fuck off, Rock."

"I'm not mad at you."

I give him a side eye while I rub my hair dry.

"Okay, I'm mad at you, but I'm not *mad* at you." He punches me in the arm. "If you'd just fucking believe in yourself—"

"I believe in myself, asshole."

"If you believed in yourself, you'd be calling my sister *right the fuck now.*"

"Or maybe I don't like your sister that much."

He glares at me.

Dude's totally fucking pissed at me, and he's lying to himself if he thinks he's not.

"Is that really the problem?" Cooper Rock doesn't do deadly calm. Cooper does happy as a golden retriever. He does arrogant as a lion. He does zen as a goddamn monk, but he doesn't do deadly calm.

Until now.

"Yeah," I lie. "That's the problem."

"Or is the problem that you're afraid if you commit to someone as awesome as Tillie Jean for real, you'll have to face that you *can* be better than what your old man made you think you could?"

Rossi leaps between us. No idea where he came from too —they don't start practice for another two days—but there he is. "Enough, Cooper. Back the fuck up."

"No. *No.* I'm right, and he knows it. He hides behind thinking he's worthless so he doesn't have to be good at anything except baseball. You're gonna be Trevor Stafford one day, dude. And what the hell are you gonna do then?"

"I said *back up*," Rossi growls.

"Let him talk," I tell Rossi. "I'd have to care for it to hurt."

Luca gives me the *don't be a dick* glare. "So if Tillie Jean said the same thing, you wouldn't care either?"

I flinch.

"Thought so." He shoves Cooper. "Let's go."

"Friends don't abandon friends, Max," Cooper mutters. "I'm still here, even if you're being an asshole."

Fuck. "I'm not your friend."

"You've always been my friend, idiot."

Rossi doesn't tell him to leave again.

Doesn't have to.

Cooper's already gone.

"So why the fuck wasn't I good enough for his sister?" I mutter.

Rossi gives me another look, this one a classic *duh* number. "*You* told him you weren't enough times that he believed you."

Jesus.

Fuck.

I did, didn't I?

And I was right.

I pack up and head back to the complex, declining six dinner invitations along the way, and hole up in my room.

Music doesn't help.

The email from my therapist asking if I'd like to talk again tomorrow doesn't help either.

Nor does one more damn knock on my door.

"Go away. I'm jacking off," I yell.

"Not very well if you can still talk while you do it," Tripp Wilson replies.

Fuck.

I'm gonna get myself fired.

Maybe that'd be a good thing.

I could just disappear.

Head off to Tahiti.

Make a living setting up umbrellas on the beach.

Be fucking lonely, RAWK! a parrot voice replies inside my own head.

I yank the door open. Fully clothed, for the record.

"Bad time," I tell the Fireballs' co-owner.

"You're not regretting this, are you?" He lifts a copy of *Arena Insider* with my bare ass on the cover.

Fuck. *Fuck.* My fingers start tingling.

I forgot that was coming out today, and I've been ignoring the calls from my agent.

He tucks the magazine under his arm and leans in the doorway. "Good article. Read it yet?"

I shake my head.

"Made me realize I'm being an ass in pretending I'm not a recovering hypochondriac."

My shoulders are getting tense. So are my lats. My pecs. My quads. Not about to tell my boss I don't want to be the guy everyone talks to about their own mental health issues.

Not when I'm cracking myself.

Should've had my agent pull the article. I am *not* in for this.

Tripp hands me the magazine. "You should read it."

He doesn't say anything else.

Not about his own issues. Not about mine.

Just hands me the magazine and walks away.

I toss it on my chair and fling myself onto my bed, right under the ceiling fan. Florida's fucking hot.

That article isn't about me.

It's about a guy I thought I was for a month or two this winter.

A guy you wish you still were, RAWK! the damn parrot says in my head.

I snort back at it.

When the parrot's in my head, reading a damn article won't help.

Will it?

Tillie Jean

"Great job, ladies," I say on a gasp as I fall back onto my exercise mat. "Way to kick booty."

"I hate you," Aunt Bea gasps.

"I didn't know I still had muscles there," Mom says between pants.

"Isn't this supposed to get easier?" Aunt Glory demands.

"Wimps," Nana says.

Mom lifts up on her elbows and glares at Nana, who pulled something in her groin—do *not* ask—and came to supervise instead of participate today. "Go walk the plank, Nana."

It's so normal.

Except nothing's *normal* anymore.

Everything's a little hollow. It's harder to make myself come to senior aerobics. It's harder to smile at customers at Crusty Nut. I don't want to paint.

Even coffee is dull.

This is *nothing* like breaking up with Ben.

That was my injured pride and my fear that I'd be alone. Being without Max?

It's like someone borrowed part of my soul and is holding it for a ransom I can't pay.

I can't make Max love me.

And I can't pretend I didn't fall in love with him.

"Same time next week?" I push myself up onto my hands and knees, then onto my rubbery legs while the class around me does the same.

"Tillie Jean, I need to talk to you about the twins," Dita says. She's still bent over huffing and puffing. "Can you paint them for their birthday?"

"Like face painting, or like paint their portraits?" Mom asks.

"You should do both," Nana declares. "Portraits of kids with their faces painted."

"Talk later," I tell Dita with a nod. "Alone. No help. Peanut gallery."

She gives me a thumbs up.

I head home to shower, ignoring the empty house next door. Max sent someone to pack up the rest of his stuff, and according to Uncle Homer's daughter, the house is rented out off-and-on to vacationers starting in mid-March, and then she's thinking of selling it permanently.

And then there's no chance Max will ever come back to that little house.

I press through one more quick shower that doesn't get the lingering glitter out of my hair or off my eyelids.

My bedroom is back to normal. Mostly. True to his word, Cooper had a replacement bed delivered the next day and brought in a forensic clean-up crew to tackle the glitter.

But it's still glitter.

And I still catch glimpses of it in the cracks between the slats of the wood floor, or on the blinds, or twinkling in the curtains around my bed.

And every time, all I can see is Max's face.

Horrified.

Angry.

Ready to slay dragons.

And then Max ready to slay me the next day.

I rush through getting dressed and head to Crusty Nut. It needs a makeover—brighter colors, happier music, mood-boosting *anything*—but I want someone else to do the work.

Not me.

"Morning, hon." Dad waves at me with a spatula when I slip in the back door. "Your mom says I should put pickle juice in your coffee this morning. Made 'em all work hard at aerobics, eh?"

I lift my glittery coffee tumbler that doesn't make me smile like it used to. "Nice try. Already brought my own."

"I figured. But maybe don't get a refill from Muted Parrot today if you want it to be drinkable? And maybe go lighter on the Zumba next week?"

I put on my apron and head for the bar. "Only until Nana's fully back. Then it's game on."

"Good plan."

I start to head to the bar, but pause. "Dad?"

"Yeah, hon?"

I start to open my mouth, to put voice to the words that have been tumbling in the back of my head, but it's terrifying.

I thought I was ready. I thought I'd be brave when the time came. I thought I could do this.

So why do half a dozen little words feel so heavy?

"Tillie Jean?"

"I think it's time I quit," I whisper.

Rip off the bandaid, right?

He blinks slowly, then nods even slower. "You know what you want to do?"

What I *want* to do?

Yes.

Yes, I know exactly what I *want* to do. It came to me in a blinding flash that felt so undeniably right that there was no question this is the direction I'm supposed to go.

But only half of it is in my control. "Yes."

I don't elaborate.

He doesn't ask.

"Okay." He wipes his hands on his apron, a familiar gesture that makes my chest ache for knowing it's not a sight I'll have dozens of times a day every day for the rest of my life, but I'm not going far.

And possibly not for a while.

But I will go.

Max pushing me to try new things? To be better? To open my world wider?

Every step I've taken the past four years, every shift I've made, they've all been here.

At home.

And this is where I belong.

It's where I'll belong until my dying day.

But not as the manager at Crusty Nut. And not every day for the next couple years while I go back to school.

It's where I'll return though.

And when I come back—

When I come back, I'll take everything I've learned here, at school, from Max, from the world I'm about to experience, and I'm running for mayor.

Shipwreck has only just begun growing and expanding.

I want to make sure we stay true to our roots while welcoming the wide world in to join us.

"Are you quitting today?" His voice is thick, and it makes my eyes burn and my sinuses threaten to drip, but I shake my head.

"No. Not today. Soon, but not today."

He smiles. "Well, good, because your mother's in no

shape to come over and help take care of all of those customers out there."

I swipe my eyes quickly, nod, and reverse course, passing through the kitchen door and out behind the bar to check on the breakfast crowd when the lone customer sitting at the bar makes me drop my coffee.

He leaps to his feet. "Shit. Sorry. I'll buy you a new one. I'll—"

"What are you doing here?"

I'm shrieking.

Max is sitting at the bar when he's supposed to be in Florida and I just told my dad the hardest thing I've ever told anyone and my feet are coated in hot coffee and I'm shrieking.

He freezes, his hair still as glittery as mine is, but his eyes —*oh, god,* I can't look at his eyes.

"You're right," he says quietly. "I'm afraid. No, not afraid. Terrified. I'm terrified that if I let you all the way in, you'll realize I'm not worth it, and you'll walk away, and I'll never be able to put myself back together again."

This isn't what he's supposed to say.

He's supposed to not be here at all, so I can get over him and not fall back into the same on-again, off-again pattern with him that I had with Ben.

Except this doesn't feel off-again, on-again.

"You hurt me," I whisper.

He flinches. "I know. I'm sorry."

I don't hear my dad join me from the kitchen, but I know he's there. The door to Crusty Nut opens, and my mom and Nana and Aunt Bea and Aunt Glory and Annika and Sloane and Georgia and Grady all pile in.

What do I *want* to do?

I want to leap over the bar and kiss his face and hold on so tight that he can't ever shake me away again and tell my family to go easy on him. He looks every bit as miserable as I am.

Bags under his eyes. Lips tight. Hair mussed. And his T-shirt looks like he slept in it.

He's hurting too.

But I've done the *don't talk about it* merry-go-round before, and I know we can't make this work if we can't face the hard stuff. "Everyone struggles sometimes, Max, but you can't just —you can't push me away, disappear for two weeks, then come back like everything's fine."

"I know." Still so quiet.

So *beaten*.

"What do you want?" I step out of the coffee mess, leaning back against the shelf under the mirror, giving myself just a wee bit more space. "Why did you come back?"

His Adam's apple bobs. He glances to my right, then slides a look at the growing group of my relatives and friends pouring in the door. "You told me once that I challenge you. That I make you want to try new things and help people more. And I thought you couldn't challenge me back. That I already had everything else I needed. I don't need money. I don't need a job. I don't need a lot of people. But I didn't know what I was missing until you challenged me to let you in. And then I found something I didn't even know I needed. I found where I belong. I don't *belong* anywhere, Tillie Jean. I don't have a place I call home. I don't have people who worry when I disappear. And I thought I liked it that way. But you— you gave me peace. You gave me belief. You gave me a home. You challenged me to be enough, just me, and to trust people to accept me no matter what. And I failed. I wasn't up for it. But I want to be. I want to learn. I want to be where you belong. I want to be *your* family. I want to be *your* home. The same way you're mine."

He looks down and rubs his palms into his eyes. "Jesus.

Just *being* here. Just seeing you—that's all it takes. You make me okay. You make me want to work hard and stay okay."

"And you left spring training behind to come all the way here and tell me that?"

"Fuck baseball. I don't need it either. I just—I don't care what it takes. I don't care what I have to do. I need—I just need you."

The door swings open again and Pop walks in the door. "Tillie Jean, that asshole who didn't know what he had when he had you has anxiety. Did you know that? It's all over this here magazine with his naked—"

Mom, Aunt Bea, and Aunt Glory leap all over him and shove him back out the door.

Max is looking down again, thrusting his hands through his hair.

I reach across the bar and tug on his wrist until he lifts his head and looks at me.

"I didn't know you did the article."

His hand grips mine like it's a lifeline, hot and firm but shaky. "I'm tired of hiding. I'm tired of letting the demons win. You asked me once who I'd be if I wasn't afraid of who I thought I was. I'd be the guy who chooses happiness. I'd be the guy who believes. I'd be the guy not afraid to say *I'm sorry* and *I love you* and *please give me one more chance*."

My eyes are burning again, my heart whirling like it's riding a helicopter blade ten thousand feet up in the air while I lean closer across the bar. "Are you saying all of that to me right now?"

"Yes."

I swallow hard. "Okay. Go ahead. I'm ready."

The corner of his mouth hitches up, but his eyes are still shadowed and haunted. "No shortcuts?"

"I'd expect nothing less than that to come right back at me, and you know it."

He licks his lips. Sucks in a breath. And then meets my

gaze. "Tillie Jean, of all the regrets I have in my life, the biggest is walking away from you like an asshole—"

"Like a festering boil on an asshole's asshole," Nana interrupts.

"*Nana*," I hiss.

"Let her go, TJ," Grady says. "You'll appreciate this so much more ten years from now if you let her help."

"Do you want to go out back?" I whisper to Max.

"No." He squeezes my hand. "Of all of my regrets, the biggest is walking away from you like a festering boil on an asshole's asshole—"

"Much better," Nana declares.

"—And if I could do it all over again, I'd take your phone calls after I left the scene of the glitter bombing, and I'd tell you I was afraid your brother would hate me, but that you were worth that risk, and if he did, that would be his problem, not mine. I don't want to hurt you. I want to love you. I want to make you happy. I want to travel the world with you and laugh with you and joke with you and give you jars of pickles for your birthday because it would confuse the ever-loving fuck out of you, and I want you to retaliate by giving me a bag of potatoes with your grandfather's face on them because it's the weirdest gift I can think of. I want to go to The Grog and challenge you to a game of pool instead of standing on the sidelines wondering what people would think if I did. I want to fall asleep in your arms every night and wake up to your *give me coffee so I can live* face every morning."

"That's a seriously ugly face," Grady says like he's trying to be quiet, except we all know he's not. "Have you seen it, Aunt Glory?"

"Too many times, young man." Aunt Glory shudders out loud. "Too many times."

"I love that face," Max whispers to me.

"It's really not a pretty face," I whisper back.

"It is to me."

"It's even worse than blotchy tear-face."

He smiles. "I love all of your faces."

It's the smile that seals the deal.

Growly Bear Max?

He's hot.

Smiling Max?

He's everything.

Everything.

And I want to kiss that smile every day until I'm old and gray, and probably a lot more days after that too. "You know smiling is cheating, right?" I whisper.

"Not when it's an honest smile."

"I love you, Growly Bear."

"I'm going to love you forever, Trouble Jean." His lips brush mine, and all of the shadows and clouds I've been living with fade away.

We're not perfect. So far from it.

But he's everything I've been waiting for.

It's time to leap headfirst into the adventure of love.

EPILOGUE

Max

HEADING BACK TO SHIPWRECK AFTER THE BASEBALL SEASON ISN'T quite the same this year as it was last year.

For one, we only have limited time here since she's enrolled in classes for the public administration degree she's working on at Copper Valley University. For two, we're both in her house instead of me moving in next door, though I made the offer for nostalgia's sake. For three, there's a hell of a lot less pressure, which I attribute one hundred percent to TJ's lessons on *do what you can do, be responsible for only the things you can affect, pay attention when the universe steers you, and let the rest go.* And four, I'm not an outsider.

Turns out getting caught shopping for diamond rings makes a guy official around here.

But I still roll over in bed on the fourth Thursday of November, back in Shipwreck since TJ has the whole week off from classes, waking up and feeling off-kilter.

It's like my body *knows*.

But unlike last year, two bright blue eyes are staring at me when I finally peel open my own eyelids. "Happy morning, sunshine," Tillie Jean whispers.

Hard not to smile back at that. "Somebody's already had her coffee."

"Nope. No coffee yet."

My brows go up.

That's unusual. "But you're coherent."

"Because it's important."

She has my full and undivided attention.

Tillie Jean coherent before coffee because of *something important* is cause for concern. I reach for her under the sheet and tug her close. "What's up?"

"I need to know what you want to do today."

"Why?"

"I know you hate holidays. So I want to do whatever will make you happy today."

I frown. "You don't want to do Shipwreck's Thanksgiving?"

"Do *you*?" she counters. "If you want to be alone, that's fine. Just tell me, and I'll go. If you want to go, we can both go, but only if you *want* to go. I don't want you to feel obligated. But if you want me to stay here with you and skip everything, I'm good with that too. I just need to know so I don't drink coffee if I shouldn't."

"You love Thanksgiving."

"Bah." She wrinkles her nose. "I love every day in Shipwreck. If I miss anything, I'll hear six versions of it by this time tomorrow. I *am* leading senior aerobics tomorrow morning before Nana and Mom and Dita head out for shopping in the city. I promised all the menfolk I'd wear them out so they can't spend as much."

This town.

I fucking love it. And when my contract's up and TJ has her degree, the first thing we're doing is moving right back here so I can help her get elected mayor and watch her take all the good she loves doing around here to the next level.

But I love Tillie Jean more than I love anything. "Never too late to replace shitty traditions with good ones." I squeeze her ass. "Like starting holidays with dessert before breakfast."

"Can you eat pie? That's more sugar than I've seen you eat in the last year combined."

I duck my head under the covers. "Not talking about pie, Trouble Jean."

I find what I *do* want to eat for dessert before breakfast, and her breathy, "*Ooooh, yes,*" solidifies it.

Every Thanksgiving morning from here on out will start with me eating Tillie Jean's pussy.

And then a nap.

And then sex in the shower.

And then both our phones start blowing up.

"We can go," I tell her as she's drying her hair.

"But do you *want* to?" she presses.

Do I?

I don't know.

I do know she hasn't had her coffee yet though, so I kiss her shoulder and head out to the kitchen, where I almost jump out of my skin. "*Jesus,* goats."

"*Rawk! Jesus goats are holy goats. Rawk!*"

Goatstradamus and his two best pals don't stop gnawing on the kitchen table. The back door is hanging wide open, and Long Beak Silver is perched on the kitchen faucet.

"Tillie Jean, I'm buying you a new lock, and there's no arguing," I call. I lure the goats out with half of the collard greens in the fridge, then lock the door and shove a chair under it.

I'm *not* getting her a new lock today.

"*Rawk! Help! I've been kidnapped! Rawk!*"

I stare at the bird. "That, I believe. You don't sound like Long Beak Silver."

"Rawk! Batten the hatches! Rawk!"

"He had remedial training." Tillie Jean slips her arms around my waist from behind. "Did I forget to tell you, or were you tied up in that crazy West Coast trip?"

"I would *never* forget a *single word* you've ever told me. Clearly, this is on you."

She snorts with laughter. "Uh-huh."

And then she shuffles along behind me while I make my way to the coffee pot, her arms still linked around my waist.

She does this at least three times a week, and I love it.

"We really don't have to leave the house today," she says.

And I finally get suspicious.

I start her coffee, but then I unhook her hands, turn around, and grab her by the cheeks. "Matilda Jean Rock. What did you do?"

Her eyes dance, and her smile lights up the whole damn galaxy. "Absolutely nothing."

"Yet?"

She winks.

I scrub a hand over my face.

On the one hand, if she's thinking of doing what I think she's thinking of doing—though I don't have an exact *what*, merely a thematic idea—then yeah, Cooper deserves it and more.

The minute I got back to Florida for spring training with Tillie Jean in tow in February, he nodded, clapped me on the back, told me not to be a dick, and went back to being the Cooper he'd always been.

We still haven't paid him back for the EGB.

That's the *Epic Glitter Bombing,* and yes, it's capitalized every time, because it's not toppable.

Probably.

Maybe.

Tillie Jean *has* had some extra thinking time this year.

But on that other hand—Cooper's had one hell of a year, and he could probably use a break.

Probably.

Maybe.

Or maybe not.

All's fair in baseball, love, and prank wars.

"Tillie Jean?"

"What? I didn't hire someone to dig up his driveway and replace it with plants to make it look like his house has disappeared. That would be *too far*."

She makes air quotes around *too far*, and I'm suddenly choking on my own laughter. "Is this a regular reminder to not piss you off?"

"Max. I *only* give my best pranks to the men I love."

"And are you trying to keep me here so you can prank me all day?"

"No, but I do have a Thanksgiving present for you. If you want it. I'm completely serious when I say you get to tell me what to do today. I don't have to hang onto old traditions. I just want to hang onto you."

"So let's go."

"Where?"

"Thanksgiving dinner. Show me your traditions. Can't reject it if I don't know what I'm missing."

Her eyes light up even more. "Brilliant. And if anyone annoys you and you want to leave—"

"I'll do my best Long Beak Silver impersonation and call them a fucking fucker."

"Rawk! Profanity is for the weak! Rawk!"

"Okay, that's seriously creepy," I whisper.

"Apparently Nana kidnapped the bird and made him watch some annoying kid show on repeat until he cried uncle."

"Huh. And I thought maybe she kidnapped him and made him hang out with Estevez for a day."

She snorts with laughter as her coffee beeps. "Ooh, life juice!"

We chase Long Beak Silver out of the house too, and then I indulge in a cup with her—yeah, it's hard to resist that smell —while we snuggle on the couch watching a few episodes of *Ted Lasso* again until it's time for the Shipwreck festivities to begin.

Tillie Jean leaps off the couch. "But first—your Thanksgiving present."

She disappears down the hall, and comes back a minute later with a small pink gift bag.

I shake my head in mock disappointment. "Not Thanksgiving colors, Trouble Jean."

"Shh. Just open it."

My birthday present this year was a box of pasta.

Regular ol' spaghetti noodles from the grocery store.

Not even kidding.

It was so random, I laughed until I cried, which was apparently the point. *You can buy yourself anything, but you would* not *have bought yourself spaghetti noodles for your birthday*, TJ had informed me.

And then she gave me the best blowjob of my life.

And I got a pirate pillow with her face on it for Talk Like a Pirate Day.

Apparently it's an important holiday here in Shipwreck.

She got a blow-up hammock that looks like a vagina for her birthday.

I told her it was better than a car or a boat since it would keep her humble.

We might not be normal, but *fuck*, do we laugh a lot.

I take the pink bag from her and peek inside, but all I see is more pink tissue paper, so I dig in.

And I'm very confused when I pull out a gray T-shirt.

"Turn it around." She's practically on top of me, bouncing and smiling, which suits me just fine, but when I turn the shirt around to look at what's printed on the front, she goes still.

And then I do too.

Growly Bear Daddies Are The Best Daddies, it says.

I open my mouth.

Shut it.

Open it again.

Glance at her.

And the sight of her face wavering between utter excitement and utter panic sends my heart flying to the stratosphere.

"Trouble Jean," I breathe.

"You don't have to wear it today," she whispers. "I mean, you probably shouldn't. Not for another couple months. And school might get complicated in the fall, so it's a good thing I have three more years to do two years' worth of work. But... do you like it?"

She bites her lower lip and watches me.

I have to swallow twice to find my voice, and once more to make it work. "Are you—is that—are we...?"

She blinks shiny eyes and nods, then reaches into the bag and pulls out a short stick with a message printed clearly on a digital read-out.

"Holy fuck," I mutter.

She loops her arm through mine and presses a kiss to my shoulder. "I know it's not exactly in the plans, but..."

"*Coffee.*" I jerk back and look down at her. "You can't—"

"One cup," she sighs. "I can have *one cup.*" She squints at me. "Are you okay?"

I blink at her again.

Am I?

She's right.

A baby isn't exactly in the plans, but fuck the plans.

I start to smile, and then I laugh. A year ago, this would've freaked me out worse than the EGB. But today?

After a year of talking and working and falling more and more in love with Tillie Jean every day? "A *baby*?"

She nods. "It's entirely possible I'll be puking my guts out this time next week."

"A *baby*." I can't stop grinning. Until a new thought hits me. "Is your father going to kill me?"

She tips her head back and laughs. "No. He likes you. And he likes that you make me happy. And in case you haven't noticed, both of my parents are basically in love with being grandparents."

A baby.

Tillie Jean and I are having a baby.

I have a diamond ring hidden in my workout bag.

The one that never leaves the closet, for the record.

I pull Tillie Jean into my lap and kiss her until we're both breathless. "I fucking adore you," I tell her.

She runs her fingers through my hair. "That's very convenient, because I happen to be madly in love with you."

The only thing I feel right now is complete and utter joy.

No panic. No worries. No fear.

Just *right*.

Happiness. Contentment. Love.

Everything.

BONUS EPILOGUE

Cooper Rock, aka a dude headed to his house after grocery shopping about the same time his dear, wonderful, favorite sister is giving her soon-to-be fiancé all of that good news in the previous epilogue

There are seventy million things I love about Thorny Rock Mountain, starting with, it's where I came from.

Yep.

I was birthed by this very mountain, and I gave it no labor pains, and we high-fived each other the minute I came out, and we've gotten along great ever since.

Don't tell my mother I'm making shit up, okay?

Not that she'd be surprised. I tell her something like this every Mother's Day to watch her laugh at me.

I'm whistling through the switchbacks.

Much as I love the city, home is where my heart is, and I'm almost home.

I pass the first house I picked up on the mountain once I decided I wanted to own the whole pile of dirt that birthed me. This one's a normal-size two-bedroom log cabin that families from the city come out and rent on weekends. "High five, Bear Cottage," I call to it.

Rents better on those vacation rental sites when it has a name.

Plus, who wouldn't want to stay in Bear Cottage?

"High five, Cedar Chalet," I call to my next rental property down the way.

All those people in the city have no idea what they were doing giving up their weekend properties to me.

They've let me buy almost my entire mountain.

Grady and Tillie Jean keep telling me it's bad for my ego, but let's be real.

There are very, very few things in life that can ding my ego.

That's all I'm saying about that.

For the record.

I take two more switchbacks, and there's one more driveway.

"High five, Beck Ryder's house," I call to one of the few properties I don't own.

"High five, Cooper, you magnificent beast," I reply to myself in my best Beck Ryder impersonation.

I like Beck.

Good dude. His wife's awesome. Their baby is too. Not that I've gotten much time around the pipsqueak, but she came from good genes, so you know she'll be awesome when she morphs from a little cute blob that eats and sleeps and blows out diapers to a walking, talking toddler who sticks her fingers in light sockets and gnaws on things she finds on the floor.

Like dirty jockstraps.

I grin. Darren Greene has his hands full these days. And yeah, his kid is how I know what toddlers do.

Heh.

I slow down and turn into my driveway, except my driveway isn't there, so now I'm slamming on the brakes, angled hard in the middle of the road, staring at my mailbox.

Mailbox is there.

But where my driveway belongs, there's no driveway. It's undergrowth and a giant pine tree and fallen leaves and *how the fuck did she pull this off?*

I look up the road.

Then down the road.

This is definitely where my driveway belongs.

I am *not* confused.

That's my mailbox.

She didn't just move my mailbox, did she?

Oh, and make no mistake.

I know exactly who *she* is.

Tillie Jean.

Tillie Jean, who has yet to learn that you don't awaken the beast in November.

Not if you don't want to spend the rest of your life looking like a toddler who had an accident in a glitter factory.

I whip out my phone and send a quick text.

Vengeance will be mine, Matilda Jean.

Vengeance will once again be mine.

Exes and Ho Ho Hos

The Bluewater Billionaires Series
The Price of Scandal by Lucy Score
The Mogul and the Muscle by Claire Kingsley
Wild Open Hearts by Kathryn Nolan
Crazy for Loving You by Pippa Grant

Co-Written with Lili Valente
Hosed

Hammered

Hitched

Humbugged

For a complete, up -to-date book list, visit www.pippagrant.com

---

Pippa Grant writing as Jamie Farrell:

The Misfit Brides Series
Blissed

Matched

Smittened

Sugared

Married

Spiced

Unhitched

The Officers' Ex-Wives Club Series
Her Rebel Heart
Southern Fried Blues

ABOUT THE AUTHOR

Pippa Grant is a USA Today Bestselling author who writes romantic comedies that will make tears run down your leg. When she's not reading, writing or sleeping, she's being crowned employee of the month as a stay-at-home mom and housewife trying to prepare her adorable demon spawn to be productive members of society, all the while fantasizing about long walks on the beach with hot chocolate chip cookies.

Find Pippa at...
www.pippagrant.com
pippa@pippagrant.com

CPSIA information can be obtained
at www.ICGtesting.com
Printed in the USA
BVHW080538160721
612047BV00007B/133

9 781955 930000